Night Machines

Kia Heavey

UNFILTERED
creative

Gratitude

…to Tasos, for teaching me that I could do whatever I wanted.

…to Karen, for setting the creative example and standard.

…to the Internet and sites like Amazon and CreateSpace, for opening the gates up to the unwashed masses.

…to Jim, for everything else.

Gratitude

Acknowledgements

Some people were very helpful to me as I put this project together. Among them were my friend, Robert Bomgardner, who passed along everything he learned as he worked on his own project. Editor Joyce Shafer (www.freewebs.com/editmybookandmore) gave me critical readings, hooked me up with feedback readers, and most of all, gave me optimism and confidence. I was also lucky to come across Jan Kardys, who has expended great energy to make the world of publishing accessible to beginners. Although I ultimately decided to self-publish, I learned much from her that has helped me maintain professionalism in the execution of my project. I'm grateful for the feedback and great ideas of my friend, Sheryn MacMunn. Good luck with your project, Sheryn! Thank you to Karen for the final edit as well as her expertise about the pharmaceutical industry. Thanks are also due my husband, who patiently answered my questions about law enforcement and crime investigation.

Acknowledgments

I.

1.

Maggie was dreaming again.

This was not unusual. Maggie was a prolific dreamer, both awake and in her sleep. A creative and loving soul, she seemed to pour her heart into the visions. She immersed herself in them and went where they took her, becoming thoroughly seduced by the intense experiences.

These journeys added a treasured facet of limitless possibility to her rich (if otherwise predictable, one might even say mundane) life. She reveled in the soaring freedom of her unfettered, dreaming mind and awakened feeling alive and inspired.

It would never have occurred to her that her dreams might one day lead her astray, might turn on her, might even become menacing.

Now Maggie was dreaming that she and Rowan walked by the lake. Hazel skipped ahead and Charlie trundled along beside them. Rowan held Charlie's hand and bent to point to the carp. The fish were so fat Maggie wondered how they bent their turgid bodies to swim. Charlie laughed the belly laugh of a toddler. He dropped breadcrumbs onto the water for the carp to rise to. Bright scarlet, incandescent white, the fish glowed like lanterns in the murk.

Shimmering willows enclosed the family in a rustling green chamber. There was no sound but the whispering of the leaves. Farther out on the lake, sunlight glanced off the rippling surface in a thousand directions. Charlie dropped more crumbs; the glowing carp rose. One especially large fish hung just below the surface with only its o-shaped mouth opening and closing above the water. Charlie squealed and dropped crumbs directly into its mouth. The fish were so funny!

The summer day thrummed with warmth and light. Maggie watched, transfixed, as the colorful carp rose from the olive-brown depths, flashed in the clear shallows, and vanished into the gloom again. One specimen had shiny, brass-colored scales etched in black and swam with jerky, robotic movements. It looked as though it could have been assembled by a Swiss clockmaker.

"Rowan, look at that fish. Doesn't it look like it's mechanical?" asked Maggie. "It looks like someone made it."

"It does," agreed Rowan.

The better view they got of it, the more evident it became that Maggie's suspicion was correct. "My goodness, it *is* mechanical." Maggie laughed with delight—what would they think of next?

The robotic carp cruised among the feeding fish and began to mouth the breadcrumbs as they did, unaware of itself as an automaton that could draw no nourishment from food.

Maggie hugged her son and pointed. "Charlie, look at that silly machine-fish. It thinks it's real."

Snug in bed, Maggie Moore opened her eyes, shook off the last vestiges of the dream, and looked out the window. Tree limbs tossed in a fitful wind and a miserable combination of snow and rain blustered over the yard. She grimaced: *snain*, as she and her friend, Vicky, called it. That winter had been so dreary, with cold rain frequently mixing into the snow and ruining it, they had felt compelled to create a new word for this prevalent weather phenomenon.

Asleep beside her, Rowan breathed loudly through his nose. Maggie slipped from bed, crept to the hallway, and pulled the door shut behind her. Her husband hadn't gotten home until long after she was asleep, and she wanted him to rest a bit more. Sometimes his work kept him out quite late, even all night on occasion.

She peeked into the other two rooms on the second floor of the house. Her five-year-old daughter and toddler son were also sleeping soundly, their cheeks flushed. It was too early for them to be up, so Maggie went downstairs alone.

She made a cup of coffee and headed for her favorite overstuffed chair by the living room window. Seated sideways across it, her back against one arm and her legs hanging over the other, she could look out at the backyard. Warmed by the coffee and lingering visions of her dream, she savored the quiet inside the house and the muted sounds of the tempest without.

Yet even in the glow of such domestic contentment, she eagerly began to contemplate the appointment she had that day. If all went well, she would once again use her professional skills, would be among intellectually accomplished adults, and might even have the occasional stimulating conversation.

Rowan was the only man Maggie had ever met that she felt she could marry, but he would never be all things to her. Nor did she expect this of him. She didn't believe married couples were sufficient human contact for one another, and that was as it should be. Everyone needed a range of social interactions to be fully realized. Much as she loved and admired her husband, he wasn't one for rambling conjecture about such topics as literary analysis or the just-so composition of a perfect measure of music. A lawman for sixteen years, Rowan worked as a detective in Stamford, Connecticut, a mid-sized city fifteen miles from Vale, where they lived. In his world, men said what they meant and meant what they said, and Maggie appreciated the concise, unmistakable purpose of such talk.

Still, she missed idle, abstract conversation at times. She knew she had been blessed the past few years to have her peaceful home and plump babies. But a part of her that had been packed away, unused, all this time was more and more impatient to get out again.

"Why don't you wear something pink, Mommy? Do you want to borrow one of my barrettes? You can borrow the one with the butterflies on it. It's soooooo pretty."

Hazel's fashion advice, while perhaps useful to a five-year-old girl, didn't help Maggie as she struggled to dress for her interview. Not having worn anything vaguely office-appropriate in several years, she no longer knew what a working Maggie Moore would look like. At last, she slipped into her one tailored suit, praying it wasn't hopelessly out of style, and stepped into a pair of sling back heels. She shook her hair loose and it fell in a glossy, chestnut wave over her shoulders. The mirror rewarded her with the sight of a long limbed, elegant woman who was still self-conscious of the voluptuous new curves motherhood had given her. Excitement glowed in her hazel eyes and she smiled at her reflection. She hadn't thought of herself as a woman in quite a long time, only as a mother. She wished Rowan were home to see her, but he had long since departed again for work.

"You look beautiful, Mommy," said Hazel.

Maggie's father showed up at ten on the dot.

"Hey, Pop. Thanks for coming over to watch the kids." Maggie kissed her father and children, received everyone's hearty wishes for good luck, detached Charlie from her leg, and handed him to her father. She waved as she backed out of the driveway.

She drove along the back roads until she reached the main route through Vale. The morning's bluster had given way to a windy day under a leaden sky that threatened more rain at any moment. Maggie hardly noticed the colorless early March scenery passing.

Wooded hills yielded to open land with scattered stands of trees and ever more buildings. Maggie passed the garish new strip mall and sped up the entrance ramp to the parkway. The acceleration felt good and she pushed the station wagon harder than was necessary. She leaned forward to turn on some music. One of Hazel's CDs began to play, a cloying female vocalist backed by a sappy chorus of children's voices. Maggie hit the button for the radio and the car filled with power-chord rock from the local station. She had grown up listening to this station. The familiar song made her feel young and brave. She sang out loud as the wagon sailed down the road.

At the north end of Stamford, Maggie left the parkway and drove a couple miles toward the center of town. The city here was fairly open, home chiefly to corporate parks younger than she. Mid-sized office buildings stood back from the road at the ends of long driveways. Even with trees still bare, the landscaping looked expensive.

Maggie began to read the corporate name signs at the road's edge. An immense slab of white marble stood next to a driveway on the left. Towards the top of the stone, a name glowed in blue letters: *NarcoDynamics*. Maggie signaled and turned.

The straight drive led to a four-story building, constructed of the same white, glimmering marble as the stone at the end of the drive. The weak sun had broken through the clouds to illuminate it further and it gleamed white against the gray sky. Maggie parked in the visitor lot at the side of the building. She checked the dashboard clock; she was twenty minutes early. To pass the time, she pulled a file folder out of her bag and opened it to review the job description one last time.

Part-time writer wanted for corporate communication work. Three to five years experience preferred, medical/scientific writing a plus. Responsibilities include editing study reports and writing corporate newsletter, plus other projects on an as-needed basis.

The job sounded like just the thing to ease back into the work force. Maggie put the folder away and fussed over her appearance in the rear-view mirror. She felt a wave of nervousness coming on and decided it would be better to be a few minutes early than to lurk in the parking lot until she was a basket case. She gathered her things and stepped out of the car.

The lobby of the NarcoDynamics building was a soaring, luminous space. Milky sunlight flowed unchecked through a four-story high wall of glass and warmed Maggie's shoulders as she sat on a bench, filling out an application. She glanced up whenever employees or their visitors passed through the bright lobby. Sophisticated, clever and professional, they walked with purpose, talking in confident voices. Maggie compared herself to them and began to have doubts. Suddenly, she felt inferior, shabby and provincial.

A bright flash caught her attention. In the center of the lobby floor, directly in front of her, was a round pool. Maggie had barely been able to pay attention to the paperwork, so compelling did she find this small oasis. Lilies and water hyacinths grew among smooth rocks. Colorful koi lolled in the limpid water in the plants' shadows.

A large, golden fish had angled into a rogue sunbeam. Reflecting off its scales, the light had drawn Maggie's gaze. She stared at the carp while it lay suspended in the warm, amniotic pool, its elaborate fins rippling like intricate fans. Abruptly, Maggie was weary of the endless, cold winter. She longed for warmth and comfort. That morning's dream of red and gold fish idling in a summer pond came back to her and the sense of peaceful contentment once again filled her. She smiled; surely the carp in the pool was a sign. She was meant to be here, to work for this company, to find fulfillment within this gleaming white building.

Confidence surged through her. It was preordained. The job was as good as hers.

"Ms. Moore?"

"Huh? Yes?" Maggie put a hand over her eyes to cut the glare. "I'm Maggie Moore. Yes?" She rose to her feet and stepped out of the direct sunlight.

A trim, middle-aged woman stood before her. She held out her hand. "Hi, Maggie. I'm Cindy Sherman. Thank you for coming to meet with us today." Cindy's friendly voice rang with proficiency and her gaze was discerning. She wore a plum-colored suit and matching pumps. Her hair was cropped into a short, chic style.

Maggie shook the woman's hand and smiled her brightest smile. "Hi, Cindy. It's good to meet you." She gathered her things and followed the woman past the reception desk to the elevators, the winsome koi in the pool forgotten.

"So, tell me a little about your background." Cindy looked up from the application she had been perusing to smile encouragingly at Maggie.

"Well, as you can see from my resume, I have an advertising copywriting background. But we did have a pharma account, and I worked on the medical language for the backs of their ads and their pamphlets."

Cindy looked again at the sheet of paper on her desk. "Uh-huh, I see. That was when you were at the Saint Chapelle Agency, right here in Stamford?"

Maggie nodded. "Yes. I was Senior Copywriter there for five years."

"Looks like most of your clients were in the beer and spirits industry, however."

Maggie couldn't read her tone—was this a statement of disqualification or a simple, friendly question? "Well, one could make an argument that those clients represent a medication industry."

To her relief, Cindy laughed. "Okay, let's get you down to the lab to meet Dr. Rajagopalan."

Dr. Rajagopalan was of medium height and late middle age. Though otherwise slim, he had a pot belly which pushed his white lab coat out in front of him. He shook Maggie's hand when Cindy introduced them. When they were both seated and Cindy was gone, he launched into a dry recounting of the work that went on in his department.

"This where we are seated is the office area," he said. Maggie noticed the musical cadence of his speech was underscored by a faint British accent. "You will have that desk over there." Maggie turned to look where he pointed. She saw a desk identical to the others in the room, surmounted by a computer.

She nodded. "Okay."

Dr. Rajagopalan continued. "Looking through there, you will see the laboratory." This time he pointed to the other side of the room. Maggie peered through a glass partition and saw an enormous space. One entire wall was windowed, as was the adjoining office area where they sat, allowing abundant natural light to enter. Structural columns and long black counters described the space within the lab. Intriguing equipment covered the counter tops. Against the distant wall were rows of small cages.

"What do you have back there? In the cages?"

"That is where we keep the mice."

Maggie strove to overcome a sudden pang of pity. "Oh, of course. I guess you have to kill a few mice every now and then to cure human beings."

"*Sacrifice*," the researcher corrected her. "Dr. Cuthbert forbids us to use the word *kill*. The lab animals are sometimes, sadly, *sacrificed* to further science."

"I see. Good to know. So this is where you conduct your research?"

"Some of it."

"Is this where Anadreme was invented?" Maggie referred to the company's best-known product, a clinical sleep aid they had developed half a dozen years earlier.

"No, Dr. Cuthbert himself invented Anadreme."

"Cuthbert?" The name had a ring of familiarity about it, although she could not think why.

"Yes, Dr. Cuthbert. He invented Anadreme in his small start-up facility. With the medicine's phenomenal therapeutic and commercial success, he built up his company into the NarcoDynamics Corporation."

Maggie imagined what kind of man the daunting Dr. Cuthbert must be, a venerable, silver-haired scientific genius as well as a formidable businessman.

"This is only one of many labs in this and the other NarcoDynamics facilities," Dr. Rajagopalan continued. "In here, we are exceptional scientists. But we have much reporting to do and not enough time to write the reports nicely or verify their complete accuracy."

Maggie nodded. "Which is where I come in?"

"Yes, I will need you to edit the ezobees."

"I'm sorry, edit the what?"

"The ezobees, the ezobees." Dr. Rajagopalan became frustrated at the look of incomprehension on her face. "The standard operating procedures."

"Oh, the S.O.P.s," Maggie exclaimed in relief.

"Yes, the ezobees. Also, there are the reports to the evdi-ay."

This time, Maggie surmised he meant the F.D.A. "Sure, no problem. I can clean those up for you."

"Splendid. There can be no decimal out of place for the evdiay. Do you have any questions?"

Maggie glanced around the room once more. She looked over at the desk he had indicated would be hers if she was hired, the one nearest the door. She pictured herself seated at the computer, typing industriously as she wrought concise English from the scientific gibberish Dr. Rajagopalan handed her. She envisioned herself as an integral part of a professional, productive, cutting-edge team. She sighed and gave a happy shrug. Turning back to her interviewer, she said, "Nope, no questions."

"Dr. Cuthbert will be overseeing the corporate newsletter himself, so he would like to meet with you before we make a decision." Cindy led Maggie down the hall from Dr. Rajagopalan's lab at a brisk walk. Maggie followed diligently, gauging the importance of the next meeting by the urgency of her guide's pace.

They rode the elevator from the second floor to the fourth. "Is the newsletter the only other responsibility for the writer's position?" Maggie asked.

"According to the job description." The personnel director surged through the elevator doors as soon as they opened, drawing Maggie in her wake. They traversed an increasingly lavish executive area, halting at last before the massive desk of the assistant who controlled access to the head of the corporation.

The slender blonde rose from her chair. "Hello, Cindy."

"Hi, Jill. I've brought—"

"You must be Maggie Moore." Jill's demeanor matched her appearance, cool, polished and professional. "Hello. I'm Jill Fairburn."

Maggie's confidence faltered. What was she doing here, among all these sharp, elegant people? She should be at home, speckled with dirt in the backyard, digging the spring garden with the children, or covered in dust, cleaning under the beds. She shook the woman's manicured hand. "Hi, Jill. It's nice to meet you." She glanced down at her own hands, half-expecting to see crescents of dirt beneath her fingernails; but her hands looked as clean and capable as any in the room.

Jill picked up the telephone handset and pressed a button. "Dr. Cuthbert, Maggie Moore is here to see you. . . . Yes, I'll send her in now." She hung up and stepped from behind her desk. "Cindy, I'll give you a call when they're done. Thanks for bringing Maggie up."

"Great. Thanks, Jill." Relieved of her charge, Cindy spun and retreated down the hall.

Jill stepped to the gray door a few yards beyond her desk, knocked once, and opened it. She leaned into the room and announced, "Maggie Moore, Doctor." Turning back to Maggie, she smiled and gestured for her to enter.

Maggie did as she was bidden. "Th-thank you, Jill," she murmured. The door closed behind her with a soft click as she turned to look towards the man seated behind the desk in the far corner.

He was difficult to see clearly in the glare from the walls of windows that flanked him. The sun battled through the steely sky behind him, obscuring him in its glare. Maggie could make out few details but was surprised to note that his hair was black and glossy.

She drew herself up straight. "Hi, I'm Maggie Moore."

The man said nothing. He neither rose nor invited her to sit in one of the leather chairs facing his desk. Rather, he remained seated, his chin resting on his folded hands, regarding her. She shifted her weight onto one foot, then pulled herself up straight again. And still the silence stretched on.

Just as she opened her mouth to speak again, a low chuckle broke the stillness. Dr. Cuthbert spoke. "Well, well, well. Maggie Cooper." He had a rich, deep voice. "Who would have thought it?" Again he laughed, low in his throat, a lion's playful growl.

"Um, it's Maggie Moore now. I haven't been Maggie Cooper in seven or eight years." She tried to put it all together; *Cuthbert . . . Cooper . . .* she wished she could see him more clearly, but the glare was too difficult to penetrate. She shielded her eyes with her hand. "I suppose I know you, but it's escaping my mind . . ." She waited for him to enlighten her, but he said nothing more.

She was about to ask if she could sit down when he stood and came from behind the desk. As he approached, Maggie was struck by his height; a tall woman at five-foot-seven, she had to tilt her head far back to look him in the face. His lithe movements suggested a powerful physique controlled with superb coordination. He came nearer and she could see keen eyes under dark brows, a roguish smile in a strikingly handsome face. His presence was so intense that she took an involuntary step back.

Horrified that she couldn't remember who he was or how he knew her, Maggie despaired of recovering her poise to interview effectively. And still, Dr. Cuthbert advanced. He halted at last within inches of her and put out his hand. She took it, intending to shake it. But he covered her hand with his other one and held it, grinning down at her. "You don't remember me, do you?" He mingled a comical look of hurt feelings with his smile.

A cold, prickly heat ran along Maggie's hairline. *Who the hell was he? He looked familiar, yet so different. He had been so tall and gangly then, pale and awkward.* She spoke before the thought had fully coalesced. "High school?"

He beamed with pleasure. "Yes, of course. Schofield High. See? You do remember me. It's Cambien! I was a year behind you—we were in calculus together." He finally released her hand, only to take her arm. "Come. Sit down." Together, they moved to a pair of tufted leather chairs and sat facing one another.

Maggie made much of setting her bag beside her on the floor. She let her thick hair fall forward to screen her face as her mind raced to bring up information. But Cambien spoke again, giving her no time to collect her thoughts.

"So, it's Maggie Moore now? Good for you. I always wondered what became of you. I don't wonder about most of the people we went to high school with," (a bitter edge to his voice for a moment), "but you were one of the nice ones. So, tell me what you've been up to. Married, I take it. Kids? Working? Run away with the circus? What's Maggie Cooper up to these days?"

By now, Maggie had willed herself back to a calm state. She sat up straight and faced her interrogator. As she met his glance she couldn't help but return his friendly smile. *He surely hadn't been this good-looking in high school, or I would have remembered him.* The unbidden thought turned her cheeks pink, but she didn't feel self-conscious. Cambien's long-lost-friend greeting had put her at ease, and she fell into comfortable conversation with him.

"Well these days, I'm not up to much." She stopped, started again. "I mean, I'm busy with the kids. I've been home with them for five years, but I really think it's time for me to get back to work."

Cambien watched her face intently while she spoke. Flustered, she looked up at the ceiling. "Oh, let's see. After high school, I went to Barnard College in Manhattan—"

"Did you know I almost went to Columbia?" he interrupted. "I would have been right across the street from you."

"Really? Why did you change you mind?"

"Oh, I don't know. It didn't really fit in with my plans at the time." He looked at the floor as he said this. As he revealed himself in profile, Maggie was surprised to see that he wore his long, ebony hair in a tight knot at the nape of his neck.

He leaned back in his chair, crossed one long leg over the other, and returned his gaze to Maggie. "What did you think of Barnard?"

Her face lit up. "Oh, I loved it. I loved studying literature and writing to my heart's content. I loved living in the city. But then, of course, I graduated and had to start earning a living."

"Ah, yes, reality sets in."

They chuckled together. "Yes, it has a way of doing that. So, I wound up in the advertising business, writing copy. I worked in the city for a couple years after graduating. Eventually, I moved back to Connecticut and started working in Stamford.

"I did take a break about five years ago, when my daughter was born. Then we had a son—"

"One of each. Nice."

"Yes, we were pretty happy about it. But as glad as I am that I could be with them when they were little and as much as I love them, I really do miss working. For years, I had been trained and skilled at using this part of my brain—the writing and editing part—and then I wasn't using it at all. At first, I didn't miss it. But after a while, I began to crave words, writing, and editing again.

"I had barely started to think about going back to work, and the first time I went online to look, there was this listing of a perfect job for me. I mean, not that I have a great deal of scientific writing experience, but I do have some from advertising, and I took bio chem at school. And most of all, I can bring some logical cohesion to the sort of technical writing I assume goes on here. Is that what you're looking for?"

Maggie paused to allow Cambien to speak about the job, perhaps elaborate on the nature of the work that went on in his company. But he continued to sit and grin at her. Increasingly self-conscious, she tried another tack. "So . . . what have you been up to since Schofield? Building up quite an empire, eh?" She swept her arm to indicate the well-appointed office and the company that was run from it. "Most impressive," she half-teased, half-complimented.

Cambien lowered his eyes for a moment in a manly display of humility. "Yes, I have been hard at work, that's for sure. And I've been most fortunate in my enterprises. As you may recall," (Maggie gave no indication that she didn't), "I went to Yale from Schofield, and I stayed there through med school. I did my residency at a big urban hospital but as soon as I could, I went to work in the research labs. Specifically, sleep clinics. I have always been fascinated by sleep disorders and how the human brain is affected by them."

"My goodness. How did you become so interested in sleep disorders?"

Cambien paused and glanced away again. For a moment, it seemed he wouldn't answer. When he finally spoke, his tone was subdued. "There was someone I once cared about, a beautiful young woman I knew at Yale. She was brilliant, too, one of the greatest minds I've ever known. There was no telling what gifts she would bring to the world." He sighed heavily. "But with that degree of intellect, unfortunately, sometimes there are problems."

Captivated, Maggie nodded in understanding.

Cambien bravely continued. "She had . . . nervous problems. They arose from too much thinking, from an inability to turn her incredibly powerful mind off. She became more troubled as time went on. And eventually, the disruptive thoughts made their way into her dreams. I remember the drastic change in her at that time. She lost a lot of weight, went about with a haunted look. That she no longer got any respite, even in sleep, was the last straw for her." He became quiet for a long moment, his gaze far away, before concluding. "One night, tormented beyond her endurance by one nightmare too many, she got out of bed and just . . . stepped through the open window."

Maggie gasped. "Oh, how horrible!"

He nodded sadly. "It was. And I never forgot her." Maggie watched the struggle on his face as he manfully gained control over the painful memory. "But that experience totally focused me. I had observed firsthand how much harder it became for her to cope, once she lost the ability to heal herself through sleep. I realized that, if a person can't get any peace in his own mind, at least at night, it's only a matter of time before he loses control. I became obsessed with the idea of giving frantic people back the power to rest at night. And that's how I wound up a researcher in the sleep clinics."

He sat back in his chair as he moved to a new subject. "Around that time, my father passed on and left me an inheritance, so I was able to start up my own little lab. I focused on dreaming, and I eventually figured out a way to turn dreams off. The medicine that came out of that research was, of course, Anadreme."

"Ah, yes, we've all heard of Anadreme," interjected Maggie.

Dimples appeared around Cambien's sculpted lips, momentarily beguiling her. He began to speak of his invention. "This drug has been a God-send to people whose rest is chronically disturbed by intense dreaming, night panics or nightmares. These are generally patients who have been through a traumatic incident or have anxiety disorders that manifest themselves as bad dreams. And as insufficient rest leads to a worsening of anxiety symptoms, these poor souls are caught in a vicious cycle of sleep deprivation and worsening distress. But Anadreme shuts off the part of the brain that creates nightmares, just like that—" he snapped his fingers "—so these unhappy people can get some rest." He sat back in his chair, smiling triumphantly.

Maggie thought about what he had been saying. "But I thought dreams were supposed to be important to people who are working through something. Don't they help the brain process information or emotions, or something?"

"So went the popular scientific thought on the subject. And it may even be true under normal circumstances. But people who have post-traumatic stress or severe anxiety are already tormented by disturbing visions during the day; the last thing they needed, in my opinion, was to lie down for some much-needed rest, only to continue to be tortured all night."

"I guess that makes sense."

"Turns out it didn't just make sense, it even produced unanticipated benefits." Cambien leaned towards her and gestured with his hands as he spoke with increased passion. Intimidated, Maggie sank back into her chair. "When these patients were allowed to sleep—really *sleep*, without any panic or nightmares to disturb them—their brains actually began to heal themselves of the chronic cycle of disturbing thought they'd been stuck in. The toxic patterns were disrupted, and the brain could start with almost a clean slate upon waking. Like rebooting a computer. And over time, the once-tormented brain began to reroute the damaging thoughts and feelings into healthier patterns, patterns which carried over into the patient's conscious, daytime thought." He paused and straightened slightly. "Of course, it's a bit more complex than that, but I'm trying to explain it in layman's terms for you."

His tone had become patronizing, but Maggie forgave it under the circumstances. In truth, she was awed by his accomplishments and the life restoring relief he provided to otherwise wretched and hopeless patients, people who would go mad without his invention. She felt humiliated by the glaring contrast between what he had built since high school and the little or nothing she suddenly felt she had accomplished in the same time.

"Wow," she said. She cringed at her own lack of intelligent commentary, which made her feel like more of a dunce than Cambien's excusable patronage had.

He leaned forward and took both her hands in his. His eyes shone. "It's good to see you again, Maggie."

She couldn't think of a single thing to say.

2.

Cambien was pleased. The interview had gone well. Maggie had just left and he was taking a moment to bask in the memory of her admiration. It had been plain on her face.

The only sticky point had been when she asked him why he had focused on sleep disorders, but she seemed satisfied with his explanation. She believed his sappy made-up tale of a lost love, a beautiful and brilliant young woman who had fallen victim to a headful of harrowing dreams.

In fact, Cambien had only ever loved one woman. And he had never once answered the question of why he studied sleep disorders truthfully; he had never told a living soul the real reason he had invented Anadreme.

⌒⊀

The rain had returned. It pelted the windshield of the station wagon so that she could barely see the road. As Maggie drove north on the parkway, she mentally berated herself for her poor performance during the interview. She had met with Cambien Cuthbert—the esteemed Dr. Cuthbert, the founder of NarcoDynamics—and had done nothing but become increasingly star-struck. She groaned as she realized she hadn't even shown him any samples of her writing. All she had done was to be awed by the successful man and scientist a casual high school acquaintance had become, and she had appeared less and less intelligent in the process. Cringing, she remembered sinking into the leather armchair, becoming tinier and more insignificant, finally to deliver the brilliant insight, *Wow*.

It was still pouring by the time she reached Vale. She pulled the wagon into the driveway. Pop's car was the only other one there. She went in the front door, kicked off her shoes and dropped her briefcase in the entry. "Hello," she called. Shoulders slumping, she headed for the kitchen. She could hear her father's whoops and the kids' shrieks as they roughhoused in the living room.

What a complete failure of an interview, she thought. *I am so out of it.*

As she entered the kitchen, the children ran to greet her and the phone rang. She kissed them quickly and picked up the receiver. "Hello?"

"Maggie? Hi. It's Cindy Sherman. Do you have a minute?"

Maggie's heart sank. "Hi, Cindy. Sure, what's up?"

"The boss wants to know when you can start."

⌒▼≺

Maggie hummed as she fixed dinner. Pop had left several hours earlier, delighted to hear her good news.

Rowan generally came home by six, kissed the children, and went through his mail before they all sat down to supper. Maggie looked at the clock and frowned; it was six forty-five. Just before the food got cold, she brought it to the table.

Maggie and the kids occasionally ate alone. Sometimes Rowan got hung up at work. A detective, he was home most evenings and weekends, but if a case came in, it meant extra hours. Stamford was home to many illustrious people and innovative enterprises, but it had its share of blight. So Rowan's overtime was not uncommon.

After they ate, Maggie cleared the table and put the dishes in the dishwasher. Charlie was cranky and clung to her leg while she worked, whining for her to pick him up.

"Stop it, Charlie. I can't pick you up while I'm working," she said in a stern voice.

Hazel came into the room. "Mommy, can you get my paints? I want to paint a picture."

Images of spilled paint, messy children, and colorful, tiny handprints on the walls flashed into Maggie's mind. "Not now, sweetie. It's almost bedtime."

"Mom! I really really really really really really want to paint a picture. Pleeeeeease!"

A dull ache began to fill Maggie's head. "I said not now, okay? It's getting late, and I don't want to have another mess to clean up." She took a step towards the open dishwasher and almost toppled over as Charlie reattached himself to her leg. "Darn it, Charlie! Knock it off." She hoisted him onto her hip, slammed the dishwasher shut, and turned it on. "Okay, come on, you two. Upstairs."

She put Hazel and Charlie into the tub together, bathed and dried them, and got them into their pajamas. She cuddled them in her and Rowan's bed and read to them. Half an hour later, she carried the sleepy children to their own rooms, tucked them in, and kissed them goodnight.

Back downstairs, she looked out the living room window at the driveway, but there was no sign of Rowan's truck. Maggie sighed.

It felt like years since anything of interest had happened in her life. When she and Rowan went out, it was mostly to social functions with other police officers and their wives, or recognition dinners for the various organizations he belonged to. He had been promoted to detective six years ago and she had been overjoyed for him. But now it was she who had news, and she needed her husband to share it with.

She went into the kitchen and poured a glass of wine. She picked up the phone and dialed Rowan's cell phone, but it went straight to his voicemail. It was now nearly nine o'clock; he must be working something important. She drifted back to the living room and turned on the local news.

The headline story came on at nine sharp; a child's body had been found in Stamford. Maggie drew a sharp breath in horror. The child had been a young girl and authorities said she had been the victim of a violent crime.

Maggie's mind reeled. Ever since her daughter had been born, the very thought of anyone hurting a child made her almost physically ill. She cringed with pain for the girl's mother. She pictured Rowan, working the scene with the other detectives and officers. They would stand at a distance from the covered body and use brave words with one another, trying not to be affected by the tragedy.

Rowan wouldn't be home for hours. The happy excitement Maggie had been feeling evaporated in frustration. Tears stung her eyes. Now she wouldn't see her husband until tomorrow, and then only briefly as he dressed and went back to work early. He would be in no mood to celebrate her good news. *Damn it, why did this have to happen now?*

A wave of shame struck her for feeling self-pity when a little girl had been murdered. Disgusted by her self-centeredness, Maggie turned off the lamp, left the porch light on, and went up to bed.

The night passed in fits and starts. Maggie fell asleep easily—she had always been a world-class sleeper, Rowan said— but Charlie woke her an hour later, crying and shouting out. She went to his room and soothed him back to sleep. When she got back into her bed, she was kept awake a bit longer by a keening wind that had risen. She stirred again an hour or so later, when her husband finally crept into bed beside her. She tried to rouse herself enough to talk to him, but was only able to murmur, "Heard it on the news."

"Yeah, it's pretty bad." Rowan spoke in a low voice. He kissed his wife and rolled onto his side, clutching the quilt around him. Maggie drifted back into unconsciousness.

And again she was wakened, nearly at dawn, by Hazel calling from her room. Maggie, long in the habit of being first responder to the children at night, ("I'm not the one who has to be carrying a gun tomorrow," she would say if Rowan tried to get up), lurched from bed and went to her daughter. Hazel was sitting up, her eyes wide in the dark, fear from her nightmare still upon her. Her mother sat on the edge of her bed, covered her up again, and stroked her hair until she slept once more.

Maggie crawled back into bed beside her husband. She looked at the planes of his face in the dim pre-dawn light and saw that, even in sleep, his brow was furrowed. Poor guy, she thought. It must have been a horrible night. She draped her arm over him and passed at once into a dream.

She sat by a clear stream that tumbled over mossy stones, surrounded by ancient forest. Still wearing her simple cotton nightgown, she bathed her feet in the quick-running water.

She looked up to see that a large, sleek buck had emerged from the trees to watch her. Maggie was alarmed at the size and branching antlers of the beast. She sat frozen as it stepped surely across the stream.

When it reached her, it lowered its face to hers and she saw that it had the shining, dark eyes of her new employer, Dr. Cuthbert. A thrill of recognition passed between her and the stag. Her anxiety gone, she now felt warmth and affection.

The great beast bent to lay its head in her lap and she put her hands on its neck, burying her fingers in its silken coat. It felt so luxurious and sensuous that she pressed her cheek to the deer's.

And thus engaged, Maggie did not wake when her husband rose at dawn, dressed quietly, kissed her flushed cheek, and returned to Stamford.

3.

Maggie tried to connect with her husband over the next few days, but he was as hard to hold as mercury. He spent long hours in Stamford, working the dreadful new case. Sometimes he came home for dinner, only to return to work right after. Mornings, he would watch local news and read the paper in the living room while the rest of the family ate breakfast in the kitchen. He'd kiss everyone when it was time to leave and drive off in his pickup truck. For the distance in his eyes and manner, he may as well not have been home at all.

The girl's body had been found on Thursday; by Saturday night, Maggie was desperate. She hadn't spoken more than a dozen words with her husband since the murder. Before retiring, she wrote a note and left it for him on the stairs.

Rowan – hope it's going as well as it can. Do you think you can hang around a little tomorrow? I'd like to talk to you. If not, I understand. Miss you, Maggie.

When Maggie woke the next morning, she found her husband sleeping beside her. She kissed his forehead and crept from the room. As she passed Charlie's door in the hall, she heard the toddler starting to fuss. She went into the room and plucked her drowsy son from his bed. He smiled at her as she held him close and carried him downstairs.

Soon, Maggie lay across the armchair, back resting against one arm, legs hanging over the other. Charlie sat on her stomach. He giggled conspiratorially as she tucked the afghan over them both. They sipped coffee and warm milk and woke up together, looking out the window at the sun working across the yard. Maggie could see signs of life creeping into the bare branches; no buds yet, but definitely a change of color.

An hour later, Maggie sat across the kitchen table from her husband. They ate breakfast in their pajamas while the children watched cartoons in the living room.

She broached the subject of his work. She knew better than to ask too many questions; a well-placed word of encouragement here and there, and she teased the story out of her husband as gently as she would remove a splinter from Charlie's foot.

Rowan looked out the window as he told her the rudiments of the case. He spoke as though he were discussing a book he had read in college or a news story from a country as remote as Singapore. Abruptly his spoon clattered onto the table as he locked gazes with his wife, his eyes bright with tears. "Maggie, for God's sake, she wasn't any older than Hazel." Incredulous, he held her gaze. The moment passed. He went back to his bowl of oatmeal and the view through the kitchen window.

"I know, Rowan, I've been just sick about it." Maggie knew there were no words. She willed her silent companionship to give her husband strength and comfort. She waited. Then, sensing he might welcome a change of subject, she launched into her news. "So, I had that interview on Thursday."

Rowan's attention returned to her. "Oh, that's right—the writing job at the sleeping pill company. How did you do?"

"Well, I got the job." Maggie couldn't suppress her triumphant smile.

"Maggie, that's great. Congratulations! I know how much you wanted that job." She drank in the sight of her husband, his graying regulation haircut and the crinkling around his slate colored eyes. His pleasure in her accomplishment was the affirmation she had craved. "I better start figuring out how I'm going to spend all that extra money," he kidded. "Let's see, I can get that new scanner that just came out. . . ."

Maggie laughed. "Don't get too excited, pal. It's only part-time. We're not looking at a whole lot of money here. It's mainly just to get my foot back in the marketplace, or something like that."

"Fine, fine. So, when do you abandon me and the children to go back to your glamorous world of literature?"

"Tomorrow, actually."

Rowan was taken aback. "Really? Tomorrow? What about the kids?"

Maggie felt sudden guilt that she had failed to keep him informed. "I'm sorry, Rowan. I wanted to tell you, but you had that horrible case come up. Don't worry, though, I'll drop Hazy at pre-K on my way to work, and Pop will watch Charlie. The daycare at Hazy's Pre-K is going to have an opening in the toddler room next month. So if it works out and I stay at this job, Charlie can go to school with Hazy on the days I'm working."

"Both kids at school? I guess it costs money to make money," Rowan teased.

"Even with both kids in daycare, we'll still make a little money. And besides, that's not the point. The point is for me to be able to start working again. I don't want to get so rusty that I'm not fit for anything by the time the kids are in elementary school."

"Okay, you're right." Rowan started on his oatmeal again.

Maggie went on. "The interview was kind of a surprise."

"Oh yeah? How so?"

"Well, I met with HR, then with a research doctor in the lab. Then they had me meet with the head of the entire company, the guy who invented Anadreme and founded NarcoDynamics and everything. So you can imagine, I was really nervous. But it turned out that he's an old friend of mine from high school."

"Really? What's his name?"

"Cambien Cuthbert . . . Doctor Cambien Cuthbert."

Rowan chewed his cereal thoughtfully. "That's funny; I don't remember you mentioning him." Since they lived in Maggie's hometown, he thought he knew all of her school chums who still dwelt in the area.

"Well, I actually didn't remember him at first. But he remembered me. It kind of came back to me as we spoke, so I guess I did well enough in the interview." She stared at the table and remembered back almost twenty years. "As I recall, Cambien was a bit of a nerd in high school. I don't know that he had any friends, really."

"Oh, *Cambien,* is it now? Awful chummy, aren't you two?" Rowan snorted.

Maggie chuckled. "You're right, I probably shouldn't call him that. He's my boss now. Well, I guess I must have been nice to him back in school. Like I always tell the kids, treat everyone the way you want to be treated. Hey, you never know who might wind up being your boss."

Later that morning, they piled into the station wagon and drove the two miles to church. Hazel, with her large eyes and tawny curls, was an angelic vision in her Sunday dress. During the service, Charlie was fussy, and presently he fell asleep on Maggie's shoulder. She exchanged the kiss of peace with her husband and children, and savored every minute of it.

～❧

The next day, Maggie began work at NarcoDynamics. Dr. Cuthbert came down to the lab to see how she was settling in. He sat on the edge of her desk and chatted with her for quite some time. He made her promise to address him only as Cambien and insisted that she come to him personally if she required anything to facilitate her work. Then he walked over to Dr. Rajagopalan and his team. He asked for details of their progress and recommended several minor adjustments. Dr. Rajagopalan was not amused.

Maggie smiled to herself as she typed on her keyboard. As if Dr. Cuthbert needed to show off. She thought he had already accomplished more in his mid-thirties than most men would in their entire lives.

She settled into the routine of the employed. She came in early and got to work on whatever reports Dr. Rajagopalan had left for her to edit. He generally arrived about an hour after she did and nodded good morning as he donned his lab coat.

Maggie worked at her desk as Dr. Rajagopalan and his assistants worked with the lab equipment on the other side of the glass partition. Sometimes she conferred with them about the reports she edited for them. (They were preparing to release the company's next major product, Somnusol, a milder sleep aid based on the same inhibitors that made Anadreme so effective.) At other times, she worked on the monthly corporate newsletter. She set up interviews and visited employees in their offices or labs, then wrote about their functions within the organization or the corporate philanthropic programs they directed. Typing away at her computer, Maggie felt a deep contentment with her new role as a productively employed citizen.

～

"Why do you admire these silly fish so?" Cambien asked her.

"I don't know. I just think they're so beautiful."

"They spend their entire lives in one small pond, never going anywhere new or trying anything different."

Maggie gazed down at the red, gold, black and white koi swarming the water's edge at their feet, begging for breadcrumbs like the tame pets they were. "Yes, but that's what's nice about them. They're so peaceful and content. Maybe there isn't anything better to try than their safe, comfortable pond. After all, everything they need is right there. Maybe the wisest and healthiest thing they can do is to stay put."

She knew she was dreaming; there was no other explanation for this surreal conversation with her employer on the banks of the carp pond in Vale's town park.

"And you, Maggie? Are you content in your small pond, in your little house, in Vale?"

Maggie didn't answer right away. Was she?

Cambien moved closer, whispering now. "Do you ever wonder what else is out there? Do you ever want to try something new?"

～

Vicky Bertrand ate an enormous forkful of baby lettuce and goat cheese, somehow making the maneuver look ladylike, and said, "So, tell me how the new gig is going." She sat across the table from Maggie on the patio of Tess's, a trendy spot for Stamford office workers. The long winter had finally relented for a day, and Maggie and Vicky had decided to enjoy an early taste of spring weather.

The two women had first met ten years earlier, when Maggie started working at the St. Chapelle Advertising Agency. Vicky was the Human Resources manager who interviewed had her, and they became friends right away. They used to shop together at lunchtime and organize people to go out for drinks after work. Maggie was frequently free in the evenings back then, since Rowan did shift work as a police officer. Vicky was keen to socialize, coming off the collapse of her first marriage and wanting to spend as little time alone as possible. A pretty woman with blond curls and an easy laugh, she seldom wanted for male company, though none of her lovers seemed to stick around very long. Maggie could never figure out if Vicky subtly drove them away or was just adept at picking the ones who wouldn't stay. But she could always be counted on to rally people for a night out.

While Maggie was pregnant with Hazel, Vicky became restless at St. Chapelle. There was only one executive position above her in the Human Resources department, and the sitting executive wasn't going anywhere, so she decided to take her considerable personal skills elsewhere. She obtained her certification and left the ad agency to sell real estate. Born and raised in Stamford, Vicky knew the various neighborhoods like the back of her hand. She was smart and personable, and she made a killing in her new profession.

When Hazel was still an infant and Maggie was a newly minted stay-at-home mom, Vicky became enamored of one of her clients. Donald was a divorced businessman from Chicago. Vicky sold him a high-end condo on Long Island Sound and then never really left it. For a while, Donald and Vicky were deliriously in love. They married just before Hazel turned one. By Hazel's second birthday, they had separated. The divorce became final the following year.

Maggie tried to be a comfort to Vicky during that time, but she was by then pregnant again. The bawdy nights out that had cheered Vicky through her first divorce were now beyond Maggie's endurance. She invited Vicky over for homemade meals or a quiet glass of wine, but was all the while either worried that Vicky was bored, or self-conscious about the contrast between her domestic contentment and her friend's lack of prospects. Vicky smiled and fussed over Hazel—Charlie too, when he came along—but she and Maggie had fallen out of their common situation. Even so, they maintained a loose friendship, Maggie to stay in touch with the fast-paced world of grownups and Vicky to keep herself grounded.

Now, seated at a coveted patio table amid the smart buzz of countless conversations, Maggie was glad she hadn't lost touch with her sophisticated friend. She reveled in being part of this world again. She finally had a purpose in her life besides cooking and cleaning for her family.

She swallowed the bite of gourmet pizza she had been chewing and answered Vicky's question. "I love it. I mean, I'm not exactly writing the next great American novel, but I'm so happy to be writing and editing again at all. And I'm helping a really cool organization. It's nice to be part of something bigger than me, you know? My company comes up with some great medicines. They really help people, and I love contributing to that."

"Well, bully for you," Vicky intoned sarcastically. "I like to think I do my little part, finding huge McMansions for the chronically overpaid to spend their embarrassing riches on." She snorted and picked up her glass of wine.

"Oh Vicky, I wasn't trying to put you down. You asked me how I liked my new job, that's all." Maggie's worry that she had insulted her friend was allayed when Vicky winked at her from over the rim of her glass.

"Of course not, babe. I'm just messing with you. Seriously, I'm glad you're so happy. Are you full-time yet?"

"No, I just work Monday, Wednesday and Friday for now. But I'm hourly, so I can be flexible if they need me to work extra, to cover a project or something. Like right now, we're getting ready to launch a new product. We just got FDA approval this year, and we're wrapping up the packaging and advertising. Too bad we didn't go with St. Chapelle, huh? That would have been a trip. I'd be working with the old crew again but this time, I'd be the client. They'd have to kiss my butt. Ha!"

"Yeah . . . uh huh."

Maggie followed Vicky's gaze as it flitted restlessly across the crowd of business people eating lunch before getting sidetracked by the flow of traffic on the nearby street. "So, what's new with you? Sell any monstrosities lately?"

Vicky came back to the conversation. "Oh my God, you should see the absurd 'center hall colonial' I just pawned off on some yuppie couple from the city. It was all I could do to keep a straight face when I showed it to them. The woman's expression was priceless when she saw the butler's pantry, complete with built-in wine fridge. Ooh la la, we have arrived, baby!" Vicky took another swallow of wine. "I'm sure they're ordering their framed prints of fox hunting scenes for the study by now," she added drily. She snickered at the recollection and drained her glass. As much as she was an expert at moving the high-end spec houses the builders churned out, Vicky herself lived in a tidy, 1930s cottage on a quiet side street not far from the center of town. Maggie loved that about her.

～✕

Rowan was not faring as well at work as his wife was. The sensational case of the murdered girl eclipsed all the cases he and the other detectives had been working on.

At first, the path of investigation was straightforward enough. This was certainly not the first homicide they had worked. Rowan and his partner, Mike Nickerson, had begun by interviewing the girl's parents.

The girl's mother, who had been home with her two children and had found her daughter's body, had been eliminated as a suspect fairly quickly. She was plainly in shock and had exhibited no behavior that would raise a red flag.

She told the investigators that she was upstairs with her younger child, an eighteen-month-old daughter. The five-year-old was watching her favorite cartoon in the family room and all the doors were locked, so the mother felt comfortable curling up with her toddler for a quick nap. She sometimes did this, and there had never been a problem. But she slept longer than she had intended:

dusk had fallen when she and the baby woke. She went downstairs to check on her older daughter and found the TV on and the room empty. She began to search for her, calmly at first, then more frantically. She noticed a French door to the backyard was open and went outside in the rain, calling her daughter. She ran through the empty yard and began to search the trees at the back of the property. Her screams brought the neighbors running, and they called 911.

Likewise, the girl's father was not a suspect. He had been in meetings all afternoon, surrounded by respectable citizens who could vouch for his whereabouts. A corporate attorney, he wasn't exposed to disturbed criminals who might hold a grudge against him.

The couple seemed to have been happy and had no known enemies. When questioned separately, neither admitted to any affairs or behavior that might bring an aggrieved third party into the picture.

Rowan and Mike believed both parents to be telling the truth. All the doors had been locked, and there was no sign of forced entry, so they assumed that the girl had been lured outside. Once in the shelter of the trees, she had been bludgeoned. A bloody chunk of granite about the size of a football lay nearby. It bore no fingerprints. Investigators spent days working the site, combing the wet leaves and evergreens for forensic evidence. They found nothing. The thick carpet of leaves held no footprints. The police dog found a weak scent that trailed off in the rain-drenched undergrowth and disappeared.

After a week had passed and all the family's friends and neighbors had been interviewed, the police had precisely nothing. It appeared that a happy, stable family had had the most heinous of crimes visited upon it for no apparent reason.

The inscrutability of the offense was its most disturbing aspect. The mayor of Stamford spoke through the local media and assured people that there was no reason to panic. They need only observe basic security precautions and otherwise go about their business. The police would have the fiend in custody soon.

But people were not reassured. 9-1-1 calls increased ten-fold as every raccoon knocking a lid off a trashcan in the night became a bloodthirsty, homicidal maniac. Elementary schools were crammed with cars every morning and afternoon while worried parents personally delivered and picked up their young children. The frequent fender-benders from the increased traffic put the daytime officers under as much stress as the night shift. At one school, a little boy was pinned between two cars as parents, desperate to get to the office, lost patience with the congestion. Fortunately, he was not injured seriously and was back in school the next day.

In a separate incident, a man came home early from a business trip only to be shot by his wife, who did not expect him that night. Having been out of the country for a week, he was unaware of the town's heightened state of vigilance. The couple lived only half a mile from the scene of the crime. The man spent several days in the hospital.

Rowan thought the investigation couldn't come to an end quickly enough. He also knew that, barring unexpected contact from a witness, it wouldn't any time soon.

4.

Cambien swept into the lab office, good humor animating his handsome face. "Come on, Maggie, you're getting a behind-the-scenes exclusive today," he boomed. He took her coat from the rack by the wall and held it out for her with a chivalrous flourish.

Maggie stood slowly. "Where are we going?" She glanced from Cambien to the complex report on her computer screen. "I–I think Dr. Rajagopalan needs this report edited by the end of the day."

"Nikhil," Cambien called across the lab space. The researcher looked up from his work, scowling. "I need to borrow Maggie for the rest of the day. Your report can wait, can't it?"

Dr. Rajagolpoulon gave an exasperated nod.

"Great, thank you so much." He turned back and proffered her coat again. "Maggie."

"Um, okay. Let me just get my things."

Then she was gliding down the parkway in the back seat of a gleaming black car, Cambien beside her. "Can I get you something? Mineral water? Juice? Champagne?" he asked. He opened a compact but well-stocked refrigerator that was built into the console in front of them.

Giddy from the luxury, Maggie considered the champagne before resigning herself to her sense of professionalism. "A water would be great, thanks." He opened a bottle and handed it to her. She took a swallow before speaking again. "Now will you tell me where we're going?"

Cambien had opened a mineral water for himself and took a long pull before answering. "As I said, you're getting a behind-the-scenes exclusive for the newsletter. I'm filming a spot for our new ad campaign. We're trying something different, and I think it's an exciting new direction for pharmaceutical advertising."

Maggie's interest as a former ad professional was piqued. "Really? What are you doing?"

"Well, think of all the commercials you've seen for sleeping pills."

Maggie thought. "They're mostly female actors pretending to wake up completely refreshed after a good night's sleep. Maybe some nighttime footage, some corny animal motif."

"Exactly. I can hardly tell one from the other, can you?"

"No, not really. So what are you going to do?"

"I'm going to make a direct appeal, as a doctor, to our potential customers. I'm going to speak frankly and plainly to them, explaining how I can help them sleep. I'm going to put a human face on the research behind our medicine."

"I have to admit, that's a fresh approach, for sleeping pills or any pharma."

Cambien grinned. "And it doesn't hurt that most of our clients are ladies. I daresay my stunning good looks will have their effect as well." He tilted his chin up and struck a heroic pose for Maggie's benefit. She couldn't help but laugh, though she also couldn't help but think he was right.

They alighted in front of an industrial-looking building on Manhattan's west side and rode the elevator to the top floor. A receptionist greeted them from behind a combination desk and espresso bar, which she shared with an enormous, tattooed man who offered them coffee. They each took a cup and proceeded into a cavernous studio.

Maggie's head swiveled. She had been to one or two shoots before, but nothing on this scale. People swarmed everywhere, scurrying from task to task. Before she could get her bearings, an energetic woman with a fixed smile and hair a shade too red greeted Cambien. A tall, sardonic-looking man with short, bleached hair sidled up beside her. Both were in their late thirties and dressed head-to-toe in black.

"Maggie, meet Tandy and Bruce from A.D., our ad agency. Tandy is our account executive and Bruce is the creative director. Guys, this is Maggie. She's our internal communications writer. She'll be doing an interest piece about the shoot."

"Nice to meet you." Tandy flashed her tight grin on Maggie before turning back to Cambien. "Hope you got your beauty sleep, handsome. We need you looking your best today." She took Cambien's arm and steered him towards the corner of the studio devoted to the stylists.

Bruce offered a handshake and a platitudinous greeting as he looked Maggie over. At a loss for small talk, they stood awkwardly, side by side, for a moment before he excused himself and ambled off after Tandy and Cambien.

Alone amidst the bustling set, Maggie wandered to an unoccupied sofa along one wall. She put her bag down, took out her cell phone and note pad, and surveyed the room. Her gaze swept over the prop stylists, director, cameraman, techs, and lighting assistants before it found Cambien. He sat twenty feet away, in a high chair in front of a brightly lit mirror. A thin, young man was blowing his hair dry while a painfully fashionable woman applied makeup to his face. Meeting Maggie's gaze, he winked. Maggie smiled back. Even ensconced in something as emasculating as a stylist's chair, Cambien was the epitome of manly charm.

The morning passed and lunch was laid out before the shooting began. Holding a plate of flank steak and fennel, Maggie stood with the idle members of the crew, watching.

Seated in a white upholstered armchair, Cambien looked directly into the camera as he delivered his lines. He would speak, the director would interrupt, light would be adjusted or direction given or his collar straightened, then it would begin again. After an hour, the major players broke to eat. Several more hours of shooting followed. At last, Cambien delivered his final line, ". . . and get the rest you need to be yourself," reached up, and snapped off the lamp on the table beside him.

In the suddenly dark and silent studio, Maggie still saw the image of Cambien's earnest expression and heard his promising words as he spoke to the millions of insomnia sufferers in the country. When the studio manager called out, "That's a wrap," and everyone applauded, Maggie realized she had been holding her breath. Cambien had been that compelling. She laughed and clapped with everyone else. The man was good.

~~~×

There is an old saying to the effect that every man must face his own demons. In Cambien Cuthbert's case, this was quite literally true. Since as early in his life as he could remember, he had been haunted by an actual demon.

The demon only appeared to him in his sleep. It was a masculine demon, taller than the tallest person Cambien knew and bulky with muscles. It had a neck as thick as a bull's. Its skin was a reddish brown color, thick and coarse, and its yellow eyes, divided by pupils like a cat's, were unblinking and pitiless.

As a baby, Cambien would howl and scream in his sleep. His parents would shake him awake, pick him up, and soothe him. As he got older, he learned to wake himself from the demon's nightmare visits. The fiend would insert itself into Cambien's dreams and scare the tiny boy nearly senseless before he would realize he was dreaming and rouse himself.

The night Cambien's mother died, when he was just three, his father allowed him to sleep in bed with him. As Cambien began to dream, he became aware that the demon had joined him. But the creature was subdued this night, silently cradling Cambien in its arms.

After that peculiar instance, the beast disappeared for almost a decade. It reappeared as Cambien entered puberty. An adolescent dream about a pretty girl in his class was interrupted as the monster lurched into the scene. Cambien recognized it at once and sank immediately into the familiar terror and despair. The demon stared at him with its awful eyes, opened its fanged mouth, and roared with malicious laughter. Cambien felt like the puniest, most pathetic wretch on earth. He cowered before the creature, trying to roll himself tightly into a ball before it attacked him, waiting to feel its teeth and claws rip the flesh from his back at any moment.

In his bed, he tossed and called out, sweating heavily. Finally he woke up. The night demon hadn't touched him, but he could not shake the feeling of helpless wretchedness it had invoked in him.

After that, the fiend appeared to him several times a year. Each visit was so terrifying that Cambien went about shakily for days afterward, anxious and cowed. He feared sleep and stayed up as late as he could, reading in his room. He dozed in the wee hours of the morning, his room ablaze with every lamp turned on. He stumbled down school halls, pale and clumsy, with pasty skin and dark rings under his eyes. The blackness of his hair and irises made him look even paler.

In addition to being wan and nervous, Cambien grew tall quite rapidly. He stretched out long and thin as he grew and his muscular development was hard pressed to keep up with his skeletal growth. He became gangly in appearance and clumsy in manner.

But he also possessed a brilliant intellect. He honed this gift during the long nights spent awake, reading and studying to pass the time. He strove to discipline his mind, hoping he might reach a point where he could control his thoughts enough to banish the monster from his dreams.

Meanwhile, he easily outperformed his classmates in almost every subject. By the time he entered high school, he had a reputation for being a nerd. The high school he attended was regional; kids from his neighborhood went there with kids from other towns. Most of the students were from Vale, a sprawling, working class town of old farmhouses and new developments. Cambien lived in the nearby hamlet of Lauren, which was wealthier and more rarified than the surrounding area. Between his nervousness, his pale, gangly appearance, his superior academic performance, and his posh address, he was often a target of the Schofield High School bullies.

Most times when he was pushed around, he kept his eyes down and waited stoically until the ruffians were satisfied and left. (They were, after all, rank amateurs compared to the beast he faced in his sleep). He would then gather up his scattered books and papers, or dredge his parka from the mud puddle, or pick himself up from the ground, and go about his business. He said nothing but had anyone looked into his eyes at those times, they would have seen a black fire burning in their depths.

By tenth grade, Cambien learned to stay near teachers or other adults, to avoid being caught alone and vulnerable by teenaged predators. In his junior year, his father gave him a second-hand car for his sixteenth birthday. He now drove himself to school and avoided the tough kids on the bus. By this time, his body had begun to fill out and he became more coordinated as he grew accustomed to his height. Less clumsy and insecure, he was picked on less frequently. Most kids simply ignored him.

To keep him from being bored, the school administration advanced him to classes for older students. In eleventh grade, he was placed in calculus, a class otherwise populated by seniors who were capable of doing mathematics on the college level.

Cambien was more contented in calculus than he had yet been at Schofield High. The kids there were a year older and hence, a year more mature. They were also the brightest in their grade and regarded academic prowess as an asset, rather than something to be scorned and belittled. Not that Cambien was suddenly popular—he was, after all, just a junior—but he was afforded a measure of respect and otherwise left unmolested.

By the second week of calculus class, Cambien realized he wasn't going to be a target. He sat up straight and raised his eyes to look around the room at the other students. This was when he first noticed the pretty, chestnut-haired girl sitting in the second row, over by the windows. She gazed outside as often as she looked at the teacher, a sweet, dreamy expression on her round face. She had bright hazel eyes and a smattering of freckles across her nose. When she stood at the end of class, he saw that she was taller than most of the other girls. From listening to kids talk, he learned that her name was Maggie Cooper, and she lived with her grandmother because her mother had died when she was young and her father was away a lot. Cambien began to feel a strong affinity for her.

Around that time, the demon visited Cambien in an otherwise innocuous dream he was having about eating a bowl of cereal. The man-like beast materialized across the table from him and roared, "Surprise!" It howled with unkind laughter. Cambien was so terrified, he fell backwards to the floor and tried to scuttle, crab-like, away from it.

The demon yelled at him in a voice as loud as a jet engine. "You have got to be kidding," it said. "Do you presume to think about that girl? Do you really fool yourself into believing she could ever possibly care for you?" It laughed maniacally again, making Cambien's ears ache. Then it flung the table aside and advanced on him. He had gotten to his feet by now, but the foul creature still towered over him. "You pathetic, ugly, little worm! You filth! You cowardly little prick!" Each word struck as painfully as a blow.

For the first time in one of his nightmares, from somewhere within his terror, Cambien felt the stirrings of anger. He stopped retreating backwards from the beast.

"No one will ever care about you, you disgusting little piece of shit. You—"

"SHUT UP!" yelled Cambien.

The demon paused in its tirade, unused to defiance from its victim. Its eyes widened in outrage and its lip curled back over its sharp, uneven teeth. Cambien did not move as he stood, waiting.

"How dare you?" shrieked the fiend, hurling itself onto him.

It was like being hit by a truck; Cambien was knocked onto his back by the force of the blow. The beast reared up and struck him with a fist like a pile driver. He felt the bones in his face shatter. He was unable to scream or even breathe through the wreckage.

He woke gasping for air. His room was black, since he had lately gotten out of the habit of sleeping with the lights on. Frantically, he turned on his bedside lamp and stared all about. His sheets were soaked with sweat, his pillow with tears and spittle. He leapt up and looked in the mirror. His unmarred face looked back at him. Shaking, he returned to his bed and sat down. His breathing slowly returned to normal. The hysteria abated. He was okay.

He had defied his demon, and he was okay.

5.

The halls of NarcoDynamics were buzzing. The upcoming launch of their new product, Somnusol, was almost upon them.

Maggie sat at her computer, editing. In her peripheral field of vision, she was aware of Dr. Rajagopalan taking readings at one of the research stations. The door to the lab, which they customarily left open, admitted the lanky form of Dr. Cuthbert. He flashed a grin at her as he passed. "Hello, Maggie."

She returned his smile. "Hi, Dr. Cuthbert."

He stopped in his tracks. "Tut tut tut, it's Cam—"

"Cambien, yes, I'm sorry. You told me to call you Cambien. Hi, Cambien."

"That's better." Satisfied, he strode on his way to Dr. Rajagopalan. "Nikhil, do you have a minute?"

Dr. Rajagopalan ceased his work. "Certainly, Dr. Cuthbert. What may I help you with?"

Maggie detected a whiff of annoyance in the Indian doctor's posture, but this apparently went unnoticed by his employer. She also noticed that Dr. Cuthbert—sorry, *Cambien*—didn't insist that Dr. Rajagopalan call him by his first name. Maggie shrugged and went back to her work. Doubtless this issue had been resolved between the two men years before she started working there. Dr. Rajagopalan called her Mrs. Moore, after all. He evidently preferred a degree of formality in his interactions with his colleagues. Maggie was comfortable with this arrangement, as she had great professional respect for his intellect and degree of education, and little or no knowledge of his personal life anyway.

She went back to the report she was editing and the sound of the men's conversation was pushed from her consciousness. She needed to pay the strictest attention to the scientific reports she edited. And so she didn't notice at first that Cambien had come closer and was addressing her. She suddenly realized he was standing right behind her and had just asked her something. Maggie swiveled in her chair and looked up.

"I'm sorry, I didn't realize you were talking to me. What did you say?"

Cambien was pleased by her reaction. "That's what I like to see; my team completely absorbed in their work. I knew I did the right thing when I hired you, Maggie. You're a steady worker. You always were. I remember watching you in class. The other kids were so gossipy and silly, and just plain mean sometimes, but you always kept your eyes on your work. You never got drawn into that nastiness. I admired you very much for it."

Maggie went pink, pleased by his compliment. Cambien continued. "I was asking you whether you thought this report was complete enough for FDA compliance."

"I, um, I guess I'm not really the one to answer that. I mean, I'm not as informed about this data or the FDA requirements as you guys are. Heck, let's be honest, I hardly even understand most of it. You guys are the brains of this operation; I just tidy up after the fact."

Cambien chuckled, charmed by her humility. "Don't belittle yourself, Maggie. There is considerable technical skill as well as a natural gift required to do what you do for us. We eggheads have spent our whole lives surrounded by test tubes; we're hopeless when it comes to constructing a halfway decent English sentence."

Maggie turned pinker still under his praise. He leaned over to point to the monitor in front of her, questioning whether a data set was complete. Startled by his closeness, she leaned back in her chair to make room for him. She answered his questions as best she could, though she became more and more flustered. It was surely unintentional, but Cambien's shoulder kept brushing against her upper arm as he reached to indicate something on her monitor. She leaned back further in her chair and found herself staring at the way his lab coat pulled taut over his wide shoulders. His voice was a deeper rumble than usual, as he was so near to her and speaking softly. She could smell the detergent and bleach from his spotless lab coat and beneath that, a combination of soap-clean skin, subtle but expensive-smelling cologne, and something else. Something very faint and difficult to identify; it put her in mind of an exotic spice. She fought to focus on his words and somehow answered all his questions to his satisfaction. Finally, he straightened up. He gave her shoulder a friendly squeeze as he thanked her for her time. Then he strode out through the open door.

Maggie looked after him for a moment. Out of the corner of her eye, she noticed Dr. Rajagopalan doing the same thing. She turned to look at the researcher and saw an expression of something akin to contempt on his face. He met her glance. "Never he came here to muddle so much with my work," he muttered. Now he looked at her as though she were somehow the problem.

Maggie wasn't sure what his point was. "I imagine he's just anxious about the new product launch, don't you think? It is a bit nerve-wracking, making sure everything has been taken care of."

The doctor looked at her another moment, then shrugged as if to say, who knows? Both Maggie and Dr. Rajagopalan returned to their work.

⤙

Maggie met Vicky for a quick drink (or two, in Vicky's case) at Tess's after work. Vicky was meeting someone for dinner. She didn't give Maggie any details and Maggie didn't ask. Vicky was usually meeting a man for something or other and Maggie had long ago stopped bothering to learn their names. The friends talked about people they both knew, a scandalous love triangle at town hall, and the case of the murdered girl.

"So they still don't have a clue, huh?" Vicky asked. Maggie shook her head. "Man, Rowan must be having a hell of a time."

"Who?"

"Rowan? Your husband?"

"Oh yes, Rowan. Of course. For a minute, I forgot I was married, since I haven't actually seen my husband in days."

"Wow, that bad, huh? I guess these things are hard on cops' families, too."

Maggie dropped her snide attitude and spoke plainly to her friend. "It really is hard, Vicky. I swear, I feel like a single mom these days. I love my kids more than anything, but they drive me nuts after working all day, and Rowan's never there to give me a break. The kids miss him, too. And even worse, I actually have a life of my own now—a job, a social life with friends I made myself, interesting stuff to talk about, you know? But it's so frustrating to have no one at home to talk to. Sometimes I really start to feel sorry for myself and the kids." Her eyes glistened as she stared down into her wine glass. "But then I think of that poor little girl and her family, and I get over myself pretty quick."

"Whew, I'll bet. Man, we think we have it bad sometimes." Vicky shook her head. She took a swallow of her bourbon and diet Coke.

Maggie checked her watch. "Speaking of kids, I better hit the road or no one's having any supper tonight."

"Oh shit, I better get going too. I only like to keep them waiting fifteen minutes or so on the first date. Bottoms up."

The two friends walked out to their cars together and went their separate ways.

Maggie got home half an hour later. She kissed her kids and father. "Want to stay for supper, Pop? We're getting tired of staring at Rowan's empty chair every night."

After dinner, Maggie walked her father out onto the porch. They looked up in surprise as Rowan's truck pulled into the driveway.

"Hey, Ro," Maggie called to him. "Nice to see you home so early. The kids are still awake."

Inexplicably, Rowan chose to take offense at her greeting. "What's that supposed to mean? Is that some kind of sarcasm? If you don't want me here, I can leave."

Maggie and her father exchanged puzzled looks. "Well, I don't want to take up your time together," said the older man. "You hardly have enough of it these days. Take care, Rowan.

'Night, Maggie." He kissed his daughter on the cheek, got into his car, and drove off.

Maggie hugged herself in the chilly night air as her husband got his things out of the truck and came towards her.

"You've been complaining to your father that I don't spend enough time with you?" Rowan growled.

"I was complaining that I miss you, if that's what you mean," Maggie answered softly. "Certainly not that it's your fault."

Rowan stopped next to his wife. He put his overstuffed briefcase and his laptop down and turned to face the same direction she was facing. He leaned back against the wall of the house, sighed deeply, and stared out at the night. Maggie leaned back next to him and stared out at the same patch of dark sky. After a moment, Rowan spoke quietly. "I miss you too, babe."

The next day, Maggie took the children to buy new shoes for the warmer weather. The nearest good children's shoe store was in Stamford, the same one her mother, then later her grandmother, had bought her shoes from when she was a child. There was a discount shoe store in Vale, but the sales people there didn't know or care to measure a toddler's foot properly. So Maggie told herself as she passed the Vale Shopping Plaza and pulled onto the southbound entrance ramp to the parkway.

After the children's feet had been properly measured and they had selected a pair of sneakers and a pair of shoes each, Maggie felt antsy and reluctant to go directly home. The weather was spring-like but not yet nice enough to spend a lot of time out in the yard. Nor did she fancy the prospect of staying indoors all afternoon. She decided to take the children to the diner for lunch. As the waiter set an enormous cheeseburger before her, she exclaimed, "Good heavens, how am I supposed to eat this?" Yet before she knew it, only crumbs remained on her plate. She rubbed her stomach and groaned. "Come on, kids, let's walk this off."

Maggie knew there was a store in this neighborhood that Hazel and Charlie might like to see. She held one small hand in each of hers and the threesome ambled along the sidewalk. As they reached the hobby shop, both children stopped in their tracks.

In one of the store's windows stood a miniature world of lords and ladies on horseback. A mail-clad army laid siege to a castle with a tiny tower and trebuchet. On the other side of a forest, elves and fairies danced and feasted. A dragon and a griffin did battle outside a nearby cave. On a white horse with lavender mane and tail sat a winged princess, crowned with a floral wreath. Hazel gazed at the plastic pixie and sighed.

Charlie, meanwhile, stood enraptured by the intricate model train layout in the other window. A long freighter ran a loop through a rail yard while above it, a streamliner pulled coaches along an elevated track that passed above the town and through a mountain pass.

Maggie stood next to her son, keeping him out of the way of the pedestrians on the busy sidewalk. "In!" shouted Charlie. He pointed and tried to move to the door. Maggie did not want to go into the store as she was already lugging a large handbag and two shopping bags full of shoeboxes. After a couple near misses where Charlie was almost trampled by customers leaving the shop, Maggie placed herself between him and the door. She knelt with one arm around the little boy and pointed out details in the train layout. "See, Charlie? Look at the bridge over the river. Do you know what kind of bridge that is? It's called a *trestle*."

Looking into the window, Maggie saw the moving reflections of people who passed behind them on the sidewalk. One long reflection stood still as its source came to a halt. She turned her head to look up and felt a thrill as she recognized Dr. Cuthbert. He smiled down at her and Charlie. "Oh, hello," said Maggie. As she rose to her feet, her heart thumped in her chest—surely from standing so abruptly.

"Hello, Maggie. Who are these little guys?" Hazel, shy around the tall, strange man, left her window, hid behind Maggie, and peeked out from behind her mother's leg. Charlie looked up, up, up at the stranger. He pointed into the window at the trains.

Maggie was always gladdened when someone took notice of her children, more so when it was someone she respected as much as Cambien. She introduced them. "This is Charlie, and this one back here is Hazel. Kids, this is mommy's boss, Dr. Cuthbert."

"Hi," Hazel said quietly, staring up at him with unblinking eyes. She stayed behind her mother and reached out to shake the hand Cambien held out before she snatched her own hand back to safety.

"Hello, Hazel. It's a pleasure to meet you. Hello, Charlie. Do you like trains?" Charlie stared up at the lofty stranger and nodded his head. He turned back to the display. Cambien came next to him and stooped to look into the window. "Charlie, do you know what kind of train that one is, up on that mountain track?" Maggie stood back a step, her arm over Hazel's shoulders, and watched Cambien with her son. The sight touched her somehow.

Hazel soon let rivalry overcome her shyness and went to Cambien. Taking his hand, she pulled him away from her brother. "Come over here, Dr. Cuzbert. You have to see this." Cambien let himself be dragged to the store's other window. "Look at this princess on the horse. She's the queen of the fairies over here. And that's her husband, and they're having a big party."

Cambien met Maggie's gaze and, flanked by her children, smiled as if to say, *what can I do? I'm utterly enthralled.* He took each child by the hand and said, "Come along, kids. Let's go inside and see what else there is."

The kids squealed with delight and went into the store without a backward glance. Maggie was flummoxed. She scooped up her packages and followed. Burdened as she was with bags, she couldn't keep up with the three of them. Cambien looked to be having more fun than the children as he took the lead in a race from display to display. Over Maggie's protests, he directed the children to place several toys each on the check out counter. Maggie was exasperated, yet amused by the fun Cambien and the kids were having. Poor guy, she thought. So busy building up his empire, yet she'd bet nothing would make him happier than to have children of his own. And Hazel and Charlie hadn't had such a spirited, carefree outing in quite some time, so Maggie let them have their fun.

Cambien and the children left the store ahead of Maggie, who came outside just in time to hear him say, "Now, who wants some ice cream?" Hazel and Charlie hollered their approval. Maggie knew there would be no way to reign in such excited children.

She could not stay annoyed, however, when she saw the delight on Cambien's and her kids' faces.

One hour and several sundaes later, Cambien walked the Moores back to the station wagon. He carried Charlie the last two blocks on his wide shoulders. Two elderly ladies walking in the opposite direction smiled at what looked like a handsome young family. Cambien held the car door for the kids. They each hugged him before they climbed in. He leaned into the car and buckled Charlie into his booster seat. Finally he turned to Maggie and for an awkward moment, she felt as though she ought to kiss him and thank him for a wonderful date. But he simply smiled.

"Well, I certainly had a great time. Thank you for letting me hijack your beautiful children. I hope I didn't hold up any plans."

"No, not at all. I hope we didn't keep you from anything important at the office."

"Maggie," he said, looking quite serious, "there's nothing more important than the children." Then he broke into an easy smile. "See you at work tomorrow."

"You bet. And Cambien—thanks. That was really fun."

"The pleasure was all mine." He held her door as she got into the driver's seat.

"Bye, Dr. Cuzbert!" they shouted out the windows. All three of them waved. Cambien waved back until they were out of sight.

6.

Maggie thought about the trip to Stamford as she fixed supper. Funny, how much she had enjoyed herself. She had always been one to stick to the plan, to be conservative with time and money. Yet Cambien had come along and waylaid her little platoon with ease. She didn't even want to think about how much he had spent on the toys he bought the children. And then, the extravagance of ice cream–not just ice cream, but huge, fudge-covered, candy-sprinkled, whipped cream-smothered and cherry-topped sundaes–well, Maggie couldn't remember the last time she and Rowan had been so carefree with the kids. This made her sad, and maybe a bit angry, too. But she was quick to chide herself. Poor Rowan, he was going through hell these days. She'd be grim, too, if she were under so much pressure to solve such a wretched case.

At that moment, she heard Rowan's truck pull into the driveway. She smoothed her hair back and straightened her shirt. She dumped spaghetti into the boiling water and stirred the sauce as she waited for him to come into the kitchen. "Hi, honey," she called as he came into the room.

"Hey, Mags. What're we having?" He came up behind her and put his hands on her hips, looking over her shoulder at the pots bubbling on the stove. Then he gave her a kiss on the cheek.

Maggie breathed deeply. Rowan seemed almost normal this evening. Damn, she missed him.

She turned and put her arms around his neck. "Spaghetti and meatballs. Don't tell Hazel, but I snuck some zucchini into the sauce." She kissed him on the lips. For a moment, he put his arms around her and kissed her back, but he broke the contact quickly.

"Did the mail come today?"

"It generally does." Sighing, Maggie went back to her cooking. "It's on the kitchen table."

Rowan walked to the table and began sorting through his mail. "So, what did you guys do today?" he asked, his attention on the return address of an envelope.

"I took the kids to Stamford to buy shoes. You won't believe it–Charlie has grown two sizes since last winter. Not one, but two."

She glanced at Rowan. "Uh huh," he muttered. He opened an envelope and began reading.

"That's pretty much it." No point in telling him about the rest of the day; he wouldn't be listening anyway. And suddenly, Maggie realized she didn't want to tell him about running into Cambien and spending the afternoon with him. Not that she had done anything wrong, but Rowan might take it the wrong way. So she left him to read his mail in peace while she finished cooking.

But at dinner, Rowan asked the children, "What did you guys do today?" They both began talking at once. Charlie blurted out "Toys!" and Hazel launched into a lengthy monologue about mommy's friend, Doctor Cuzbert, who bought them toys and took them all for ice cream.

"What's this? Who?" asked Rowan.

Maggie felt a guilty surge of panic. She began to talk quickly over the children. "I tried telling you. I took the kids to Stamford to buy shoes—"

"Yes, I heard you. Charlie grew not one, but two sizes since last winter."

"I didn't think you were listening, so I stopped talking."

"Of course I was listening."

"Well, how am I supposed to know that? People usually look at people when they're talking to them," Maggie snapped. The children stopped gibbering and the room grew quiet. Maggie hurried on. "Anyway, we ran into my boss and he insisted on taking the kids into the toy store and buying them stuff. Then he bought us all ice cream, and the kids and I went home." She hoped Rowan would settle for her account; after all, it was the truth.

After a pause he said, "Well, who could blame him? Our kids are exceptionally adorable. I'm not surprised they charmed an innocent man into showering them with gifts and treats. Look what they do to your father all the time."

Maggie laughed gratefully at his joke as relief washed over her. Hazel piped up. "Doctor Cuzbert gave Charlie a ride on his shoulders!"

"Did he now?" asked Rowan. He reached across the table to the bowl of grated cheese and spooned a generous amount on his pasta.

"Mommy, may I have some more milk?" Hazel asked. Maggie took her cup into the kitchen.

~~~

If Rowan seemed distracted or cross with his family when he was home, it wasn't by choice. The truth was he could barely stand the sight of them. Not that he hated them or was angry with them, but quite the opposite; they were so beautiful, soft, content, and healthy, and he loved them so much. It was unbearable.

He was a police officer because there was nothing else he could have been. He had always understood the world to be peopled with a daunting proportion of evil, dangerous, nasty monsters, and his years in the New Haven and Stamford Police Departments had more than verified this conviction. With each new inhumanity he responded to, he withdrew emotionally, an almost imperceptible amount, from the world. He had to, or he would go mad.

He and the other cops made shocking jokes about their work. They wryly referred to the segment of the public they dealt with as their "clients." They shuttled disturbed people and maltreated children to the appropriate social services. In their personal time, they kept themselves relentlessly busy; some were avid hunters or kept small boats for fishing on the sound, some drank, some volunteered for additional rescue services in their own neighborhoods, some carried on illicit affairs, some were deacons, some were military reservists. Usually, after twenty years on the force and only in their mid-forties, Stamford police officers retired. Some of them had to if they wished to retain their humanity.

Rowan had sixteen years on the job and was not yet ready to retire. He still had a rich reserve of human emotion and, though he had seen much, he was not so calloused that he was beyond feeling. This turned out to be unfortunate because, when he responded to the call of the murdered girl, his heart was very vulnerable to what he found. Which led to the trouble at home.

He used to come home at the end of the day and feel the world slide off his shoulders. If he had been disturbed at work, he had only to look in on his young children and watch them play together to feel human and peaceful again. But now, if he incautiously raised his eyes from the television and looked through the window at his daughter's head bent over her latest garden project, he saw only a small girl's brown hair matted with blood and clumped together with rain and dirt. He used to be able to join his wife in the kitchen, taking her in his arms as she turned smiling from the stove to greet him, and find solace. But now, Maggie's bright eyes and wide smile dissolved into the wrecked eyes and sunken face of the dead girl's mother. He could no longer accept the whim of fate that was his own life. The human condition was too painful. There was so much pain that it had, inevitably, forced its way into his world. Rowan's beautiful wife and children were now, by glaring contrast, intolerable reminders of the pain.

Desperate to avoid the pain and not one to turn to drink or drugs, Rowan kept up a compulsive surveillance of the media coverage of the case. It would have been impossible to pick a more fascinating victim for the news to obsess over. The young girl had been the daughter of respectable people who lived in a safe neighborhood. Her father was a well-known, wealthy attorney in town. Her mother had been a vice president of a large Stamford marketing firm before she left work to raise her children. She had become involved in several charitable organizations and enjoyed a certain social standing. Because of the stature of the family, the youth and innocence of the victim, and the mystery surrounding the dreadful act of violence, the media coverage of the incident was intense.

Recently, the story had spilled out of the Stamford media and been picked up by the big, New York City-based stations. Rowan and the other detectives and officers avoided reporters like the plague, leaving Chief Stankiewicz to speak for them. As he grew tired of having no new answers to the reporters' questions, the Chief became increasingly foul-tempered and abusive with the detectives. Rowan could hardly blame him. He was ashamed of having accomplished nothing of consequence, as far as finding the killer was concerned.

And so, after checking into headquarters the following morning, Rowan drove to the north of town, to the forested lanes, antique houses and gleaming mansions of the well-to-do, to the dead girl's neighborhood. He would re-canvas today, interviewing anyone he could find, trying to find someone who remembered something that would help. He would start by checking in on the girl's mother. This decision was oddly comforting. Rowan would never consciously admit it to himself, but he only felt normal these days in a house of heartbreak.

That Sunday, Rowan did not go to work. He made his famous ultra-cinnamon French toast and the family sat to eat breakfast together before heading off to church. Father Bill gave a homily about assuming the burdens of less fortunate people, and Maggie thought about how Rowan had made the murdered girl's family's burden his own. After church, she suggested they go to the park and take a walk by the lake. She missed the beautiful spot, not having been there since the previous fall. But at the park, they found winter still clinging to the earth in shadowy spots beneath trees and alongside boulders. A northerly breeze tore ragged bits of cloud across the sun and cold light flickered over the yellow lawns.

Undaunted, Maggie herded her family resolutely down the lakeside path. She looked into the opaque water, trying to catch sight of the bright carp that lived there. But the wind chopped the water's surface and nothing beneath it could be seen. Hazel complained that she was cold. Charlie stopped every few paces and whined, raising his arms to convince his father to carry him. "Oh come on, Charlie. Give me a break," Rowan barked. He and Maggie strode ahead, leaving the children to straggle behind them.

"Rowan, I know how busy you are lately," began Maggie, "but I really need you to come to something with me."

"What?"

"It's a launch party. NarcoDynamics is launching our new sleeping pill. They've been working on it for years and it's finally hitting the market. It's a really big deal. So we're having a fancy party and we're supposed to bring our spouses."

Rowan groaned. "Really? They specifically said to bring spouses?"

"Yup. My invitation was addressed to Maggie and Rowan Moore. And my boss even wrote a personal note on it, saying how much he hoped we'd come. Both of us. So you see, we kind of have to go. It's a corporate culture thing."

Rowan laughed mirthlessly. "Oh, great. We have to immerse ourselves in NarcoDynamic culture," he sneered. "Very well, when and where?"

"It's at the Chisholm Gallery, in Greenwich."

"I know where the Chisholm Gallery is."

Maggie checked her temper and continued. "It's on the twelfth. It might even be fun. The catering will probably be incredible, there will be musicians, and it coincides with a great new exhibit. In fact, we get to preview it before it opens to the public. It's called Morpheus, after the Greek god of dreams. It's also a play on words–*morph us*–to focus on the transformative properties of sleep and dreaming. Really quite appropriate for our new product launch."

"Well, now I know why they call it 'corporate culture.' La-di-da." But Rowan sounded slightly interested. "Is it just for the employees?"

"Oh no, there will also be the PR firm, a bunch of local doctors, some editors from the medical journals, if we can get them, and some local media. Maybe even some of the New York news stations, if we get lucky."

"Black tie?"

"No, not quite. You can wear your good suit. I'll get you a hip new tie, if you want." Maggie started going through her closet in her mind. She would have to get a new dress, maybe some shoes. She began to look forward to a sophisticated night out with her husband. They hadn't been on a proper date in ages. She took Rowan's arm and huddled close to him against the stiff breeze. "Who knows, Ro? It might even be fun." She nuzzled his ear and gave him a quick, playful kiss. Rowan turned his head and briskly returned her kiss. They simultaneously looked back to check on the children. Hazel had taken Charlie by the hand and was leading him along the path behind them, explaining various items of importance in a steady stream of prattle.

"Dear God, when does that girl breathe?" asked Rowan. Then his gaze snapped back to the space in front of him. Maggie saw his eyes fix on something that lay beyond the horizon. She still held his arm and she could feel the ever-present tension in his muscles, the sinews taut, through the fabric of his sleeve.

Maggie felt more alive lately than she had in a long time, reconnected with the adult world as she now was, but she was all the while cognizant of her husband's struggle. It was the one thing that kept her from being completely happy, for she couldn't be content while he was foundering. "So, Ro . . . how's it going?"

He exhaled a noisy "Phfft!" in reply.

"That good, huh?" Maggie searched for the right words. "I mean, how about you? Are you okay?"

Rowan sighed deeply. "No, Maggie, I'm not really okay." He walked on in silence.

Maggie longed to draw him out, to make him talk about it, but that was not Rowan's way. He was a man and he would work through his problems himself, period.

It was Maggie's way to share burdens, to ease a loved one's pain by taking some of it on. But she couldn't take what Rowan wouldn't give. "Have you thought about getting some help with it?" she continued gingerly. "Aren't there special counselors to help cops deal with stuff like this?"

Rowan took a quick look at her. "Yes, Maggie, there are critical incident stress counselors and there are shrinks who work with cops. But there's also no way I can start going to a shrink. I'm a supervisor. How am I going to have any authority with guys who think I'm nuts?"

"Oh come on, Ro. They aren't still in the dark ages like that at the PD, are they? You would think, after what happened to Schmidt . . . " Maggie referred to an officer who had committed suicide a few years earlier.

In a patronizing tone, Rowan said, "Maggie, I am not going to kill myself." He scowled and returned his gaze to the vanishing point. Maggie held onto his arm as they walked, lamenting her inability to connect with her there-but-not-there husband.

Fourteen miles from the park where Maggie and her family walked, Cambien stood on the bank of a stream that rushed to the salty sound. Like Maggie had done, he peered into the water, looking for fish: herring, in his case. This particular waterway was a route they had taken to return to their vernal spawning grounds for thousands of years.

Cambien had first come here as a boy. In an uncharacteristic display of paternal interest, his father brought him to see the phenomenon. On that occasion, Cambien remembered, the herring were so thick in the water that he felt sure he could walk across the brook on their backs. His father told him to go ahead and try, so he rolled up his dungarees and stepped in. The fish did not support his weight after all and he drew in his breath as he stood in the rushing water up to his knees, shocked at how cold it was. But though his legs ached to the bone, he was so taken with being part of the rushing stream and the living current within it that he stayed in the icy water. Before long, he found that he could hold his hands still beneath the surface and then, at precisely the right instant, snatch a silver and blue herring from the water. His father watched from the bank, amused, as his young son triumphantly held out fish after fish for him to admire. Finally, when the boy's lips were plum colored and he trembled visibly, his father made him get out and go home to warm up.

Cambien begged to return, but his father only brought him a few times after that. Once he was old enough, he rode his bike to the spot. After that, he drove there. He never stopped coming to the stream to watch the spring migration, and it never ceased to resonate within him.

Now he stood still as a statue and stared, unblinking, into the water. He imagined himself among the rushing current and frantic fins and sparkling, dislodged scales drifting lazily back downstream. The urgency of the quicksilver herring coupled with the inevitability of their migration soothed him. He watched the fish as they were drawn to the waters where they had hatched, to spawn themselves and complete their life cycles.

Cambien Cuthbert had been an uncommonly still child. When he was an infant, his worried mother sometimes held her ear to his mouth, to assure herself that he was breathing. And this wasn't only when he was asleep; sometimes he would lie perfectly still in his crib and stare at the ceiling with wide, somber eyes. The doctor said there was nothing wrong, that indeed, Cambien was hale and hearty. But still, his mother worried.

As Cambien learned to sit up, he began to interact with the people around him. His mother thought she noticed something odd in the way he did this. Her friends' babies instinctively returned the smiles their parents lavished on them; her son appeared to study the expressions of people around him. It seemed he then applied what he had observed to his own interactions. So now when his mother cooed and sang to him, or his father heaved him onto his shoulders and made much of him, Cambien worked his tiny features into the appropriate expression. As he got older, he became so proficient in normal human behavior that his mother found his actions nearly indistinguishable from those of other children. And yet, he always seemed a bit aloof, watching the goings on around him with a cool detachment in his dark eyes.

Even when Cambien's mother died, his grief only seemed to go so deep. His parents had wondered why a brother or sister hadn't followed their son, and the doctor found that his mother was mortally ill. Cambien had bouts of tears when she died, especially at the funeral, but he would return to his calm state the instant the storm passed. It's the still waters run the deepest, an old aunt said. Indeed, Cambien's eyes appeared quite bottomless as he looked up at his parents' friends who tried to comfort him. Disquieted by the child's unblinking gaze, the adults would tousle his hair, straighten, clear their throats, and find a conversation to join.

Cambien's father didn't take his wife's death well. He was not cruel or abusive to the child, nor did he indulge in hysterical displays of grief, but rather, he simply withdrew. His hair and his demeanor grayed. He made sure his son was fed and clothed, dutifully kissed him onto the school bus, donned his colorless overcoat and made his way, shade-like, to his office in Stamford. He worked with numbers and papers all day, shuffling people's savings accounts and retirement plans and dreams like Hades shuffling the pale souls in the underworld.

Upon returning from school in the afternoon, Cambien would be greeted by Mrs. Byrne, the gray-haired matron his father had hired to mind the boy until he got home from work. Father and son dined silently in the evening, eating whatever Mrs. Byrne had left in the oven for them, neither tasting nor talking. Occasionally, Mr. Cuthbert asked Cambien about his day. Cambien obligingly provided a brief account of his activities at school, but neither of them particularly heard the words.

Cambien grew as tall as his father. Though his complexion was spotty and pale, his adolescent features held the promise of becoming handsome someday. He had inherited the sable hair of his mother's people, but his eyes went beyond mere heredity. They were so dark as to appear black; when he spoke to someone and fixed his gaze upon them, the person would become mesmerized, trying to discern the point at which Cambien's iris ended and his pupil began. Only in full sunlight could it be seen that his irises were in fact the deepest blue-gray, the color of the sea at night.

Father and son passed the years in peace. Cambien grew taller and his father grayer. Their somber evening meals continued, uninterrupted by the riotous social life one expects of a teenager. After meals, Cambien went back to his studies in his room and his father sat in the armchair in the den, unseen television images flickering across his face. Other homes in the neighborhood rang with the heated shouts and slamming doors of adolescent growing pains; the Cuthbert's house endured in the silence of a young man who felt no call to rebel and a father who had no impulse to constrain him.

7.

The night of the NarcoDynamics product launch party arrived. Maggie and Rowan stepped out of the truck, Rowan handed the keys to the valet, and they made their way into the lighted art museum in Greenwich's upscale cultural district. An animated crowd of smartly dressed men and women flowed through the open doors beneath the bold portico, from which the din of many voices and strains of music poured forth onto the cool evening air.

As soon as Maggie entered the crowded gallery she had the curious sensation that she could feel Cambien watching her. She couldn't see him and had no idea where he was concealed in the lively crowd, but she was aware of him.

She and Rowan shed their coats and handed them to the woman by the door. Maggie smoothed her gleaming chestnut hair. She had recently had it cut into a mass of chestnut waves that rolled down her back. She wore a deep crimson dress, a simple gown of subtle sheen, sleeveless and cut on the bias, that skimmed her figure and flattered her white throat and arms. Her bright hazel eyes sparkled. She looked so striking that even her stoic husband was moved to words.

"You look really good, Mags."

Maggie flushed with pleasure. "Thanks, Ro. I'll take a Scotch on the rocks, by the way."

They had been carried along by the crowd and now stood in front of a well-stocked bar. Rowan got their drinks and they moved to the wall where they could watch the guests drift down the gallery. Occasionally, Maggie greeted someone she knew from work and they introduced their spouses to one another. Ever resourceful, Rowan ran into several acquaintances of his own. "That's Dr. Manson, he used to work at the ER," he said. Or, "Oh brother, there's Chad Hallopen from the *Champion*. That's all I need." They recognized several personalities from the local news channels and one man from a New York station.

As Maggie watched people join the throng, she recognized a woman with aggressively red hair, accompanied by a tall, blond-haired man who wore a sarcastic expression. She leaned against Rowan and pointed with her chin. "See those two? They're the people from the ad agency I told you about. Tandy and Bruce, I think."

As the strange looking pair passed before them, Maggie called out, "Tandy! Bruce! Hi." They turned to her expectantly but came up blank as they made eye contact. "It's Maggie, from NarcoDynamics. I met you at the commercial shoot," she explained.

Elaborate smiles and air kisses ensued. After the briefest possible encounter, the sophisticates moved on to the bar. Though feeling slighted, Maggie wasn't surprised. She turned to Rowan. "Like I told you, not exactly warm and fuzzy, those two."

Rowan smirked. "Come, now, Maggie. I hope you didn't think Bruce would invite you to his Tupperware party or something. After all, you can't do anything for them."

The Scotch was good stuff and Maggie sipped it with gusto. White-shirted caterers passed a selection of gourmet hors d'oeuvres as a trio of cello, violin and flute wove a musical spell through the glowing atmosphere. Rowan stood beside his wife, casing the crowd and making droll comments. He elbowed her in the ribs and she followed his gaze to see a woman in a green dress. The woman's neckline plunged to just above her navel, exposing an obscene portion of her unruly breasts. Maggie gaped as the exhibitionist passed. "Good Lord," she exclaimed. She and

Rowan chortled together. She tugged on his arm and said, "See that guy who just came in? That's Dr. Rajagopalan. I work with him almost every day. My desk is in his lab.

Dr. Rajagopalan handed his overcoat to the lady by the door. He took the coat from the woman behind him, evidently his wife, and handed that to the coat check lady as well. They worked their way up the gallery, Dr. Rajagopalan leading the way and nodding stiffly to acquaintances he passed. As he approached, Maggie stepped forward, smiling, to greet him.

"Hi, Dr. Rajagopalan. So nice to see you somewhere besides work." She turned to his wife and offered her hand. "Hello, I'm Maggie Moore. I work in the same lab as your husband."

Mrs. Rajagopalan shook her hand modestly. "Hello, I am Nala." The woman's accent was heavy; Maggie suspected she had a limited English vocabulary. She was half a foot shorter than Maggie as well, so she had to stoop to speak with her. Undaunted, she complimented the older woman on the beauty of her richly colored and ornamented garments, which she indicated with a hand gesture as she spoke. Nala got the gist of what she was saying and nodded several times, murmuring "Thank you very much."

Maggie turned to Dr. Rajagopalan and introduced him to Rowan. The two men shook hands and looked each other in the eye, both recognizing a seriousness in the other that they respected. Dr. Rajagopalan said, "Maggie tells me you are a police detective. That must be very interesting work. Are you involved in that terrible case of the murdered girl?"

"Yes, but it's very slow going," Rowan answered. Maggie cringed at the reminder of his job as the familiar shuttering came over her husband's face.

Dr. Rajagopalan, sensing that Rowan did not wish to discuss that particular subject, moved the conversation along briskly. "I had a friend in medical school who went to work in forensics. He works now with the police department in New Haven. Perhaps you have heard of him? He is quite well known in his field and has written several books on the subject. He has also worked on some very well-known cases."

Rowan brought himself back to the conversation. "Maybe. What's his name?"

"Dr. Max Tan."

"Oh sure, I know Dr. Tan. He did the analysis on the Simmons case a couple years back. He kept that guy from walking."

"Yes, that is my friend. Always in school, he had a little television in his room, and he would watch all the detectives shows. He loves the police, he said. If he were a big, strong man, he would be a police detective. But he was little, so he studied to be a doctor detective." The men chuckled and began trading stories about Dr. Tan and other scientists with whom the police consulted.

Maggie listened to their talk. She watched her husband's face, pleased to see him relaxed and chatting. She smiled at Nala, who smiled back politely before resuming her effort to follow the men's conversation. Maggie's gaze was drawn to the far end of the room; through the dense crowd, she thought she had seen a tall figure. There were several large, dark-haired men in the throng and she casually surveyed each, but none was Cambien. Again, she had an almost physical sensation of being watched. She turned her head quickly in the other direction and saw a man in a black suit vanish into a packed section of the gallery.

Rowan and Dr. Rajagopalan continued to talk, now joined by another of the NarcoDynamics chemists. Nala stood by them and watched. Maggie interrupted. "I'm getting another drink. Would anyone else like anything from the bar?"

"I'll take another," said Rowan.

Along the way to the bar, Maggie paused and looked down the side gallery where she had seen the tall, black-haired man vanish into the crowd. This room was mobbed and Maggie could see why; the new exhibit had been installed there. Large canvases were illuminated on the walls and myriad sculptures stood on pedestals.

She allowed the flow of the crowd to carry her into the space as she drifted from piece to piece. She found herself vaguely disturbed by the works. The canvases were mostly full of dim, unformed shapes and barely discernable suggestions. Suddenly she came upon an exquisitely rendered painting that depicted a woman not much older than herself. The woman lay asleep on a daybed in a garden. The cold light of a high, full moon bathed the scene. Colorless blooms perched atop black plant shapes. Maggie paused before the painting; clearly, the woman had meant only to enjoy an afternoon nap. Deep in a narcotic slumber, she had forgotten the time and in turn had been forgotten, left to spend the night outdoors. Maggie felt sure the woman in the painting would wake at any moment, disoriented, knowing neither the time nor where she was.

A deep voice rumbled in Maggie's ear, "This one is my favorite, too." She spun to see Cambien beside her. "Don't tell Chisolm, but I haven't got much use for the rest of this so-called 'art.'" He smiled at her. "Maggie, my dear, I am so glad you've come." He bent to hug her, placing a kiss on her cheek. Maggie reflexively returned his hug, meaning only to be sociable, and was horrified to realize that she felt blissfully happy in his arms. Unable to snap herself out of it, she stayed in the embrace a second longer than one generally did when greeting one's boss. Cambien graciously took no notice. Maggie blushed; but surely a man as handsome and successful as Dr. Cuthbert was used to women throwing themselves at him. He probably no longer noticed such things.

Maggie spoke. "What do you think of your launch party?"

Cambien startled and looked about wildly. "Oh, is that what this is? I was wondering what the hell was going on."

Maggie laughed. A tray of pickled and peppered crudités was proffered, but the server moved on when neither of them acknowledged him standing there. Cambien tucked Maggie's hand into the crook of his arm and guided her from painting to sculpture to painting. Amid the densely packed crowd, they drifted in a bubble of privacy. Cambien's discourse showed both a cultured knowledge of modern art and a subtle disdain for the pretensions of the genre—something Maggie tended to agree with, even if she couldn't summon the vocabulary he commanded on the subject. She felt hot disappointment with herself; how was it that she, a trained professional writer, was at such a loss for words around him?

A sleek couple joined them, a vaguely exotic woman and her gray-haired husband. They were austerely dressed in expensive-looking clothing and appeared to be in their late forties. Cambien kissed the woman on both cheeks and shook hands with her husband. "Thanks for coming tonight. May I present Maggie

Moore, our star scientific writer. Maggie, meet Doctors Peter and Marie Broadbent," said Cambien.

Maggie shook hands with the Broadbents. "Nice to meet you."

"Besides being an old friend, Peter is also Editor-in-Chief of the *American Journal of Pharmaceutical Therapy*," explained Cambien.

"I'm sure that had nothing to do with your invitation though. Right, Cambien?" Peter's brittle face smiled, though Maggie could not be certain he was joking.

Cambien grinned confidently at him. "Believe me, Peter, once Somnusol hits the market, you will be thanking me for letting you attend this historic event. If nothing else, I hope you at least enjoy the food. Pulling this reception together was more involved than planning a wedding."

"Any food would be delicious after the place we visited for lunch," said Marie. Maggie could not place her accent: perhaps eastern European?

"Marie and Peter drove up from Philadelphia to be here tonight," Cambien explained.

"They had all this B-list memorabilia everywhere, as though it would create an atmosphere of sophistication. But you don't look too close, or you see a layer of dust an inch thick on everything."

Rowan suddenly sidled into the group, next to Maggie. She started and smiled when she saw him. "There you are," she said, as though she had been scouring the room looking for him.

He handed her a fresh glass of Scotch. "I think you forgot about this," he said, giving her a significant look. Maggie smiled gratefully, just then realizing how much she had wanted another. Rowan turned to the other three and held out his hand. "Rowan Moore."

"Pete Broadbent. Glad to meet you." He shook Rowan's hand, half turned, and said, "My wife, Marie."

"Nice to meet you," said Marie. She took Rowan's hand and gave him an appraising look.

"Likewise," said Rowan. He turned to face Cambien. "And you must be the esteemed Dr. Cuthbert. It's good to meet you." He flashed a gallant smile.

Cambien, who had watched Rowan since the moment he came into view, gave a tight, knowing grin. He took Rowan's hand in his own, shaking it firmly. "The pleasure is all mine," he intoned in a deep, chesty voice. "I want to thank you for lending your beautiful and gifted wife to my little venture. She has been a most welcome addition."

"You're quite welcome. Anything to get her out of the house for a few hours," Rowan kidded. His cool gray eyes remained alert.

There was a momentary pause when no one said anything, then Marie picked up her story about the odd restaurant. She continued uninterrupted through the account, concluding with, "and the server actually asked us if we wanted dessert! Can you believe it?"

Everyone laughed, Maggie the loudest. "Speaking of dessert," Rowan segued, "I hear you took the kids for some great ice cream the other day, Cambien."

The Broadbents were confused. "Kids? Cambien, you don't have children. Is there something you haven't told us?" Marie teased.

Cambien met Rowan's glance for a moment, then spoke to Marie. "Of course not, Marie, dear. Rowan's talking about the Moore children. I ran into Maggie and her kids the other day, and we spent the afternoon together."

Rowan held back the impulse to say *my kids*.

"We had the nicest time, actually," Cambien continued. His gaze had softened and shifted to Maggie. She returned his look, nodding in agreement with his account. He smiled into her face, remembering. "They were looking in the windows of the hobby shop. The kids were utterly charming. They were fairly drooling over the toys. So I took them inside and let them each pick something out. Then we all went up the street for ice cream."

Maggie concurred. "The nicest afternoon we've had in a long time." She and Cambien were now speaking to one another as though they were the only people in the room.

"And you do make the most beautiful children, Maggie," he said in a solemn tone.

Peter shifted uncomfortably on his feet and Marie suddenly found something on the other side of the room to look at. Rowan had had just about enough. "I like to think I had something to do with it." The temper in his voice belied his humorous words.

"Yes, of course," drawled Cambien. He did not bother to look away from Maggie as he spoke. She glanced down, suddenly self-conscious. "You must be so proud of them all." He pulled up his French cuff and checked his watch. "And now, if you all will excuse me, I must go and make a few remarks."

He left the little group with nods to the ladies and made his way across the gallery. Maggie followed him with her eyes, watching as people repeatedly stopped him, men to shake his hand, women to throw their arms around him. The woman in the obscene green dress embraced him. Her arms draped around his neck, she arched her back to look into his face while she spoke. Disturbed, Maggie looked away.

Rowan watched his wife watch her boss. He made small talk with the Broadbents and, after several minutes, he excused himself and Maggie, took her arm, and steered her towards the center hall.

The trio stopped playing and Cambien's amplified voice filled the space. The Moores paused on their path to the exit.

"This is truly an amazing and humbling sight." Cambien gazed out over the crowd, his handsome face flushed with accomplishment and pride. "Thank you all so much for coming here tonight and being part of our celebration. I especially want to thank anyone who traveled to be here, and also the dignitaries in our industry and the media who made time to join us tonight." He greeted numerous prestigious people in the crowd by name. Then he launched into a personal account of his company's history. Maggie and Rowan stood captive in the motionless sea of admirers. Everyone looked at the man of the hour. Gracious and charismatic, he held the room in thrall. When his remarks concluded, the room erupted into applause and scattered cheers.

"Okay, let's go," said Rowan. Maggie, who had been mesmerized by Cambien's speech along with the rest of the crowd, didn't feel like leaving. But she saw her husband's patience was exhausted, so she followed him to the door.

Maggie and Rowan quarreled in the car on the way home. Neither wanted to, but they were both tired and the effects of the cocktails were wearing off. "That's a hell of a crowd you keep company with, Mags." Rowan started.

"What do you mean by that?" Maggie tried and failed to keep the edge out of her voice. "I think they're excellent people. Successful, cultured, intelligent . . . I think we could do worse than to rub elbows with them every now and then."

"I think your creepy boyfriend wants to rub more than elbows with you."

Maggie was confounded. "What, do you mean Cambien? You've got to be kidding. First of all, he's more of a gentleman than anyone else we know. He's also an old friend of mine. And anyway, every woman in that room was all over him."

"Jealous?"

Maggie was grateful for the darkness as she felt herself flush red. "Of course not, Rowan. Don't be ridiculous." She tried to change the subject. "I thought you got on pretty well with Dr. Rajagopalan, anyway."

"He's a good guy. You have my permission to continue working with him," Rowan kidded tersely.

Maggie was relieved to feel the conversation de-escalating. "Thank you so much. I sincerely appreciate your approval. You also seemed to like the Broadbents."

"What, those two pompous blowhards? If Pete were any stiffer, you could scrape paint with him. And that wife! Does she ever have anything nice to say? Or does being stuck up pass for a sense of humor with her?"

Maggie thought about it and found she agreed with her husband. "They were a bit snobby."

By the time they got home, they were both exhausted. The children were sleeping over at Pop's house, so they had only to undress and fall into bed. As Maggie had hoped, the evening had taken Rowan out of his obsession with solving his case for a little while. He had been himself for entire sweeps of time, and Maggie felt closer to him than she had in a long while, the issue of his jealousy of Cambien notwithstanding. (Certainly not *her* jealousy, as he had suggested.)

Maggie was almost glad Rowan was jealous; lately, she felt as though he didn't notice her at all anymore. She turned to him and he put his arms around her and kissed her. In the darkness of their room, they bonded for the first time since before Maggie was hired at NarcoDynamics and Rowan started working the wretched murder case.

⌁

Back in college, Maggie had been a bit of a wild girl. Turned loose in Manhattan, she let her newfound liberty lift her like an updraft beneath a fledgling bird's wings.

Like Cambien, she had lost her mother at a young age. Her father sent for his own mother when his wife was clearly succumbing to the renal failure that plagued her kin, and Nan had come from England to ease his burdens. When Maggie's mother passed on, Nan kept the house running smoothly while her father traveled. A ship's engineer, he was away at sea for months at a time. Nan did her affectionate best to fill the void left by Maggie's departed mother. And as if to make up for her father's frequent absence, Nan saddled her with greater regulation than any other kid she knew, pushing her hard to achieve as much as possible. While her friends were outside eating popsicles in the twilight, Maggie was at her desk, finishing extra credit work for school. She knew that Nan did this partly to encourage her to achieve as much as she was capable of, but mostly to keep her safe indoors.

By Maggie's sixteenth birthday, Nan's mind began to fail and she grew frail. Now Maggie was coming home from school to care for her grandmother while her father traveled. Then Maggie came home one day and found Nan on the kitchen floor, where she had lain since falling off a chair she was using as a step stool. Maggie called the ambulance and did what needed doing. By the time her father returned a week later, Nan had been treated for a fractured hip and wrist and was preparing for transfer to the rehabilitation center.

Maggie's father retired from the shipping company for which he had worked for twenty-six years. He found a new job with the city of Bridgeport, working as a mechanic on the port authority's boats. The following year, Maggie was accepted at Barnard College, a small, distinguished women's school in New York

City. ("See, all your hard work paid off," said Nan, when Maggie told her the news). In the fall, she moved into a dorm with the other freshmen and began her undergraduate work.

Maggie worked hard and did well academically. She joyously immersed herself in the greats among English and American literature and took pleasure in incessant discussion and analysis of the material with like-minded people. But more than that, she reveled in her new freedom. After her mother had died, Nan had come and nearly smothered her with attention. Later, as Nan's health failed, she had had to struggle to keep up with her advanced coursework, the upkeep of a household, and the care of an elderly woman.

But in college, Maggie only had one job, and that was to be a student. Meals were prepared for her and dishes were cleared away in the cafeteria; bathrooms were cleaned and hallways vacuumed by the maintenance staff. Once her class work was done, Maggie was free to do as she pleased. Not only that, she was in New York City, where there were unlimited possibilities for spending one's free time.

She cast off years of pressure to be a good girl and let go of what she ought to do without a backward glance. Maggie dove into the city's nightclub culture. Weekends found her downtown in bars and ballrooms, drinking all the underage alcohol she could get her hands on and dancing madly to any hard-rocking band she could afford to see. She loved the loud music, the chaos of a thrashing crowd, the power of amplified instruments, the pounding of drums, the zany dress codes, and the reckless love affairs. It was all one big release from the rigors of her good-girl life.

During this period of time, Maggie dated wild boys. Longhaired, black jeans-clad, guitar playing, love song writing guys seemed like a perfect fit to her. Being with such a person made Maggie feel like she was wild, too.

Of course, young men such as those are not known for responsible behavior. Not that Maggie was looking to get married or anything—she had lived her whole life responsibly and maturely and had had her fill, thank you. But nonetheless, the series of misbegotten, incautious liaisons took their toll on her emotionally. By senior year, she had ceased dating altogether.

After returning to the Connecticut suburbs, Maggie renewed some high school friendships and made new friends where she worked. Hours could be long at the St. Chapelle advertising agency and the employees grew close to one another. It was during this period of time that Maggie became friends with Vicky. They and some other St. Chapelle associates formed a softball team to blow off steam and socialize somewhere besides a bar.

Maggie first met Rowan when St. Chapelle played the Stamford Police team. She noticed the sternly handsome, sharp-eyed man looking her way on several occasions. He was not the type of man who caught her eye, with his short haircut and orderly way of dress. In fact, he was the very opposite. But he found a way to begin a conversation with her group of friends before the game was over. Plans were made by some St. Chapelle employees and police officers to meet up at a nearby pub. Maggie tagged along, and she and Vicky spent the next several hours at a table full of burly cops who swapped wildly entertaining stories of their work.

This was all new to Maggie. As she sat listening, it dawned on her that she had never personally known a police officer. In her quest to be a wild girl, she had naturally avoided people whose job it was to keep order. But here were these gallant young men, telling uproarious stories of their professional adventures, and Maggie found herself entranced.

Rowan had maneuvered his way to sitting next to her without obviously doing so and told a story about a possible terrorism call he had once been on. After September 11th, there had been many such calls, always false alarms, and that had been the theme of the last few stories. In this case, Rowan heard a broadcast over the police radio that someone had reported a stranger running through their neighborhood and casting handfuls of white powder on the ground. The caller feared that the white powder was nothing less than some sort of biochemical warfare. Just as Rowan heard the announcement, he saw the very fellow running towards him. Sure enough, the runner reached into a pouch and threw white powder on the ground as he ran past Rowan. "So I tackled him," Rowan related.

Maggie hardly heard the rest of the story (the man turned out to be from a runner's club, and he was merely marking a route), she was so struck by what Rowan had done and how he had done it. He had flung himself onto a suspected terrorist without hesitation. Forget all the rock and roll, long haired, leather jacketed musician-types she had ever dated; this man beside her was wild. And more than that, he was also a *man*. It dawned on her that, in the real world, being strong enough and brave enough to do such a thing was, truly, *wild*.

Maggie couldn't believe it when the bartender hollered for last call, the evening having gone by in the blink of an eye. She and the one or two ad agency friends who were left said goodbye to their new law enforcement friends. She did not exchange contact information or make plans to meet again with Rowan (although Vicky celebrated the acquisition of new acquaintances by going home with one of them).

Over that spring and early summer, Maggie saw Rowan at softball games, or when her group and his group overlapped at a local watering hole. If the St. Chapelle team had a game, he would sometimes pull up in his cruiser. "We had a report of open containers," he would say in his deadpan, cop's voice, and Maggie would self-consciously hide her bottle of beer behind her back, though she knew he must be joking.

Since her epiphany the night she and Rowan met, when she had realized that he was the most intense man she had yet come across, Maggie avoided becoming involved with him. She skillfully derailed conversations that seemed to be heading towards discussion of going out for dinner. In Maggie's life, parents came and went, and boyfriends were cads; she had no desire to tie herself to another human being in any meaningful way. And she sensed that, with a man of integrity and courage such as Rowan, she would not be able to have anything less than a serious relationship. He was too rare and honorable a thing to mistreat.

After months of allusions and retreats, Rowan came right out and asked for her phone number. Caught unaware by his abrupt change of tactics, Maggie gave it to him. I'll just go out with him once, to get him off my back, she told herself. But of course, that wasn't what happened.

Rowan had been the youngest of six children, surrounded by cousins, growing up in Cincinnati. His home was loud and messy and tumultuous. There was entirely too much drinking, yelling, and slamming. Some children look to their parents or older siblings as role models; Rowan took his as examples of what not to do. He endured through eighteen years of domestic turbulence, keeping his own little corner of the dilapidated house scrupulously orderly. He watched his older siblings drift off one by one, weed seeds on the wind, landing wherever to take root and start messy, chaotic families of their own.

By the end of high school, Rowan was ready. He had decent grades and several thousand dollars in savings. He left home to attend a state university in the northeast that had a respectable criminal science program. Rowan worked as a dispatcher with the New Haven Police Department while he completed his Bachelor of Science degree, then was hired on as an officer. He completed his training at the police academy and spent a couple years in New Haven before transferring to the Stamford Police Department.

Time passed and Rowan settled into his career and adoptive home. He took an apartment in a quiet neighborhood and hung around with the other cops when he was off duty. He volunteered in community outreach programs sponsored by the police department and the union, met with neighborhood representatives, taught drug and alcohol awareness to teenagers, and helped out at fundraising events. His department sponsored a Boy Scout Explorer post and he had a great time working with kids who thought they might be police officers when they grew up. Married cops and their wives invited him over for steak. So Rowan was content.

When he first saw Maggie playing softball, she was up at bat. She leaned gamely over home plate, waving the bat back and forth. She wore a T-shirt and shorts, her long legs splayed and her feet planted firmly in the dust. A breeze kept blowing her hair across her face and, laughing, she would shake it back over her shoulder, never releasing her grip on the bat lest a quick pitch catch her unprepared. The more Rowan watched Maggie the more he liked her. She seemed bright, lively and fun, but she also had a certain dignity. Rowan was drawn to that quality, it having been so rare in his life.

8.

Easter came. The house was filled with the scent of rosemary from the leg of lamb Maggie was roasting. Pop came over and sat with Rowan in the living room. As usual, Rowan had the TV on, the volume competing with the omnipresent crackling and hissing from the police scanner he kept beside him on the end table. But for once, the news wasn't on the screen. Pop had convinced Rowan to put the pre-season Red Sox game on, and they watched together. Maggie brought them cold beers. Pop smiled and said thanks. The kids played on the floor with their new toys. Maggie left them to it and returned to the kitchen to put the final touches on the meal.

At the table, Rowan was talkative. Maggie watched him interact with her father and the kids. She knew it was a show, mostly for Pop. When company was over or they were out socializing, Rowan was, as always, a skilled conversationalist. Between his endless supply of stories and his quick mind, he could keep an entertaining rapport going for hours. But at home, alone, he retreated morosely to the sofa in the living room, watched the local news and listened to the scanner, his laptop on the coffee table in front of him. He alternated between keeping vigil and dozing on the couch and came to bed in the wee hours, long after Maggie was asleep. They hadn't been close since the night of the Somnusol launch party, several weeks earlier.

Maggie felt her husband slipping away from her. If there were another woman, at least she'd have a face to put to her rival. If he were a workaholic, she could despise his employer. If he were a drunk or an addict, she could hate his disease. But it wasn't anything she could put her finger on. And so she watched him converse with her father and children, loving the dynamic sound of his voice and the animated movement of his features, knowing that it would all disappear shortly. Her father would go home, the show would be over, and Rowan would withdraw to his sofa.

Later that night, Maggie sat beside him on the couch while he watched TV. The kids were asleep and she was ready to nod off herself. She stood up and stretched, her loose hair tumbling down her back. "Well, I'm turning in," she said pointedly.

"Okay," said Rowan. "I'll be up in a bit."

Maggie bent down to him and placed her hands on his thighs for support as she leaned forward to kiss him goodnight. She tried to find words. "Why don't you come to bed at a normal time? You always stay up so late, lately."

"I can't sleep," he answered matter-of-factly, his eyes seeking the screen beyond her.

"Well, that sucks. Anything I can do to help?" she asked with a suggestive grin.

"No, but thanks." He kissed her again, and she knew she had been dismissed. There was nothing else to do; Maggie went up to bed.

At work the next day, Maggie felt loneliness draped over her shoulders like a heavy mantle. As often happened, she and Rowan had barely exchanged two words in the morning hustle out of the house.

She had been trying to meet Vicky for lunch or a drink for days, but her friend had no time for her; between the spring housing market and the latest man she was dating (same one for a month now), Vicky was simply too busy. Lunchtime and right after work were the worst times for her, but they were the only times Maggie could get out.

She couldn't look forward to meeting with Cambien because he was traveling all week. He might be just a professional acquaintance, but any time she spent with him gave her joy. Even Dr. Rajagopalan was at a conference, leaving her alone in the large lab. The only sound was the hum of the fluorescent lights on the ceiling. Maggie frowned at her monitor. She found herself wishing her mother were still alive.

At 4:30, she could no longer take the isolation and left the office. She drove north on the parkway, looking forward to the affectionate greeting she would get from her children. But even this was depressing, in a way; Charlie can hardly even talk yet, she thought bitterly.

For the first time in years, Maggie couldn't sleep. This was especially distressing, because she had always had the gift of falling deeply asleep within minutes of laying her head on her pillow. But now, when she desperately wanted to escape her thoughts, she was trapped by an unwelcome consciousness.

Rowan lay beside her. He had, as usual, been terse and uncommunicative all evening, and though Maggie had declined to argue with him about it, she felt raw and abandoned. She had been exerting all of her will to be understanding while her husband was going through a difficult time, but it was becoming harder and harder. It seemed the more she excused his abruptness and short temper, the more abrupt and short-tempered he became. And tolerating Rowan's boorishness came at a heavy toll; lately she felt an almost constant rage tightening her chest. She sat up and looked at her sleeping husband. Rowan's mouth dropped open and he began to snore. She scowled and, abandoning any hope of falling asleep, got out of bed and went downstairs.

Moonlight seeped into the dark living room through the house's rear windows. Maggie sat sideways across the overstuffed chair and stared dejectedly outside. The backyard glowed in the light of the nearly full moon, the surrounding trees black and unfathomable against the midnight sky.

Maggie worried about Rowan. He had been distant and testy in the past when he was going through something, but it had always been enough just to give him space. When he had resolved his internal torments, he returned to her, and she welcomed back her strong, warm husband.

But this time, the dead girl had taken him farther away than he had ever gone. She could hardly bear to think the thought: *What if he can't come back this time?* The anger that had been simmering in her breast dissipated as an ache replaced it, and Maggie yearned for her Rowan.

And then, there was another consideration: *What about Cambien?*

She had long ago admitted to herself that she found Cambien attractive. His long, lean frame, his glossy jet hair and bottomless eyes, his rich, growly voice, his chivalrous manner, his professional and scientific accomplishments—he had grown into such an impressive man since high school. She still couldn't understand why no woman had snapped him up, and knowing he was available was eating at her constantly.

Because now, as surely as she knew she was a woman, Maggie knew that Cambien wanted her. She could see it in the way he found reasons to meet with her, the way his gaze sought her, the way he hung on her reactions to his words, no matter who else was speaking. This was devastating. If she were available as he was, they would surely be together now. What would their life be? Who would Maggie be, linked to a man as intelligent and sensitive as Cambien? Would her unused gifts flourish? Would she be as accomplished as he was, in her own right? A more fully realized human being? Would their union be richer, truer, more intimate than the life she had with Rowan? Right now, it seemed certain.

A horrible thought formed itself in her mind. *What if she had married the wrong person?*

Maggie's eyes stung and a ragged sob tore itself from her throat. She had felt Rowan getting farther and farther away from her for so long, and she had been sadder and lonelier than she had wanted to realize. And now she thought of Cambien and the obvious crush he had had on her in high school, and she felt as though she had missed the greatest opportunity she had ever had.

Why had Cambien reappeared in her life now? Was this some sort of second chance? But bound to Rowan by marriage as she was, she did not see how she could go to him. Indeed, the very idea made her ache for her husband even more. She wanted to be strong, but she had always had Rowan to help her. But he was fighting his own battle, and his strength was unavailable to her.

A hopeless despair overcame her and she curled up miserably into the cushions of the chair. What would become of her? She wanted two men and could have neither.

In the morning, Maggie woke knowing that she would try to get her husband back. He had been in a dark place for so long, he had lost sight of the light and beauty in his life. She loved him and would bring him back to her by showing him her love. She would show him how good their life together was, how blessed their home was, how lovable their children were.

As usual, Rowan shuffled downstairs and checked the news, summarily kissed his children, and headed for the door. Maggie caught him there, put her arms around his neck, and gave him a goodbye kiss. She only held him a moment, sensing he would panic if she tried to block his escape to work, but it was long enough to make him take note of her. His eyes briefly connected with hers and a taut smile flitted across his lips. "See you tonight," he said. He turned and left.

"Call me if you're going to be late. I'm making a good supper," Maggie called after him.

Maggie was not scheduled to go to NarcoDynamics. She spent the day cleaning the house and marinating steaks. She laid a pretty table outdoors and set the children to plucking spring blooms for the centerpiece. She boiled baby potatoes, tossed salad, and uncorked a bottle of wine. Singing, she pictured the family dining al fresco, surrounded by beauty and contentment. Then, after the children were asleep, she would take her husband by the hand and lead him to bed; poor Rowan desperately needed to clear his mind for a while, and she knew just the thing.

Fifteen minutes before he was due home, Maggie changed into a romantic lace blouse. She called the kids in to scrub their hands and faces. A clean T-shirt for Charlie and they were as cute as buttons.

Six-thirty, and Rowan had not yet arrived. Maggie checked the coals, which were perfect. She needed to put the steaks on soon. The familiar anger began to build in her throat, but she forced it back down. She took a deep breath and called Rowan's cell phone. He answered on the second ring, which was encouraging, but his "Hello" was terse and angry sounding.

"Hi, honey. I was just checking where you were. I wanted to put the steaks on soon."

"I'm sorry, Maggie. I got a late start home, and the goddamn traffic was already backed up." He pulled the phone away from his mouth and Maggie heard him yell, "Nice job, asshole," to a fellow motorist. He spoke into the mouthpiece again. "Ugh, today just sucked. The chief was all over us because the goddamn news is all over him. He has no clue how much worse he makes everything. The man is utterly clueless. He really needs to retire already, let someone with a clue do the job." And on he ranted.

Rowan's mood was not improved when he got home. He barely allowed Maggie to peck his cheek as he stomped through the front door. He sat in the living room, sorting his mail with the news on. Maggie kept her voice cheerful. "Listen, Ro, I've set the dinner table out in the backyard, since it's so nice this evening. Why don't you sit out there? The children made a lovely centerpiece—you should go see." Rowan grimaced as though she had asked him to do something particularly distasteful. Grunting, he heaved himself off the sofa and went to sit outside. He shoveled Maggie's carefully prepared meal into his mouth, barely chewing his food before swallowing, and was disinclined to talk. Maggie chatted bravely about the day she and the children had had, but the recounting of their mundane activities failed to penetrate the pall around Rowan.

Maggie felt horrible for the poor little girl who had been killed but damn it, that was no reason for her whole family to be miserable. *Easy Maggie*, she told herself, carefully tamping down her growing agitation again. Rowan finally opened his mouth to holler at Hazel, who had been tickling her little brother with a dandelion she had pulled from the centerpiece, which caused him to knock over a glass of milk. Rowan righted the cup and slammed it back onto the table. "Look what you did, Hazel! Now go inside and get a rag and clean it up!" In tears, Hazel ran into the house.

Maggie had had enough. "Was that really necessary, Rowan? It was an accident."

"When is she going to learn, Maggie? That is unacceptable."

"Oh, for heaven's sake, Rowan, she's five. She's learning every day. Must you make everyone miserable, when we've worked all day to make a nice meal for you?" She tried to stop there, but the long-simmering rage kept talking. "It's not like your manners are so great these days, you know."

Fighting words were just what Rowan had been looking for. "Oh, what's that supposed to mean?" he shot back gleefully. "You sure know how to make me feel even more like crap, after the chief and the news and everyone else piles on and makes me feel like crap all day. The last thing I need is to come home and have my wife make me feel like crap, too!"

By now, Charlie was crying and Hazel, who had emerged from the back door holding a dishtowel, hesitated by the wall, her eyes as big as walnuts and her lower lip bulging out. "You have no idea what I go through every day," Rowan wailed.

But Maggie had thought of nothing except what he was going through for so long, she was at last past caring. She was no longer able to keep down her hurt and rage at his abandonment. "My God, you'd think you were the only one who was having a hard time here! You haven't spoken twenty words to me since this case came in and the only time you talk to your children is to yell at them. You've been a complete jerk for weeks now. How much longer are we all supposed to live in limbo, waiting for you to feel better?"

"I don't need this," screamed Rowan.

"Cut it out. You're upsetting the kids, and the neighbors will hear you. It's embarrassing," Maggie hissed.

Rowan seized on this new umbrage. "Oh, so now I'm an embarrassment. Well, that's just great." He sprang from his chair, seized his plate and cup, and slammed past his sobbing daughter, into the kitchen.

Maggie let him go. She went to Hazel, picked the weeping little girl up, and sat her next to her brother at the table. She stood between them, rubbing their backs and holding cups of milk for them to sip. "Don't be upset, kids. Daddy's just having a hard time at work. He doesn't feel very well right now, but he loves us all very much."

Maggie wasn't even sure this was still true. A cold white fury burned behind her eyes. When the children had settled down a bit, she told them to wait outside while she went in to check on their dad.

Inside the house, Maggie saw that Rowan had gathered his briefcase and keys. "Where are you going?" she asked.

"I'm going back to work. Haven't you heard? A kid's been killed, and us lazy, stupid cops haven't found the murderer yet." His face was mottled red, his eyes wide with frenzy. "The goddamn reporters were asking me where I was going when I left headquarters to come home for dinner tonight, like I had no right to eat or see my family until we catch the bad guy. So I'm going back to look at everything we've got for the one hundredth time, since God knows we got nothing new. Besides, I don't want to hang around here and be an embarrassment to my wife."

Maggie was through excusing Rowan's temper tantrums. "Give me a break, Rowan. How much more of this are we supposed to take? I know you're angry, but we didn't do anything wrong."

"I'm sorry I'm a lousy husband and a lousy father. Jesus, I'm doing the best I can, trying to make you happy, the chief happy, the papers happy, the kids happy, everybody has to be happy! Everybody but me. I got nothing left inside of me to give." He turned to go.

Maggie stopped him. "Do not leave without kissing your children. You just scared the crap out of them. Now go out there and tell them you love them, and kiss them goodnight."

Rowan did as his wife told him. Maggie followed him out back to make sure, her arms folded across her chest, the lovely blouse long forgotten. Rowan squatted down level with the children, told them he was sorry for yelling and that he hoped things would be better soon. He kissed their wet cheeks, straightened up, and rumpled their hair. As he passed Maggie, he was even able to come up with a perfunctory "I'm sorry" for her. He went back through the house. Maggie and the kids heard his truck start up and drive off into the cooling twilight.

⌒▅⃥

Cambien slouched in an armchair in his paneled living room. He listened to the stereo and sipped amber liquor from a crystal snifter. A night breeze stirred the floor-length silk draperies by the open windows as it crept across the room to caress his heated brow.

He had left his thoughts to rise unchecked on symphonic waves of music and they had flown directly to Maggie. He hadn't bothered to rein them in, but had allowed himself to imagine being with her. And now he was filled with hopeless desire.

Cambien drained the snifter and stood. He switched off the stereo and walked upstairs to his bedroom. The rooms in his gracious old house were large and high ceilinged, and it took several long strides for him to reach the granite-tiled bathroom. He shed his clothing and faced the mirror. A tormented visage looked back at him. "You have to get control of yourself," he pleaded with it. He turned the shower on and stepped into the cold stream. His eyes closed, he let the water beat against his face for a long time.

Still damp beneath his silk robe, Cambien emerged from the bath. He walked to an antique wooden cabinet in the corner. Procuring a key from his pocket, he unlocked it and drew forth a miniscule bronze brazier, which he set on the cabinet's surface. Into its base he shook several nuggets of charcoal. He lit them and blew out the flame. Once they glowed brightly, he dropped several translucent yellow pellets onto them. Immediately the scent of exotic herbal incense wafted through the room, borne on plumes of blue smoke.

Cambien walked across the thick Persian rug to his bed. Sitting cross-legged in the center of the bedspread, he lay his hands, palms up, on his thighs. He closed his eyes, cleared his mind, and began to meditate.

⌒▅⃥

Maggie couldn't sleep. She lay in her empty bed in the dark, staring at the ceiling. A week ago, she would have wept at that evening's scene with Rowan. Now she felt nothing. She hated the numbness where she used to feel love, or at least anger.

There was also the frustration of having been without contact for so long. She had hoped to connect with her mate this night, yet here she was alone, both empty and full of longing. Giving up, she sat up on the edge of the bed and then stood. Her nightgown fluttered about her ankles as she wandered from the room.

A quick glance into each of the children's rooms told her they slept soundly. She looked up through the window at the end of the hall; the bright moon beckoned her. Maggie descended the stairs and went without pause through the kitchen to the back door.

Stepping outside, she breathed the thrilling night air. A teasing breeze swept her hair from her face like a lover's hand. She closed the door behind her and walked barefoot across the cool, damp grass. Standing in the middle of the yard, Maggie surveyed the indigo world about her. Shapes and forms were impossible to discern when she looked directly at them and could only be seen obliquely, from the corner of her eye, like unearthly things. Lifting her gaze to the blackness of the woods, she began walking again. Soon she was among the dark trunks, the leafy branches tossing and chattering above her. Her naked feet made no sound on the debris of the forest floor. Drawn from one patch of moonlight to the next, she proceeded through the dark wood. She could see a large area of silver light through the trees and bent her steps towards the clearing.

"Maggie."

She couldn't yet see into the clearing but was certain the voice had come from there. It was a hoarse voice, a man's voice, carried to her on the wind. A few more steps and she emerged from the trees into the luminous circle of a lost meadow. Feathery grasses, driven by the wind, tickled her legs. Maggie had grown up playing in these woods but had never known this glade was here; had it been called forth, Brigadoon-like, by the brilliant moon?

"Maggie."

She turned to see who called her. From the dark of the trees across the clearing, a man's form materialized. She knew the panther-like silhouette immediately. As he stepped forward, Cambien moved into the moonlight. He came to Maggie and stood looking down at her, his jet hair whipping around his face, his black eyes reflecting the white moon as surely as a forest pool at midnight. Helpless, Maggie looked up into them.

No pretense or barrier of civility between them now, Cambien grasped her arms in his strong fingers. He stared intently into her face. "I knew you would come." He said it simply, happily.

Maggie, already drained by frustration and abandonment, felt utterly weak. She vaguely knew she should pull free from Cambien's grasp. As though drugged, she felt a dim thrill of alarm, but an even stronger force kept her still. Deliberate, rational thought was impossible. "Cambien, I . . . what are you doing here?" She realized she sounded as ambiguous as she felt.

Holding her with his look, he smiled. "I came for you, of course. I could tell, I knew that you were alone. I hope I'm not being presumptuous, but you are, clearly, very much alone." The smile disappeared, replaced by a solemn gaze. "And I can't bear that. Maggie, you must know you can come to me if you need anything." He bent his head so that his black hair mingled with her chestnut hair in the night wind. *"Anything,"* he whispered into her ear.

The softest of kisses—barely a breath—he placed on her neck. His hands left her arms to encircle her, one spanning her back through the thin fabric of her gown, the other pulling her close by the waist. Maggie was held to the spot as firmly as if she were in irons. In a last defensive measure, she placed her hands, balled into fists, between her chest and his. She felt the pounding of both their hearts in her hands. She couldn't remember ever wanting anyone as badly as this. She barely knew what it was that stopped her anymore, but she still recognized, somehow, that she wasn't free to yield.

Cambien, who had pressed his lips against her heated neck, pulled far enough back to peer into her face. His eyes burned with desire and Maggie looked away. "Why do you hold yourself back?" he growled.

She met his gaze again, defiant. "Cambien, you know I'm married. I . . . we . . . we can't be together." Desperate, she appealed to his honor as a gentleman, mutely pleading for mercy. She would not be able to withstand him much longer. Her legs trembled against his and, humiliated, she knew he could feel it.

Cambien looked at the ground, shaking his head bemusedly, a wicked smile playing about his lips. "Maggie, don't you know what this is?"

She wasn't sure what he was referring to. "What? What is this?"

He looked directly into her face. "Maggie, you're dreaming. This is just a dream."

"Dreaming? But how? I was awake."

Cambien shook his head. "No, Maggie, you are asleep. You came here in your dream." He stepped back, releasing her with one hand to gesture behind him. "See? How else did this get here?" A heavy, carved wood bed stood just behind him, the decadent linens turned down. Now Maggie saw there were candles burning in tall, iron stands alongside it. Miraculously undisturbed by the wind, the tiny flames lent their gold to the silver of the moon, casting the scene in an enchanted light.

"I have no idea." Maggie stared at the incongruous objects, unable to make sense of them. Gradually, a delicious possibility dawned on her. "So . . . this really is just a dream?"

"Yes, Maggie." Cambien put his arms tentatively around her again and bent forward to brush her lips with his. "And if this is just a dream," he breathed, "it doesn't really matter what we do, does it?"

This time, Maggie brazenly returned his gaze. Slowly and clearly, she said, "You're right, Cambien. It doesn't matter what we do."

She could see that her answer pleased him, was grateful to have the power to please him at that moment. He burned her with one last lustful look before bending to kiss her mouth. Their hair blew about their heads and Maggie's gown wrapped around her form in the wind as Cambien pressed her body to his. She was struck by such an intense wave of desire that she nearly lost consciousness. She panicked lest she fall back into the oblivion of sleep, losing her grasp on this moment. She didn't think she could bear that final frustration, to have Cambien in her arms and then lose him, even if it wasn't real.

With the wind flailing the leaves above them and the ghostly light bathing the bed, Maggie abandoned herself beneath him. She looked up at the night sky and was rewarded with the glorious sight of Cambien Cuthbert throwing back his splendid head, the stars pinioned in his black mane, wholly losing himself in her. She felt a surge of power; she knew he was bound to her now with a finality as powerful as death. Maggie closed her eyes.

II.

9.

As Maggie shamelessly embraced the pleasures of her nocturnal vision, she did not pause to consider the implications of her actions. Chasing her own fulfillment, she gave not a thought to where it led.

But where, exactly, did she go when she dreamed? Did she wander the rooms and expanses within her own mind, circumscribed by the confines of her skull? Or did she project her desires, anxieties, and wishes—her very soul—beyond her physical presence? Was she utterly alone as she wandered, the creatures she met mere conjurings of her restive brain? Or were they, like her, projections of other flesh-and-blood beings, sent forth into the ether by fevered minds to seek freely, uninhibited by conscience or consciousness?

Such thoughts did not trouble Maggie the next morning when she woke, the man next to her having transformed from the wild-haired, sonorous-voiced Cambien to the stern-eyed, careworn Rowan.

Maggie's first tryst with Cambien may have occurred while she was asleep, but she was wide awake when she made the decision to have an affair with him. Not an *actual* affair; Maggie was, after all, a woman of principle, and such tawdriness was not a behavior she cared to engage in. She would never be the cause of that kind of pain for her husband and children.

Rather, Maggie decided to have an *imaginary* affair, a relationship that existed only in her mind. No one needed to know, not even her lover.

She had woken the morning after her dream feeling luxuriously sated. Rowan had slunk in at some point during the night and was as far over on his side of the bed as he could get, making subdued snorkel sounds as he slept. Maggie almost felt guilty for a moment, but chided herself. How ridiculous! It wasn't as though she had actually cheated on her husband. In fact, her nocturnal romp had left her more relaxed and, well, happy than she had been in weeks. She felt she might now be able to get through the day without becoming exasperated at Rowan's churlishness. Who knew? Maybe this was a good thing for all of them.

Maggie further planned her fantasy infidelity as she sat sideways in the armchair by the living room window, sipping her morning coffee. The night wind from her dream had materialized with the light of day and a lively spring breeze rang the wind chimes she had hung from several low branches. She gazed across the lawn to the encircling trees, idly trying to spy the fairy path she had trod in her dream. But the woods seemed pedestrian in the morning light, evenly dark and unbroken.

Who was hurt, if she decided to carry on a torrid affair in her mind? Maggie believed in marriage, and she believed in her marriage to Rowan. Maybe they were going through a rough patch right now, but she took her vows seriously.

Even so, since she had gotten to know Cambien, the bonds of matrimony were, for the first time, beginning to chafe. There were moments when she positively ached to be with him. And if Rowan was temporarily unable to provide the affection a woman needs from her man, maybe an imaginary affair would be just the thing. She could ease her frustration, even imagine herself loved and cherished, while her husband worked through his problems. She would no doubt be bored with the whole thing by the time

Rowan was ready to come back to her. But in the meantime, if last night's dream was any indication, there would be plenty to distract her from the unhappiness in her home.

Maggie put on a flattering dress and brushed her hair until it rippled in silky waves over her shoulders. She hummed as she spritzed perfume on her wrists, even putting a dab in her cleavage. She giggled at herself. (Look at you, Maggie! You're acting like you're getting ready for a hot date). Rowan's alienating himself in the living room, ignoring her and the children, hardly bothered her this morning as she gathered her things, lined the kids up to kiss him goodbye, and left the house.

It seemed to take forever to drop off the children and drive to Stamford. Maggie arrived at the office early enough to get her favorite parking place, in the celadon shade of a magnificent old willow. She stepped brightly off the elevator and went to her desk. Once seated, she was disappointed not to find any emails from Cambien, only a stack of editing from Dr. Rajagopalan. But she set to and greeted Dr. Rajagopalan in a cheery voice when he came in an hour later. The old researcher looked at her curiously before returning her hello.

By lunchtime, Cambien still hadn't found an excuse to stop by the lab, and Maggie's buoyant mood began to wane. She got a sandwich to eat at her desk, worked, and waited. By two o'clock she grew impatient. Now that she had decided to allow herself to be (not really) seduced, she wanted to see the object of her imaginary affection, to look him in the eye, to draw inspiration for her musings. She printed out a draft of the newsletter she was working on and headed for the elevator.

On the fourth floor, Maggie stepped jauntily up to the massive executive reception desk. "Hello, Jill. Do you know if Dr. Cuthbert has a free minute? I'd like to get his opinion about some editorial I'm thinking of for the newsletter." She waved the printouts in the air between them, tangible corroboration the sleek executive assistant hadn't requested.

"I'm sorry, Maggie, but Dr. Cuthbert isn't in today."

Maggie kept her voice bright, hoping Jill didn't notice how crestfallen she suddenly felt. "Oh, that's okay. Is he ill?"

"I don't know, dear. He just left me a voicemail last night, saying he would be out today." Jill's tone let Maggie know that, even if anything were amiss with the founder of the company, she was far too professional to discuss it with the employees.

"Okay, no big deal. Thanks anyway." Maggie turned and walked back down the long hall. She was surprised at how disappointed, even foolish, she felt; it wasn't as though Cambien had really slept with her, only to abandon her the next day.

Anyway, the nice thing about imaginary lovers is that they are, by definition, at the imaginer's beck and call. As soon as she had a moment to herself, she could conjure him right up.

Maggie smiled. She had just decided she had a date with her new lover that very evening.

Maggie took up her imaginary affair with the rapture and intensity of a new love. Her step was lighter, her hair glossier, her dress tidier, her eyes brighter. She savored the way she felt, giggling to herself when coworkers asked what she had done to look so good. Had she lost weight? Gotten a haircut? Bought a new blouse? No, said Maggie, smiling inscrutably.

She was now thankful that her husband was so distracted by his goddamn job, or problems, or whatever it was. She was grateful for every minute alone she had in the evening, with the children asleep and Rowan out, left undisturbed with her thoughts. These became more intense and romantic by the day, so that far from her initial plan to have a merely sexual imaginary affair, Maggie now had an entire relationship in her mind.

She and Cambien were intimately involved, intertwined (she imagined). They told each other everything about their days and their dreams, and what's more, they were fascinated with each other. Sometimes, they were carrying on a naughty affair behind Rowan's back. But even though this was a fantasy, it still made Maggie feel guilty, so most of the time, they were a passionately happy married couple, Rowan and the children never having existed at all. They lived in a gracious Victorian house in North Stamford, surrounded by gardens, lawns and woods, from which Cambien tore himself daily to attend to his pharmaceutical empire. Counting the moments until he returned in the evening, Maggie wrote her bestselling novels in her study, sunlight and the scent of roses pouring through the French doors.

Into this fantasy world, Maggie packed everything she fancied was missing from her life; romantic love, creative opportunity, a dream house, intellectual stimulation, total intimacy, prestige, and recognition. Whenever she was alone, at night in bed, driving to work, or even during a quiet moment in the lab, she would visit the perfect life she had created. And all the while, she congratulated herself on her cleverness. Now she truly had the best of both worlds, she believed.

～✎

At the office, Maggie looked forward to meetings with Cambien almost ravenously. She craved the sight of him, the clean, exotic smell of him, the rumble of his manly voice, and the infinite depth in his black eyes when he looked at her.

Cambien returned from his brief absence (it turned out he had been traveling to one of the NarcoDynamics manufacturing plants in the mid-west) and came to see her his first day back. He had several supervisors with him from the factory, and he was giving them a tour of the Stamford office.

"This is Dr. Rajagopalan's lab," he explained as he strode unannounced into the room, leading a group of white-coated men and women. Dr. Rajagopalan looked up from his work and scowled, but Cambien didn't notice. "And over here is Maggie Cooper—I'm sorry, I mean Maggie Moore." He smiled at his gaffe with a studied self-indulgence. "Maggie and I have a bit of a history, so I sometimes think of her by her unmarried name. Anyway, Maggie writes the bulletin you've been getting." Maggie stood and nodded, smiling, to the guests. They smiled back, some of them speaking up to say how much they enjoyed the newsletter, or how pleased they were that the company's other functions were being communicated to them.

A few days later, Maggie was summoned to Cambien's office by his executive assistant, Jill, to review some editorial ideas he wanted her to include in the next issue. Maggie entered his office with a confident stride, looking him in the eye as she greeted him, privately amused by the notion that she was intimately familiar with him and he didn't even know it. The poor, innocent man, she thought to herself.

"Don't you look like the cat that ate the canary?" he said. He stood to greet her. "Have a seat over here, next to me, if you don't mind. That way, we can spread everything out on my desk and both look at the same things right side up."

"Works for me," Maggie said. She moved compliantly to his side and sat in the chair he had pulled up for her.

Cambien laid several leaves of paper on his desktop, the next issue of the newsletter crudely sketched out on them. "First of all, I was thinking you could do a feature piece on the Somnusol launch."

Maggie laughed. "I was thinking the same thing. In fact, I've already started it."

Cambien gave her a simpatico look. "Great minds thinking alike, right Maggie?" He began to discuss his ideas for the rest of the newsletter. Maggie offered her professional opinion where appropriate and made notes on the sheets of paper. As they worked, Cambien's arm or leg sometimes brushed against hers. Where Maggie would once have chastely moved away to avoid the contact, she now welcomed it. It made her feel sophisticated and in control. It was also, she had to admit to herself, pleasurable to have physical contact of any sort with the attractive man beside her. And perhaps she also hoped that she was having an effect on him, too; there was no headier thought than the idea of this great man weak with desire for her.

"Well, that should get you started, anyway," Cambien concluded. "How are things going otherwise? Keeping up with the study reports okay? We're not overloading you, are we?"

"No, I'm fine. As you know, I've added a day to my workweek, so I can keep up."

"Yes, and you should put in as many hours as you need to handle the workload. Don't worry about your fee. We'll pay whatever it costs to get the job done." Cambien hesitated a moment, then went on. "And Dr. Rajagopalan—is he working well with you? Any problems there?"

Maggie was surprised by the question. "Of course not. Dr. Rajagopalan is fine to work with."

"Then you haven't experienced any attitude problems with him or anything of that nature?" Cambien paused. "I probably shouldn't say this in front of other employees, but I know I can trust you; we've been having some insubordination issues with

Nikhil. So if you find yourself having any trouble with him, please come and see me about it."

Maggie was taken aback. She thought about it. "I mean, he's not exactly chatty, but that's fine with me. I'd much rather share workspace with someone who minds their own business and lets me do my job than with someone who interrupts me constantly to talk."

Cambien gave her leg a friendly squeeze. "That's my girl. Keep your eyes on your work, and just take anything Nikhil says with a grain of salt. All right, I guess that's it for now."

Maggie felt bereft now that the meeting was ending. She had been lulled by the cozy mood in the office and the time alone with him. "Okay," she said. "I'll start writing this up. I'll email you the first drafts in about a week."

He nodded. "Great. We'll meet up again to go over them." They stood and he walked her to the door. An intimate aura lingered as she said goodbye and turned to leave. She had to remind herself that the closeness she felt was a figment of her imagination, for it certainly felt as though there was something real between them.

10.

Maggie leaned back against the counter, dropping her gaze demurely. Before her, Cambien stood shirtless, dressed only in black cotton sleep pants. He moved closer, his bare feet teasingly overlapping her own. He took the coffee cup she was holding and placed it several feet away. Then his broad hands were spanning her lower back, pulling her to him.

She looked up at his chest and spread her hands across it. His skin was warm, tan, and fragrant, with just enough dark hair to underscore his masculinity. Drawn, she trailed kisses along his breastbone before turning her head and laying her check against him. She felt the quickened beating of his heart. Past his shoulder, she saw a charming old farm table before a bank of windows. Outside, a sloping lawn dropped away to a blooming strip of meadow, woodlands visible just beyond. She saw several deer grazing along the edge of the trees before Cambien lifted her face to him. He kissed her in earnest this time and Maggie, seduced by the domestic idyll and the delicious man at its center, returned the kiss with increasing fervor. Cambien's strong hands lifted her to the countertop as he pressed himself against her.

It was always difficult to drop the kids off at daycare on Tuesdays, let alone after a dream like the one she had been having when the alarm clock buzzed.

The children were home with Maggie, sometimes Rowan too, all weekend, and Pop came to watch them on Mondays. So after three days of being at home, Charlie was disinclined to do without his immediate family. Hazel was old enough to act like a big girl most of the time, too cool to need her Mommy, but Tuesdays were hard for her as well. Today her eyes welled up, but she valiantly held back the tears. This display of courage rent Maggie's heart more than sobs could have done.

"I love you, Hazy," she murmured, kissing the top of her daughter's head. "Look, Sandy's here. Go say hi." Hazel turned to see her best friend come into the room. She gave her mother one last hug and ran off.

Charlie had a very hard time. "No go, Mommy! No go!" he wailed, clinging to her legs. His little face was red and blotchy, tears and snot running down to his jiggly jowls. Maggie was almost in tears herself.

"Charlie Bean, please," she pleaded. "It's only for a few hours. I'll be back to get you before you know it."

"Noooooo! You stay!"

Maggie scooped him up, holding him to her chest like a baby. She wiped his face with a tissue and kissed him. Then she used a brusque, business-like tone. "Charlie, Mommy has to go to work now. Her boss is waiting for her."

"Doctor Cuzbert?" Charlie asked between sniffles.

"Yes, that's right, Doctor Cuthbert. If I don't go to my job, all the work Doctor Cuthbert needs done won't get done. Then he can't run his company any more, and he'll be so sad."

Charlie considered what she had said. "Okay, Mommy."

Kay, one of the women who worked at the daycare, came over to facilitate the leave-taking. She took Charlie from Maggie's arms and hoisted him onto her hip. "Guess what, Charlie? Guess what we have over here? New blocks! Look at these. They're special blocks that can make a big castle, if you're careful when you build it." Charlie agitated to be put down so he could get his hands on the new blocks. Kay set him on his feet and gave Maggie a wink.

"Thank you," Maggie mouthed silently. She turned and left quickly.

She was almost to the door when Charlie noticed her gone. She heard his howl: "Mommy! Mommy! Mommeeeeeeee!" Without looking back, she left the facility hastily, letting the door close behind her to silence her son's cries. Tears stung her eyes as she walked briskly up the path to her car.

Later that afternoon, the phone on Maggie's desk rang. It was her husband.

"Hey Rowan. What's up?"

"Just giving you a heads up. I have to finish a ton of reports before I can leave tonight. The captain is right up my ass, so I can't leave until they're done."

"Yup, do what you have to do. Want me to fix a plate for you to eat when you get home?"

"No thanks. I'll get something here."

"All right, see you when you get home."

"No you won't. You'll be asleep. See you in the morning, Mags."

"Mommy, will you please play race cars with us?" Hazel's plaintive tones were so grating that Maggie relented.

"Just a minute, Pumpkin. Let me finish up the dishes." She dried her hands and went into the living room. Hazel and Charlie had dumped a bin of toys onto the floor. Tiny cars and loose sections of racetrack were in a heap between the coffee table and the sideboard the television sat upon. Sighing, Maggie took up the instructions and set to assembling the track. Charlie and Hazel, attempting to help, grabbed pieces from one another and joined them to other pieces in such a way that they would never form an oval. Maggie lost her temper more than once. "Knock it off, you two. Give me that." She tore a section of track out of Charlie's hands with a force that made his eyes well up. "Sorry, but for Pete's sake, let me do this." Finally, Hazel and Charlie sat still and watched while she finished putting the track together.

The air was humid and heavy, and Maggie twisted her hair up off her sticky neck as the children snatched up racecars and tried to put them on the track. The mechanism that locked the cars onto the track was complicated, so Maggie had to do it for them. She put on an announcer's voice, speaking through cupped hands to simulate a loudspeaker. "Ladies and gentlemen, we bring you the fiftieth annual Moore Track Five Hundred." She hissed into her hands, imitating the sound of a massive arena full of screaming fans. The kids squealed, each grasping a control. "On your marks . . . get set . . . go!" Overexcited, the children sped up their cars too quickly, both of which derailed and leapt the track on the first curve.

Maggie patiently replaced the cars and started another heat. After several trials, the kids got better at controlling them. But Charlie's still went off the track fairly frequently, which required Maggie's assistance. The muggy air felt stifling and her head pounded as she leaned over the track for the twelfth time. She tried to focus on the game, but Cambien wouldn't keep his hands off her.

He had started teasing her earlier, while she did the dishes, coming up behind her to press against her and kiss the back of her neck. He vanished momentarily when the children insisted that she play with them, then lurked nearby, smoldering, as she put the track together and started the race. Once the kids were able to run the cars themselves, he was all over her again. Maggie retreated to the sofa, watching the children's game with her eyes only. She left the light off next to the couch and sat in the dimness, envisioning her lover beside her. His ardor was so intense it ignited her passion as well.

"Mama! Car," shouted Charlie for at least the twentieth time. He pointed to his tiny dragster, flipped on its back beside the track.

"Oh, for God's sake, can't I have some peace?" Maggie snapped. "Here, why don't you guys watch a cartoon?" She picked up the remote and turned on the TV, flicking through the channels until she found one of Hazel's favorite shows. "Take a break and watch TV for a little while."

"No! No! No like!" protested Charlie.

"Well, Mommy needs some time to herself. Hazel, can you please help Charlie with his car, then?" But Hazel was already watching the cartoon, slack jawed, in the way small children do. And Charlie was now doing the same in spite of himself.

Maggie left them in the living room and went into the downstairs bathroom, locking the door behind her.

As time went on, Rowan and Mike's case of the murdered girl grew cold. Nearly three months had passed, every lead they had followed went nowhere, and new clues were nonexistent. Life in Stamford went on, and fresh cases arose and began to take up their time, making it harder to concentrate on the unsolved murder. The girl's family, heartbroken, had moved to another town. Their house sat on the market, unsold, its horrible history repelling buyers.

The girl's mother had given Rowan a key before she left town so he might examine the scene freely and frequently. He often went to the house in the afternoon, approximating the time the crime occurred, and sat among the trees at the edge of the backyard. He told no one he did this, not even Mike.

He would sit motionless a few feet from where the little girl had been found, imagining he could still see the small depression in the pachysandra where she had lain. Then he would raise his eyes to the surrounding area and concentrate on every detail: the secretive evergreens, dense and full even last March, giving cover to the murderer; the litter of leaves and pine needles on the ground, muffling the sound and shape of footprints; in the distance, above the canopy of the trees, the silent steeple of a small white church and the peaks and chimneys of the taller houses in the venerable old neighborhood. The ground in front of Rowan sloped downward into the woods, eventually diving into a dry ravine before rising on the other side and gradually becoming another lawn. No other houses could be seen through the trees.

Behind Rowan, the ground was level, a lush green carpet thirty yards deep, ending at the flagged stone patio of the empty house. An abandoned wooden play set stood tastefully to one side on its bed of cedar shavings.

It should have been a wonderful house for children.

11.

Maggie had never before had the knack of choosing what she dreamt about. But now, she willfully wandered the passageways of her dreamscapes, willing herself to encounter her lover. And with astonishing frequency, he came to her. The dreams were lucid and realistic, rich and detailed. Maggie, often conscious that she was dreaming and thus able to direct her actions, immersed herself in Cambien, sating every craving and feeding every desire. She woke feeling deliciously ravished and ravenous for more. She supposed his prevalence in her dreams could be explained by the fact that she fell asleep most nights thinking of him.

The trick was getting enough sleep to be able to be with him. Rowan kept his odd hours, often waking Maggie when he came to bed, much as he tried to be quiet. And nearly every night, one of the children had nightmares. Hazel would materialize silently by the side of the bed, startling Maggie out of her slumber. Or Charlie would shout and toss until Maggie went and roused him. The little boy would weep with the fear of his nightmare still upon him and she would lie beside him, comforting him until he was asleep again. She would drift off, only to be wakened by

Charlie's kicks and out-flung arms; he was a restless sleeper on the best of nights.

When she finally crept back to her own bed, the slight movements she made disturbed Rowan. His resulting snores drove her downstairs to the sofa. Once she managed to doze off again, as often as not, there would be more commotion. Rowan's police scanner, always on, would crackle to life with the urgent, disembodied voice of the dispatcher. Or a fresh terror would seize one of the children. Maggie would mount the stairs, zombielike, to the second floor and start the whole thing over again. It amazed her that Rowan was able to sleep through all the goings-on, but although he only slept five or six hours a night, he slept like the dead.

Maggie drove to work in the mornings with her eyes stinging, already looking forward to going to bed that night. She craved sleep. She craved her dreams, and she longed for Cambien.

She went through a box of old CDs from college and found a David Bowie album. There was a melancholy, wildly romantic song on it that she had shunned back in her crazy days because it was rather corny. But having now rediscovered it, she couldn't get enough of it. She played it over and over again in her car, driving to and from Stamford on the parkway. *Love me, love me, love me, say you do,* sang Bowie, and Maggie sang along. *Like the leaf clings to the tree, oh, my darling, cling to me.*

Maggie drove south in the morning, north in the evening, blinking in the daylight, singing along, and aching for Cambien.

〜✕

She stared at her computer screen. The afternoon sun, stymied by the blinds, cast a sneaky glow through every gap and seam. The motor in a refrigerator hummed softly on the far side of the room. She was alone today, Dr. Rajagopalan having taken the week off.

She squinted at her monitor, which displayed a pharmacokinetic analysis she was supposed to be editing. But the words in front of her became nonsensical, blurring into fuzzy shapes, meaningless to Maggie's sleep-deprived eyes. Maybe a cup of coffee, she thought.

Cambien peered around the doorframe. "May I come in?" he asked in his mellifluous voice.

She straightened up, barely able to suppress the grin that tried to steal over her face. "It's your building," she answered glibly.

He came into the room, shaking his head. "You're the funny one." Pulling a chair beside her, he sat very close and looked over her shoulder at her computer screen. "What are you working on?" he asked. And as though it were perfectly natural, he rested his chin on her shoulder.

Surprised, Maggie laughed. "I do hope you're comfortable." She tried to sound casual, though a hot flush rose up her body. His face was mere inches from hers, his breath in her ear, and she turned quickly back to her work. "Dr. Rajagopalan left me this analysis, and I'm trying to—" Her explanation was cut short as Cambien splayed his long fingers over her cheek and turned her face to him. Maggie's lips parted in surprise. Smoothly inclining his head, he kissed her. The kiss was gentle but it burned her like fire. The feeling swept through her, weakening her limbs, tightening her chest, making her heart thump painfully. Captivated, she did not resist.

The kiss deepened. Now both of Cambien's hands were on her, one entangled in her hair, the other stroking the soft skin of her throat. Maggie had dreamed of this for so long, had wanted it so badly, she felt powerless to stop it. Her hands left the keyboard—she couldn't help it—and her fingers spanned his wide chest. His mouth left hers to sear her neck with kisses. He dipped his hand into the neckline of her blouse. Maggie's head lolled back wantonly and she gasped with pleasure.

Cambien stood in the doorway, his arms folded, one leg crossed over the other, watching her from under dark brows. "Are you all right, Maggie?" he called.

Maggie's head whipped upright, her mouth agape and eyes wide. Good Lord, how long had he been standing there, watching her? And what the hell had just happened? Was that a daydream? Had she fallen asleep?

For several seconds, she was too flustered to answer. "I'm so sorry," she finally stammered. "I don't know what . . . my God, I think I was asleep. Oh, you must think I'm horrible. I swear, I never sleep on the job. I don't know what just happened."

Concern showed plainly on his face. "Are you sure you're okay?" He took in the dark circles under her eyes and her pale, puffy face. "You don't look like you feel so hot."

"The kids have been waking me up every night with nightmares," she explained, humiliated; she didn't believe an employee's personal problems were the concern of his or her employer. "I can't apologize enough. It is absolutely not my habit to doze off on the clock."

Cambien wasn't angry. "My dear, I certainly did not mean to make you feel guilty. If anything, I feel guilty for taking you from your beautiful children so often to do my work for me. But of course, you are a mother first, a scientific editor second."

Maggie's panic began to subside. "You are far too understanding."

"Nonsense. I'm only glad to see that you're okay. I was passing the lab and saw you with your head lolling, and I was afraid you had fainted or something."

Well, at least she hadn't been writhing in her chair. Her moans must have been only in her head. The wicked pleasure she took in knowing a secret about Cambien that even he didn't know began to return. He stood before her, touchingly concerned for her wellbeing, while moments earlier he had been ravishing her where she sat. She congratulated herself yet again on having invented such a clever way to conduct a guiltless affair. She smiled knowingly, amused by the puzzlement this added to his look of concern. "Well really, I am fine. I must have dozed off but I promise, I won't do it again, Boss."

"Are you sure you're alright? If you need to take the afternoon off, please do."

"No, I'm good. I really want to wrap this up before I leave today. Thanks anyway."

"Okay then. Hope you get a good night's sleep tonight." He flashed his charming smile, turned and was gone.

Maggie smirked. He was completely unsuspecting. He had no idea that she had just been engaged in an ardent embrace with him, would probably do more than that with him while she lay in bed that night, waiting for sleep.

Cambien strolled cheerily down the hall, away from Maggie's office, an irrepressible grin stealing across his face.

Rowan came home in time for dinner that night, something he had been doing with greater frequency lately, although he remained emotionally distant from his family. Maggie had long ago resigned herself to letting it be and going about her own business. At nine-thirty, she emotionlessly kissed him goodnight and went to bed. She read for half an hour, turned off the light and, thinking of Cambien, nestled into her pillow.

He had been worried for her today when she had nodded off at her desk. He cared for her. This made her inordinately happy. She drifted into unconsciousness, Cambien held firmly in her mind. Little surprise, then, that she began to dream of him.

Tender morning light washed the room. Cambien reclined on his side, leaning up on one arm to look at her. He was speaking to her but his words faded in and out of audibility, making no sense. Maggie realized there was something between them in the bed, something warm and soft. She raised herself up onto an elbow and looked down to see a beautiful child. It was a tiny girl, with coal black hair and amber eyes, wearing a white linen gown that was so long, it hid her feet. Although she was no bigger than an infant, she looked to be three or four years old. She was too young to speak, yet the light of understanding shone in her eyes as she returned Maggie's gaze. A peaceful smile curved her little rosebud mouth.

Maggie looked at the enchanting little girl, at her fair skin and jet hair, her coral little lips. She was beyond beautiful. Maggie was awash with love and longing for the tiny creature.

Cambien was still speaking, his words coming into focus like a radio being tuned to a station. "What do you think of her?" he was asking.

Maggie was at a loss for words to describe the feelings the child evoked in her. "I love her so much," was all she could say.

"As do I. So . . . will you stay with her?"

"I would like nothing better." Maggie sighed.

". . . because I will too. I'll stay with our child."

Maggie looked at the baby girl in disbelief. "Is she ours, then? Yours and mine?" The child smiled puckishly at her and Maggie's heart heaved.

"Yes, my love."

Bliss flooded Maggie. She bent and placed her forehead against the girl's, eye to eye, the tiny nose rubbing against her own as softly as a flower petal. They giggled together.

"And me, Maggie? What about me?"

She looked up at Cambien, struck as always by the hewn beauty of his face and the sheer strength of the attraction she felt to him. She saw anxiety in his eyes. "What about you?"

"Do you love me?" Even as he said it, the emotions she felt crystallized and she knew it to be so. Awestruck at the realization, she nodded mutely.

"Then say it, my love." Joy began to dawn on his face, chasing the fear from his eyes. She knew herself to be the source of his fear and his joy, and her yearning for him intensified. She could not refuse him. She paused only fleetingly at the edge of the chasm behind the words.

"I love you, Cambien."

He gave her a beatific smile, which she returned. There was nothing to keep her from staying in this bed, with these beloved people, forever. She looked into his midnight eyes and knew she needed nothing more.

When Rowan joined her in their bed she remained asleep, reclining in the glowing embrace of her phantom family as her husband of flesh and blood lay breathing evenly, steadfast, beside her.

12.

In June, Charlie turned three. Maggie and Rowan had begun a tradition on Hazel's first birthday of inviting their own friends over for a meal and some adult libation. Their friends did the same, and a child's birthday became a rally for former drinking buddies to socialize in a more mature way, at a private home instead of a bar or nightclub, and to include their children in the festivities.

Taking advantage of the fine weather, Maggie and Rowan bought hamburgers and hot dogs, made potato salad, and invited several couples they knew to the party. In the late afternoon, their driveway began to fill with cars. Pop had already arrived and was setting up the gift he had given Charlie, an inflatable wading pool. He got it blown up and filled with three inches of frigid water from the garden hose. He pulled up a lawn chair and sat with a bottle of cold beer in one hand, resplendent in an orange t-shirt that had the word "LIFEGUARD" printed across the back, gaudy tropical-print swim trunks, black socks, and a pair of rubber garden clogs. He and the children splashed each other savagely. Maggie laughed to see her father in such a rambunctious mood.

Rowan's partner, Mike, arrived with his wife, Claudia, and their three children. Claudia, having been tipped off by Maggie that the party would involve water, had dressed her children appropriately. They ran to join the Moore kids in the pool.

Several more people arrived, walking around the side of the house to join the party in the backyard. Maggie greeted them, Rowan got them something to drink, and more children joined the screaming, thrashing throng in the pool. The grownups sat in the shade of the tall maple and oak trees that ringed the yard, drinking beer and talking. Rowan had tuned the radio to the local station and rock music drifted through the yard. After getting the hors d'oeuvres passed and placed on tables near the guests, Maggie finally sat with the grownups, enjoying a glass of wine and cooling down from her stint in the kitchen.

Next to her was a couple she knew only casually, the Adamses. Their three-year-old daughter was Charlie's close friend at daycare, and Maggie often chatted with them while dropping her kids off in the mornings or picking them up in the evenings. The Adamses seemed like her kind of people—unpretentious, down-to-earth, with a good sense of humor. So she had invited them to the party and was now glad she had. They were wonderful company, full of funny stories and good humor. Chris Adams worked down in Westchester County as an information technology director for a large corporation. His wife, Melanie, edited a magazine for wine connoisseurs. They had brought three bottles of sparkling white Spanish wine to the party. Melanie was seven months pregnant with their second child.

Maggie found herself gazing at Melanie's swollen belly. She and Rowan had talked about it years ago and had settled on two children as their goal. This plan had been solidified when the ultrasound showed their second child would be a boy. "All done," Rowan had said smugly, clapping his hands as though he had just completed a demanding task. Maggie was generally in agreement with him on this point—after all, children are exhausting, expensive, and quite painful to bring into the world. Furthermore, she had finally gotten herself back into some sort of shape and was happily back at work, building up her career as a scientific writer. A baby now would completely derail the progress she had made and strip her of the identity she had been painstakingly reclaiming these past few months.

But still, sometimes, Maggie thought about another baby. She missed the immensely creative feeling of making a new life. She missed the aura of magic around a new baby. And most of all, she missed the intimacy she had shared with her husband during the charmed time of creating a new human being together.

Maggie looked up from her thoughts to see Vicky round the corner of the house and come into the yard. "Hi, everyone," she called in her raspy voice.

Maggie leapt up to greet her friend. "Yay, I'm so glad you made it. I know a little kid's party isn't always the most exciting place for a swingin' single gal to spend her evening."

"Oh, please. Like there's anyone better to see than you guys. Sorry we're late . . ."

"We?"

" . . . and I hope you don't mind, but I've taken the liberty of bringing a guest with me."

Maggie was intrigued. "Of course I don't mind. Who did you bring? Not that guy you've been seeing?"

Grinning widely, Vicky nodded. "Yup, the same." She seemed practically incandescent with happiness.

"Wow, this must be getting serious," said Maggie. It gladdened her to see her friend so content.

Vicky gave a little shiver of excitement. "I sure hope so." She lowered her voice and spoke in an animated, hushed tone. "Maggie, I know I've been through a lot of men—a couple husbands, even—but I'm not kidding, this guy is like no man I've ever met before."

"Well, where is he?" Maggie craned her head, trying to see who was coming up the path behind Vicky.

"I think you may even know him. He's just getting Charlie's present out of the trunk of his car. Here he comes."

Dear God, this couldn't be happening. Maggie looked past Vicky and beheld a grinning Cambien striding up the flagstone path, carrying a huge gift-wrapped box. Her heart contracted into a cold, hard lump of stone, radiating pain through her chest. *Breathe, Maggie.* Somehow, she kept the smile frozen on her face.

He was upon her in a wink. "Hello, Maggie. Hope you don't mind me party crashing like this," he crooned. He bent to kiss her cheek and she mechanically returned his greeting. "So, this is where you live. What a charming old house."

Maggie struggled to draw breath, smile convincingly, speak appropriately. "Cambien, my goodness. I had no idea you . . . and Vicky . . . Of course I don't mind you tagging along. Please, come in. Well, I mean, come in the yard, we're not actually in the house." Vicky began to laugh and Maggie tried to play humorously off her tied tongue. "Oh, you know what I mean– come join the party." Cambien watched her coolly, smirking. If Maggie didn't know better, she would have thought he was enjoying her discomfort.

Turning, she saw that Rowan had come over to greet the newcomers. He, too, seemed taken aback at the sight of Cambien but recovered immediately, extending his hand in greeting. "Dr. Cuthbert, we meet again. Hey, Vicky." He gave Maggie's friend a warm hug. "Welcome to Sea World. Hope you brought your swimsuit. What can I get you to drink?"

Maggie had no idea how she got through the evening. If Cambien had come to her house and punched her in the gut with all the force he could muster, he couldn't have demolished her more. And no matter how many times she told herself she was being ridiculous, the feeling of devastation wouldn't let up.

She and Rowan laid out food on the table and their guests filled plates and returned to their lawn chairs to eat. Vicky helped herself to many glasses of wine and flitted about the yard, catching up with the Nickersons, introducing herself to the Adamses, flirting with Pop. Cambien followed suit, imbibing and tagging along after his girlfriend (Maggie shuddered at the word) from guest to guest, charming everyone with his quick wit and striking good looks. Maggie couldn't bear to look at them.

Rowan, on the other hand, tracked Cambien with a shrewd gaze all evening. Mike was perhaps the only other person who wasn't charmed by the good doctor, watching Cambien suspiciously as he conversed with Claire.

Unable to mingle lightheartedly, Maggie got a plate of food and went to the wading pool on the pretense of feeding her children. Pop greeted her from his lifeguard post. "Hey, Pop," she said as brightly as she could. She sat in an empty chair next to his. "Hazel, come here and have something to eat." She went back and forth between her children, coaxing them to eat a few bites between bouts of leaping and splashing. She remained poolside, neglecting her guests as she sought composure.

"I think he likes his present," said Pop. He reached into the pool and heaved a wave of water at his grandson. Laughing, Charlie turned his face away and splashed back with both hands.

"I think they all do," said Maggie dully. Unbidden, her gaze wandered to the deep shadow at the back of the yard where Vicky and Cambien had retreated to a bench. Maggie drew in her breath; her boss and her best friend, drunk on her wine, were making out on her garden bench. She felt sick.

What's wrong with you, she chided herself. *You should be happy for Vicky. And you should be happy for Cambien. How many times have you told yourself it was a shame he was single? Well, now he's not. Good for him.* But she couldn't shake her misery and waves of prickly heat washed over her periodically.

"Are you alright?" her father was asking. He stared at her clammy complexion.

Maggie nodded. "I'm fine, Pop."

She worked harder at being convincingly merry. At last, it was time for cake. Maggie set Rowan to collecting all the children around the table while she went into the kitchen and lit the candles. Everyone sang as she carried the orange frosted, steam shovel-shaped confection to the table. Charlie blew out all four candles (three for being three, one to grow on) on the first try. Everybody cheered. As Maggie began to cut the cake and serve it to the children, Vicky and Cambien came over to her, their arms around one another. Maggie forced herself to look at them and smile. "Hey guys. What's up?"

"Maggie, I hate to eat and run, but we're going to take off," Vicky said. "You don't mind, do you?"

"Of course not. It was nice of you even to come. Now run along and have some fun while the night is still young." She and Vicky embraced.

Cambien stepped close. "Thank you for a lovely evening," he said. He gave her a warm hug and a kiss on the cheek, as a family friend would be entitled to do.

Maggie felt no pleasure in his contact now; she had to fight the urge to shrink from his touch. "I'm so glad you could come," she said stiffly. He stepped back to stand beside Vicky, putting his arm around her, a sly smile on his face. Vicky merely looked ecstatic. They both grinned at Maggie for another moment, and she felt the need to say something more. "Well, you two certainly win the prize for the element of surprise," she added. "You could have knocked me over with a feather when you came around the corner." Vicky and Cambien looked at each other and laughed.

"In all honesty, I didn't even know you two knew each other," said Cambien. "Vicky and I only figured it out the other day. And she thought it would be funny to surprise you."

"Me?" said Vicky. "It was your idea."

"Was it? I thought you thought of it, dear." Cambien gave Vicky an affectionate kiss—Maggie's stomach lurched—before he addressed his hostess again. "Well anyway, thanks again. See you on Monday."

"Yup, bye, guys," said Maggie, turning quickly back to the table full of small children clamoring for cake. Arm in arm, Cambien and Vicky sauntered across the darkening lawn to the path that led to the front of the house. Maggie looked after them several times, a lump the size of a golf ball in her throat.

In another part of the yard, Rowan, in the lawn chair next to Mike, also watched Cambien's retreating back. "My wife's boss," he said. Mike snorted. They both took a swallow of beer.

After cake, it was time to open presents. Naturally, Charlie opened the biggest package first, the one Cambien had brought. It was the train set from the hobby shop window.

The Nickersons were the last to leave. They sat in the yard until nearly ten o'clock. Every moment was agony for Maggie, who forced herself to sit with her friends as though nothing were amiss. Finally, she excused herself and took the children inside to watch a movie. Claudia followed her, bringing in the last of the dishes. The kids watched a cartoon while Maggie cleaned up the kitchen. Claudia kept her company. Fortunately, she was a talker. She prattled away while Maggie wrapped plastic around the leftovers and put them in the fridge.

Claudia started an unwelcome new topic of conversation. "So, that was your boss?"

Maggie leaned over the sink to wash dishes. A thick hank of hair swung in front of her face. "Yup, that's Dr. Cuthbert."

"Wow, he sure is a hottie."

"You think so?" Maggie said quickly. "I hadn't thought of him that way." She scrubbed a pan with steel wool so hard it shone like a freshly minted dime.

Claudia fanned herself. "My God, how could you not? How the hell did Vicky snag him?"

"Probably because, unlike us, she's single." Maggie couldn't keep the bitterness from her voice. She rinsed the pan and banged it in the drain board.

"Well, hell, Maggie. Just because we're on a diet, doesn't mean we can't look at the menu."

"Claudia, would you mind checking on the kids? They're too quiet."

"Sure, Mags." Claudia stepped into the living room and returned a minute later to report that everyone under four was asleep. She went out back to fetch her husband, who came in with Rowan. The Nickersons gathered their swimsuits, towels, sippy cups and toys into a huge tote bag. They took their leave with sleeping children slung over their shoulders.

"I'm going to check the news," Rowan announced.

Maggie almost sang with relief. "Fine, I'll take the kids to bed. I'll probably stay up there, too, so goodnight."

"'night, Maggie." He already had the distant expression he wore while watching TV and shutting the world out. Maggie picked Charlie up and was able to rouse Hazel enough for her to climb upstairs under her own power.

Charlie slept right through his change to pajamas and Hazel fell asleep as soon as she got into her bed. Finally, Maggie was alone with her feelings.

What she felt was a detestable brew of some of the most excruciating emotions in her repertoire. She felt stupid. Abandoned. Bereft. Betrayed. Hopeless. And above all, utterly wretched.

At least the prickly waves of nausea had receded. She realized that these had been surges of terror; she had feared her agitation would be noticed, so deeply disturbed was she. And once her distress had been noted, it would have been immediately apparent to everyone what was wrong with her. She dreaded either Cambien or Rowan seeing her misery, seeing right through her. She didn't know which of them would have been worse.

Exhausted by the emotional toll the evening had taken on her, she fell into a merciful and dreamless unconsciousness.

~~~

The next day, Maggie longed to be alone. She needed to sort her feelings and patch up her demolished psyche enough to keep functioning, so that no one would know.

She had awakened so early that the pale light outside had an unworldly, colorless quality. She slipped out of bed and went down the stairs in the disorienting twilight. With a mug of coffee, she sat sideways on the armchair where, not long ago, she had blithely planned the imaginary fling she would have with Cambien.

What a fool she had been. Did she really believe she could immerse herself in feelings and fantasies about a man as exceptional as Cambien and escape unchanged? She had made a fatal miscalculation, and now she had to face the consequence she had refused to acknowledge all this time; she loved Cambien, beyond all hope or reason.

Even from the depths of her wretchedness, she knew her misery was utterly inappropriate. Her single, dearest friend and her single, extraordinary employer had found love with one another, and only the most selfish wretch could be unhappy for them. Worse, she had no business having feelings for Cambien in the first place, married and a mother of two as she was. So not only was she in unbearable torment, she had no one with whom she could talk about it. For the second time in recent months, she wished her mother were alive.

There was no option but to salve her injury and limp on. A vision of the rest of her life revealed itself to her. She saw herself shuffling through an endless string of empty days, bearing a painful wound that never healed, enduring an endless hunger that calcified into a constant, corrosive ache in her very soul. The future seemed quite hopeless. Maggie chuckled mirthlessly; perhaps Vicky would ask her to be matron of honor someday. Maggie did not know how she would get through it.

Later that morning, Vicky stirred in her massive, four-poster bed. Bright sunlight and a late morning breeze flowed into the room through open windows as she drifted up slowly from a luxurious slumber. Opening her eyes at last, she took in the rumpled state of the bedding, the throw pillows and bedspread and her own clothing strewn about the floor. Two half-full wine glasses and an empty water glass stood on the nightstand. Images of the previous night began to fill her head and she smiled, stretching sensuously.

She sat up, savoring the way she felt. She half-remembered Cambien gently waking her in the pre-dawn, already dressed, to say goodbye. And before that . . . *ah, before that.* She hugged herself, smoothing her hands down her bare arms as she recalled the sumptuous lovemaking: the first time with great urgency, a long-simmering flirtation finally given its head to erupt into flame; a brief rest in one another's arms, then a tender, more intimate interlude. Vicky remembered falling helplessly into black eyes as her body responded to a touch that had unprecedented power to move her.

She gathered the cushions and sat up, her smile widening, her eyes dreamy and unfocused. She was glad she had waited before inviting this man into her bedroom. Maybe she had known from the moment she met him that he was different, that this time it would be about more than carnal attraction and a couple of sweaty nights. Maybe this time it was about feelings. Perhaps the month or two of waiting to become lovers had allowed physical attraction to mature into a real connection (which was doubtless why the sex had been so good). Surely neither she nor Cambien could deny the goodness of their relationship or the happiness they brought one another.

Oh Vicky, you're in it deep this time. But instead of the usual anxiety she felt at the prospect of becoming attached to a man, she felt nothing but joy. She adored Cambien, longed to be with him, and couldn't wait to see him again. She felt, for the first time in a long time and maybe more genuinely than ever, that she had a future with this man. An image of her own hands, spread white against his broad, bare chest, flashed into her mind and her entire body tingled with remembered sensations. She closed her eyes and shivered, enraptured.

Okay, take it easy, Vick. Play it cool, so far, so good. Lord, it would be hard, but she would need to hold herself back. She must use every scrap of self-control she could muster to keep herself from appearing on his doorstep that very evening, begging for more. She eyed the phone on her nightstand, longing to hear her lover's voice. *No, Vicky,* she told herself firmly.

As though her wish were its command, the phone rang. Vicky knew who it would be. She let it ring three times before answering, using her raspy, still-naked-in-bed voice. "Hello?" She said this as though the caller might be anyone at all.

"Good morning. How are you feeling?"

Vicky curled up kitten-like, the smile so wide now she didn't know how it fit on her face. "Hi, Cambien. I'm feeling pretty good today. How about you?"

"No complaints here." Vicky giggled into the phone. Cambien spoke in intimate tones. "I was calling to thank you for a lovely evening. Best 'nightcap' I've had in a long time."

"The pleasure was all mine." Vicky tamped down the urge to add, there's more where that came from. *No pressure to get together again,* she reminded herself firmly

Luckily, Cambien broached the subject. "I also wanted to let you know that I'll be a bit busy for the next couple days, but I hoped you might be available for dinner on, say, Thursday?"

Happiness flooded Vicky. He wanted to see her again, and not just for a late-night drink and another screw. *Keep it cool, Vick,* she reminded herself. *Like a cucumber.* "I don't have my calendar in front of me, but I believe I'm free that night," she answered.

"If I recall correctly, you don't have much of anything in front of you at the moment."

Vicky laughed, intrigued anew by his suggestiveness. "You would be correct, Doctor. But I'll put dinner into my schedule as soon as I get out of bed."

"You naughty girl, still in bed. I've been up for hours already." He feigned indignation.

"Surely you knew what kind of woman you were getting involved with, Doctor."

"Oh, I can't wait to find out more about what kind of woman I'm getting involved with. So far, everything I've discovered has been utterly fascinating." Vicky thrilled at his words. "So until Thursday, then."

"Until Thursday." She hung up the phone, glowing with pleasure.

Oh yes, she was in it deep this time. And dared she cautiously hope that Cambien was in it with her? That phone call was certainly encouraging.

Reluctant to break the spell, Vicky stayed in bed a while longer. She knew what it was she felt. She hadn't felt it in years and certainly never as strongly as now, but she knew it for what it was. And it wasn't nearly as scary as the other times.

You love him, she admitted matter-of-factly to herself. *And that's good enough for now, and the future is wide open.*

This simple admission clarified the rapture she felt, the repletion this man brought to her, body and soul, simultaneously creating a yearning for more. She foresaw nothing but increased happiness, joy heaped upon joy, as she and Cambien discovered everything about one another. Vicky sighed contentedly. She couldn't wait for the future.

13.

Maggie sat despondently at her desk. Over two weeks had passed since the devastating birthday party, and the pang of loss hadn't lessened. She went to bed forlornly every night, telling herself that surely, tomorrow she would feel better. And every morning, the ache was there before she could open her eyes.

At work, Maggie now avoided contact with Cambien as studiously as she had once sought it. The mere sight of him wracked her with longing and plunged her into anxiety that he would see the yearning she knew must be plain on her face.

But as hard as she worked to avoid him, the more she seemed to see of him. The first workday after the party, almost the instant she reached her desk, her phone rang. It was Jill, saying that Dr. Cuthbert would like to see her. Caught unprepared, Maggie stammered of course, she would be right up. Still reeling from the shock of seeing Cambien with Vicky, she had barely dragged herself to work that morning. She groaned aloud, gathered her unkempt hair into a clip, straightened her wrinkled blouse as much as possible, and departed for the stairs.

When she presented herself at Jill's desk, she noticed the executive assistant take in her disheveled appearance almost imperceptibly. Always professional, Jill smiled in welcome. "Dr. Cuthbert is expecting you. Go right in."

"Thanks, Jill." Maggie lifted her chin, determined not to look as beaten as she felt, and walked through Cambien's open door. "Hey, Boss," she said brightly, striving to sound normal.

Cambien, who had been thumbing through some papers on his desk, looked up. "Hello, Maggie," he greeted her robustly.

Maggie noticed him looking at her a beat too long, doubtless taken aback by her slovenly appearance. "Sorry I look so casual today," she began apologetically. She rebuked herself silently for drawing attention to her appearance. "I just couldn't get it together this morning. Charlie was up all night with a virus," she explained lamely. She was appalled at how easily she cast the blame on her own son.

Cambien gallantly dismissed the issue. "Nonsense, Maggie. You don't have to dress up for me. We're old friends, you and I. Come, sit beside me while we go over this editorial." He patted the seat of a chair he had already drawn beside his own in anticipation of her visit.

Their once intoxicating habit of sitting side by side when working together now promised to be as excruciating as lying on a bed of nails. Maggie did as she was bidden, moving woodenly to Cambien's side and sitting in the chair.

"I read through your story about our PR campaign for the Somnusol launch and its effectiveness. It's an excellent analysis, really well-researched and concisely written."

Maggie spoke spiritlessly. "I didn't do much. I got the data from the PR people. They had already done all the heavy lifting. I just wrote it up."

"Of course, that's what we pay them for. But your write up is just the right voice for our newsletter. Maggie, really, you mustn't be so modest." His voice today was rich, mellifluous, animated. He seemed to be in an exceptionally good mood, his eyes bright with high spirit.

Of course he's happy, thought Maggie miserably. *He's in love. But then again, so am I, and it's causing me no end of sorrow.*

"There is, however, one passage here that I think could be deleted, and another that ought to be expanded." Maggie sat resignedly beside him, inhaling his clean, exotic scent, feeling the rumble of his voice reverberate within her own chest. As he so often did, Cambien leaned close to her, circling his edits with a pencil and brushing his upper arm against hers. Maggie jumped as though she had been burned. He turned to her, his face inches from hers, the very picture of affectionate concern. "Maggie, my dear, what is it? You're as jumpy as a cat today. Is everything alright?"

Of course it's not, she felt like screaming. *I'm head over heels for you, and you love my best friend, and she loves you, and I'm married anyway, and my husband doesn't love anyone, and my whole life is a huge mess.* But instead, she answered quietly, "Yes, I'm fine. I'm sorry I'm so out of it. I—I'm just tired."

"I hope you didn't overdo it at Charlie's party. I did notice at the time that you looked a bit pale." He stared at her intently. She must have been seeing things, for it looked as though the shadow of a smirk flickered over his face.

Had he noticed how devastated she had been when he made his appearance? Had he guessed how she felt about him? Maggie swallowed, trying to moisten her dry mouth. "No, it's not a big deal. I just didn't sleep so well last night, that's all."

"Tisk tisk, we can't have our employees not sleeping soundly at NarcoDynamics. What does that say about our company? You know, Maggie, I'm not just your friend, I'm also a doctor. I'd be happy to give you something if you need help sleeping at night. On the house, of course."

"I'm sorry? What?" Although she worked at a company famous for its sleeping draughts, it had never occurred to Maggie to take the medication herself.

Cambien noted her reluctance. "Just the Somnusol, Maggie. I wouldn't prescribe anything like Anadreme for a simple case of sleeplessness. No reason for you not to enjoy your dreams, after all."

"Oh, no thanks, Cambien, really. That's not necessary. I'm sure I'll sleep like a baby tonight. If my kids let me, that is." Again she had offered her own children as the cause of her distraction. She was disgusted with herself.

"Very well, suit yourself." Cambien took her shoulder in his firm grasp, an earnest expression on his face. He looked directly into her eyes. Maggie stared back, helpless. His voice was tender and solicitous. "I just want you to know that if there's anything bothering you, you can always talk to me about it. No matter what it is, work-related or otherwise, I'm here for you."

Her misery being the one thing she couldn't possibly talk to him about, Maggie wondered whether he tormented her on purpose. She heard herself thanking him for his concern, saying she would bear it in mind but that really, nothing was wrong. Cambien smiled kindly at her. After a pause, he asked if she wanted to get on with the editing. "Yes, by all means," she answered.

By the time he finally dismissed her from the meeting, Maggie was shaking from the strain of maintaining her composure. The atmosphere between them had been, as always, affectionate and intimate. And what reason would Cambien have to behave otherwise? Why would he think anything had changed between them, innocent as he was of her feelings for him? Maggie slunk into the stairwell, forbidding herself to run. In its cool, florescent privacy, she descended the two flights to the lab level, stifling sobs and wiping tears on her shirt hem.

Maybe she should quit, she thought as she sat at her desk. The pain of seeing him was intolerable. Maybe she should just give up and stop inflicting this torment on herself.

But she rejected the idea as soon as it occurred to her. She could not possibly quit, as there was no credible reason for her to do so. If she abruptly left her job at NarcoDynamics, the job she had been telling everyone she simply adored, people close to her would wonder why. People like Rowan, and Vicky. And certainly, Cambien would demand to know why she was leaving him. She had no faith in her ability to look him in the eyes and conceal the truth from him.

She had no choice but to stay. So there she sat, a fortnight later, forcing herself to edit Dr. Rajagopalan's research reports, willing herself to write stories for Cambien's newsletter, praying for strength to keep going, and holding onto a faith that someday, somehow, it wouldn't hurt so much.

Hearing a knock on the frame of her open door, Maggie looked up and was surprised to see Vicky. "Hello, Maggie. I finally get to see where you work," she said. She walked into the room. Maggie couldn't help but notice she looked radiant. Her blond curls shone, her blue eyes sparkled, and a bright smile lit her face.

A mixture of sadness and pleasure at seeing her friend washed over Maggie. Ignoring the flare up of the ever-present ache in her heart, she stood and came from behind her desk. "Hey, Vick. This is a nice surprise. What on earth are you doing here?" Maggie abruptly realized that Vicky must be in the building because she was visiting Cambien. The pain struck at her anew, but she fought hard for outward equanimity. Forcing the smile to remain on her face, she continued, "Oh, of course– you must have been upstairs seeing your boyfriend." Vicky grinned wider and blushed at the word. "Well, how do you like that? I've been working here for three months, and do you ever come to see me? No. But now that there's a man involved, all of a sudden you have plenty of time to drop by NarcoDynamics."

Vicky looked like a chastened little girl. "You make it sound so mercenary."

"Oh Vicky, I'm just busting your chops."

"I know you are. I'm sorry I never came before. But anyway, it's not like you ever invited me or anything." She tossed her curls, turning her nose up in mock indignation.

"You got me, I never did invite you." Maggie capitulated, inwardly amazed at her ability to banter with the woman who had stolen her imaginary lover and broken her heart for real.

"So there, we're even." Vicky laughed. "Now show me around."

"Sure, come on in. As you can see, this is my desk." Maggie presented her workspace to her friend with a flourish, and Vicky ooh'ed and ah'ed as if beholding a great marvel. "That desk there is Dr. Rajagopalan's and that one's Mark's. He's another doctor on the team, but he's only here sometimes." Maggie stepped over to where the large room transitioned from office to lab space. "This is where Dr. Rajagopalan and his team do their lab work. And there's Dr. Rajagopalan and Mark."

The two men, who had been hunched over their work on a counter about twenty feet away, looked up. Vicky smiled and waved at them. "Hi, I'm Vicky Bertrand. I'm an old friend of Maggie's."

"Hello, Vicky. Nice to meet you," the men replied.

Vicky turned back to Maggie. "Okay, tour over, grab your bag. We're going to lunch."

Maggie had been having trouble eating lately. The prospect of trying to choke down her food while sitting across from Cambien's real-life romantic interest, who doubtless wanted to go to lunch only so she could babble about the details of her love life, was not an attractive one. Maggie tried to squirm out of it. "I don't know, Vicky, I'm up against a bit of a deadline."

"You already have orders from the top to go out for lunch." Vicky lowered her voice to a conspiratorial whisper. "It's okay, I know the boss." She winked. "Come on, we're going to Tess's. It's far too nice out to sit inside all day."

Outmaneuvered, Maggie got her handbag and the two women went down to Vicky's car. At Tess's, they got a coveted patio table and sat looking at menus. Maggie ordered soup, figuring it would be easy to swallow no matter how dry her mouth was or how large the lump in her throat became. "That's all you're getting?" Vicky asked.

"I'm not that hungry."

Vicky shrugged, ordered soft shell crabs and a glass of wine, and handed the menus to the waiter. Then she set her elbows on the table and folded her hands, her eyes alight, like someone settling in for a long-awaited feast.

Maggie drew a deep breath, steeled herself, and said, "So, tell me. How's it going with you and Cambien?"

The floodgates opened. Vicky talked and talked and talked. She spoke in earnest tones, dreamy tones, infatuated tones, questioning tones, and kittenish tones. She related details and episodes and scenes. She repeated amorous things Cambien had said to her. The food arrived and she barely ate, so busy discoursing was she.

Maggie bore it like a trouper. As Vicky's best friend, she knew it was her duty to listen to this at least once (leaving aside the fact that she had already listened to it through two previous husbands, and the downside too, as they became ex-husbands). She forced herself to pay attention, asked the occasional question, and made incidental remarks of encouragement. At least Vicky's focus wasn't on her, Maggie; it was on herself. Maggie was able to stare into her soup as though listening intently while shoring herself up emotionally. After all, it was very hard to hear Vicky gush like this, to learn intimate details of Cambien's style as a lover, to have it driven home so cruelly that he was romantically involved with someone other than herself.

When Vicky began to describe the scene in her bedroom over the weekend, Maggie could take no more. Desperate not to hear, she stood abruptly, grasping her handbag. "I'm sorry, Vicky, would you excuse me a minute? I have to run to the ladies' room." Without waiting for an answer, she turned and fled into the restaurant. Inside, she blundered through the closely spaced tables, pulling someone's linen napkin and fork to the ground as she passed. "I'm sorry," she called over her shoulder without slowing. In the restroom, she leaned over the sink, splashing cold water on her face. Looking up, she saw a haunted woman in the mirror.

A girl in an expensive-looking dress came into the bathroom. Her eyes met Maggie's in the mirror. The younger woman turned away and disappeared into a stall. Maggie shook her head, toweled her face off, and returned to her table. As she got there, Vicky had just paid the tab. "Hey, what are you doing? We always split the bill," Maggie protested.

"Lunch is on Cambien today," Vicky answered. "It was his idea that we go out. And anyway, I talked your ear off the entire time."

"You didn't talk my ear off."

Vicky dominated the car ride back to NarcoDynamics as she described assorted ambiguous statements and actions that Cambien had made and taken, then recruited Maggie's help in divining their true meanings. "What do you think it meant, when Cambien said he couldn't meet me for lunch last week, and Jill said he wasn't there when I called to say hi?" she asked. Or, "I wonder why he never stays all night. He'll fall asleep with me, but then he always gets up and leaves. He never stays for breakfast. Why do you think he does that, Maggie?"

Maggie could only shrug. She didn't want to think about it. The Herculean control she had exerted over herself throughout the ordeal was fast ebbing. The hurt in her gut, which she had painstakingly tamped down to a manageable ache, had been rubbed raw by the unwelcome view into Vicky and Cambien's relationship which she had been force fed the past two hours. By the time they pulled up in front of the entrance to NarcoDynamics, Maggie couldn't even bear to look at her friend. "Bye, Vicky," she said. She hopped out of the car. Once free of the confined space, she turned around. "It was good to see you."

"You bet. See you later." Vicky smiled, waved, and drove off.

Feeling like she had been mugged, Maggie slouched into the building. Her shoulders slumped, her eyes on the floor, she saw no one around her. She took no notice of the lovely fountain and bypassed the elevator, instead walking up a flight of steps in the secretive peace of the stairwell.

Emerging on her floor, Maggie shuffled along in a daze down the hall. She watched her feet pass one another on the carpet beneath her, propelling her resolutely towards her office. In this downcast posture, she didn't see Cambien approaching from the other end of the hall.

"Back so soon?" he called merrily.

Maggie looked up, startled. Unguarded as she was, she knew her face was not properly composed and her posture must convey her downheartedness. Cambien was walking briskly towards her. With no time to recover, she simply answered, "Yes, I'm back."

"Well, I trust you ladies had a nice time." He never broke his stride and, grinning, tossed out a playful comment as he passed. "I hope you girls didn't talk about *me* the whole time."

＞ﾟ

At home that evening, Maggie again felt grateful for the distance that had set in between husband and wife. She made it through the evening in an outwardly normal manner, though she was inwardly wracked with pain. Rowan gave her the customary fraction of his attention when he came home, reading his mail and watching TV until dinnertime. He focused mainly on the children at table and retreated again to the living room after the meal.

Once the children were in bed, Maggie sat beside her husband on the sofa and watched the news. An odd sort of unspoken companionship had emerged between her and Rowan, damaged as she now was, like him. Each trying to elude his pain, they shared an unconscious empathy for one another's motivations and behavior. Sitting on the sofa and focusing on the flickering screen was far preferable to letting one's thoughts take command. A mind left free to wander would relentlessly return to the object of misery, teasing it, replaying it, reliving it; that way lay madness.

Only when Maggie's eyes drooped with sleepiness did she say good night and go up to bed. Her head on the pillow, she willed her mind to stay blank until unconsciousness overcame her, keeping any thought of Cambien at bay. Mercifully, she hadn't dreamed of him since Charlie's party. She hadn't dreamed much of anything since then.

Maggie would have been surprised to know how often Rowan thought of her. It seemed to her as though he were little more than a roommate, a boarder with his own life and concerns who merely shared living space with her and the children. But although he made little contact with her, Rowan thought about his wife all the time. Even when he wasn't consciously thinking of her, he was aware of her presence in his life. He missed her terribly, but the pain blocked his way to her. The sight of her burned his eyes and forced him to turn his face away. Much as he needed her, thirsted for her, he was helpless to go to her.

Now he watched her leave the room on her way to bed. With her back to him, he could look at her safely. He stared longingly at the curves of her body moving fluidly beneath her nightgown. He gazed at the brown hair curling down her back, recalling its fragrance. He wanted to call her name and coax her back into the room with him, to hold her close and press his face to her neck, to feel the vibrant life force coursing through her veins. But he remained mute, thwarted.

He had noticed a change in Maggie's mood lately. She was quieter, holding herself in. He figured it had something to do with her creepy boss dating Vicky. No doubt Maggie had enjoyed the obvious crush the man had had on her, and her nose was probably out of joint. Well, Rowan would give her privacy to work through it. Not that he had any choice these days, standing on the far side of a bottomless chasm from her.

He sat and stared at the screen, thinking about his wife. He wondered how much longer he would be estranged from the world like this, wondered if he would ever feel like himself again. Maybe a new Rowan had been forged and this was who he now was, his feelings forever cauterized. Even if he got lucky and found the little girl's killer, perhaps it would no longer matter.

But dear God, he hoped not. Rowan closed his eyes. He made a valiant effort to focus on the longing he felt for his wife, isolating the feeling and clinging to it, holding it tight as proof that his humanity lived on somewhere within him. He would use it as his beacon, guiding his way back to her, someday, when the pain had at long last been vanquished.

Several hours later, Rowan went upstairs. He sat on the edge of the bed in an old t-shirt and some track shorts. Various insignificant sources of light combined to illuminate the room softly; a distant streetlight, a sliver of moon, the night light in the hall. Rowan looked down at his wife as she slept. Her thick lashes made spiky, crescent-shaped shadows on her cheeks. Her hair fanned out on the pillow beside her. He watched her for a long while before cautiously getting into bed beside her. Ever so softly, he put his arm over his wife, his hand resting on her hip. In her sleep, Maggie made a soft purring noise. Rowan nuzzled into her fragrant hair, placing a silent kiss on her neck before settling his head beside hers on the pillow. He drifted off to sleep.

～━━✕

"Mommy?" Hazel looked up at her mother.

"Yeah, babe?" Maggie asked absent-mindedly. She was concentrating on evenly submerging the loop of an oversized bubble wand in a tray of soapy liquid. She had bought the giant bubble kit for the children the day before, on her lunch break in Stamford, from the same hobby shop where they had once met Cambien. Now she carefully lifted the wand from the tray, confirming that a film of soap stretched across its opening.

"Why are you so sad?"

Maggie, surprised by the little girl's question, did not answer right away. Slowly at first, then with a fluid increase of speed, she drew the wand through the air, an enormous, rainbow-infused bubble appearing in its wake. Charlie squeaked with awe and ran to catch the bubble in his arms, laughing hysterically when it burst all over him.

"Charlie! You broke it!" scolded Hazel. "Mommy, can I try?"

"Here you go, sweetheart." Maggie handed the wand to her daughter.

She had been taken aback by Hazel's question. She had thought that, all this time, she had successfully concealed her personal devastation from everyone around her. Yet her young daughter had seen right through her. This was unnerving–if a little girl could see her sadness, who else could?

A damp southerly breeze blew across the yard. Maples, tulip trees, and hickories gently waved their greenery-laden branches. Watching Hazel try to weave a giant bubble, Maggie reviewed her interactions with the important people in her life over the last couple of weeks. She did not recall any difference in Rowan's behavior. He kept to his routine of long hours at work and distant demeanor at home.

She thought about Vicky. The truth was that it was too difficult for her to see much of Vicky. Maggie had become a wizard at finding excuses why she couldn't meet her friend for lunch or a drink. The only exception had been that day when Vicky had shown up at NarcoDynamics and dragged her out to Tess's. Maggie remembered everything she could about that outing and concluded that Vicky had been so absorbed in herself and her new love that Maggie could have collapsed dead on the table and she wouldn't have noticed.

Then Maggie thought about Cambien (something she hadn't allowed herself to do since Charlie's birthday party). Although the very sight of him caused her egregious heartache, it seemed as though he was turning up more than ever. Maggie couldn't be sure—she knew she was even more sensitive to his presence now than when she had been in the throes of her imaginary affair—but it seemed that way. She remembered how he had summoned her to his office for a meeting the first minute of the first day back at work after the party. She thought about what they had discussed at that meeting, several trivial items about the newsletter. Surely, Cambien could easily have emailed her his comments. And he had seemed determined to maintain the aura of closeness that usually permeated their interactions, rubbing shoulders and using affectionate terms like "dear" and "old friend" with her.

Cambien had also turned up in Dr. Rajagopalan's lab almost daily, much to the old researcher's chagrin. He always made a point of stopping on his way out, sitting on the edge of Maggie's desk and smiling grandly down at her, asking her about this or that in a congenial tone.

During one such visit, as Maggie tried desperately to avoid looking at him by pretending to focus on her computer screen, he asked, "Are you trying to avoid me, Maggie?"

Surprised, she glanced up at him, only to be skewered by his penetrating gaze. Mesmerized, she sat helplessly in her chair. "Of course not, Cambien," she answered, without any of the force she had meant to put into her reply.

There were other instances that came to mind, now that she was thinking about it: Cambien calling on her repeatedly at a staff meeting, even when she was not the most appropriate person to speak. Cambien appearing at her elbow from nowhere, just in time to walk to the parking lot alone with her. He even managed to be marching briskly upward as she descended the usually deserted stairwell on several occasions.

And every time she came across him, he was thrilled to see her. He insisted on speaking with her in a personal, friendly, and often tactile manner. He asked shrewd questions about how she was feeling or what she was up to, hinting that he knew she was hiding something and urging her to open up to him, practically smirking at her assertions that things were fine.

Maggie considered Cambien's behavior in the past few weeks. She supposed it was possible that he had noticed something was bothering her. But even so, he couldn't have any inkling that he himself was the cause of her unhappiness. No one but she knew the extent of the liaison she had had with him. She was sure she had said and done the right things when he and Vicky had revealed their relationship to her. No, Cambien couldn't possibly know that she was as love sick as a teenager over him.

Lost in thought, Maggie didn't notice that Hazel had abandoned the wand to Charlie's hands and was looking up at her again. "Mom?" Her soft voice broke through Maggie's reverie.

"Yes, Hazy?"

"You look sad again."

"I do? I'm not sad, babe. How could I be?" Maggie scooped her daughter up, squeezing her in a playful hug. "I have you."

14.

"Are you ever going to invite me over?" Vicky batted her eyes at Cambien over her plate of warm duck salad. Her face was flushed with excitement and wine. Cambien returned her look with a steady gaze and a slight smile, arching an eyebrow as if encouraging her to continue. "I mean, you've been to my house any number of times. I'd like to see where you live." When he still said nothing, Vicky continued to plead her case. "I'm a realtor, for chrissakes. Where someone lives means a lot to me. It tells me a lot about that person."

Cambien broke eye contact, looking down at his plate. "Ah, but Vicky, I'm a private man."

Undaunted, Vicky tried one more time. "Come on. Take me home with you." She reached across the tablecloth to stroke his hand. "I'll make it worth your while."

Cambien couldn't help himself and chuckled at her forwardness. He met her gaze again and she returned his smile. She could feel the tide turning her way. "Fine, fine, I know when I'm beat." He laughed. He signaled the waiter and paid their bill. As they strolled across the gravel parking lot, he said, "Now I know how you unload so many houses. You're quite a saleswoman."

Vicky took his arm. "I certainly don't use that strategy with just anyone. Only my most discerning clients require the hard sell." Cambien looked at her with raised brows. She laughed. "I'm kidding, of course. That particular technique is reserved just for you." She stood on tiptoes to kiss him.

They drove in Cambien's sport car, through the gathering twilight, back through the woods of Westchester County to the Connecticut state line, to the enclaves of North Stamford. They didn't speak, both taking in the warm beauty of the summer evening. Vicky rested her hand on Cambien's thigh as he drove. Eventually he turned onto a twisty lane that lead through dense woods. A brook appeared and followed alongside the road for a while before hurling itself over a waterfall and into a small lake.

After several miles, Cambien turned again onto a wider street with gentler curves. Most of the homes along it were tall farmhouses with peaked roofs or tasteful Colonials with manicured lawns. The houses were set back discreetly from the road and commanded generous yards, separated by barriers of woodland. The road finally ended in a cul-de-sac, in the center of which stood an enormous weeping cherry tree. Its mossy trunk was as wide as the car and its massive boughs reached high into the twilight sky.

"What a gorgeous old tree," sighed Vicky.

"I'm told they planted it when they built the house," Cambien replied. He navigated the coupe around the tree and a handsome Victorian house that had been concealed behind it came into view. He pulled into the long, straight driveway.

Vicky gaped, open-mouthed, at the magnificent dwelling as they drove through the apple orchard scattered on either side of the driveway. It stood taller than the gracious trees around it. Its wooden shingles were painted teal, the trim dark green. In the Second Empire style, it had a slate mansard roof on its high third floor. There was even a square tower on the right side of the structure. "Oh, my, Cambien. What a beauty."

"Is that your professional opinion, Madame?"

"It's my professional, personal, and every other kind of opinion."

They stepped out of the car and Vicky wandered onto the front lawn to admire the grand building. Several enormous beech trees spread across the darkening grounds. Stars had begun to punctuate the royal blue sky above the tall house, mimicked by the fireflies flickering above the lawns.

Cambien came up behind her and put his arms around her. He spoke softly in her ear. "Would you like to see more?"

Vicky leaned back against him, smiling. "As much as you'll show me, baby." She followed him up onto the wide porch, waiting while he unlocked three large locks. Once inside, he stepped briskly across the entry hall to a beeping panel and punched in the code to turn off the alarm. "My, that's some heavy-duty security you've got there. Surely, this can't be considered a bad neighborhood. And I know what I'm talking about."

"As I said at dinner, I like my privacy. I don't like surprises." He turned and walked further into the house, turning on lights as he went. Vicky followed, turning in circles to take in the fine detail and generous proportion. They passed through a walnut-paneled dining room and into an expansive living room. She could smell leather and wood polish. French doors lined an entire wall. Cambien didn't turn any lights on in this room, as there was still just enough light outside to look over the grounds. Vicky thought the property was one of the most beautiful she had seen, serene and private, with a wide lawn dotted with mature specimens of various trees. Through the gloaming, she could make out an oval pool set into a flagstone patio. Beyond that, the lawn sloped down a gently rolling hill to an expanse of woods. The tops of several other large houses could be seen intermittently peeking above the leaf canopy at a genteel distance.

Cambien went to the center door and undid several bolts. He pulled it open and cool evening air poured into the room. Vicky came and stood next to him. "Is that a pool I see?" she asked. Without waiting for an answer, she pulled her blouse over her head and dropped it on the floor. She sashayed out onto the flagstone path, shedding garments as she went, arriving at the pool wearing nothing at all. She turned to look back at Cambien, who leaned in the doorway, a black silhouette against the faint light from an inner room. "Well? Are you coming?" she called.

She saw him begin to come forward, a lanky shadow moving sinuously down the path. Turning, she dove gracefully into the reflection of the starry sky.

The water was surprisingly warm, gliding as sensuously as silk along her body as she swam beneath the surface. She came up on the far side of the pool and turned to look back. Cambien stood at the edge, removing the last of his clothing. He, too, dove into the pool, barely rippling the reflected sky. His sleek head popped up beside her a moment later.

"Well, hello," Vicky greeted him.

"Hello, yourself." His voice was deep, husky. She could see his eyes easily in the dark because they were darker still. He moved closer, grasping her, pulling her to him. Vicky drifted weightlessly against him, her wet mouth open to his. He crushed himself into her, pressing her against the rough concrete edge of the pool. Moaning, she welcomed him. She felt a drowning sensation that had nothing to do with being in water.

Later, they lay on their backs on the grass, on a blanket that Cambien had pulled from somewhere. Vicky looked up at the stars. The night sky was full of them, more than she had ever seen. She lay beside the tall, dark-haired man, overwhelmed by the preponderance of stars.

When she opened her eyes, dawn had arrived and colored the world misty pink. Cambien stood over her wearing the pants he had discarded the night before, holding a bundle of her clothing.

Vicky looked up at him, blinking sleep from her eyes. "Hi," she said.

"Good morning," he rumbled back. He sat beside her on the blanket, placing her clothes within easy reach. "I'm afraid everything's a bit damp from the dew. What did we expect, though, sleeping outside like wild animals?" He grinned.

Vicky sat up, tucking the edge of the blanket under her armpits. In the early light of day, with Cambien half dressed, she felt modest. But she returned his rueful smile. "I'd say 'wild animal' is a fit description for you."

He chuckled. "Well, I'll be in the kitchen, making breakfast. There's a bathroom off the front hallway, and the kitchen is through the dining room." He kissed her, stood, and walked back to the house.

The private yard in the dawn twilight seemed as discreet to Vicky as any dressing room. She stood and put her clothes on before following Cambien back up the flagstone path. Her bare feet left prints in the cool condensation on the flat stones.

He fed her breakfast at a massive, antique table in the large kitchen. They sat in front of a bank of windows that looked out over the back and side yards. She sipped the coffee he had brewed and watched a group of deer grazing along the edge of the lawn, where the trees began. He brought bowls of granola, yogurt and fresh fruit to the table. Vicky tried a spoonful. The yogurt was creamy and rich, the fruit succulent and sweet. Though simple, the meal was as good as anything served in the high-end restaurants she frequented. She ate and drank, looking alternately at the tranquil grounds outside and the shirtless man seated across from her. *I could get used to this,* she thought. *Oh boy, could I get used to this.*

After they had eaten, Cambien said he hoped she didn't mind if he took her home, as he had an appointment that morning. "Of course," Vicky agreed. "But won't you show me the rest of your amazing house first?"

He smiled. "Sorry, not this time. I wasn't really expecting company . . . it's kind of a mess upstairs." He moved to her and kissed her, effectively quelling further protest.

Vicky sat quietly in the car on the ride home, a feeling of loss stealing over her as the coupe took her further and further from Cambien's enchanting home. She made a mental note of where the house stood, 56 Linden Lane. She vowed that she would return, dared to hope that, maybe one day, she would return for good.

She glanced at the man sitting beside her as he navigated the twisty old road through the woods. He noticed her look and smiled at her, placing a warm hand over hers as his gaze returned to the road. Happiness washed over her. She was consumed with a longing to be intimate with this man in every way, to be fully and irrevocably united with him. She looked out the window, lest he read her thoughts in her face.

At her cottage, Cambien walked her to the door. He kissed her once again before taking his leave. "Do you have time to come in? I'm not afraid to show you my bedroom," she teased.

Cambien declined the invitation good-naturedly. "Duty calls," he said. He turned and walked back to his car. Vicky watched him go before she went into her tidy house.

～✕

It's no use, Maggie thought. She lay in her empty bed (Rowan having already left for work) in the gloom of a gray morning. As she did every day, she had woken with an ache in the place between her chest and belly, longing for Cambien. She had tried for a month to push him from her thoughts, to go on with her life, to redirect her insistent love to the people in her home. Her recalcitrant heart beat a constant refrain: *that's not good enough.*

She dragged herself out of bed and went downstairs to make coffee. A southerly breeze, warm and wet, had been commanding the weather for days. Now even the sullen draft had died, leaving the atmosphere close and stagnant. Maggie peered at the leaden sky; at least the sun wouldn't come out today and make it unbearably hot. Gray mist obscured the trees on the far side of the yard, robbing the July foliage of its splendid greens. She was thankful for the oppressive day and the colorless world it created. It suited her mood.

It's no use, trying to get over Cambien. She sighed, her untouched coffee cooling in the mug she held. It was all supposed to have been a lark, a simple device to buoy her through a marital low, a harmless way to placate her hurt feelings at her husband's emotional abandonment while acknowledging the attraction she felt to her boss. But the device had grown in the dark, unchecked, until it had become a machine of monstrous proportions. A towering contraption, it was now beyond her control. Indeed, it had sucked her into its maw, caught her up in its gears, maimed and mangled her, and yet refused to let her out. Once set in motion, it chugged along relentlessly, mechanically, processing her without mercy to an end known only to it. Trapped, Maggie could only pray it would be over soon.

Without heart, she went through the motions of feeding and dressing her children. She dropped them at their preschool and drove south on the parkway towards Stamford. She fished around in the debris in the car's console, finding the old David Bowie CD. She put it in the player and skipped forward to the song she had listened to repeatedly while she was conducting her fantasy fling, turning the volume way up. Bowie crooned to her. *For our love is like the wind. And wild is the wind, wild is the wind.*

Maggie reached her desk. An email from Jill indicated that Cambien wished her to be present at a briefing one of the research teams was conducting that morning. Maggie would once have bridled at the short notice; now she simply replied that she would attend. She would do whatever Cambien asked, whenever he asked it. The fight had quite gone out of her.

The day was so dismal that the conference room was nearly dark. Dr. Ziegler, a man with curly gray hair, increased the gloom by pulling the shades. Soon the only light came from the screen he projected his presentation onto.

There was no formal conference table in this room, but rather several smaller tables, a dozen upholstered chairs, and a desk. Eight more people were present, some taking notes, others heckling Dr. Ziegler good-naturedly. He returned fire whenever he could.

Maggie sat passively in an armchair, her spiral-bound notebook open in her lap, her pen at the ready. Cambien lounged against a desk on the far side of the room and she determinedly avoided looking in his direction.

Dr. Ziegler stood in front of the screen, onto which he had projected a slide reading *Nonbenzodiazepine Therapy and Geriatric Insomniacs.* Maggie copied the words into her notebook.

"Today I'm presenting the team's progress as we pursue development of a nonbenzodiazepine hypnotic that is better tolerated in elderly patients," began the researcher.

"Crash the Volvo again, Doctor Z?"

Everyone chortled. Maggie could just make out the person who had spoken in the darkened room. Perhaps a few years younger than she, he sat up smartly, his brown eyes mischievous behind his glasses.

"Har-dee-har-har," retorted Dr. Ziegler in a deadpan voice. "What Steven is referring to is the unfortunate history of negative side effects in older patients taking hypnotics, which we hope to overcome in this study." He pressed a button on the remote control in his hand and a catalog of side effects appeared on the screen. "As you can see, the list of problems is extensive, which has led the medical profession to turn away from this class of drugs as a suitable treatment for their elderly patients."

Forcing the constant awareness of Cambien from her mind, Maggie squinted at the screen. She was unfamiliar with at least half the terms. She jotted in her notebook: *Extensive side effects– get copy of presentation from Dr. Ziegler.*

"We think this is unfortunate, since this medicine has great potential to knock out insomnia quickly in older patients. Now as most of you know, we've been focusing our research on Cyclopyrrolones . . . "

Maggie wrote: *Studying cyclopeer . . ?*

"We believe in this class because of its superior ability to bind to the benzodiazepine site of the receptor complex. . . ."

Maggie's pen moved haltingly across the page: *Binds to benzocaine?* . . . Finally she scrawled: *Make appointment to interview Dr. Ziegler.* She then spent several minutes struggling to make sense of the diagrams flashing on the screen but soon gave it up. Thwarted, she concentrated on trying to look as though she knew what Dr. Ziegler was talking about.

Before long, as it always did, her persistent heartache pushed into the void in her unoccupied mind. Resignedly, she looked across the room at Cambien. Seated casually on the edge of the desk, his long legs stretched out to the floor, he watched the presentation. He snickered along with everyone else while two of the research assistants mocked Dr. Ziegler's hand-drawn diagrams.

Undaunted, the doctor slogged through his program. A new slide filled the screen. Maggie thought the crudely sketched molecules looked like spaceships. "Now here we see the core structure of our sample cyclopyrrolone, as opposed to the benzodiazepine–"

Cambien interrupted. "My God, man, the entire fleet is under attack!" The whole room, even Dr. Ziegler, erupted into laughter.

Maggie alone was not laughing. She watched Cambien as though she were watching a movie, mesmerized, the voices in the room fading to a background murmur. A surreal feeling overcame her. His striking face, animated by the light from the screen, was cast in relief against the darkness of the room. He still grinned as the laughter he had inspired died down and the presentation continued. She could not look away from him. He was so desirable to her, so commanding and confident, his lithe frame poised gracefully on the edge of the desk. *Oh Cambien, do you know how badly I want you? Do you know the pain I'm in? The hole you've carved in my soul?*

Once everyone's attention was back on the screen, inevitably, he turned to meet her gaze. She made no effort to conceal the fact that she had been staring at him, and his expression told her he knew it anyway. He returned her look questioningly, and she was certain there was a smile of encouragement on his lips. As clearly as if he had spoken, she heard his voice inside her head: *Don't worry, Maggie. We'll be together again.*

She smiled back uncertainly before turning away to pretend she was following the presentation. Out of the corner of her eye, she saw him watching her now. She would not risk another direct look at him, but her peripheral vision told her he was amused at her effort to appear as though she knew what Dr. Ziegler was talking about. She nodded as though he had made a good point, distinctly saw Cambien smirk, and was wracked with self-consciousness.

When the meeting was finally over, she fled the room. She returned to her desk to pick up her bag, told Dr. Rajagopalan she was going to lunch, and left the building.

Outside, the steely sky continued to glower. The air was so oppressive that she looked at everything through a haze. She drove to a deli and bought a sandwich and a bottle of water. A short walk brought her to a bench beneath a spreading dogwood in a nearby park. She chewed her sandwich and stared despondently into the pond in front of her where an enormous snapping turtle made its ponderous way through billows of algae in the mucky shallows.

She couldn't shake the invasive feeling she had had when Cambien looked at her in the conference room. Even now, he possessed her mind, holding her apart from the world around her. She stood abruptly and began to walk briskly on the path around the lake. Sweat ran down her face and still she strode on. She sought motion, trying to walk fast enough to move the air past her, to generate a wind that would winnow the specter of Cambien from her thoughts. But the air was too heavy to help. She felt as though she were shouldering her way through wet towels on a clothesline. In the breathless closeness, she was suffocating. The effort finally sapped her strength and she returned, head bent, to her car.

That night, she filled the bathtub with cool water and bubbles. She undressed Hazel and Charlie, put them in it, and sat on the closed toilet lid, watching them play. The heaviness of the atmosphere left her lightheaded. When she stood to lift Charlie from the tub, she fought off a wave of dizziness. Glancing out the open bathroom window, she saw a flicker of distant lightning.

Once the children were in bed, Maggie stripped down and went to soak in a bath of her own. The cool water eased her, chasing away the lightheadedness she had been battling. Gratefully, she saw a breath of air stir the bottom of the curtain. Thunder growled in the distance.

Dressed in a sleeveless nightgown, Maggie descended the stairs and went to the front door. "Where are you going?" Rowan called from his lair in the living room.

Maggie paused. "I think there's a storm coming. I'm going out to watch it." She stepped out onto the dark porch.

With the light off, she stood in the dense night, watching the western sky. Miles away, she saw turbulent clouds illuminated by frequent flashes, marching from southwest to northeast. She heard the booms and caught whiffs of the rain-laden wind driven beneath the system. But the storm moved ponderously northward, never veering from its course.

She paced in frustration as the clouds receded into the distance. Back inside, she drifted into the living room to perch on the arm of the sofa. "Where's your storm?" Rowan asked facetiously.

"Very funny. What are you watching?"

"Nothing. Just the news."

Restless and drained, Maggie stood. "I'm going to bed." She bent and gave her husband a quick kiss. By the time she had labored up the stairs, the cooling effects of her bath had worn off and she was again sweating and panting in the airless night.

In the bedroom, she put the fan in the window, aimed it at the bed, and turned it on high. She lay on top of the sheets, pulling her gown up over her knees for maximum exposure to the breeze. Hot, frustrated and empty, she stared at the ceiling, wondering how she would ever sleep.

For the first time since her son's birthday party, she gave herself permission to think about Cambien.

The feeling of connectedness she had basked in during her fantasy affair had been aroused again that day. She was certain she had not imagined the familiarity in his glance, the purpose in his smile, in the darkened conference room. The old sense of intimacy flooded through her once again. Like a heroin addict feeling the ecstatic rush of the drug, Maggie shuddered with welcome.

Yet from this very gratification, the unrelenting ache of desire sprang anew. Oh, how she longed for Cambien . . . his agile mind, his clean smell, his spellbinding eyes . . .

Stop it! Inside her head, Maggie screamed at herself. *You'll drive yourself mad. What about Rowan? What about Vicky? What about your children?*

A faint flicker of heat lightning flashed through the trees outside the window and drew her gaze. A stifled sob escaped her.

You've got to stop it. There is no place for this foolish fantasy in your life. You're only bringing pain upon yourself and tearing yourself away from your family, your friends, and your life. You've got to make it stop!

She curled into a ball and lay on her side, hugging herself. The craving she strove to suppress was unbearable; the prospect of surrendering her bond with Cambien—even if it existed only in her mind—was even more so. Again, she relived the bereavement she had felt when she first saw him with Vicky. Again, she berated herself for getting into this stupid situation. She yearned desperately for the pain to stop. There was nothing she wouldn't do to make the raging hunger go away.

Over the drone of the fan, thunder moaned tauntingly in the distance. *Please, bring on the storm. A manic, raging one, with pelting rain and wild wind, to sweep me from this hell.* Hot tears on her cheeks, Maggie buried her face in her pillow, her body stiff against the upward thrust of the cruel mattress.

Suddenly she was supported not by the mattress, but by a broad-backed horse that sped forward over a lightless landscape. Maggie grasped for the animal's mane, wrapping her hands in its silken blackness. Her storm had arrived at last, lashing the land with gale-driven sheets of rain.

The horse galloped at breathtaking speed, bearing her along. Powerful muscles rippled beneath her thighs as hooves pounded the dark land in a merciless rhythm. She held tight, gripping gleaming black ribs with her knees, leaning forward into the wind-whipped mane. It was all she could do to keep her seat, let alone slow this powerful beast.

Rain beat on her back and drove into her eyes, blinding her. She risked letting go with one hand to wipe the water from her face only to see, in a vivid flash, a craggy cliff falling away in front of her. She pounded her fists on the horse's withers, screaming futilely for it to stop, but her voice was lost in the din of the tempest. She could only cling to the animal as it gathered itself and leapt into the chasm.

She felt herself falling. She held onto the massive back with all the strength in her arms and legs, waiting for the impact. A blinding flash of light was followed instantly by a horrendous crash.

"Looks like your storm finally got here." Rowan's voice was low in the darkness of the bedroom. Beyond his black silhouette, Maggie saw another blinding flash of light. She heard the blast of nearby thunder, the rain beating on the roof, and the howl of a high wind. Her heart, still pounding from her breathless ride, was only provoked more by the storm.

She sat up, trying to look around her husband and out the window. "Oh, Rowan, you left the fan in the window. It'll get wet and short out or something."

Rowan flopped onto the mattress. "Me? How did I leave it in the window? I just got here." His voice was already thick. Piqued, Maggie got out of bed and went to unplug the fan. She looked out into the violent night. The wind blew cooling rain into her face. She pulled back from the window and lowered the sash so more water wouldn't get on the floor.

Rowan was on his side, his back to her, already snoring. Agitated, Maggie left the bedroom and went downstairs.

By the open window, she settled into the armchair to watch the storm. The wind and rain held sway. Branches tossed and cracked beyond the yard. Lightning flashed and thunder exploded in instantaneous answer. *Oh yes,* thought Maggie.

Again she rode the runaway horse, streaking through the lightless landscape, going wherever the animal took her.

They cantered up a wide lawn and came at last to a halt by a large, lightless house. Maggie tried to discern the details of the building in the gloom, suddenly wary of dismounting. She could just make out French doors, open to blackness within. Lightning flared and there was Cambien. He paced, tall and menacing, on the flagstones between the open doors and her mount, waiting for her. His head was lowered against the wind-driven rain, his hair plastered to his scalp, water running down his face to drip off his nose and lips. He glared at Maggie from under drawn brows, breathing hard, his eyes flashing with rage. She knew she had kept him waiting and her tardiness was the cause of his wrath. The thrill she had felt at seeing him turned to fear. She began desperately trying to turn the horse's head, to dig her heels into its sides and fly.

With superhuman speed, Cambien stepped forward and swept her to the ground. He dug steely fingers into her upper arm, forcing her to face him and holding her fast. Water deluged the world.

"Who the hell do you think you are?" he growled in controlled fury. Maggie could only stare into his flinty eyes.

He grasped her arms with both hands now, pulling her hard against him and leaning down to bruise her mouth with a furious kiss. His breath came hard through his nose. Maggie couldn't breathe at all; his kiss sealed her off from the world. If not for his painful grip holding her still, she would have sunk to the ground. After an age, he lifted his head, the edge taken off his rage. His glare boring into her face, he spoke in louder tones than she had ever heard him use, not quite shouting but surely having only the most tenuous grip on his passions. "Don't you ever, ever stay away that long again," he commanded hoarsely.

Maggie, sure she didn't possess the strength to stand on her own two feet, summoned all the force she could muster. Looking down, refusing to be ensnared by his ravenous gaze, she said, "But Cambien, nothing good can come of this." She had intended to say this in a tone of finality, but it came out as a soft murmur, the weakest of protests.

Enraged anew by her token defiance, he flung her before him, in through the open doors, and hurled her down onto a massive divan. Maggie heard leather creak, felt soft blankets and cushions scatter. She looked about wildly but the details of the room were lost to darkness. She could see the storm flaying the world outside, its wrath unabated. Wind tore into the room, whipping the drenched draperies and driving the rain all the way to her legs. Against the indigo rectangle of the open doors, Cambien loomed as a specter, his eyes burning brightly in the black silhouette of his head. Maggie panted with fear; he looked demonic as he advanced upon her.

She fought when he poured himself over her but she was no match for his strength. He easily captured her arms and held them over her head, forcing his knee between her thighs. He tore at the hem of her gown with his free hand, the staccato of ripping fabric competing with the roar of the storm. Maggie would have screamed but she knew there wasn't another living soul for miles around. With no recourse, she ceased struggling. Her wet face burning with excitement and shame, she found herself shivering with anticipation.

Cambien drove hard into her, again and again, pounding relentlessly. He released her arms and she held onto him with the same ferocity as she had held to the wild horse that brought her here. She was through fighting the tide that drew her to him; she no longer wished to be saved from this fate. The ecstasy she had felt the first time she dreamed of him came back to her. But that time, she had been enraptured by the sense of power she held over her lover. Now, Maggie realized, it was she who was helpless, he who wielded the power. Relieved, she shed all pretense of self-control, renounced all responsibility, and was borne ever higher on waves of unrestrained passion. Cambien ground into her, ruthlessly forcing her to acknowledge her self-abandonment, driving home the irrevocability of her complete surrender.

When it was over, he lay with his head on her chest. She stroked his sopping hair from his cheek as their breathing slowed.

Maggie and Cambien were back together again.

15.

The idea had been only to enjoy a few piquant daydreams about a man she found intriguing. But Maggie, an incautious wader, had stepped into a treacherous stream. It had seemed harmless enough from the safety of the bank, burbling invitingly with the promise of cool relief. Once she had stepped into the pebbly shallows, however, she found the current below the charming surface deceptively strong. She was pulled farther and farther from the shore, expending all her will just to keep her footing. Panic rose in her as her strength failed. Finally, defeated by the relentless undertow, she stumbled. And once she had fallen, the current easily swept her into the surging depths.

She now spent her days adrift, a passive bit of flotsam swept through a dimly lit unreality by an irresistible force. No longer master of herself, she dwelt with increasing frequency in a world apart, leaving her sensible self behind with shockingly little provocation.

Dr. Rajagopalan was the only person Maggie saw with regularity during the day. She now took full advantage of his natural reticence, greeting him briefly in the morning and then sometimes going for hours without speaking to another human being. She no longer answered her phone, checked her messages rarely, and returned calls even more infrequently. She hadn't spoken to Vicky in weeks. If Rowan left a message, she would dutifully force herself to return his call promptly, but he still kept mostly to himself.

She returned work calls and emails with greater alacrity, not wishing to jeopardize her job. Between bouts of fantasizing, she performed her duties competently. And if Jill or Cambien himself called, she suddenly became her most conscientious, responding quickly and brightly to any request. She felt most alive when she was in Cambien's presence, as he was the only link between the darkness she inhabited in her mind and the world of daylight she left her body in.

For his part, Cambien welcomed her revived preference for his company. He called Jill almost daily, telling her to summon Maggie to his office for a meeting. Maggie would report to him within minutes, not caring whether she seemed too eager. They sat side by side at Cambien's desk, rubbing shoulders and smiling too much, the glow of intimacy all about them. Although they might sit in front of the paper-strewn desk for an hour or more, very little work was discussed.

So close had their relationship become that people began to notice. Maggie and Cambien would sometimes emerge from the stairwell so intent upon their conversation that they took no notice of coworkers they passed in the hall. Cambien could often be found perched on the edge of Maggie's desk, holding forth in his deepest voice, while Maggie smilingly pretended to work. Dr. Rajagopalan became so exasperated with his employer's constant presence he had taken to leaving the lab altogether in a posture of disgust whenever Cambien appeared. And Cambien, who had once frequented the lab to find fault with Dr. Rajagopalan's scientific method, now took no notice at all of the researcher's absence.

Administrative assistants, managers, and mailroom boys fell silent when Maggie or Cambien (or, not infrequently, the pair of them) walked by. Once they had gone, the employees spoke in hushed, excited voices.

"They are definitely doing it," asserted an assistant manager of corporate services to the two other people in her cubicle. Maggie and Cambien had just passed by.

"How do you know?" asked a muscular young man. He leaned against his mail cart expectantly.

The assistant manager rolled her eyes. "Oh my God, look at her. She is *so* getting laid."

While their co-workers' assessment of their relationship was technically incorrect, it was otherwise quite accurate. Maggie and Cambien were not conjugally involved in a strictly biological sense, but this was not true metaphysically speaking. In both her conscious mind and her sleeping psyche, Maggie was with Cambien constantly, erotically, emotionally, completely. She barely knew her own husband anymore, and though she loved her children with a mother's love, she guiltily avoided their eyes as often as not.

For his part, Cambien had never lost his attraction to Maggie. For half his life, he had thought her the ideal woman. His affection for her was not like the carefully constructed, addictive world of fantasy Maggie had built for herself; it ran deep, a steady, unquestioned, fundamental part of who he was. He was a man who loved Maggie Cooper. He always had been.

━━◆

In his junior year of high school, Cambien had come back from Christmas break to find that the desks in calculus class had been rearranged. No longer in groups of four, they were now arrayed in rows and columns. He took in the new seating arrangement and also noticed that pretty, dreamy-eyed Maggie Cooper and her two friends had already arrived and selected new seats for themselves near the windows. At least half the class had by now arrived and seated themselves, and empty seats were becoming scarce. There were still several near Maggie, and without giving himself time to over-think it, Cambien boldly crossed the room and folded his tall frame into the desk directly behind hers. Head lowered, he waited for people to glare at him incredulously, bluntly tell him to sit somewhere else, or get up and move as though suddenly smelling a foul odor.

But nothing happened. Maggie continued to talk with her friends in front of and beside her with the intensity that teenaged girls bring to their conversations. Eventually, two boys sat in the seats behind Cambien, the room was filled, and the new seating arrangement had been set.

Cambien couldn't believe his luck. For that entire week, he heard nothing of the teacher's instruction. He was free to sit mere feet from the chestnut-haired girl who, like he, had lost her mother at a young age. He watched the sunlight play on her long hair, shattering into a thousand miniscule prisms. He listened to her musical giggle as she spoke quietly with her friends whenever the teacher's back was turned. And on Friday of that week, he was rewarded with an unprecedented gift. Maggie, sitting sideways in her chair to fish books out of her backpack, was facing the door when he came in. As he walked to his desk, he passed within feet of her. She glanced up as he passed and met his gaze. "Oh, hello," she said. To him. She had looked him in the face, smiled, and said hello.

Cambien was stunned and, forgetting that he had been walking, stood still, gaping, before her. He came to his senses just before fatal awkwardness set in. "Hi," he responded. But Maggie had already returned to her book bag. Cambien took his seat behind her and began to take out his class materials, an irrepressible grin crossing his face.

There was no further direct contact between them for several weeks. However, Cambien was an excellent student, and the teacher, Mr. Ross, made no secret of it. While handing back tests, Mr. Ross might say to the class, "Sorry, gang, Mr. Cuthbert has ruined the curve for you again." Without raising his hand, Cambien was called upon to answer the questions that no one else was able to answer. Once, as Mr. Ross struggled to explain antiderivatives for the second day in a row, he announced that, "Everyone should really get this concept by now. Mr. Cuthbert has understood it for weeks." Everyone turned to look at him and Cambien felt his face redden. Most of the other kids looked at him with resentment. But right in front of him, Maggie turned around with a smile and a look of frank admiration. The light played around her head, lighting her hair like a halo. A very angel she seemed to Cambien at that moment. He could have kissed Mr. Ross's shoes.

Two weeks later, Cambien got lucky again. Mr. Ross was walking from desk to desk on the far side of the room, giving students individual instruction on their classwork. Cambien pretended to read the textbook that lay open on his desk while he listened to Maggie talk with her friends. They were lamenting the deplorable food the school cafeteria served.

"I'm starving, and I know I'm going to walk in there and everything will be disgusting," complained Maggie's brown-haired friend. (Cambien thought her name might be Liz, but he wasn't sure).

Maggie's blond friend (Cambien had no idea what her name was) piped up. "Oh, totally. Bet you anything, they have those nasty green beans again. My God, they have them every day."

The three girls rolled their eyes and squirmed in their chairs, deeply affected by the prospect of another revolting lunch. "I wish we could go to Tony's for lunch," sighed Maggie. "I could really go for some pizza."

"Oh God, me too," whined the blond girl. "Liz, when's your car getting fixed?"

The brown-haired girl looked depressed. "Not in time for lunch today," she said sulkily.

"I can give you a lift."

The three girls turned their heads in unison to look at Cambien, surprised that he had joined their conversation uninvited. In truth, he had shocked himself by speaking up. He cleared his throat. "I mean, I have a car. And I was going to go get some pizza for lunch anyway. So it's no problem. If you want a ride."

Finally, Liz spoke up. "I don't know," she began. Cambien could tell by her tone that there was no way she was going to get into his car. She and the blond girl looked at each other, the blond rolling her eyes, Liz suppressing a giggle. Too late, he realized he had made a horrible mistake. Rejection and humiliation began to close in on him like collapsing walls.

Beyond anything he could have hoped for, Maggie spoke up. "Sounds good to me. Come on, guys," she said to her friends, "let's go out for lunch."

"Maggie!" hissed the blond, as though warning her that she was committing an unforgivable faux pas. But Maggie would have none of it.

"Liz, you were the one who started this whole conversation. And Tammy, you were just saying you wished we could go out. So come on. Let's go!"

Maggie won the argument. She and her two friends sat in the back seat, whispering and giggling. Cambien chauffeured them to Tony's. At the restaurant, he got two slices of sausage pizza and a large Coke and sat down in an empty booth. The girls walked past a few minutes later and sat in a booth on the other side of the restaurant. Cambien pretended to read the menu, ignoring the tittering and hilarity coming from their table. Fifteen minutes later, he drove them back to school. It didn't bother him that no one sat up front with him. Cruising up the long drive through campus with Maggie Cooper in his car, Cambien felt like a million bucks. Nothing could bother him.

As soon as he had parked, the rear doors flew open and Liz and the blond girl sprang out, hastily distancing themselves from the decidedly uncool transport they had just availed themselves of. Maggie got out more slowly, torn between keeping up with her friends and disowning their rudeness to their driver. She stood next to the car for a moment, speaking down to Cambien through his open window. "Well, thanks for the ride."

"You're welcome, Maggie."

"What's your name again?"

"Cambien."

"Oh, yeah. Well, thanks, Cambien." She spun and ran off to catch up with the other two. He sat in his car until they had disappeared inside the school, the door closing on their squeals and shrieks of laughter.

Seventeen years later, Maggie would have no recollection whatsoever of the trip to the pizza parlor, or of how she had paused a moment to extend a civil word to a fellow student who had done her and her friends a favor. To a confident and popular girl like Maggie, it had been a non-incident. But to a lonely, embattled, and sensitive boy like Cambien, it had made all the difference in the world.

As spring arrived, the seniors in calculus class began talking excitedly of receiving college acceptance letters. Keeping himself inconspicuous, Cambien listened freely as Maggie and her friends discussed their plans. Tammy, the blond, was going to take some accounting classes at the community college down in Norwalk. Liz was heading for the state university in New Haven. Neither seemed terribly excited, and both were also toying with the idea of getting a job and an apartment and blowing off college altogether. (*My God, how did they get into this class at all?* he wondered). But Maggie was utterly thrilled at the prospect of going to college. She had just been accepted to Barnard, a small Ivy League women's school. She was going to New York City, to learn to be a writer. Obviously, this prospect was more exciting to her than to Liz and Tammy, who sat impassively as Maggie told them the news.

When Cambien heard Maggie say that she would attend Barnard College that fall, he nearly shouted out loud. Although he had no friends to discuss it with, Cambien had also been getting acceptance letters. The guidance counselor had told him at the beginning of the year that he would complete the requirements for high school graduation by winter break and he need not stay a fourth year. So he had also been applying to colleges and universities, and the acceptance letters were accumulating at his house.

His letters all came from Ivy League schools, since that was all he had applied to, and among them was one from Columbia College. Cambien had been undecided about which school to attend but now he knew. He would go to Columbia, just across Broadway from Barnard. An intense joy welled up in him as he though of the next four years. He and Maggie would already know each other and no one else, and no one else from Schofield High would be around to oppress him. At Columbia, where intellect was king, he would be a star. Maggie would see him for what he was, a rare and valuable man. And when he chose her as his companion, she would be grateful for the opportunity. She would finally understand how well suited to one another they were. Their love would be legendary.

But the demon had other plans for him. Cambien, who hadn't given the beast a thought in months, was caught off guard.

Even in his sleep, Cambien had been smiling. He dreamed he was unpacking in a sunlit dorm room, placing books on shelves and clothing in drawers. The venerable stone buildings of Columbia University's upper Manhattan campus could be seen through the window. He unpacked shirts into a drawer, fantastic shirts, in colors so bright they hummed and patterns of such intricacy they glided across the fabric like automated machinery. He was overjoyed to be there and delighted to discover he owned all those great shirts. The room grew dark. He looked out the window again to see a gray, dusky sky.

Next to the window, the demon stood with his back to Cambien. As tall as the ceiling and as broad as three men, the monster tore the hutch off the top of the desk and hurled it against a wall. Cambien's carefully arranged books flew in all directions. Paralyzed with fear, he watched the creature as it dredged its claws through the freshly made bed, shredding the linens and filling the air with feathers and bits of mattress stuffing. Then it turned to the open drawer where Cambien had just been stowing his magnificent shirts. The terrified boy retreated from the monster's advance until his back was against the door. The fiend looked at him with a malicious grin. It placed an open palm on the wall above the bureau and leaned forward like a man at a urinal. Cambien heard the patter of liquid hitting fabric and saw acrid steam rising from the open drawer. A sour odor filled the room. The demon shook with malevolent mirth as it relieved itself.

Again, Cambien felt stirrings of rage in his gut but he quaked at the memory of his last encounter with the monster, its fist crushing every bone in his face. When it had finished with Cambien's clothing, the demon loomed over him. An evil smile split its hideous face. "What the hell are you doing here?" it mocked in earsplitting tones. "You think you're so smart. Ha! You don't belong here."

Cambien wanted to protest, but he couldn't move his mouth to speak. The demon stood back, stroking its chin in an exaggerated gesture of consideration. Then, as though something had just occurred to it, it spoke again. "Aha! I've got it. You came here because *she's* here. Is that it?"

Cambien's stomach heaved with humiliation. The demon looked around the trashed room. "Well? Where is she? Shouldn't your girlfriend be here with you? Wouldn't she be here, fucking you at this very moment, if she wanted to be? She should be blowing you while you unpack."

Terrified as he was, Cambien would not have Maggie spoken of in such coarse terms. "It's not like that," he protested weakly.

Pleased that it had provoked the boy into speech, the demon held one hand to its tapered ear. "Eh? What's that?" it asked as though hard of hearing.

"Maggie's not like that," Cambien answered a bit more forcefully. He stood straighter and met the demon's eyes.

"Oh, I see. A perfect lady, your little whore. Well, where is she? Maybe we should go and look for her." The beast reached Cambien in one ground-shaking step, fastened its massive hands around his arms, and lifted him as easily as if it were picking up one of the crumpled books from the floor. Cambien struggled for composure, not wanting to give the monster the satisfaction of watching him descend into uncontrolled panic.

The demon spun and stepped to the window. Using Cambien's rigid body as a blunt instrument, it bashed the panes and sashes out of the way. It reached through the opening to dangle him in the air. He looked down to see the paved plaza in front of his dormitory building, at least twenty stories below. Thin veils of cloud passed beneath his frantically kicking feet. He couldn't breathe in the thin air and the last of his control was driven from him. In a seizure of panic, he screamed and flailed. The beast had been waiting for his hysteria and it barked out a burst of cruel laughter. The deafening noise soared past Cambien and over the campus below. Even at hundreds of feet in the air, he could see the faces of students and professors looking up from brick walkways to see where the laughter was coming from. They pointed at him as he dangled and shrieked. They were amused.

"Well?" demanded his captor again. "Where is she? Isn't she supposed to be here somewhere? Isn't that why you came here?"

Even in his torment, Cambien could now see Maggie, far below him, standing with a group of students. Like everyone else, they were looking up at him. He would have given anything for her not to see him like this, helpless and out of his mind with terror. Maggie was lifting her hand to point, the students she was with dissolving into laughter.

"Hey, Mag-gie!" the demon called down to her. "I've got your boyfriend here. What do you want me to do with him?" Cambien saw Maggie's laughter disappear behind a look of consternation. Now her friends were laughing at her too. She turned and began to stalk away. "Wait, Maggie – you forgot this!"

The monster flung Cambien out into the open air as carelessly as if it were a class prankster throwing wadded up paper balls at the girls. A fleeting hatred more intense than any Cambien had ever experienced was instantly displaced by sheer terror. His arms and legs worked frantically. He screamed and screamed. Wind rushed past him, tearing the screams from his throat as he fell. The plunge went on forever, windows and brick flashing past him, breath denied him, the paved ground ever approaching.

When he finally flailed himself awake, it took him a very long time to get under control again. Every light in his room burned as he sat staring at the horizon until the sun rose completely above it. He walked to his desk on shaky legs. The acceptance letter to Columbia lay on top of a pile of similar missives. Bitter tears running down his cheeks, he picked it up, crumpled it into a ball, and hurled it into the wastebasket. He looked at the pile again. Now Yale's letter was on top. Fine, he would go to Yale. There were certainly worse places to go.

By the time he had dressed for school, Cambien had formed two resolutions that would become the blueprint for his adult life. First, he had resolved that he would be with Maggie Cooper one day. This union was necessarily delayed, but it was by no means diminished as a life goal for him. And second, he had resolved what his course of study would be; he would become a doctor, specialize in sleep disorders, and discover the way to banish the demon forever. Once this second resolution had been achieved, he would be free to focus on the first. The years of separation would be extremely difficult, but he would keep his ultimate goal always in mind. And one day, when he was in a position of power and control, he would claim Maggie as his own.

16.

Maggie was aloft in a dream. She lay on her back, her head turned to the side to see out the small window. Wisps of silver white flashed by. Her body felt weightless on the butter soft leather of the thickly padded seat, fully extended to a reclining position. She heard the drone of the jet engines and the hard breathing of the only other person in the cabin.

Turning to look above her, Maggie arched her body to meet Cambien as he moved smoothly. She closed her eyes so that his steady rhythm and the din of the engines were all she knew. There was no other world but these breathless heights. . . .

~~~

Pop sat on the porch, waiting for Maggie to come home from work. He sat in a rocking chair that had been there since before he'd sold the old house to her and Rowan. The children played with Lincoln Logs on the decking near his feet. An ice-cold bottle of beer in his hands, he watched the lowering sun and breathed the early evening breeze.

Clouds moved over the western sky, dimming the glowing atmosphere. In the premature twilight, Maggie's station wagon pulled into the driveway. Hazel and Charlie continued to build their tiny cabins. "Hey kids, your Mum's here," said Pop. "Don't you want to say hello?"

Hazel looked up from the unstable structure she had built. "I guess so. Come on, Charlie." The two children stood, holding hands, and began to move slowly towards the porch steps. Pop was surprised by their behavior. Usually, he had to restrain them until Maggie had safely parked the car.

"What's the matter with you two? Aren't you happy to see your Mum?"

Holding her brother's hand, Hazel turned somber eyes on her grandfather. "Yes, Pop. It's just that . . ." She let the sentence trail off, looking back at the driveway to see if her mother was near yet. Maggie was still inside the car, putting away her sunglasses and gathering her things.

Pop prompted the child. "It's just what, Hazy?"

Hazel turned back to him. "It's just that Mom doesn't really play with us very much anymore."

"Oh, I see. Well, I expect she's a bit busier than she used to be, now that she works full time and still has the cooking and cleaning to do."

Hazel sighed dramatically. "I guess so. But, sometimes, I feel like . . ." She sought the right words. ". . . like me and Charlie are bothering her."

"Oh?" But now Maggie's footsteps were crunching the gravel in the driveway, so he let the matter go.

Watching his daughter approach, Pop was surprised by the difference in her appearance over the last few weeks. For one thing, she had lost weight. Her curves had sharpened into angles and she looked spare and tense. And she was unusually pale for high summer, the darkness around her eyes accentuated by the eye shadow and mascara she had applied with a heavier hand than usual. Even in the dimness, she squinted against the light. Most striking was the change in her bearing. She moved in an almost surreptitious way, a wraith furtively crossing the open yard to seek the shelter of the old house. Pop watched her with concern for a moment before addressing the children. "Go on, you two. Go give your Mum a hug and a kiss."

As if they had only been waiting for his command, Hazel and Charlie yelled, "Mommy, Mommy," and bounced down the steps to her.

Maggie's wide smile brightened her face as she bent to her children. "Hi, babies," she said, kneeling and drawing them into a hug. Hazel and Charlie laughed and talked over one another, inviting her up on the porch to see the village they had been building.

Pop watched the three of them, reunited after a workday's separation. He shook off the vague alarm he had felt a few moments earlier. Everything seemed to be in order. "Hello, Maggie," he called. His daughter had finally straightened up and begun to make her way toward the house.

"Hi, Pop. Want to stay for supper? We're having fish sticks."

Rowan and Mike stalked back to their desks, silent and wrathful. Neither spoke as they sat down, staring at the piles of papers and files and photos. Rowan angrily swept a stack into a drawer, banging it shut. "Fucking Chief," Mike growled.

They were off the case. Chief Stankiewicz had called them into his office and given them the order. As they had made no progress in over three months, he told them he was delegating the investigation to the cold case team. He said they needed to focus on cases they actually had a chance of solving. There had been a series of 24-hour pharmacy robberies, for instance, and the stores' owners were pressuring him for answers. There had also been the horrifying rape of a woman who had parked her car on the upper level of the garage at the mall. And there were other, less sensational but nevertheless pressing cases that needed their attention.

Sitting sullenly at their desks, Mike and Rowan looked at each other. They simultaneously picked up their phones and hit speed dial. Each man spoke briefly with his wife, explaining that unforeseen circumstances had come up and he wouldn't be home for dinner. They left together, getting into their own vehicles and meeting up again at Mooney's, a favorite pub among cops and firemen in town. They needed to sit together, drink draft beer, eat crappy bar food, and complain about the chief.

An hour and a half later, they sat side by side at the bar, half-empty glasses in front of them and plates of picked-over onion rings and Buffalo wings shoved into the space between them. Tom Mooney, himself a retired cop, took a break from pouring beer and came over to Mike and Rowan. He gave them a sympathetic look as he cleared their dishes away. By now, the story of the Chief's half-assed decision had long been disbursed among the bar's patrons, the appropriate whistles of incredulity had been whistled, and the chief had been called an outstanding new array of derogatory names.

Rowan glanced over at his partner. Mike was clearly soothed by the support of the other cops in the bar and reveling in a combined state of self-pity, righteous outrage, and intoxication. But Rowan wasn't calmed. He would never have said it aloud but deep inside, he knew Stankiewicz was right. He and Mike were banging their heads against the wall. They had nothing to go on and Stankiewicz knew it. *We failed*, he thought grimly. *We failed, and a little girl's killer is walking free.*

Mike turned to Rowan, looking at him blearily. He spoke in a confidential slur. "You know what, Rowan? I have to admit, I'm kind of glad it's over. I'm relieved, you know? I mean, at least the pressure's off us."

Rowan gave a curt nod and Mike's gaze turned to the TV set over the bar. Rowan watched his partner's profile as he stared vacantly up at the glowing screen, twirling his mustache absent-mindedly between his thumb and forefinger. In spite of the beer and receptive atmosphere, Rowan was even tenser than when he had arrived. He envied Mike, who was able to feel relief, a burden lifted, as official responsibility for solving the murder was taken from him. Rowan felt as though nothing had changed; he had failed to catch the fiend, and the responsibility for the failure was his. The only difference was that now his failure had been officially declared, and the tools he needed to fix it had been taken away.

What could he do now? He would still see the tiny, broken victim when he looked at his own children, the devastated mother when he looked at his wife. And now he had no recourse. There was nothing for him to do to make it better. He fought down a surge of fear. Even when he had been trying and failing to solve the case, he had still had actions to take, people to call, a place to be, a distraction from his own mind. Now he had nothing but the pain, the horror, the ghastly realization that his entire life hung on a whim of fate.

He used to think smugly of himself as a satisfied man who had a beautiful family, a meaningful job, and a comfortable home. He had always thought of himself as a winner, but now he knew he was someone with too much to lose. If only he could solve the case, he could prove that the world was orderly and controllable, and that his family was safe.

As he mused, Rowan's attention was drawn to the television screen above the bar, and he was brought back to the present with a disturbing shock as he recognized Dr. Cuthbert's face filling the screen. It was the creepy commercial Maggie's company had been running seemingly non-stop since they launched their new sleeping pill. Though Rowan couldn't hear what the man was saying over the noise of the crowd, Cuthbert's gaze seemed fixed on his own, his LCD eyes bright and penetrating. With a shudder of revulsion, Rowan looked away.

It was getting late. Maggie would be asleep by the time he got home. There was no point in rushing back to be tortured by his thoughts in a silent house. Rowan ordered another beer.

~✦✕

The next day was no better for Rowan. Word had gotten out about the case's change of status. Chad Hallopen, the irritating reporter from the *Champion*, accosted him as he got out of his car. "Detective, good morning," Chad called. He came at Rowan with microphone cocked. Tall, bespectacled, and curly-haired, he resembled a long-shanked wading bird as he stepped purposefully toward Rowan.

"Chad." Rowan nodded curtly, not slowing his stride.

Chad matched his pace. "Detective, will you confirm that the Becker investigation has been declared a cold case?"

"Who told you that?" snarled Rowan. He gratefully reached the door, swiped his passkey, and pulled it open.

"I'm afraid I can't reveal—" began the reporter, but Rowan had vanished into the building, leaving the door to slam behind him.

At the dinner table that night, Maggie shared unwelcome news. "Rowan, I have to go on a little business trip next week."

Rowan had just taken a huge mouthful of pasta salad. Agitated, he tried to speak. "Wha? You ave a bidness trip? When?" This was new; Maggie had almost never been away from her family, alone, overnight since Hazel had been born.

"Next week. I'm leaving Tuesday and coming back Thursday." She waited for him to finish chewing and swallow, so he could ask his questions.

Rowan gulped the mouthful and fired off the next round. "Where are you going? What are you doing?"

"We're going to the St. Louis plant. I'm supposed to interview the production manager out there. He just won Employee of the Year, so I'm profiling him—you know, a morale-boosting corporate feel-good story. But it should be interesting. I'm actually looking forward to it. I've never really been inside any kind of factory." Maggie smiled. "Who knows? I might learn something."

Rowan brought her back to her first sentence. "Who's *we*?"

"Huh?"

"With whom are you going? You said *we*. Who's *we*?"

"Oh . . ." Rowan watched his wife assume a studiedly neutral expression. For God's sake, doesn't she know what I do for a living yet, he thought. Looking intently into her food, she spoke. "Several other people from the Stamford office are going. We all have business there, so Cambien thought it was smarter if we all traveled together. He doesn't like to take out the company plane for just one or two people, if he can help it"

Rowan chuckled grimly. "Ah, the private jet." He shook his head incredulously and muttered, "Man, that guy is smooth."

"Rowan, don't be a jerk." Maggie's casual veneer fell away, replaced by a bout of temper. "That's not fair. You go all over the place all the time, and I never give you a hard time. You're always coming home late, going out all weekend, doing whatever you need to do. You just went to Boston for three days for a conference. And last month, there was training upstate. And did I interrogate you about what you were up to? Of course not."

"No, you didn't. You never do ask about what I'm up to. It's almost as if you don't really give a crap."

The children had stopped eating and were watching their parents raptly, their eyes too big for their faces. Maggie noticed their expressions and calmed herself. Pausing for a moment, she thought about what Rowan had just said. He's right, I don't really care, she thought. Swiftly, she sought to deflect blame. In a lower voice, so as not to upset Hazel and Charlie further, she said, "Again, you're being unfair. If anyone has lost interest around here, it's you. You're never home anymore and when you are, you sit and stare at the TV, or read the papers or the mail, or go online, or listen to your scanner, or do all those things at once. It's almost like you can't stand to be around us."

Now it was Rowan's turn to admit she had a point. He sighed inwardly; there was no way he could tell her about his horror of spending time with her and the children or the terror his own thoughts inspired in him. That he fully intended to become more present in their lives again, one day, but he wasn't ready yet. "OK, touché. I have been . . . busy lately. I'm sorry, it's just been a really rough couple of months." Maggie didn't give him a hard time, but took another bite of her supper.

Rowan sighed. "Listen, I also should tell you, since you'll hear it anyway; that murder case I've been working on? Well, the Chief just turned it over to Cold Case. He says it's gone nowhere in months and there's a backlog of other stuff he needs me and Mike to get going on." He savagely speared several rotini on the tines of his fork.

Maggie's expression softened. She knew this abrupt loss of purpose and, hence, identity would be difficult for her husband to handle. "I'm sorry. I know you've been working that case like a dog. That's got to be pretty frustrating."

"You have no idea," Rowan said dejectedly. "But on the brighter side, we're pretty close to arresting a perp on an assault that's only three days old."

"Do you mean that woman, at the shopping mall, that was on the news?" Maggie asked. Rowan nodded. "Well, that's got to feel pretty good."

Now that the tension had left the conversation, Hazel wanted to be part of it. She had grown weary of her parents' encoded speech. "What woman?" she asked.

Rowan and Maggie looked at each other. Maggie ate a bite of chicken, leaving Rowan to explain. "Oh, there was a bad man who hurt a lady near the mall. But we're about to catch him. We know who he is and he'll be in jail soon."

Hazel grinned widely, proud to be the daughter of a crime-fighting superhero. "Way to go, Daddy," she said.

Later that night, Maggie went to bed and Rowan stayed downstairs to watch the news, as usual. He grimaced through the story of the murder case's reassignment, felt vindicated during the segment about how the police were near an arrest in the rape case and through it all, he was just so grateful to have something to watch.

17.

Maggie was packing for her trip. She had vacuumed the dust off her good leather duffel bag and aired it out. Now she was laying out clothing on her bed. If she felt apprehensive at the prospect of traveling out of town with the man who was driving her insane with lust, she did not allow it to distract her from her packing. She knew Rowan trusted her and she knew herself to be trustworthy.

Still, the occasion lent itself to a rich feast of imaginings and highly charged scenarios. For the next three days, she would be in a different world from her responsible, overstuffed life, where children and housework sapped her wit and energy. She would be alone (in a way) with Cambien, loose in a strange city. Tomorrow night, she would lay her head on a pillow under the same roof as he. She would wrap herself in his proximity. If she felt sadness that none of it would be real, if she even felt a bit pathetic, she did not let it deter her from her fantasies.

She packed several outfits that would travel well and strike the right note of professionalism. Then she packed dinner clothes, in case she shared a meal with her colleagues. To be safe, she packed two selections. One was a pair of black trousers and a crisp linen wrap top; the other was a cocktail dress. She held the dress in front of her and looked in the mirror. It was constructed of an overdress of olive-hued lace and burnout velvet layered over a deep amber-colored sheath. The dress fit to all her curves without being tight and teased flashes of skin through the intriguing fabrics without showing too much. Its color sparked up flecks of amber in her eyes, setting them aglow with a subdued flame. Humming, she laid out a daytime pair of shoes and packed a pair of heels.

Next, she reached for one of her customary cotton nightgowns. Dingy with age, it was soft and comfortable. As she lifted it from the drawer, her eyes fell upon a seldom-worn garment, a short, satin chemise in midnight blue that she had bought before she had children. At that time, it had made her feel powerfully enticing to wear the nightie for her husband. With a naughty smile, she tossed it into her bag as well. No one would see it but her, but it could only enhance the romantic trance she expected to spend her bedtimes in.

The next morning, Rowan came into the kitchen while Maggie was feeding the children breakfast. He kissed the top of each of their heads, saying, "Goodbye. I'll pick you up from school."

Maggie followed him to the door. "You're sure you've got everything under control? Remember, Pop is around if you need help with anything. He can get the kids if you're hung up at work or stuck in traffic or something. And I put in groceries, so you should have plenty to eat for the next couple days. There are even some frozen meals, if all else fails. You can just microwave—"

"Maggie," Rowan cut her off, "we'll be fine. For Pete's sake, you'll be gone for two days and a wake up. I think I can handle it. Even if the children ate nothing until you returned, they wouldn't starve." He looked levelly into his wife's face. His expression softened. In a reassuring voice, he added, "Really, we'll be fine."

Maggie smiled. "I know you will. I'm sorry, it's just harder to leave you guys than I thought it would be." She laughed softly. "It's probably the healthiest thing I can do, to leave you all alone every now and then. Get out of my rut." She looked into her husband's face and saw concern.

"Maggie" he said haltingly, searching for words that wouldn't offend. "Please, just be careful. With your boss, I mean." Maggie drew breath to begin arguing, but Rowan held up his hand. "I know, I know, and I'm sure you're right. He's a perfect gentleman, he's in love with Vicky," (Maggie felt a lurch in her gut), "you've been best friends since high school, et cetera, et cetera. And please don't doubt that I trust you completely." (Maggie felt a wave of guilt). "So don't get all mad at me, I'm just saying: please, be careful around that guy."

Maggie gave an exaggerated sigh of indulgence. "Yes, Rowan, I'll be careful. I promise to do my work, perform any required corporate socializing, and get back to my hotel room early enough to call the babies and say good night."

Satisfied, Rowan leaned to kiss her. "Call me when you get there." He turned and was gone.

Maggie arrived at her office building a little after nine. Since the travelers were to meet in the lobby at nine fifteen, she sat on a bench by the carp pool to wait. Before long, two members of Dr. Ziegler's team joined her. They looked to be in their late twenties or early thirties. They introduced themselves as Steven Lang and Katy Ng. Maggie recognized them from the meeting she had attended a couple weeks earlier, where Dr. Ziegler had given his progress report. Steven had been one of the research assistants who heckled Dr. Ziegler. She stood and shook hands with them, battling a pang of inferiority.

Maggie thought of herself as young, yet here were these two, several years younger than she and already doctors. And she was proud of her Ivy League undergraduate degree but as a writing consultant in the world of medical research, she felt decidedly under-credentialed. It seemed as though everyone was a doctor, and more and more of them seemed to be younger than she was. She had a niggling feeling that she had peaked years ago, that she had long since reached her potential, and it was all down hill from here.

She defied the wave of self-doubt, refusing to allow it to subdue her. She was going to St. Louis as part of a team, damn it. She had a specific job to do, for which she was uniquely trained and qualified. For all their fancy degrees and oblique conceptualizations, the brilliant people on either side of her couldn't do what she did. Maybe she wasn't curing cancer, so to speak, as they were, but she could communicate their progress to the world at large, and that was important, too

Besides, Steven and Katy were talking to her as though she were their equal. Maggie calmed down and the three of them chatted while they waited for the last member of their party.

"What's our intrepid corporate reporter covering out at the plant?" asked Steven. His brown eyes peered curiously at her through metal-rimmed glasses. He was of medium height and build, with short, thick hair that matched the color of his eyes. His smile was friendly and inquisitive.

Maggie smiled back. "I'm going to do a story about the Employee of the Year, a production manager named Don van Zandt. I hope to give a brief overview of what he does as he oversees the production process, so people in this office can learn about what happens after the research is done and FDA approved. You know, things like: How do we manufacture the medicines? What safeguards are in place? How is the product packaged and shipped out? And so forth."

"Sounds fascinating," said Steven. "If only we didn't already have intimate knowledge of the process."

"Amen," Katy chimed in. "If I never see another pill come down a conveyor belt, it'll be too soon for me." Like her associate, Katy also had intelligent brown eyes behind metal-rimmed glasses. She spoke with no trace of an accent, despite her exotic surname and appearance. Maggie guessed that she had been born in the United States.

"You guys have been out there before?" asked Maggie.

"Oh, just a little." Steven snickered.

"Yes, lucky us," added Katy. Maggie envied their camaraderie. She noticed that Katy wore a large engagement ring, while Steven wore a wedding band. Clearly not romantically interested in one another, they enjoyed a congenial working relationship. Talking to them was like talking to a brother and sister.

Steven explained further. "When our team's last product was cleared to launch, we had to spend a lot of time at the factory, making sure the manufacturing was up to scratch. After all, we developed the protocol for mixing it up. At first, Dr. Ziegler was there with us. But once he was confident we knew what we were doing, he suddenly had a whole bunch of stuff he had to attend to personally back here in Stamford."

Katy continued the narrative. "So now, whenever there's an issue, we just get sent automatically. Recently, there was a dosage fluctuation and a whole batch had to be destroyed. The factory says they've got it under control, but we have to go out to monitor it, supervise sample testing, and make sure everything's okay."

"I guess that can get kind of boring," commiserated Maggie.

"At least this time, the Big Cheese has business out there too, so we can hitch a ride on the company plane," said Steve.

Katy nodded. "Sure beats traveling coach."

A familiar, deep voice sounded from just over Maggie's shoulder. "Good morning, crew. Everyone ready?"

"Good morning, Cambien," said Steven and Katy. Maggie turned to see her boss standing beside her.

"Hi, Cambien," she said. She felt her pulse quicken and heat rise to her face.

He nodded briskly at all of them. "Great, let's hit it." He led the way through the little group and out the glass doors, pulling a rolling suitcase behind him. Steven and Katy towed similar luggage. Maggie hoisted her leather duffle bag by the strap over her shoulder and followed behind, Cambien's impersonal group greeting having left her somewhat disappointed.

A gleaming black limousine waited in front of the building. The liveried driver placed their bags in the trunk while they made themselves comfortable in the car. Maggie kept it to herself that she had never been in such a luxurious vehicle.

The sleek car purred along the parkway, buffering its passengers from the slightest bump or sway. Morning editions of several newspapers had been supplied for the passengers. Cambien took up the *Times* and began reading. Following his example, Katy and Steven were soon lost behind unfurled leaves of newsprint. Maggie leaned against the door and tilted her head to look up. Leafy trees shaded the road. Through them, she saw a handful of puffy, fair-weather clouds riding in an azure sky. She gazed dreamily out the window at the summer day flashing by, her mind on the nearness of Cambien's thigh, a mere two feet away from hers on the wide leather seat.

The county airport had never been taxing to navigate; its modest size and provincial nature had always been charming and uncomplicated, even with the new security protocols in place after September 11. The owners of private aircraft and their guests, however, didn't even report to the main terminal. Their limo drove right to the edge of the tarmac. As they walked to the steps, Maggie thought that the Gulfstream was much larger than she imagined a private plane would be. Aboard, they sat in deeply padded, cream-colored leather seats. The uniformed captain came in, introduced himself, and conferred briefly with Cambien before rejoining the co-pilot in the cockpit. A pretty young woman, also in uniform, asked them all to prepare for takeoff, walking among them to check that everyone was seated comfortably and safely before moving to her own seat and fastening her safety belt.

Again sitting by a window, Maggie watched the scenery speed past as they launched from the runway. She looked towards the front of the plane as she always did during take off, marveling at the vertical tilt of the craft. She loved taking off, was thrilled by the thrust of extreme acceleration and the dizzying exhilaration of leaving the ground behind. She closed her eyes and let the thrum of the powerful engines reverberate through her body. She was accelerating as one with the hurtling plane, racing upward through the ether. She was a part of the bright sky, unbound from the earth, an airy spirit free to roam at the speed of light. In a trance, she felt the plane level off and she with it, now suspended aloft, weightless, a soul who rightly dwelt in the stratosphere.

Resting against the cushioned back of his chair on the other side of the cabin, Cambien watched her face. He took in the lashes against her cool cheek, the graceful line of her neck, and the curve of her mouth. He knew what it was she felt. He felt it too, every time he ascended heavenward. He knew, as he always had, that she was of the same spiritual persuasion as he.

A quiet joy spread through him. As he had felt seventeen years earlier, driving onto the high school campus with Maggie Cooper in the back seat of his car, so he felt now. He reflected on the time that had passed since then, the years of planning and hard work and discipline and self-denial. Painstaking decades of preparation were now bearing fruit: Maggie, in his Gulfstream, being flown to his factory complex.

She was in his world now. She doubtlessly intuited it, although she might not yet recognize it consciously, but he was the master here. By stepping into his limousine back at the office, she had implicitly accepted his sovereignty.

Cambien turned to look out at the sky and a shiver ran through him. He felt a euphoric anticipation.

Soon.

⌒⌔

At Lambert-St. Louis International Airport, they were met by another limousine. In the car, everyone took out devices and checked emails and voice mails. Not wanting to feel left out, Maggie pulled out her cell phone and dialed Rowan's number.

He picked up on the second ring. "Hello?"

"Hey, Ro," said Maggie in a soft voice, her hand cupping the phone for privacy. "We made it, safe and sound. We're on the ground in St. Louis."

"Good to know. Hey, how was the company plane?"

Maggie turned as far away from her companions as possible, not wanting them to hear how unsophisticated she was. "It was really cool. You can't imagine how easy it is to get around like that."

Cambien's silky voice cut across the car. "Is that Rowan? Tell him I said 'hi.'"

"Cambien says 'hi,'" Maggie repeated dutifully.

"Is he right there?" Rowan asked. His voice had gone cold.

"Yes," answered Maggie. "And also two of the Stamford researchers, Steven and Katy. We're all in the car, heading for the factory."

"Then I won't keep you. Call me later and let me know how it's going."

"Okay, Ro. Talk to you later."

By now, they were on a large expressway on the outskirts of town, gliding through an industrial area that buffered the city from the rural outliers. The car exited the freeway and cruised along a service road that ran parallel to it. Eventually they came to a stretch of lush, green woodland, followed by an expanse of emerald lawn. In the center of the lawn was a huge marble monolith that said "NarcoDynamics" in glowing blue lettering, a larger twin to the one in Stamford. From this park-like setting, another road intersected theirs. The driver signaled and turned. Maggie read the street sign: *Cuthbert Circle.* She couldn't resist teasing Cambien. "You know what I like about you, boss? Your humility. It's not like you have to name streets after yourself or anything."

Cambien, who had been going through a file of papers on his lap, looked up and chuckled. "Now, don't judge me too harshly, Maggie. It's actually named for my father who, after all, provided the seed funds to start the business. I had plenty of good ideas, but I would have had to give them to an employer if he hadn't left me the means to start my own company."

Maggie looked ahead of the car again as they rounded the woodland on their right, impatient to see the St. Louis NarcoDynamics plant.

After what seemed a very long time, the factory finally came into view. It was a striking structure, built of countless planes of clear glass on a frame of green steel girders, interwoven with green-tinted concrete formed into organic shapes. The building rose like a mound of enormous soap bubbles from the grassy lands around it. Maggie gasped, struck by the immense size of the operation. Beyond the main building she could see at least three smaller structures, each larger than the corporate headquarters back in Stamford. At this time of year, with summer in full flourish, the entire complex seemed to blend into the mild hills and woods surrounding it, a breathtaking feat for such massive structures.

Pretending to type nonchalantly into his mobile phone, Cambien heard Maggie's gasp and was deeply gratified. This was a moment he had anticipated for years. It was what he had pictured in his mind when he hired an internationally renowned architectural firm to design his factory. Maggie's reaction was what he had thought about when he first laid eyes on the completed facility. Without looking up, he drawled in his most casual tone, "Well, Maggie, what do you think?"

She didn't answer at first, not being able to think of words to describe the unique structures and ingenious layout of the campus. The sheer scale overwhelmed her and left her deeply humbled. Finally she spoke in a voice of profound respect. "I think it's the most fantastic building I've ever seen. My God, who thought of it?"

Cambien allowed himself the pleasure of looking at her wondering face. "I came up with the rough sketch myself, which I handed off to the architects, Grayburn and Grasso. Maybe you've heard of them? They did the Minerva Center in Manhattan and the Pelham Museum of Fine Arts in Boston."

"Uh huh," said Maggie. She gaped at the magnificent building as it loomed closer. Signs and arrows directed traffic along the many roadways that ran through and around the complex. Cars and trucks zoomed along the roads, while golf carts and pedestrians peopled the walkways.

Their car drew up to the main entrance of the factory. Maggie and her companions stepped onto the walkway and walked up to a set of double glass doors. Cambien pressed a button on the wall and the doors buzzed. He opened one and held it for Maggie, Steven and Katy.

Behind the tall reception desk sat one woman in her twenties and another in her late middle years. Both looked up at the newcomers and gave warm, mid-western smiles in greeting.

"Hello, Dr. Cuthbert," said the younger woman shyly.

The middle-aged woman spoke in a glowing, motherly tone. "Hello, Dr. Cuthbert. It's always a sunny day when you visit us."

"Hello, Juliette." He leaned over the counter and gave her a kiss on the cheek. "Hi, Jessica," Cambien said to the younger woman. He turned to Maggie and the others. "That's Jessica, and this is Juliette, who has been with us since we started up operations out here in St. Louis." The older woman beamed. "Jessica and Juliette, this is Maggie, our corporate communications writer. Steven and Katy you already know."

Maggie shook hands with both receptionists. She moved aside so Katy and Steven could greet them. Cambien took charge again.

"Let's see . . . Katie and Steven are here to see Tom and Maggie is looking for Don."

Very good, Dr. Cuthbert." Juliette picked up the telephone receiver, pressed a key, and spoke through a building-wide intercom. "Tom and Don, please come to reception to pick up your visitors. Tom and Don, visitors waiting at reception."

Maggie heard the woman's voice amplified through the walls and down the hallways that opened off the reception area.

While they waited, Jessica produced temporary ID passes for Maggie, Steven and Katy. "Just swipe these to get through the locked doors," she explained in a soft voice.

There followed a lull in the conversation. Maggie looked towards the wall opposite the front doors. A pair of double doors stood dead ahead and hallways ran off to the right and left. There were windows along the bit of hallway she could see and in the double doors. Through these, she could glimpse a large, open space beyond. Somewhere within, automated machinery rumbled incessantly; the plant was operating in full swing.

The double doors swung open and two lab-coated men came through them. One was evidently Tom, because he went right to Katy and Steven. Tom appeared to be in his late forties, with thinning, reddish hair and a pleasant, if somewhat harassed, manner. He greeted them all, introduced himself to Maggie, and led Steven and Katy away, down the hallway to the right.

The second man, Maggie's contact, was also in his late forties. Don was a giant, with a protruding gut to match his size. He had graying brown hair on his head and in his mustache and beard. His demeanor was as large as his physical presence. "You must be Maggie," he boomed, bowing in a courtly fashion and extending his hand.

"That's me. And you must be Don." Maggie placed her hand into his giant paw and shook it.

Don turned to Cambien. "Keeping all the prettiest ladies in Stamford, are you, Doc?" Maggie laughed at the flattery.

Cambien smiled guiltily. "It's good to be the king."

"How was the trip out?" Don asked him.

"Smooth sailing."

"Good. Mostly smooth sailing here, too, just have that dosage kink to work out. Tom and your guys'll figure it out, though." He turned to Maggie and held out his arm. "And now, my dear, if you will accompany me." Giggling in spite of herself, she placed her hand into the crook of his massive arm. "I'll show you to the guest office so you can drop your stuff off." He began to lead her away towards the hallway but paused to look back at Cambien, who still stood in the lobby. "Don't worry, Doc, we'll take good care of her." Maggie looked back over her shoulder at him.

Cambien was watching them recede. "See to it that you do." He smiled possessively at Maggie as he watched her go. In high spirits, she tossed her head as she was led away by her enormous escort.

Don took her past the reception desk and down the hall to the right. Now closer to the windows, she was able to look through them and into the open space beyond. Several desks were near the windows. Further back across the polished cement floor, machinery churned, monitored by workers.

"That's where the final phases of production occur for Anadreme," Don explained, noticing the direction of Maggie's glance. "Let's get you situated, and I'll give you the big tour."

"Oh good, I was hoping someone would. I've never been inside a real factory."

"Well, I don't know if I'd call this a *real* factory, but it's what passes for one at NarcoD," Don joked. Maggie laughed.

A left turn and a right through a set of double doors, then twenty feet down a hall, and Don showed Maggie into a large, carpeted room. Katy, Steven and Tom were already there. Katy and Steven had donned lab coats and made coffee, which they were trying to drink quickly so they could get to work. "Hey, Maggie," they said.

"Hi, guys." She glanced around the room. The wall opposite the door was a row of large windows, through which she saw lawn, walkways, and one of the smaller outbuildings. The room itself was divided into a sitting area and, nearer the windows, a work area. "Is this our headquarters while we're here?"

"Yes," answered Katy. She waved towards the desks. "There are computers over there, if you need to work or check email. And Steven just made a pot of coffee. Would you like some? It's fresh."

The coffee smelled good but Maggie was anxious to start her tour. She had been fascinated by her brief glimpse of the inner workings of the plant through the hallway windows. "No, thanks. I don't want to keep my guide waiting." Don smiled graciously. Maggie set her briefcase down on the far side of the couch, put her cell phone in her pocket, grabbed her notebook, and turned to face Don. "Ready?" she asked.

"I am at your service," he answered, bowing. Maggie followed him out of the room, waving goodbye to Steven and Katy, who were trying to drink their coffee while it was still too hot.

Don walked Maggie through the facility, explaining each stage of the manufacturing process as they went along. Some areas could only be observed through glass, and the few workers inside them wore white jumpsuits that covered them from head to toe. Other areas were open, high ceilinged and bright, with people clustered around various stations. "They always work in pairs, so one can verify what the other does," Don explained. "Absolute precision is crucial when mixing up a batch." In still other areas, workers moved sheets of paste into huge drying ovens or monitored milling machinery. Every now and then, Juliette's omnipresent voice beckoned through the public address system, requesting an employee to report to the front desk or pick up line two-oh-nine.

After an hour of touring the plant, Maggie's stomach was growling and her head was spinning. Don was wrapping up his tour on the large, open floor where the packaging of the finished pills took place. "Is that it?" Maggie asked.

"For this building, it is. We still have the research building, the printing plant, and of course, the warehouse. That's my favorite; we get the golf cart for that one." He noticed the daunted look on Maggie's face. "But first, I'm sure you'll want to tour the cafeteria." She smiled gratefully.

"Can we just stop at the office? I want to grab my wallet," she said.

"We can certainly stop there, but your money is no good here. Boss's orders."

Maggie laughed. "Okay, then. Let's eat."

Don led the way through the maze of hallways, halting to swipe his ID card next to a set of double doors. At the buzzing sound, he pushed them open and he and Maggie emerged onto one of the green walkways that criss-crossed the campus. This one was encased in glass, supported by the omnipresent green steel girders, and bright with sunlight. Looking up, Maggie saw that milky clouds were filtering the light, keeping the day pleasantly cool.

The cafeteria was a free standing building, the smallest in the complex, situated behind the main building and centered between it and the other three as yet unexplored buildings. It was a large, square hall with a tall, dome-shaped roof, constructed almost entirely of glass and steel, with an unobstructed view of the sky and the landscape around it. Maggie caught her breath at the beauty of the place.

When she was in college, Maggie used to take the train to the New York Botanical Gardens when the winter chill got to be too much. She would sit with a book on a stone bench inside the huge conservatory, among the leaves of the exotic plants, and bask in the green, filtered light, the humid warmth, and the smell of growing things. Now she thought of the great conservatory as she looked around her.

Exotic, thick-trunked trees shielded the space from the summer sun. In their verdant shade, colorful blooms and large-leafed ferns filled the planting beds that ran around the periphery of the hall. In the center of the room, a pool held a water garden of lilies and lotuses. Maggie thought briefly of the pool in the lobby of the Stamford building, which paled in comparison to this one. Looking around, she saw a man and a woman in separate locations, each wearing a green coverall and tending to the plants and trees. She glanced up at the leaves splayed along the glass roof and the soft light sifting through them. "This place is stupendous," she said. "We don't have anything like this in Stamford."

"Well, we have to have our perks out here in St. Louis, too." Don chuckled, amused at her reaction.

Maggie's head kept swiveling. "I would just come here and sit all winter," she said. "It's like going on a tropical vacation, just walking into this room."

"Yep, it definitely takes the sting out of the harsher winters." Maggie looked about for several minutes more until Don steered her towards the food counter.

From a round table on the far side of the water garden, flanked by the plant's most senior executives, Cambien watched Maggie. He saw her mouth fall open as she gaped up at the atrium like a farm girl seeing her first skyscrapers. A grin spread across his face.

After lunch, Maggie and Don parted company for half an hour, each going to their respective workspace to answer emails and return phone calls. Maggie called Rowan and got his voicemail. She left him a message that the factory was fascinating and also beautiful, and that she was learning a great deal.

She spent the rest of the afternoon touring the remaining buildings and learning about Don's work. First they visited the on-site research facility. In St. Louis, the chemical engineers focused on mass production methods for the drugs developed in Stamford. As they walked along, Maggie recognized two of the researchers from a visit they had paid to Stamford a month or so earlier.

They went on to tour the packaging plant and, after obtaining Don's promised golf cart, the warehouse. This last building was a cavernous space, used to store raw materials, completed packaging, and cartons of final, packaged NarcoDynamics products. Don zipped up and down the aisles between the towering shelves and stacks, taking corners entirely too fast, narrowly avoiding a forklift that trundled across their path, and clipping a twenty-foot tower of cartons as they cut past it. Maggie turned to watch the boxes on the top sway alarmingly back and forth before settling down.

"For heaven's sake, Don, take it easy. You're going to get us killed." She laughed, holding onto her hardhat with one hand and the careening cart with the other.

Undeterred, Don proceeded with his breakneck tour until at last they rolled up to the entrance again. "So that's the warehouse. Please hand your hardhat to the nice man by the door and, as you have three minutes to meet your car, we'll take the golf cart back to the main building."

"Oh no." Maggie blanched at the prospect of the mad dash across the grounds, and it was just as bad as she expected. Don floored the pedal and the tiny vehicle leapt out onto the wide path. Her stomach dropped as they swooped over a rise in the path and briefly became airborne.

But she held on tight, and in no time Don pulled to an abrupt stop by a set of doors. "Oh, thank God," Maggie said. She leapt out of the cart, laughing.

"You're welcome," said Don.

"Aren't you coming?"

"Alas, I still have work to do here. You should be able to find the guest office by now. Just swipe your card to get in, go straight down the hall, take the first right, and you'll know where you are."

Maggie had by now smoothed her hair and composed herself. "Well, thanks so much for the tour."

"No need to say goodbye. We'll be joining you for dinner tonight, so we'll meet again in a couple hours."

Maggie was glad to hear it. "Great, I'll see you then." She waved as Don turned the cart and careered back down the path.

Maggie dashed to the waiting car, breathless, her hair flying loose and her face bright. Steven, Katy and Cambien were already inside. The driver opened the door for her and she thanked him before getting in. Good humor from Don's golf cart steeplechase animated her expression as she greeted everyone. They looked up from their various handheld devices with raised eyebrows.

"Gee, Maggie, looks like you really dig hanging around the old production facility," said Steven drolly.

"I think this place is amazing. I know it's old news to all of you, but it's all new to me." She turned to her boss. "Cambien, you've outdone yourself. This place is fantastic—so organized and well thought out. I don't think the people in Stamford can have any idea of the size of our operations. And it's so beautiful here. That cafeteria—how can you even call it that? It's more like a conservatory. And the people are so nice, too. I wish I could work here."

Maggie went on listing the production plant's assets. Steven and Katy looked at each other amusedly. But for Cambien, each word out of her mouth was a singular stroke of pleasure, though he maintained an expression of courteous indulgence as she spoke. He supposed the other occupants of the car would be shocked if they knew that her words made everything he had accomplished seem, at last, worthwhile.

They arrived at the Swanset Plaza Hotel in the center of St. Louis and checked in. Comparing their keys, they discovered that Katy and Steven's rooms were next to each other on the third floor, Maggie's was on the fifth floor, and Cambien's was on the sixth. As they rode up together in the elevator, Cambien told them all to meet in the lobby at seven. They would be having dinner with their contacts from the plant. Steven and Katy got out on the third floor and Maggie and Cambien were alone in the small space.

Having talked herself out during the car ride, she merely smiled at him. He returned the gesture, looking steadily at her from across the small compartment. Suddenly self-conscious and dreading an awkward silence, she spoke about the first thing that came to mind. "What kind of place are we eating at tonight?" she asked.

"Oh, nothing too fancy." He spoke languorously, without breaking eye contact. "It's a reliably good restaurant, specializing in Italian and American food. They also have the added benefit of offering a private room, so we can make fools of ourselves without offending the entire establishment."

Maggie laughed. "Sounds just about right. No fancy dress or anything, then?"

"No, in fact," Cambien cast an appraising glance up and down her, and Maggie felt heat rise to her cheeks, "you can wear what you have on."

The elevator opened onto the fifth floor, and Maggie stepped out. "See you at seven," she said with a quick wave.

Cambien watched her until the doors closed again.

～✕

Maggie's room was spacious and bright, though the lowering sun was on the other side of the building. Her leather duffel bag had been placed on a luggage stand near the foot of the bed. She opened it and hung her clothing in the closet. Mercifully, not much wrinkling had occurred; she had packed well. She drifted to the windows that ran across one wall. A block away, she saw a ribbon of light glinting between the buildings. The Mississippi River was reflecting the golden glow of the late afternoon sun over the city. The clock on the nightstand read 5:36. She grabbed her handbag and left the room.

Outside, she walked down the broad avenue and onto a wide bridge. Beneath it, the Mississippi undulated like a torrent of molten gold between the streets and buildings. Maggie stopped halfway across. She leaned on the iron railing and gazed upriver. The city of St. Louis adorned the manicured banks. The waterway was alive with watercraft. Pedestrians walked alongside and over it, and everywhere the dazzling golden light was reflected by its endlessly moving surface. Standing suspended between Missouri and Illinois, Maggie felt that something immense and important and interconnected to the world flowed beneath her feet.

She finished walking across the bridge, just so she could say she had been in Illinois, too. Then she made her way back to her hotel room to call her family before it was time to meet the others for dinner.

Pattie van Zandt turned out to be as petite as her husband, Don, was large. In a trim, rose print dress, tipsy on half a glass of wine, she leaned over the table and hollered outrageous comments about everyone seated there. Not even Cambien was spared, and each statement drew uproarious laughter. Seemingly cowed by his tiny wife's outsized personality, Don sat back in his chair, his beer mug as insignificant as a shot glass in his huge hand. Occasionally he corrected her or added a detail she had forgotten, but otherwise he was content to listen along with everyone else.

"Ellen, remember that time at that first Company dinner? When you almost started a fight with those guys from Des Peres?" she called across the table to Tom's wife.

Ellen, a jolly woman with a girth to rival Don's, was already shaking with laughter from Pattie's ongoing narrative. "Pattie, you know I don't remember anything about that night," she warbled. Next to her, Tom slapped his forehead in feigned mortification.

In her high-pitched voice, Pattie began retelling a story the St. Louis denizens were clearly familiar with and seemed eager to hear again. Maggie looked around the table at them all. She was warm with wine and a sense of heartfelt affection for these good folks whom she had just met that day. She noticed that the gathering consisted of couples of one sort or another. There was Don, large, friendly, and chivalrous, uncharacteristically quiet as he let his wife do the talking. Small-framed and full of the devil, Pattie chirruped beside him like an irrepressible songbird. Next to them and across the round table from Maggie sat Katy and Steven, intelligent, competent, and good-natured. To their right were Tom and Ellen. Tom's quiet, official manner never completely left him, but away from the plant, his harried demeanor was replaced with deadpan, understated humor. His wife Ellen's heart was surely as large as her bosom, which heaved with mirth at her friends' stories. And beside Maggie sat the founder of the feast, Cambien.

Maggie glanced surreptitiously at him. He was laughing at Pattie's story, as was everyone else. Perhaps it was the wine, but Maggie saw him through a haze that both softened and deepened his features. The chesty rumble of his laugh, too, reverberated within her own chest, beside her very heart, as though he were a part of her. She felt a painful wave of closeness to him.

While Pattie told her story, Maggie imagined a different life for herself, one where she had been single when she started working at NarcoDynamics. If only she were free to follow her heart, she knew that she and Cambien would sit here tonight not just as coworkers but also as lovers. Or maybe she would have met him earlier, not having lost years of her career to child rearing, and they would now be husband and wife, entertaining their employees as a team of equal partners.

Not wanting to descend into despair over what might have been, Maggie forced her thoughts back to the circle of cheery faces around the table. She focused on their bawdy tales and soon she was laughing as loudly as any of them.

After dinner, they all walked out into the balmy evening, calling good night to one another in the parking lot. The Stamford contingent got into their waiting car and drove back to the Swanset. Full of food and drink, still laughing over stories they had heard at dinner, they rode up in the elevator together. Katy and Steven got out on the third floor after wishing Maggie and Cambien a good night.

"Hey, don't forget—the car will be here at eight-thirty tomorrow morning," Cambien yelled after them as the doors slid closed. "Do you think they heard me?" he asked Maggie.

"Doubtful." Maggie chuckled. "Don't worry, they'll figure it out. After all, you did tell us what time the car would get here at least six other times tonight."

"Okay, okay, I won't worry." The elevator had stopped again and the doors slid open on Maggie's floor. Cambien watched her as she smiled and turned to go. "Good night, Maggie. Sleep well," he said softly.

Outside the elevator now, Maggie turned back to him, recalled by the tenderness in his voice and the familiarity in his words. He was staring after her, a hungry expression on his face. "Good night, Cambien." Her voice caught as she uttered the words. The elevator doors closed.

She went to her room thoughtfully, trying to decide whether she had imagined the intimacy in her employer' s voice, the longing on his face. She ultimately decided that it didn't matter whether it had been real or not (it probably hadn't, after all), because she would allow herself to imagine that it had. She readied for bed and dressed in the satin nightie.

In the dark, between the crisp hotel linens, she conjured a scene wherein she rose from her bed to answer an urgent knocking at her door. Cambien filled the doorway, a ravenous expression on his unsmiling face. "Cambien, what is it?" she asked, knowing very well the answer.

"May I come in?" His voice was husky. And Maggie, a single woman in this particular fantasy, stood aside to let him pass.

Once the vision had played itself out, she slipped into a sated slumber. And as he so often did at night, Cambien came to her. But unlike most of her dreams, which involved the vigorous slaking of carnal thirsts, this vision was of a more pedestrian nature and quite similar to the longing she had felt as she sat beside Cambien at dinner.

Maggie and Cambien, side by side, toured the plant as she had done with Don that day. And they were married; technicians and workers addressed her as "Mrs. Cuthbert." She was as much a part of the wondrous facility as he was. His hand was firm at the small of her back as they walked on.

They arrived at a large machine. A conveyor belt just above their heads descended to a sorter. The machine whirred loudly, but the belt was empty. Tom stood on the other side of it, gesturing and speaking in an agitated voice. Several technicians in white coveralls flanked him, all of whom were looking from him, to the empty conveyor belt, to Cambien and back again. Cambien tried to placate them while Maggie leaned over the belt and looked up to where it fed out of the machine. She thought she might be able to fix it.

Climbing the ladder on the side of the machine casing, she began to work the dials on top of the cabinet. Watching the effect on two gauges, she twisted knobs expertly. "I got it," she called down to the others. All discussion halted as everyone looked up. A sudden rush of pills issued from the interior of the device and swarmed down the conveyor belt.

Excited talk broke out among the onlookers and Cambien's triumphant "Ha!" was heard above all. Maggie wondered at her own skill. She watched the tablets shimmy down the moving ramp, luminous and precious as pearls.

When she woke the next morning, after spending the night as the capable Mrs. Cuthbert, Maggie was disoriented for quite some time as she acclimated to the reality of her empty bed.

⌒▼⌐

She could hardly wait to get into the car that morning, to be in the presence of Cambien and return to the magical complex he had built. She looked excitedly through the windshield, anticipating the moment when the glass and green steel structure would rise into view. Not long thereafter, she returned to the packaging area of the production facility, chatting with Don as they observed the lavender Somnusol pills riding down the conveyor belt.

One story above her, Cambien stood at an observation window and looked down on Maggie as she worked. He loved the sight of his operations in motion, the deafening drone of running machinery and the precision of the manufacturing process. Watching completed product make its way along the conveyor was as much a meditation to him as seeing the herring run upstream every spring, a ritual he never missed. The fish had no more choice than the tablets; they would follow the course predetermined for them. What should be would be, and there would be order to the universe. And so Maggie had returned to him who had loved her since they were children. He looked down upon his smoothly operating machinery and amid it the one woman, at last a willing participant in his vast operation, and he knew a greater joy than he had ever felt.

It was time. The plans had been made, the deal would be closed this very evening. The same shudder he had felt in the jet shook him again, a mixture of nervous energy and aching expectation. And Cambien, who had long worked to order and control the universe and arrange a reality where things would run according to a plan, his plan, prepared to plunge headlong into the current he had created and become one with the flow of the fate he had preordained.

18.

In his hotel room that evening, Cambien dressed for dinner with a bridegroom's care. He cleansed his body. He combed his sable hair back from his high forehead and fastened it into a sleek ponytail at the nape of his neck.

His clothing had been selected and tailored months earlier; it was crucial he look both grand and seductive this night. The dark suit of fine-gauge wool draped elegantly on his wide-shouldered frame. The crisp, white shirt of finest Egyptian cotton contrasted with his dark hair and eyes. At his throat, a silk tie shimmered in tones of raspberry, camel and amethyst, hues a woman might notice and take as an indication that the wearer was more sensual than the average man.

He checked his reflection in the full-length mirror and was pleased with what he saw. He felt a surge of confidence. No woman yet had been able to resist him, once he had decided to obtain her.

But this wasn't just any woman; this was *Maggie*. His confidence faltered slightly. It was true; this was the only woman whose acquisition had ever mattered to him. She was the reason for all of it—the lifetime of work to become successful and wealthy, the selection of a house that would impress her when she saw it, the designers who filled it with the right furnishings, the personal shoppers who dressed him in fine clothes, the care he took of his own body—all of it to present Maggie with a man whom she could not resist.

And he knew his efforts hadn't gone unnoticed. He had seen her lingering gazes and caught the notes of deeper meaning in her voice. He sensed the longing that emanated from her like a scent when she was near him. Maggie was a good woman and an honorable one, but she was also only human. He knew his finely calibrated manipulations of the past five months had been effective. He knew how badly she wanted him. And tonight, he would give himself to her.

She didn't realize that the arc of her fate had been traced long ago. And now, as her one, truly intended mate, he would joyously lead her to that fate, revealing it to her as tenderly as a new lover removing her clothes for the first time.

One floor beneath Cambien, Maggie also dressed thoughtfully for dinner.

She had spent the day wandering the campus of the NarcoDynamics plant, increasingly charmed by its civilized, industrial sort of beauty. The people she met were warm and friendly, content in their work and kind to one another. At midday, she had gone to the cafeteria for lunch. She walked through the foliage with her tray of food until she found a small table behind the man-sized leaves of a banana tree. She had eaten there, hidden and alone, feeling like an enchanted, thumb-sized maiden, lost in the feral forest.

Back in her hotel room at the end of the work day, she had called her family. Pop was with the children, as Rowan still hadn't gotten home from work. He was spoiling them so thoroughly they could barely stay on the phone with her. She let them get back to their fun. She dialed Rowan's cell phone and got his voicemail. She left him a message, saying she would be at another company dinner that evening and might not be back in time to call and say good night.

The matter of making contact with her family dispensed with, Maggie turned her attention to the evening ahead. Another round of fine dining, heady drink, and witty company lay before her.

Best of all, it would be another evening that she could share a meal with Cambien, drink in his masculinity, and fantasize that this was her life. Tomorrow morning, the car would take her to the waiting jet. The jet would take her back to her stifling, pedestrian life of buzzing dryers, distant spouse and wailing babies. But before that happened, she would savor this last night of indulgence.

She dressed in the alluring green-and-gold cocktail dress, never giving a thought to the more conservative dinner outfit she had brought. Standing before the mirror, she ringed her eyes in smoky shadow that shimmered with gold and complimented her dress. Enhanced, her eyes glowed like amber lanterns. She applied a deep red lip stain, shook her hair over her shoulders, and smiled at her reflection. She knew she looked ravishing, and knew Cambien would think so, too. She thought of the evening ahead, the flirting she and he would engage in, the conversations they would have only with their eyes—all safely in a public place, in the company of Katy and Steven, and no harm done in the final analysis. But Maggie had grown addicted to the self-affirmation she took from the attention Cambien paid her, and she planned to evoke a rich harvest this evening.

At seven-thirty sharp, Maggie stepped from the elevator and into the lobby of the Swanset. Across the airy space, Cambien stood near the doors. He leaned against the wall, his body in a casual pose but his eyes quite serious as he watched her approach. Maggie couldn't fight the smile that pulled at her mouth as she observed his expression. When she was within ten feet of him, he took a step towards her and gave a low whistle. "Maggie, you look stunning," he said. He took her elbows in his hands and leaned forward to give her a sociable kiss on the cheek.

Triumphant, Maggie stepped back. "Thank you, Cambien. You look quite dapper yourself," she said, now taking the time to look him over critically.

"Do you really think so?" Cambien struck a male model's pose for her, ostensibly goofing around while giving her time to internalize his carefully assembled presentation. Overcome with a wave of attraction to this tall, impressive man, she let her gaze travel up the sleek lines of his suit, over his slim hips, across his broad chest and wide shoulders, to be at last snared by his eyes. She remembered to laugh a beat later than she should have. Cambien silently took note.

"Unfortunately, Katy and Steven are going to have to meet us there," he said. "They had to wait for some tests to finish running."

"Oh, okay." Maggie suddenly felt apprehensive at being alone with Cambien. Dressed and made up as she was, she suddenly felt inappropriate.

"I have a rental car, so you and I can drive ahead. We'll leave the company car for them."

"Okay," repeated Maggie. She stepped through the door Cambien was holding open for her. As if on cue, a valet pulled a compact sports coupe up to them. He hopped out, came around, and opened Maggie's door for her, holding her hand to steady her as she sat down, down into the low, leather seat. The valet closed the door and Cambien handed him several rolled up bills. He came around to the driver's seat and slipped behind the wheel.

They drove onto the avenue and towards the river. The sun setting behind them threw its rays back to set the river on fire, nearly blinding them. Maggie watched Cambien handle the small car with a sure hand. He noticed her gaze and shot her a smile, which she returned before looking out her window. Neither spoke.

They sailed over the bridge she had walked across a day earlier. On the other side, Cambien drove parallel to the Mississippi until they reached a cultural district on the waterfront. He pulled up in front of a low stone building with ivy greening the walls and huge iron carriage lanterns on either side of the many-paned doors. Another valet opened Maggie's door and held out a hand to assist her as she rose gracefully from the low-slung car. Then Cambien was at her side, proffering his elbow. She took his arm and they entered the restaurant together.

A jacketed maitre d' greeted them. "Bon soir, André. Cuthbert, party of four," Cambien said in an authoritative tone.

"Yes, of course. It is good to see you again, Monsieur Cuthbert. Right this way, s'il vous plaît."

"Merci, André," said Cambien, stepping aside and placing his hand on the small of Maggie's back to guide her forward. Acutely aware of his touch, she allowed herself to feel possessed. They followed the maitre d' through the entry hall and into a large dining room. Maggie looked about her as they went, taking in the subdued opulence of the establishment and the gay laughter of the diners.

André led them through an open set of doors and onto a wide veranda. The Mississippi glimmered just beyond the railing. "Oh, it's lovely," exclaimed Maggie. The sun, now nearly extinguished by the hills and trees on the far bank, sent one last red flare into the evening sky. Pleasure boats sailed to and fro on its molten reflection. Strings of tiny white lights hung in the veranda's awning and lanterns glowed on the linen-clad tables.

Maggie followed André to a table directly against the railing and all the way to the side of the veranda, as far out over the river and as isolated from the other diners as it was possible to be. The maitre d' pulled out a chair for her and helped her get settled. "Thank you," she said, turning her head to look up at him.

André smiled in reply, struck by her beauty. He looked quickly over her head at Cambien in frank admiration. "Will you wait for the rest of your party, or do you wish to order some wine? Perhaps some hors d'oeuvres?" he asked.

Cambien looked at Maggie, who shrugged the question back to him. "We'll take the wine list, please."

"I'll send the sommelier." André left them.

Maggie looked from the face of the man across the table to the radiant evening scene on the river beside them, each view stealing her breath with its beauty. Waves lapped softly against the wall below them. She sighed. "Oh, Cambien, this place is just so beautiful." She gazed at the red line of the horizon, which had finally claimed the sun.

He also looked out over the river. "I know. I try to come here every time I'm in town. Believe it or not, this establishment has been in business for almost a century. I guess they know what they're doing."

The sommelier arrived and presented Cambien with the wine list. He made a selection and soon Maggie's pleasure was compounded by sipping a glass of tangy white wine from the

Languedoc-Roussillon region of France. The briny flavor burst in her mouth and tugged at her salivary glands. She paused to savor the taste, setting her glass on the linen-covered tabletop. Water condensed on it from the heavy evening air. She watched a large bead gather enough weight to break free of its inertia and streak down the side. She looked across the table at Cambien, who was gazing out over the river.

"I'm so glad you know your way around a wine list. I love it when someone picks a great wine, like this one," she said. He looked at her as she spoke, his face relaxed. "When I go out, I always order the same kind of wine. I always enjoy it and I'm never disappointed. But then, I never try anything new."

Cambien raised his glass. "Well then, here's to Maggie trying something new." They clinked their glasses and drank. She savored her last sip of wine, allowing it to bathe her tongue before she swallowed. Cambien refilled her glass.

"Thanks," she said, taking another taste. "I'd better slow down. I don't want to be inebriated by the time Katy and Steven get here."

"Oh, don't be silly. I'm taking you out tonight so we can relax and unwind, just be ourselves. So please, discard any reservations you have. Let your hair down. We've all been working hard enough these past two days."

"I hardly felt like I was working at all. It was like being on a swanky vacation, to be let loose in your incredible factory."

Cambien looked humble. "Thank you for saying so. I put a lot of effort into creating an environment that was not just productive, but good for the people who worked there. Something that filled their aesthetic needs as well as their work needs. So I'm really pleased to hear you say you liked it."

A companionable silence fell. They looked out over the shadowy river. Lights danced across the water from the distant bank. They sipped their wine and breathed the cooling air. There was no conversation between them for several minutes; simply being together in this beautiful place sufficed.

Cambien felt a quiet, deep joy. After all, this was only the first of a lifetime of evenings he and Maggie would spend together, just like this: happy and in love. He wondered whether she had begun to sense it. Maybe she already knew.

He made a show of checking his watch. "Hmm, I think we should go ahead and order some hors d'oeuvres. It's starting to get late."

Maggie, interrupted from her reverie, agreed. Soon several intricate dishes were placed on their table. If the setting hadn't already been mesmerizing enough, it now took on an epicurean quality. With one last glance towards the door, looking for their missing dinner mates, they set to. They ate enormous shrimp stuffed with Roquefort cheese and herbs, marinated artichoke hearts, and grilled fennel. There were stuffed mushrooms and salads of chopped endive and grapefruit, and caviar and crème fraiche on potato crisps. Cambien refilled Maggie's wine glass before adding a dash to his own. He signaled the waiter for another bottle. Maggie sighed with pleasure.

Presently, she paused in her repast. "Those guys sure are late. Don't you think we should save some of this for them?"

"Of course. You're right."

"Do you think they're okay? I mean, not that I'm not having a fantastic time, but we've been here for an hour already."

"Yes, it is getting on. Let me check on them." Cambien drew a slim cell phone from a pocket. While Maggie gazed out over the glowing water, he pretended to dial and held the phone to his ear. After a moment, he began to speak in a low voice. "Hey, Katy, how's it going? . . . Uh huh . . . So you need to run that test again? . . . right. That's too bad. We're having a lovely time." He winked at Maggie, who flushed and smiled broadly. "Well, we're certainly sorry to hear that. Please, order in something for yourselves and your team . . . Okay, we'll see you later."

He closed the phone and looked ruefully across the table at Maggie. "Looks like we're on our own."

Although wrestling with wine-loosened scruples and quite pleased at this pronouncement, Maggie was able to form her expression into one of disappointment. "That's too bad. They'll miss this beautiful food and the lovely view." The new bottle of wine arrived and the waiter filled Maggie's glass. "Merci," she said in her best high-school French.

"Don't feel too bad for them. They've been here before, but you haven't. So please, enjoy yourself." He lifted his glass in salute. Maggie did the same, giggling. She took a swallow while Cambien watched her.

"Well then, I guess there's no harm if we eat the rest of these hors d'oeuvres," she said. She helped herself to a cheese pastry.

"None at all," agreed Cambien. Another comfortable silence fell between them, only the murmur of nearby conversations and the gentle, rhythmic lapping of waves to be heard. The night fell in earnest, wrapping their table in a cloak of intimacy. They became simply two souls, communing across the glow of a solitary lantern.

With the onset of darkness, a cool breeze sprang up off the river. Maggie shivered. Cambien stood immediately, rounded the table, and removed his jacket. Facing Maggie, he reached around her and draped it tenderly over her shoulders. His white shirtfront dazzled her eyes. He placed a finger beneath her chin and lifted her face to him. "Better?" he asked, his voice deep and velvety as the darkness around them.

Maggie nodded. "Thank you." He returned to his seat and smiled across the table at her. She wrapped his jacket around herself, enfolding herself in his scent. Warmed from without and within, she let her eyes half close.

Cambien looked at her appraisingly. He opened a new line of conversation. "I trust you don't mind that our closing event has turned out to be a bit of a date."

Maggie giggled. "I guess it did. No, I don't mind at all. I've certainly been on worse dates." She took another drink of wine.

"Maggie, I . . ." and he paused coyly, shaking his head. "Oh, never mind."

She was intrigued. "What, Cambien?"

"Nothing, never mind. It was silly, really."

"Oh, come on. That's not fair. You started to say something, so say it."

"Okay, but only because you asked me to." He met her gaze once again. "Maggie, did you ever wonder what it would be like if you and I actually had dated? I almost went to Columbia, you know, when you were at Barnard. What if I had? Do you think we might have gotten together? I wonder how it would have gone."

Brave with drink, Maggie favored him with the truth. "Sure, I've wondered about that. Who wouldn't?" Thrilled by her own daring, she continued. "Let's face it, Cambien, you're an extremely desirable man. What they call a 'hell of a catch.' Of course I've thought about it." He smiled humbly at her praise. "I mean, seriously, why the hell have you never gotten married? How is a guy like you still on the market?"

Now he fixed her with a mesmerizing stare, all trace of jest gone. Maggie could not look away. Holding her with the intensity of his gaze, he spoke rapidly in low, urgent tones. "Perhaps I never married because I could never stop thinking about my first love. Perhaps no one else has ever measured up, and I can be satisfied with nothing less. Maybe I'm still waiting, burning for her with every fiber of my being, holding myself ready for the day she comes back to me. Because I know in my soul, as does she, that we are meant to be together, and that our love will be legendary and infinite."

Maggie stared into his black eyes, the victim of a hypnotist. She wanted to fall into those eyes, to drown in them, to do whatever he asked of her. She loved him so deeply and this last revelation, that he was an old-fashioned romantic of the finest sort, only made her ache for him more. She swallowed drily. In a whisper she asked, "And who is this first love?"

"Do you really not know?"

Maggie heard the tremor in his voice as he spoke. In slow motion, she shook her head.

"Maggie, we have just sat here and confessed to one another that we have both dreamed of being together. We are both adults; it's time to be honest, don't you think? To admit that I want you as badly as you want me." And without releasing her from the intensity of his gaze, he extended his hand across the linen covered tabletop and placed it over hers.

Shocked at the contact, she broke away from his mesmerizing eyes and looked down at their joined hands. A ray of light from the lantern glinted off her wedding band, just barely visible between his brown fingers.

And with his touch, as surely as if there had been a loud *crack* and a whiff of sulfur, a spell was broken.

For the first time in months, Maggie fully remembered who and what she was. She met Cambien's gaze again but this time, to his dismay, something in her face had changed. For with that physical contact, the reality of what he was proposing had burst into her consciousness.

And Cambien, builder of empires, progenitor of miraculous scientific advance, and employer of thousands, Cambien, tall and handsome, erudite and high, the great man she had admired and desired for so long, had become something different. Now he appeared to her as a common man who would sleep with another man's wife, a sleazy lecher who would place his own lust ahead of her children's need for a stable home, a man who claimed to possess a love worthy of reverence yet disrespected the most sacred vows a man and a woman could make.

In the next instant, a wave of guilt crashed over her. She saw herself now for what she was; a vain woman who gleaned self-fulfillment from the attention she garnered with her inappropriate behavior, nothing more than a self-centered tease. And now she had encouraged Cambien until he had placed himself in a wretched position. She was ashamed.

She withdrew her hand and put it in her lap. "Cambien, I— I'm so sorry," she stammered. "I seem to have caused a misunderstanding."

He was struggling for equilibrium. The world was spinning away from him. The prize that had been as good as taken was soaring hopelessly out of his grasp. He could not think about what had just happened.

Maggie was disheartened to see a mask close over his face.

"Not at all," he said. His voice had become falsely cheerful, horrible. "It's I who behaved inappropriately. Whew! You were right, we really should have laid off the wine." A mechanical laugh issued from the rictus on his face.

Maggie abhorred the artificial creature he had become. "No, don't put it on yourself, Cambien. I've been a total jerk. I'm so sorry for the way I've behaved."

"Nonsense. I had no right to speak to you the way I did. But thank you for being such a good sport about it," he said in the awful, phony voice. "Look, let's go back to the hotel–" Maggie flinched "– to our *own* rooms, and sleep on it. I trust this whole thing will look a lot less, er, disturbing in the morning."

The ride back to the Swanset seemed to go on forever. Maggie stared out the window at the blackness while Cambien kept his gaze on the road. There were one or two feeble attempts at small talk, which subsided quickly, and eventually they both abandoned the idea of speaking at all.

At the hotel, Cambien dropped her at the front door, saying he needed to park the car himself, as there were no valets available. Maggie knew this wasn't true but she readily agreed. She imagined that a shared elevator ride to the hotel's bedchambers would have been excruciating. She prepared to exit the car, then paused and turned to speak to Cambien, who simultaneously attempted to talk to her.

"I just want to say again how sorry I am—

"Again, I do hope you'll forgive any impropriety—"

They both fell silent. Finally, he bravely summoned up his rueful smile, managing to provide some comfort to both of them. "Look," he said, "everything is going to be alright. We are old friends and misunderstandings are bound to happen between people who've known each other as long as we have. It was meant to be a hypothetical conversation, and I guess I just got carried away."

Maggie did her best to return his smile. "Of course. Listen, let's just let it go and pretend it never happened."

"Deal."

"Deal."

She got out of the car, breathing great gulps of the cool night air, grateful to be alone.

In her room, Maggie kicked off her heels, stripped off her dress, and pulled on her dingy old nightgown. She went into the bathroom and scrubbed the makeup off her face. Her cell phone rang in the bedroom as she was toweling off.

Her heart pounding, she went to see who was calling. It was Rowan. At first, she didn't want to answer; he would surely hear the agitation in her voice. But then the realization that Cambien had wished to separate her from him made her want to talk to her husband more than anything. She answered the phone anxiously. "Hey, Ro," she said, belatedly trying to sound casual.

"Hey, Mags. Done with your dinner yet?"

Maggie closed her eyes and swallowed, forcing thoughts of Cambien and the disastrous evening out of her mind. "Yup, all done for the night."

"That wrapped up early, then. You left me a message that you wouldn't get back in time to call."

"Yes, well, we finished pretty early after all. Half the people couldn't make it. They got stuck at the plant. So it was actually kind of boring and we came back early."

"Well, get to bed so you can come back nice and early tomorrow. Believe it or not, we're starting to miss you out here in Connecticut."

He had spoken in a light-hearted voice, but that was the way Rowan always said the important things. The full meaning of his words resonated within her. Through the night, from her distant husband to her, heart to heart, came Rowan's call. He had been estranged for so long, she had convinced herself he no cared. But here he was, bidding her hurry back to him. Still cringing in shame for her wanton behavior and in shock over Cambien's willingness to destroy her family, Maggie was filled with gratitude. Her husband was still her husband. Their children were still their children. She still had a home to return to.

"I will, babe," she said in a soft voice. "I miss you, too." *I've missed you for the longest time,* she thought, her eyes glistening.

"Call me when you land, so I know you got back safe."

"You bet. Good night, Ro."

"'Night, Mags."

She lay in the hotel bed, the lights out. The effects of the wine were leaving her and, as Cambien made his way back into her thoughts, she felt nauseated.

They had said conciliatory words to one another when parting, trying to make light of what had transpired between them. But the truth was that something quite momentous had occurred and it had irreversibly changed the nature of their relationship. Cambien had told her that he had loved her for half his life (ridiculous, really, as they hadn't even spoken for years before she went to work at NarcoDynamics, and when she thought about it, she didn't believe they had been especially close in high school, either). He had asked her to become his lover and, in so doing, had expressed contempt for her husband and children, conferring less importance on their wellbeing than on his own lust.

And so, Maggie grappled with her anger at Cambien for threatening her family while she simultaneously mourned the loss of the man she had thought he was. She despised herself for turning away from her own husband, losing faith that he would return from his emotional retreat. And she felt mortified that she had been so flirtatious for so long with a man to whom she was not married.

This last point bothered Maggie more than anything. How complicit had she been in encouraging Cambien's inappropriate attentions? Had she secretly wanted him to suggest a tryst? After all, how many fantasies had she had of being seduced by him? How many dreams of being taken by him?

No, she told herself firmly. These were only dreams and fantasies. Maybe she had been flirtatious, but looking back, she was certain she had never been openly suggestive.

And Cambien couldn't possibly know what went on in her dreams.

The hours crept by. Maggie lay still, weathering the assault of her conscience and her growing hangover. Finally, near dawn, she slept.

Immediately, Cambien towered before her. He glowered down at her, a look of barely suppressed rage and unfathomable hurt on his face.

Alarmed, she tried to placate him. "Cambien, please, I—" But words failed her. She had no idea what she could say that might soothe him. With one last look of contempt, he vanished.

Maggie stared through the air where he had stood, her eye traveling to a vastly distant horizon where blazing blue sky met a dry, brown land. The vantage point of her dream zoomed up and out, and she saw that she was standing on a narrow bridge of barren rock, no wider than a bathmat, that protruded over a desert canyon. The floor of the chasm lay several thousand feet below her. The black shapes of vultures glided beneath her feet. A hot, high wind blew upward from the abyss and into her face, pushing her hard and threatening to knock her from the narrow spit of stone she stood on. Weak with terror, she collapsed to the ground, trying to cling to it. The canyon swept away dizzyingly beneath her while the hot wind blasted grit into her eyes and mouth.

"Cambien!" she shrieked, trembling. Sobs convulsed her. Dust caked her lips. "Goddamn it, Cambien, let me down! *Cambien!*"

But he had gone. She lay abandoned, the wind roaring in her ears, the canyon spinning under her, the sun blazing into her eyes.

Maggie woke to find that the sun was indeed shining into her eyes, and the room was indeed spinning. She lurched precipitously into the bathroom and vomited into the toilet. When the heaves finally subsided, she sat on the cool tiles a while longer, wallowing in wretchedness.

Gradually, the room stopped spinning and her stomach quieted. She got shakily to her feet, dropped her gown and stepped into the shower.

Cambien appeared in the lobby, impeccable as usual. They greeted each other politely and stepped outside to receive the little sports car from the valet.

He only alluded to the previous evening once as he drove. He seemed to have himself under very tight control.

"How are you feeling this morning? Forgive me for saying so, but you don't look entirely well. I can only apologize profusely if my poor behavior has anything to do with it." He was careful to look out the windshield the entire time.

Maggie felt hung over and guilty, but at least the former symptom was improving. She answered him in a steady voice. "Thanks for asking. I'm feeling all right, maybe just a bit hung over. And you?"

"Aside from my damaged male ego, you mean?" He chuckled humorlessly, chagrined. "I feel well physically. My only worry is that I have made you uncomfortable. I hope you can accept my sincere apology and take my word that I will never behave inappropriately towards you again."

"Apology accepted," Maggie said reflexively. She wished the conversation would end.

Cambien seemed satisfied, or perhaps he sensed her discomfort. "Good. Then onward we go."

The flight back east was a subdued affair. Neither Katy nor Steven had been able to conclude their business and both remained in St. Louis, so Maggie and Cambien were the only passengers. As on the trip out, they sat on opposite sides of the plane, reading. Maggie sipped a Coke, which settled her stomach. She suddenly remembered a recent dream of being intimate with Cambien, alone in a private plane–the twin to the one they now occupied–and she blanched at the thought.

Cambien held a newspaper in his shaking hands, willing himself to focus on the words in front of him. His mind raced as panic grasped towards his pounding heart with icy fingers.

You lost her, his frenzied mind screamed at him. *You blew it. You were so close, and you blew it.*

Shut up, he answered himself. *It's just a setback. It's just going to take a little more time, that's all.*

But the panic rose in him. *All is lost. You saw her face last night, when you touched her. She was repulsed by you. All is lost, she's gone forever. You might as well just die.*

I said SHUT UP! Cambien noticed Maggie looking at him anxiously and realized he had been muttering.

"Sorry," he intoned in a ludicrous attempt at sounding nonchalant. "Was I reading out loud?"

Maggie nodded, watched him a second longer, and returned to her newspaper. Abandoning the attempt to read, Cambien looked out the window. Cold sweat prickled his scalp. *Hold it together. It's incredibly important that you keep your cool now. You have to play this right.*

They rode, alone together, in the back of the limousine to the Stamford office. Stiff, formal, excruciatingly awkward, the trip was nearly unbearable. At last they walked into the familiar lobby. Cambien fled across the space. Maggie, who lingered a moment beside the carp pool, was quickly left behind. Without slowing his pace, he called over his shoulder to her, "Thanks again, Maggie. I can't wait to read your write up." And he vanished into the elevator bank.

Bemused, Maggie walked up the single flight of stairs to the lab. As disturbed as she might have been by the previous evening, she thought Cambien was having a worse time with it.

She put her bags down beside her desk and called hello to Dr. Rajagopalan, who was working with a lab aide on the far side of the large room. "Hello, Maggie. Welcome back," he answered.

She was deeply relieved to be back at her lab, in her home state, only a short car ride from her children and husband.

Her husband. A fresh pang of guilt stung her as she once again contended with her situation. She had taken advantage of Rowan's emotional difficulties, which had arisen from the horrors of his work. A policeman's wife, she ought to have known better. But she had used his withdrawal to justify her own self-indulgence, her spiritual faithlessness and masturbatory musings.

What she had felt for Cambien had not been love—she knew that now—merely a fantasy-fueled infatuation with a man who never really existed. But she had *believed* herself to be in love with someone besides her husband, and she had done nothing to stop it. She had embraced it, fed it, wallowed in it. This was unforgivable.

Last night, alone in her hotel room, she had been adrift in a tempest-tossed ocean of swirling regret, loss and mortification. With uncanny timing, Rowan had thrown her a lifeline. Maggie shook her head; all that time, she had been deluding herself that she and Cambien shared some sort of transcendent connection, and it turned out he couldn't have been more different from her. And when she had been most lost, Rowan, almost a thousand miles away, had reached out to steady her.

She shuddered at the thought of how close she had been to destroying that.

She dialed Rowan's cell phone. He picked it up on the first ring and the sound of his voice calmed the trembling inside her.

⌒×

Jill glanced up and saw Cambien heading toward her. "Welcome back, Dr. Cuth—"

"I am not to be disturbed." He passed her without slowing and entered his office.

"Yes, Dr. Cuth—" This time, she was cut off by the slam of the door. Her eyebrows rose when she heard the lock turn.

In the refuge of his office, Cambien abandoned his luggage and strode across the room to the bookshelves. His hands shook and he perspired freely. Opening a low cabinet, he pulled out a basket filled with NarcoDynamics products, packaged in sample sizes for doctors to give to their patients. He dumped the basket onto his desk and rummaged through the mound of packets until he found what he was looking for. Tearing open the small foil envelope, he shook two yellow pills onto his palm and put them on his tongue, then chewed them into a bitter-tasting paste. He opened a small refrigerator next to the cabinet, took out a bottle of mineral water, and washed it down.

For the next ten minutes, the founder and chief executive officer of NarcoDynamics, Inc., crouched on the floor of his office, his arms over his head, and rocked on the balls of his feet. Whimpers of panic and loss escaped him.

Finally, he felt the first merciful effects of the medication. His heart rate began to slow and his trembling to cease. His breathing became deeper and more regular. The acute emotional pain he was in became distant, muted, replaced with a feeling resembling something like hope or joy. He stopped rocking back and forth, and soon stood up. Cautiously, he made his way to his desk.

He sat for several minutes more, gratefully feeling his rigid muscles relaxing. A warm, light feeling suffused his body. He sipped the mineral water from the bottle. At last, his customary, confident smile returned to his face and he was once again the handsome and impressive scientist and businessman, Dr. Cuthbert.

He swept the pile of drug samples back into the basket and returned it to the cupboard. Appearing completely normal now, he sat at his desk and began to go through the piles of paperwork Jill had left for him. He would be able to suppress the horror of his failure for now. He would be able to do what he needed to get through the day.

At four o'clock, Maggie could no longer sit still. She rose from her desk and walked across the lab to Dr. Rajagolpoulon.

"Dr. Rajagopalan, if it's all the same to you, I'm going to head home for the day." He peered at her through his glasses. Feeling compelled to explain further, she said, "I haven't seen my kids in a couple of days and I'd really like to get home to them."

A rare smile warmed his face. "Yes, yes, of course. It is only fair. Please, go. I will see you tomorrow."

"Thanks." Before he had a chance to remember something he needed that day, she passed her desk and scooped up her bag on her way out the door.

As she drove north on the parkway, she became more nervous with each passing mile. The closer she got to home, the closer she came to looking her husband in the eye. She tried to calm herself by insisting that she had done nothing wrong; it wasn't as though she had actually cheated on Rowan. But every time she made this argument, a voice in the back of her mind remonstrated that, although she may not have shared her body with anyone beside her husband, she had most certainly shared her heart.

Abashed by this reality, Maggie was only grateful that she had not been seduced in every sense of the word. No one but she knew how far she had strayed, and she was thankful for this opportunity to reclaim her marriage. She had the gifts of a clear head and a lifetime with Rowan ahead of her, and she would never again take these things for granted. But she yet faced the challenge of re-entering her domestic life and restoring intimacy with her husband while exorcising the secret of her virtual transgression.

It would be difficult. She would never want to hurt Rowan or endanger their marriage by revealing the feelings she had once had for Cambien. But Rowan was a shrewd man and he knew her better than anyone. She both dreaded and hungered for the first moment they would share alone with one another.

~~~

Several hours later, Cambien got into his car and started his drive home. Like Maggie, he began to feel the strain on his nervous system from the events of the previous evening. But

Maggie's anxiety was born of her desire to leave that night as far behind her as possible; Cambien's fear was that she would succeed in doing so.

A light rain began to fall, and he turned on the windshield wipers. They squeaked rhythmically as they worked. His mind soon set up a chant to their cadence: *You blew it. You blew it. You blew it.* He shook his head and blinked into the grayness beyond his car. *You blew it. You blew it. You blew it.* "Stop it!" he screamed, his voice cracking.

He had to believe it wasn't over. He only needed to regroup and plan his next move. He would go to Greece tomorrow as planned (only without his anticipated traveling companion). He needed to get new incense anyway. And while there, he would figure out what to do next.

He had to believe that Maggie had loved him; that she was in love with him even now. Surely she was only waiting for him to present his case properly, to persuade her to stop clinging to her silly bourgeois notions of morality and leave her tedious family. Certainly that dull civil servant she was chained to could not provide the quality of life he could offer.

As he drove, he felt the effects of the medication wearing off. There was a definite shake to his hands now and he grasped the steering wheel harder to steady them. He struggled to stay focused on the road in front of him, which had become more treacherous as the rain intensified. *You blew it. You blew it,* the wipers chanted. His breathing became shallower and quicker as the artificial calm he had spent the afternoon in evaporated. Doubt, loss, and an utter failure of confidence descended upon him. Cold sweat ran down his neck and slicked his palms against the steering wheel.

He drove as quickly as he dared in the poor conditions. By the time he pulled up in front of his house, the last of the daylight had yielded prematurely to the gloom. He pulled his suitcase from the car and dashed through the rain to the shelter of the porch. Entering the house, he keyed his code into the alarm system and flicked on the lights. He fought to catch his breath, the panic now robbing him of the ability to respire properly.

The housekeeper had left a neat stack of mail on the entry hall table for him, but he passed it without a glance. His only thought was to reach the sanctuary of his room, where he could relax; he could meditate, burn incense, and even resort to additional medication if it came to that. He desperately needed to clear his head, or he would go mad.

At the top of the stairs, he smelled an unfamiliar, sweet scent. Turning on the lights in his bedroom, he saw several large vases ranged around the chamber, each full to bursting with fat red roses in full bloom. Their cloying scent filled the room.

Ignoring the flowers, Cambien shed his clothing as he passed through the room to the bath. He took a long, bracing shower, the water so hot it scalded his skin red. Finally, telling himself he felt calmer, he turned off the water and toweled dry. He wrapped his black silk robe around his still-damp body and came out of the bath.

The sight and smell of the roses assaulted him anew. The memory of instructing the housekeeper to fill his bedroom with red roses for his return came back to him now, taunting him. He had anticipated a triumphant return, with Maggie on his arm; the roses were to have been a surprise for her as they retired to bed together. Now he felt foolish beyond measure.

The belittling voice in his head began to lambaste him as brutally as the demon had ever done. He leaned on his dresser and glared at his reflection in the mirror. What a stupid fool he was, he derided himself. Did he really think Maggie would ever be interested in him? Would love him? A pathetic piece of shit like him didn't deserve to breathe the same air as her, let alone share a bed with her. And he had been so presumptuous as to think they would lie here, together, this very night, and that she would allow him to touch her actual body.

From the depths of his despair, the bile of bitter disappointment grew, boiling up inside him. He felt, as surely as if it were really happening, his innards liquefying, seething, bubbling up into his throat like hot acid. His eyes burned. A painful pressure blossomed beneath his Adam's apple. Unable to contain the detestable torrent, Cambien opened his mouth, not knowing whether he would vomit or gag. But he did neither. Instead, he gave vent to a broken cry of rage.

19.

Vicky knew she shouldn't.

But the rain made a melancholy pattering sound outside her window, which begged to be listened to with a lover in a shared bed. And although she had sworn to remain cool and aloof and not to tip her hand, she had missed Cambien terribly while he had been on his business trip. And she knew that he was to have returned this morning, and was doubtless alone in his spectacular house even now, listening to the same melancholy pattering as she. And as sometimes happened in the evening, she was a bit tipsy.

And so, with romance in her heart and a mischievous smile on her lips, Vicky poured a few more fingers of scotch into her glass, added fresh ice, and took it into her bedroom. She sipped the scotch and set the glass atop a tall dresser. Half the liquid sloshed out, but she didn't notice. Humming, she pulled a tiny red camisole and matching thong from a drawer. She stripped off her clothes and, a few sideways hops later, pulled on the thong. She slid the camisole over her head and paused for another swallow of her drink. From her closet, she selected a black sleeveless dress. Although it appeared to close with a long row of buttons up the front, the buttons actually concealed snaps. Vicky smiled naughtily as she snapped the dress up over her red lingerie, envisioning the look on Cambien's face when she whisked it off again.

She stepped into a pair of high-heeled sandals and admired herself in a mirror. Her tousled blond hair fell into her eyes and her full, red lips grinned knowingly. Oh, she was going to get it good tonight.

And so, although she knew she shouldn't, Vicky was soon weaving her car along the wet night roads towards Cambien's house. She giggled as she drove. Who could blame her, really? She was powerless to fight the attraction that drew her through the night—she was in love, after all. And unless she missed her guess, so was Cambien.

Who knew? Maybe he had missed her as much as she had missed him. Maybe tonight, he would say the words. She stopped giggling and sighed deeply as she drove.

Vicky found 56 Linden Lane again without much trouble, though the night was dark and rainy and she light-headed. She dashed through the rain and onto the porch, where she paused to shake the water from her hair. She reached for the doorbell but noticed the door was ajar. The naughty smile back on her face, she pushed it open. The door was well maintained and glided inward silently.

Amused by the realization that she held the element of surprise, Vicky stepped out of her shoes and crept silently into the entry hall, barely suppressing giggles. She padded quietly into the kitchen, found it empty, and proceeded to the living room. When that, too, proved uninhabited, she went back through the dining room to the entry hall. She peeked into the parlor, but all was dark. The hall light was on, and she realized that Cambien must be upstairs.

The thought of surprising him in his bedroom brought on a strong new urge to laugh, which she stifled with great difficulty. She crept up the stairs, the thick Persian runner muffling any sound. She paused at the top of the steps. Four doorways opened off the hall. Only one was lit, and she made her way noiselessly to it. She saw Cambien on the far side of the room, leaning on a dresser, his back to her.

Vicky leaned against the doorframe, propping a raised foot in a provocative pose and inclining her head to the side so that her hair fell over one eye. In her sultriest voice, she said "Hey, there." She waited, her smile wide and lewd, to savor Cambien's reaction when he turned and saw her.

He spun at the sound of her voice. She was surprised to see that he looked as though he had been, of all things, crying. His face and eyes were red and wet. Even his lips were deeply colored and swollen looking. And his expression was the last thing she expected, a mixture of misery and perhaps rage. He looked at her as though he couldn't believe his eyes, staring intently at where she stood, unable to make sense of what he saw.

In truth, Cambien had been so far outside himself that he was having difficulty comprehending Vicky's sudden, unannounced presence in the sanctity of his bedroom. At the first tones of a female voice, his overwrought heart had thought, for the most fleeting of moments, that Maggie had reconsidered and returned to him. But even as he turned, his brain had begun to recognize the timbre of a voice belonging to a different woman. As his eyes fell on Vicky, he struggled to remember who she was to him, even as outrage at her presumption began to swell within him. "You!" he sputtered incredulously. "What are you doing here?"

A sober person might have recognized the danger in Cambien's voice and face, but Vicky was besotted with single malt and love. All she perceived was that the man she adored was unhappy. She made the dreadful mistake of entering the room, clumsily moving towards him. "Ooh, honey. What's the matter?" she cooed. She reached him and laid her hands on his chest in an effort to soothe. "Oh, my, you are tense." She attempted to steer him towards the bed. "Here, come lie down and I'll give you a massage. And you can tell Mommy all about it."

Cambien wouldn't budge. He continued to glare at her with that horrible look of disbelief on his face. Thwarted, Vicky stepped back and considered him. With her wild blond hair across her blurred vision, she completely misread his expression. "What's the matter, baby? Need a little persuasion?" She took another step back and, as she had planned, zipped open the snaps on the front of her dress and let it fall to the floor with a flourish.

She posed for a long moment, eventually becoming confused by his lack of reaction. "Wow, you really are in a bad mood."

Cambien couldn't move, couldn't think what to do.

Turning from him, Vicky began swaying about the perimeter of his room, looking at framed prints, handling curios. "Hey, this is a nice room. How come you never invited me up here?" She drifted to the cabinet in the corner and halted in front of the huge vase of roses that rested on top of it. "Oh my God, these are beautiful. Are they for me?" she added coyly. She buried her face in the blooms and breathed deeply.

The sight of the vapid, drunken slut in the vulgar, red, whore get-up, pawing through the flowers that were meant to be a consummatory gift for his Love, sundered the last vestige of Cambien's restraint. "How dare you?" he roared. He sprang across the room, seized Vicky's arm, and spun her to face him.

"Ow, hey!" The painful force of his fingers snapped her from her reverie. "What the hell is up your ass tonight?" she squawked at him. Vicky was out of patience. She swept her hair out of her eyes and looked defiantly into Cambien's face. "Oh that's right, I forgot . . . *you don't like surprises*," she taunted, imitating his voice for the last four words.

Cambien's eyes blackened. Even through her haze of impairment, Vicky at last sensed she was in trouble. But before she could do more than register the thought, Cambien's large fist backhanded her jaw. The force of the blow spun her around and she crashed against the cabinet, knocking the vase to the ground with her as she fell.

Her head swam. She had heard a wet crunching sound when she was hit and now could not close her mouth. She saw the vase lying next to her. Cushioned by the thick Persian rug, it had not broken but merely disgorged its load of roses and water onto the floor. She had the disjointed thought that the rug was an exceptionally fine one before Cambien's guttural shouts began to rain down on her. "They're not for you . . . who the hell you think you are . . . look what you did . . . how dare . . . not for you . . . what!"

Vicky rolled onto her back, one arm shielding her face. She looked into the flailing mass of fists that descended on her, desperate to make contact with the human being that had once been there. "Cambien," she tried to say. But her jaw would not move and all that came out were shapeless sounds of injury and fear.

In a transport of rage, he sank his knees into her stomach and rained blows upon her head. He hacked disconnected words and phrases at her as he struck. "Whore! Stupid bitch! Drunken slut!" Vicky's arms waved ineffectively about her head as though she were warding off a swarm of gnats. One of the endless blows caught her in the throat with another ghastly crunching sound and she found she was no longer able to draw breath. Her hands clutched at her broken throat, her eyes staring up into the barrage.

Unable to exorcise his rage adequately with his fists, the monster that had once been her lover hoisted the heavy ceramic vase from the floor and raised it into the air. Vicky had another odd, disjointed thought—*What a pity! After it survived the fall*—before the vase began its descent.

Later. Rain still falling outside. Cambien's flailing fists had finally ceased their frenzy. Panting, he sat back on his heels beside the body. His rage spent for the time being, thoughts materialized and swarmed, besieging him.

How did he let this happen? How did she get in here? With a grimace, he remembered entering his home in such a state of distress he had neglected his customary security protocols; not only had he forgotten to set the alarm, he had left the door open.

God, what an idiot he was. He needed to get control of himself. Leaving the door open had been a bad enough mistake, but now look what he had done; Vicky lay dead on his bedroom floor.

Sacrificing the child had been one thing—it needed to be dead to serve its purpose. (And who could deny that it had served brilliantly? Maggie's fool of a husband had been as good as gone, so preoccupied had he become with investigating the child's murder).

But the corpse beside him needed to be alive to be useful. Vicky had been instrumental in fanning the hellfire of jealousy in Maggie's heart, bringing her to her knees and leaving her frantic for his attention. Now Cambien had lost a vital weapon from his arsenal. Vicky was no use to him dead.

His breath came fast, refused to slow, and he felt the familiar clammy fingers of panic grasping at him. Quickly, he clambered over the body to the cabinet, pulling the key from the pocket of his robe. He opened the doors with shaking hands.

Among the things inside glinted the incense burner he used when he meditated, fashioned of bronze and semi-precious stones. There was also a bowl filled with packets of medicine, similar to the one he kept in his office cupboard. As before, he pawed through them until he found what he was looking for. He staggered into the bathroom, the pills on his tongue, cupping water in his hands to swallow.

He looked up into the mirror over the sink. Blood spatters mottled his face. He dropped his robe and stepped into the shower.

When he re-entered the bedroom, he was calm and clear-headed. First he looked at the windows. Good, the shades had been drawn all this time. He dressed quickly in a dark sweat suit.

He sat on the edge of his bed, his back to the body. The hot shower and the pills had done their work. He took several deep, relaxing breaths, using his meditation techniques to concentrate. He had a lot of cleaning up to do.

～✖

The sun rose, burning through the last of the clouds from the previous night's rain. Cambien sat at his kitchen table and ate a bowl of yogurt while watching the mists creep out of the woods at the edge of his sloping lawns. He poured a fresh cup of coffee and brought it back upstairs with him.

The bag he had brought to St. Louis lay on the floor. He hung the carefully chosen outfit he had worn to dinner with Maggie in the walk-in closet. *The Seduction Suit*, he had called it to himself. He shook his head. How could he have been so mistaken? Maggie had certainly given every indication that she was ready to give herself to him. Why else would she have worn that tempting little dress and that vampy red lip color? Surely she had known what the deal was.

Aggrieved, he dumped the rest of the bag's contents onto the floor. Angry with himself for misjudging Maggie and furious over his loss of control the night before, he began stuffing the bag with clean clothing. He muttered excoriations to himself as he worked.

At 8:00 a.m., he sat behind his desk at the NarcoDynamics Stamford headquarters. Suitably medicated, he performed his duties as Founder and C.E.O. most convincingly. Only someone who knew him well might notice anything amiss in his demeanor, but as no one really did know him well, his masterfully suppressed agitation went unremarked. Perhaps Jill, leaning over his desk to place a stack of reports on it, observed the pulsing in his temple as he silently clenched and unclenched his jaw. But she was professional to her core and said nothing.

At three, Cambien left the office. He drove himself to the county airport, past the commercial terminal, and up to the gates that demarcated the private hangars. He was expected and waved through. He parked in his usual space and carried his bag to his waiting plane.

At five, Cambien was soaring over the Atlantic Ocean. With altitude and distance, he was able to relax and gain perspective on the strains and disappointments of the past forty-eight hours. He ate the light meal his cabin attendant served him as he looked out over the endless expanse of deep blue water. Darkness came quickly as he flew east.

He pulled a small case, the size of a compact, from his jacket pocket and opened it. He took out a cornflower-blue Anadreme tablet and washed it down with the last of his wine. He hadn't slept without taking Anadreme first for six years.

He knew it wouldn't have worn off entirely by the time he arrived in Athens. As the inventor of the drug, he was aware that a conscious patient who had taken Anadreme would have difficulty with abstract or arcane concepts, but would be able to perform simple tasks like reading and following directions.

He would be fine.

He watched the sky blacken where it met the sea. The dismay of the recent past became indistinct in the transformative darkness, losing its sharp edges.

A thousand miles lay between him and the instrument of jealousy he had once wielded, now only a broken corpse in a wrecked car sunk in a woodland swamp.

Two thousand miles lay between him and the look on Maggie's face when he had touched her hand.

A thousand miles lay between him and Maggie now, at home with her people (he could not bring himself to think the word *family*). She would be thinking of him, he knew. She would be hugging the children and maybe even kissing that loser she lived with (Cambien shuddered convulsively), but she would be thinking of him. And when she went to work the next day, she would discover that he was gone for an undetermined amount of time, and the longing would begin to gnaw at her again. He would see to it.

So that when he returned, she would be waiting.

His cares falling away from him into the lightless ocean waters, Cambien closed his eyes and, at long last, slept.

It was all going to be fine.

III.

20.

Culpability.

The late summer sun warm on her face, Maggie pondered the principle of culpability. She sat on a bench by the elementary school playground and watched her children clamber up jungle gyms and over seesaws.

The previous evening, when she had returned home from her fateful business trip, she had felt both emotional and awkward. She could not get enough of her children, never having been away from them for two nights before, and she hugged them fiercely and frequently. Rowan stood by, allowing her to re-acclimate. She straightened and gave him a shy embrace, kissing him without meeting his eyes.

"How was the big business trip?" he asked in a conversational tone.

Maggie gratefully took the opening he provided and talked about the numerous neutral details the topic provided. She described the journey out, the excitement of the private jet, and the beautiful factory. She told about meeting Don, the tour he gave her, the fascinating operations of the plant, and the breathtaking golf cart ride. As they sat at the dinner table, she expounded on the beautiful conservatory in the cafeteria, the friendly people of St. Louis, and the Mississippi River twisting in the golden sunset.

She left Rowan to clean up the kitchen and took the children upstairs. They spent a boisterous hour together, bathing, dressing in pajamas, and piling into Maggie and Rowan's bed. She read to them and carried them to their rooms. After kissing them goodnight, she went back to her room to unpack. She dragged it out long enough that it was nearly bedtime when she went back downstairs to rejoin her husband.

He was sitting in his usual spot on the sofa, watching the news. Maggie sat next to him, trying not to appear self-conscious. She wanted to be close to him but feared the intimacy, lest he somehow divine the guilt she was hiding. They watched the news together, not speaking. After several minutes, Rowan, keeping his eyes on the screen, placed his arm around his wife.

Like a dam breaking, love and gratitude for him flooded her. Maggie turned and wrapped herself around him. She kissed him on the mouth. The evening news was forgotten.

"Looks like you missed me while you were away on your fancy trip, huh?" Rowan teased.

"I did, more than I expected to," admitted Maggie.

She leaned in for another kiss, but Rowan pulled his head back. "My, my. Where did all this come from? Do private jets make you horny or something?"

Maggie closed her eyes. "Please, I don't want to talk," she murmured. Her mouth found his again. He let it go, marveling as he felt passion coursing through him once again. It had been so long.

The following morning, a Friday, Maggie called Dr. Rajagopalan's voicemail and left a message that she would not be coming in that day. She told Rowan she had too much to do, but really she was wary of returning to Cambien's domain.

Rowan smiled at his children and kissed his wife fondly as he left for work. Maggie fed and dressed the kids and got them into the car. It was now mid-August and time to register Hazel for kindergarten.

Once the paperwork had been completed and they walked out of the school building, Charlie and Hazel begged her to let them play on the playground. Maggie saw no reason not to and she sat on the bench to watch them.

And now, sitting in the morning sunlight, unobserved, Maggie felt brave enough to confront her confused thoughts. She thought about the night before, and how blessed she was to have her strong, steady husband in her life. She was elated they had connected again, Rowan having been emotionally absent for months, and she having been distracted by her fantasy life. She wanted only him, from now on. That much she was sure of.

But there were several lingering problems. One was the unease that would be unavoidable between her and Cambien whenever they met at work. There was no way for him to take back what he had said and no matter how he tried to explain it away, they would both always know he wanted her. And that he was willing to destroy her family to get what he wanted. Never mind that she had once believed she wanted it, too; that had only been a game she had played with herself. And even if it had grown beyond her original intentions, even if she had felt admiration, lust and – she once thought – love for Cambien, she was sure she no longer did; the glimpse she had gotten of his selfish and amoral nature had disabused her of such feelings.

So the question of whether she would be comfortable continuing to work at NarcoDynamics was something she needed to address. She thought again of resigning her position but again met the same roadblock: if she quit her job, Rowan would want to know why, and she had never been able to lie to him. Worse, if she quit right after returning from a trip with Cambien, Rowan would quickly deduce that the two events were linked. As emotionally dense as he could be, he certainly wasn't stupid. And although she was angry that Cambien had thought she would cavalierly abandon her family, she didn't want to arouse Rowan's anger at him, too.

Because the truth was, it wasn't entirely his fault. She could not shake the conviction that she bore some of the blame as well.

And so she sat in the warm sun, wrestling with the concept of culpability. How culpable was she? How wrong was what she had done? If her part in the imaginary affair was all in her head, then was her guilt also only a figment of her imagination? What about her heart? Had she not also (unintentionally, but nonetheless) put her heart into the affair? Had she not, in some way, cheated on her husband after all?

Lost in her thoughts, Maggie didn't at first see the black-clad figure making its way up the path that led from the sidewalk to the schoolyard. Gradually she took notice of its approach, registering a middle-aged man walking a small, shaggy terrier on a leash. *Why is he dressed in all black?* she wondered before noticing his white clerical collar. She felt a jolt as she recognized her priest, followed immediately by embarrassment as she realized she hadn't been to church in months.

"Father Bill, good morning," she called out to him as he neared.

The priest looked to see who had spoken. The sun glinted off his steel-framed glasses and steel-colored hair. "Why, Maggie Cooper. What a pleasant surprise." By now he had come close enough for his little terrier to sniff at her feet. Maggie reached down to pat him.

"He's cute. What's his name?"

"Lazarus. I call him that because he got hit by a car when he was a puppy and they thought he was a goner, but here he is again."

At the sight of the dog, Hazel and Charlie had abandoned the playground and come running. "Guys, look who's here," Maggie said. "It's Father Bill. Say 'hello,' please."

The children obediently looked up from Lazarus long enough to say, "Hello, Father," before giving their full attention back to the dog.

The priest sank down companionably onto the bench next to Maggie, who moved over to make room for him. "Lovely morning, isn't it?" he asked, looking up into the scrubbed blue sky.

"It certainly is." Maggie showed her children the right way to meet a strange dog ("See, Charlie? You hold your hand out so he can smell it. That's right, Hazel") to mask the self-consciousness she was feeling. Father Bill had come upon her just as she had been wallowing in guilt.

"Father, may we take Lazarus for a walk?" Hazel asked.

"Sure you can, sweetheart. Here, you just put your hand through this loop, like this. That way, he can't get away from you."

"Stay where we can see you," called Maggie. Flustered further by being left alone with the priest, she searched for a topic of conversation as her children ran off, giggling, the shaggy little dog half-pulling them. "How's the church these days, Father?"

He looked placidly up at the treetops shimmying in the golden light. "Oh, much the same . . . except we haven't seen you in quite a while." His tone was not accusatory, merely friendly and matter-of-fact, and he gave her a half-smile. Maggie felt herself softening and her concerns pressed into her thoughts again. Bound by them, she said nothing more.

From across the playground, the children's laughter carried to them on the warm breeze. The sun embraced them in its comforting rays and the rustling leaves whispered. She and the priest sat together, saying nothing.

At length, Father Bill broke the silence. "I always knew I would be a priest, you know. Since I was a little kid." He watched the children as they tried to coax Lazarus into a miniature police cruiser mounted on a giant spring. "You've probably heard people say it's a 'calling.' Well, since I can remember, I've always felt the call. First, it was other kids on the playground who were maybe having a tough time with the bullies, or their big brothers, or understanding their class work. Later, it was bigger people with bigger problems. When someone needed encouragement, or understanding, or hope, or spiritual guidance, God always had a way of calling me to them."

Maggie remained mute. Sparrows landed at their feet, looking up hopefully as they hopped about, searching for errant crumbs in the wood chips.

Father Bill's gaze now rested on the birds as he spoke. "This year is my thirty-second year in the priesthood, you know," he said quietly. "I'd be a pretty poor excuse for a priest indeed, if I couldn't tell, after all these years, when someone needed spiritual counsel."

Maggie stared at the ground. Hot tears fell on her clenched hands, surprising her. Suddenly, gratefully, she began to talk. "Oh, father, I'm so ashamed. And I didn't know who I could talk to." She gave a great, wet sniffle and began rummaging through her bag for a tissue.

"Shame isn't something God wants us to feel, Maggie. After all, we're all human, and we all make mistakes. God knows that and He loves us in spite of it." He paused a moment to let her blow her nose, then asked soothingly, "Would you care to tell an old man about it? Maybe I can help."

"Oh, come on. You're not old." Maggie gave a soggy smile and took a moment to gather her thoughts. "Actually, since you asked, I would like to tell you about it. But I'm so afraid. I don't want anyone to know," she finished in a whisper.

He smiled. "Well, we may not be in the traditional darkened booth, but I think," and he opened his arms to indicate the surrounding trees, the grass, the open sky, "that God has provided us with a serviceable confessional. Please, feel free to speak what's on your mind. Of course I'll keep your confidence. It's what I do."

Maggie kept her gaze on her children, some fifty feet away, while she spoke. "I don't know how this happened. I swear I wasn't looking for that kind of attention or anything, but, well . . . my husband hasn't been himself for a while. He's been really distant, and even mean to me and the kids when he's around. I know he doesn't mean it. He was upset about something that had nothing to do with us. But I guess I let my pride get hurt, and I—" Maggie fought to put her transgression into words. "I started a new job, and my boss turned out to be an old high school friend of mine. And he seemed to really like me, so I guess I started flirting with him, and he flirted back, and, um, I think I really liked it. It made me feel attractive and like I was interesting to a man again . . ." She trailed off.

"Are you trying to say that you've had an affair?" Father Bill prompted gently.

"No! Good God, no. I mean, I didn't sleep with him or anything. But I don't feel like I'm completely innocent, either. I think I really led him on, maybe I let him think we would have an affair. He actually asked me to, and I got really mad, like I was disgusted with him. But the more I think about it, the more I think it . . . it was my fault, too, for acting the way I did and leading him on. I mean, it's not like I didn't think about him. A lot, actually. I feel like he must have been able to read my mind or something, and I can hardly blame him." She faltered, not sure how to word the crux of what was bothering her.

"Were you in love with him?"

Hearing her torment plainly spoken stung Maggie and fresh tears rolled down her cheeks. "I thought I was in love with him," she sobbed. "And I'm married. I'm a mom. What the hell was I doing? I should be in love with my husband. All I can think of is what a horrible person I am, that I could be so . . . unfaithful to my family." She cried great, heaving sobs of shame. "I've been telling myself I'm di-disgusted with him for not thinking my family was important, but maybe I-I'm disgusted with myself." She fished a fresh tissue out of her purse and mopped her face.

The priest sat quietly as she pulled herself together. After a few moments, she spoke the last thing that was bothering her. "And now, I'm having trouble facing my husband. He doesn't know any of this, and I don't want to tell him. I don't want him to know. It would hurt him terribly, and what if he never trusts me again? Father, I'm really having a hard time with this . . . did I somehow cheat on my husband?"

Father Bill spoke in a comforting tone, but his words were disturbing. "Well, this is a tough one, and you're right to take it seriously. If your husband doesn't have your heart, what does he have? In Matthew, we read that if you look at someone and desire him, you have already committed adultery in your heart."

Maggie began to cry anew. "Oh, no," she moaned.

The priest reached into his pocket and handed her another tissue. "Okay, okay, don't be so hard on yourself," he soothed. "You're certainly not the first married person to have feelings for someone besides your spouse. Believe me," he added sardonically. "Listen, whatever transgression you have committed, it's quite clear that you have seen it for what it is and rejected it. And it's also clear that you do, in fact, love your husband and place him above all else."

"I do," Maggie murmured. She was calming down again.

"Great, so, most of the heavy lifting is already done," he said bracingly.

"But what if Rowan finds out about how I felt? What if he never trusts me again? What if he can't forgive me?" Maggie asked.

"I think you have one more thing to do before you worry about that," he said. Maggie looked at him questioningly. "First, you need to forgive yourself."

She thought about it. He had a point; she had rejected the inappropriate behavior and moved past it. She had reaffirmed her bond with her family. It did seem that the problem she wrestled with now was her own unrelieved guilt. But when she thought about how very deeply she had been involved—emotionally and erotically—with her illusory lover, she cringed with regret. "I'm not sure I can," she said quietly.

"Maggie, what do we know about God? That He loves us no matter what stupid thing we do, right? That He forgives all." She nodded in agreement. "Now, if God thinks it's okay to forgive you, then who are you to say He's wrong?"

Her tear-streaked face broke into a smile. Although she knew her faith to be imperfect at best, she felt a sense of relief nonetheless. He was right; who was she to say she wasn't forgiven already?

But one more thing troubled her. "I guess I can work on forgiving myself. But what about Rowan? Do you think I should tell him what happened? Will he be able to forgive me?"

The priest sighed. "My dear, when the time is right to tell your husband about it, you will know. In the meantime, just try to give yourself a break, all right?" He favored her with a warm smile of understanding. Then he rose to his feet with a great groan and several popping sounds from his creaky joints. "And now, I believe Lazarus is returning to us," he said. Indeed, the little dog was racing toward his master through the playground, his unmanned leash whipping along the ground like a snake, Maggie's laughing children galloping after him.

Her burden considerably lightened, Maggie watched Father Bill and his dog recede along the pathway toward the distant houses. She took a child's hand in each of hers. "Come on, kids, we still have to do the errands." The three of them walked towards the parking lot.

Hazel looked up at her mother. "Mommy, were you crying?"

"Was I? I don't know, maybe a little. Nothing's wrong, though, baby. Everything's okay," she answered, smiling.

Several hours later, Maggie pulled into her driveway and was surprised to see Rowan's truck already there. It was far too early for him to be home from work. Rowan himself was waiting on the porch for her. The children, surprised to find their father home early, ran up the steps to him. He hugged them and sent them into the house to watch cartoons. Then he turned to face his wife.

A feeling of foreboding overcame her. "Is it Pop?" she asked tensely.

Rowan shook his head.

"Well, who is it? What's wrong?"

In a low voice, Rowan told her that a call had come in that morning about a car off the road in the woods of North Stamford. He was only half-listening to the radio when the responding officer reported a fatality, and the tag was radioed in. He had been shocked to hear Vicky's name crackle back over. He had gone to the scene himself to make sure.

Maggie sank back to sit on the porch railing as the world took an ugly spin. A numbing grief descended over her and at the same time, a sickening fear blossomed in the pit of her stomach. In spite of the warm summer day, she began to shake.

Rowan stood before her, looking into her face with concern. "You okay, Mags?" he asked quietly. He laid his hands on her shoulders.

Maggie looked at him and saw tears sliding silently down his cheeks. She fought to compose herself, nodded once. "Please tell me what happened," she said quietly.

He sat on the railing beside her, staring into the same middle distance as she. "They're still trying to put it all together, but it looks like it happened late last night. It was crappy out. She was on a little-used, twisty road in the woods. She must have gotten lost and confused. Anyway, she went off the road—maybe she was even trying to pull over to get her bearings, who knows—but it was a really bad spot. There's a wicked drop-off, almost a cliff, and her car went over the edge. Some guy who lives out in the woods called it in this morning. Noticed it from a distance, while he was having his morning coffee on the patio." He misinterpreted her knitted brows. "But it looks like she died on impact. It's not like she would have been okay if someone had noticed it sooner."

"Rowan, Vicky would never have gotten lost. You know that. She knows Stamford like the back of her hand," Maggie protested. "*Knew*," she added with a half sob, half laugh.

"We still don't know exactly what happened. The accident guys are out there putting it all together, but it takes a while."

Maggie shut her eyes and pinched the bridge of her nose. "Was she drunk?"

"We don't know that yet, either. Toxicology'll take a couple of weeks."

The merciful numbness was wearing off as Maggie realized that she hadn't spoken to her friend for weeks, and now she never would. For the second time that day, she began to cry wretchedly. Rowan put his arms around her, pulled her close, and hugged her fiercely. He laid his chin on top of his wife's head as she sobbed and heaved against his chest, fighting his own grief as he strove to comfort.

21.

Cambien was climbing, climbing. The hot Mediterranean sun beat down on the brown hills. Sweat dripped from beneath his hat. Hiking briskly, he worked his way up the baking hillside. The narrow way he trod was little more than a goat path. Wild thyme and sage grew over it in most places. Each footstep crushed the herbs, releasing their fragrance into the hot, dry air. Presently, he paused in the shade of a small grove of olive trees. He removed his rucksack, took out a bottle of water, and drank deeply.

He looked back down the hill he had been climbing. It tumbled to the edge of low cliffs, which descended almost vertically into the crystal blue of the sea. So much clearer than the Atlantic Ocean Cambien had grown up with, the Mediterranean Sea allowed one to look directly into its depths, guilelessly revealing submarine features hundreds of feet deep. His eyes followed the craggy line of the cliff as it continued its vertical descent beneath the surface of the water, until it was finally lost to view in the blue-blackness.

He turned to look ahead, up the path he ascended. It scaled the hill for another half mile or so before leveling off on a brush-covered shoulder. Beyond that, more craggy heights climbed into the azure sky. Clusters of fig, olive and cypress trees broke up the rocky landscape.

Cambien took a final swig of water before replacing his rucksack and continuing upward. As he approached the hill's shoulder, he heard the metallic clanking of bells. To his right, he saw several goats tethered in the shade of an olive grove, which grew in a hollow not visible from below. The goats wore metal bells around their necks, clanging and clinking as they foraged about.

Setting his sights on the steep trail ahead of him again, he now saw the form of a man at its summit, silhouetted against the blueness of the sky, watching his approach. Turning to his left, he saw another man atop a tall, stony crag. Looking once more at the goats to his right, Cambien saw a third man, previously unseen, emerge from the crevices between the boulders beyond the grove. He looked around the landscape for the other two—there were five brothers in all—but he saw no one else. With a brief nod at the man in the olive grove, he continued upward.

Shortly, he was within hailing distance of the man at the trail's summit. "Yiassou, Yianni," he called as he closed the distance between them.

Yianni, the oldest brother, stood motionless, watching. He wore a coarse linen shirt, the sleeves rolled up over his brown forearms, the tails tucked into loose trousers. A wide-brimmed, canvas hat shielded his head from the sun. His feet were shod in leather sandals, a canteen hung at his side, and a rifle was slung across his back. He nodded as Cambien came to a halt in front of him.

The man who had stood on the rocky outcrop to Cambien's left made an impressive leap from its height, dropping to the ground several yards away. He strolled to his brother's side, making a show of his nonchalance. The third oldest, he was outfitted similarly to his brother. "Hello, Nikos," Cambien greeted him.

"Hello, Dr. Cuthbert," the man replied in a heavy Greek accent. Of the five brothers, his English was the best, so it was he who dealt with visitors such as Cambien. "We heard that you were in your residence yesterday. How was your trip?"

"Pleasant, uneventful. It's always nice to get back to the island, though."

The men in front of him nodded. Their dark eyes remained fixed on his own. While not menacing, they communicated the information that he was on their territory, but that they would allow this for now. "Yes, we like it here very much," Nikos replied.

Yianni pulled a packet of cigarettes from his pocket and offered one to Cambien, who shook his head. "No, thank you." Shrugging, Yianni lit one and smoked thoughtfully, looking past him at the sea beyond.

Cambien spoke to Nikos again. "Is your father at home?"

"Yes, he is just up the path. He expected you would come. You wait here, I will go and tell him." With a look at Yianni, Nikos turned and hiked briskly to the top of the path, where he disappeared over the summit.

Cambien stood beside the oldest brother. He took his water bottle out again and had another long drink. Side by side, the two men gazed silently over the breeze-swept hillside. Ten minutes passed before Nikos came back down to fetch Cambien.

As they crested the hill's shoulder, the ground leveled into a large plateau, at the distant back of which the land rose again in rocky stages for nearly another mile before it peaked. The land before them, sheltered in the lee of the island's summit, was surprisingly green for this dry, scrubby place. Here were many more olive trees, and trees bearing figs, almonds, pomegranates, and peaches. The thyme and sage shared the ground with grass, and a small flock of sheep rested in a shady enclosure. The air buzzed with the song of countless cicadas.

The two men walked through the humming groves towards an ancient-looking, whitewashed house, which was built into the base of the ascending cliffs. In front of the house, an arbor sheltered a large patio from the sun. Grape vines grew over it as thickly as actual walls and roof. In their shade, in the center of the patio, a man sat at a wooden table. His hair and mustache were silvery white. He stood to greet his guest.

"Welcome," he said, opening his arms and smiling graciously. Unlike his sons, he had eyes of blue, bright as the Mediterranean Sea. Cambien went to him and the men embraced, kissing one another on both cheeks.

"It's good to see you again," said Cambien. He smiled broadly. "You're looking well."

The old man smiled back, looking at him with an almost paternal affection in his hawk-sharp eyes. "You look healthy, but perhaps a little disturbed. Please, sit down." He indicated an empty chair at the table. To his son, he said, "Nikos, bring wine and *mezedakia.*" Nikos disappeared into the house, leaving Cambien seated across from the old man.

Cambien had first sat in this chair, across from this old man, thirteen years earlier.

The summer after he graduated from Yale, his father treated him to a trip to Europe. He chose to visit Greece, to meet the few relatives he had on his mother's side: an ancient uncle and a morose cousin in Athens, with whom she had never been close. His mother's family had moved to the United States when she was just a baby.

After spending a week in the hot, noisy city, visiting the Acropolis and the museums, Cambien was ready for a change. His mother's cousin, a dour woman about his father's age, mentioned that their family originated on a large island in the Aegean Sea; perhaps Cambien would like to take the ferry boat out and spend a few days. There were distant relatives still to be found in the dusty hills.

Two days later, he had rented a room in a small inn on the large island. After talking to his landlord, whose English wasn't bad, he did indeed track down some second and third cousins. Mostly fishermen and farmers, they laughed to see their dark hair and eyes and striking features reproduced on the face of their bright, young American relative.

Cambien stayed for a month, slipping into the peaceful rhythm of life on the island. He slept late, spent his mornings swimming or exploring, ate huge dinners, napped through the heat of the day, and stayed out to drink and talk with the men or walk the starry beach until late at night. Far from the lights of any city, he watched open-mouthed as meteor showers spangled the black velvet heavens, the same sky that had kindled the minds of the ancients who had dwelt in this place.

He rented a scooter and toured the sage-covered highlands, discovering villages and terraced olive groves, tiny whitewashed chapels, herds of goats, and bat-filled caves. He gorged himself on local food and wine; fried fish and giant beans, grilled meats, savory tomato salads and tangy goat cheese, crusty bread, and on everything, the rich, fragrant olive oil. He swam in the clear, blue water and hauled himself onto salt-encrusted rocks to doze in the sun. He shed his customary pallor for a deep tan and a glow of health.

If not for the demonic horror that still disturbed his nights on occasion, he would have been utterly content.

But no matter how far Cambien traveled, the demon came with him. Soon the deep sleep he had been enjoying was ruptured by its loathsome presence. As he was battered by repeated nocturnal visitations, he began to deteriorate once again. Darkness encircled his eyes, and his movements became clumsy and unsure.

One day, he rode the scooter to the far end of the island. He left it lying at the road's end and continued on foot to the top of a craggy hill. From its peak, he saw a smaller island, about a mile away from the one on which he stood.

The next morning, he walked to the marina near his lodging and engaged a fisherman to take him out to the small island on his boat.

Cambien lit on a much smaller dock amid several tied-up boats and walked into the tiny village. He sat in the only cafe and ordered coffee and a pastry. As happened in the small island villages, word spread of the stranger's presence. Cambien did not want for company and cheerily answered all questions put to him.

After an hour or so, he left the cafe on foot to explore. Passing through the small town in the blink of an eye, he was soon laboring up the rocky slopes. He aimed to gain the crest of the large, central hill and thus have a view of the entire island. But after his meanderings brought him to a lonely trail though a rocky ravine, he found his way barred by four sturdy men, with hair and eyes as black as his own.

One of the men (Nikos, it later turned out) asked him, in heavily accented English, what he was looking for.

"Nothing, really," replied Cambien, returning his unblinking gaze with sleep-deprived eyes.

Just then, another man, who resembled the others except for being a generation older and having eyes of Aegean blue, came around the bend in the trail and walked up to the group. The four younger men parted, so that he might approach Cambien.

The newcomer looked gravely into Cambien's face. He smiled beneath his graying mustache. "I know who you are," he pronounced, in the best English Cambien had yet heard on either island. "And I can see that you are having trouble." He stepped to the side, indicating the way forward. "Come, we will go to the house."

Intrigued by the man's air of wisdom and understanding, Cambien accompanied him along the rocky trail, the four black-haired men following silently several paces behind.

He spent the afternoon in the shade of the grape arbor, talking, eating, and learning.

"I heard that a stranger had come to the island and I had an idea who it might be. When I see your face, I know who you are. You are Helena's son." Cambien smiled in delight at the man's perception. "You have her face. I remember how she looked one summer, when her family came here to the island. She was a beautiful young girl."

And later: "You have a problem, no? A problem in your sleep?"

Cambien was speechless. "How do you know this?"

"I see, I know. This rock, this island, that we live on," (he swept his arm in a wide arc as he spoke) "has been here forever. This island has seen many things, and it has told me some of them." Sipping the homemade wine in his glass, Cambien could believe it. "So I recognize in you, perhaps, someone who has an unwelcome visitor."

Cambien sat up abruptly. "How do you . . ."

The old man smiled. "I see that I am right. You do not have the quality of life. You are not free."

Cambien's tired eyes burned. "No, I'm not," he said brokenly.

By now, the sun was lowering in the sky toward the big island. An early evening breeze lifted the silvery leaves of the olive trees and clanged the bronze bells hanging in their branches. The sheep bleated gently in their enclosure.

The old man leaned forward. "You go back now. You come again tomorrow. There are some things I can maybe teach to you."

Cambien went, and returned the next morning. And so his tutelage began.

The old man showed him many things. He took him to the apex of the island's central mountain and showed him how to look peacefully and detachedly down upon the blue world. He crushed bunches of dry, late-summer herbs in his hands, combined them this way and that, and gave them to Cambien to inhale. He led Cambien deep inside a cave, beyond the point where any light reached, and showed him utter blackness, perfect emptiness. He lit a lantern and showed him a crevice in the cave floor that apparently had no bottom.

"In the ancient times, a very famous oracle lived here, in this cave. She knew the correct plants to burn, and she dropped them into this hole. Hades, the Underworld, sent its secrets back up to her on the smoke. She would open her mind in her dreams to the images that were sent."

Cambien brought an overnight bag and spent a week on the island.

The old man explained the sleeping mind and the freedom from earthly restraint that it gave. He taught Cambien to meditate and train his mind to access this same freedom, but in a conscious state. He burned incense he made from an ancient recipe, using the fragrant plants that grew on the island, and taught Cambien use his mind to climb onto the ascending plumes of smoke. Thus, he learned that the door of his mind worked two ways; it let things like the demon in, but it could also let Cambien himself out.

Aloft on the blue smoke, he coursed over the surface of the earth. Miles of sea sped beneath him. He soared over darkened villages and cities, observing the people as they slept, their minds innocently open to whatever visitations occurred.

The old man was impressed with his progress. "Never have I seen anyone learn so well, so quickly. I love my sons, but they have never been able to understand the way you have. You came to me feeling as though you have a curse, but really you have a gift."

At the end of the week, Cambien and the old man sat on a cliff, watching the moon rise over the gently rippling sea. The teacher had packed a parting gift for his pupil; a bottle of homemade wine, a packet of mellow sheep's milk cheese, and a generous supply of the incense he made. They talked of the things Cambien had learned.

"Please don't think that I'm not grateful," Cambien said. "You've shown me parts of my mind I had never seen and taught me to use abilities I never knew existed. You taught me all about the mind's door, and how to go through it and make the world my own. But there's one thing I still don't understand."

"What is that?" asked the elder.

"How do I close the door?"

The old man seemed bewildered. "But why would you want to close such a marvelous gift?" Then he remembered the nature of his student's torment. "Oh, of course." He looked out over the dark sea, drew a heavy breath. "I am afraid I do not know how to close the door."

A week later, Cambien began his coursework at Yale School of Medicine. And eventually, with the things he had learned on the island and the information he absorbed as he trained to be a doctor, he figured out a way to close the door. It was called Anadreme, and it made him very wealthy.

Once he had invented Anadreme, he truly came into his own. He took the medication every night before sleeping and finally banished the horrific demon that had disturbed his peace for his entire life. At last, he felt a sense of power over the direction of his own destiny and began to plan its course.

He also continued to explore and hone his traveling ability, as he had come to call it. He would light the charcoal granules in the tiny bronze brazier, drop several lumps of the old man's incense on top, and settle down to meditate. By experimenting, he learned that he could add certain things to the burn to influence and guide his travels as they altered the composition of the smoke. He rose heavenward on the vapor, drawn in the wake of the essence he added as it sought to return to its place of origin.

With a small portion of his wealth, Cambien purchased a one-room cottage on the shore of the little island, which he used as a retreat. Although years might pass without him visiting it, he was made easy by knowing he could go there at any time.

To this rustic paradise he had planned to withdraw with Maggie, once she had surrendered to him. There they would explore one another in a Mediterranean Eden. But not only had this plan failed to unfold properly, he had been so distraught he had left the door to his house open, and the trouble with Vicky had ensued. Hence, his retreat to the cottage had been a haphazard, desperate flight.

Once he had reached his simple bed, he had taken his medication and gone to sleep, his dreamless slumber restoring his exhausted body and wracked nerves. He slept quite late the next day. When he woke, he walked to the cafe for breakfast.

He needed to see the old man. Really, he needed to see Maggie. But he had foolishly allowed his supplies to run dry, assuming that he would have the real, flesh-and-blood Maggie in his arms by now. Since that had not transpired, he needed the means to travel to her again. And for that, he needed to see the old man.

And so it was that Cambien was seated at the wooden table beneath the grape arbor, gritting his teeth through a visit he could barely wait to conclude. He drank the old man's wine and ate his cheese and olives. They talked about what they had been doing, not having seen one another in perhaps two years. Cambien brushed aside his host's concerned questions about his somewhat edgy demeanor, saying he had been working too hard and had come to the island for a bit of rest.

The old man bragged that he had become a bit of an oracle himself, as his reputation drew seekers of spiritual wisdom from near and far to his island.

Cambien had noticed, over the years, that his clothing had become finer and employees now maintained his house and kitchen, rather than his feral sons. Having prospered considerably over the same period of time, Cambien hadn't commented on it. But now he used the old man's bragging to turn the conversation to the reason for his visit.

"Since you do seem to be running a bit of a cottage industry, I will admit that I have come here partly to discuss business with you," Cambien segued.

"Is that so?" The blue eyes gleamed with the spirit of enterprise. "What can I do for you?"

"I would like to buy more incense. I've used up the generous gift you gave me, years ago." He tried to sound as though it were a matter of little consequence to him whether or not his errand was successful, but the old man's eyes narrowed slightly.

After a pause, his host spoke again, now in a more business-like tone of voice. "Very well. Come with me."

He led Cambien along a path that ran away from the house, in an easterly direction, along the base of the cliff-like hills. Cambien had been on this path before. After walking for a quarter mile, they left the trail and wound in among some large boulders until they reached the mouth of a cavern. Inside, it was about the size of a large room, high enough for a man to stand upright and have several feet clearance. Woolen rugs covered the floor, several chairs and a table were ranged along one side, and a heavy, wooden cupboard stood against the back wall.

It was in this place that the old man had first taught Cambien about traveling. Looking about, he saw that it had been spruced up a bit; the walls were freshly whitewashed, the floor was swept more conscientiously, and the rugs were newer and nicer.

The old man went to the cabinet against the back wall and unlocked it. He brought forth a bottle of ouzo and two small glasses, which he placed on the table. He turned to his guest. "Before we do business, we have a drink together." The licorice-flavored liquor burned Cambien's throat, warming him and taking the edge off his nerves.

"Now, what exactly do you want?" asked the incense maker, leading the way back to the cabinet. The smells issuing forth were mostly familiar to Cambien, the exotic herbal bouquet of the incense he sought, with pungent undertones he did not recognize. Looking inside, he saw shelves crammed with earthen containers, brass incense burners, dried plants, a bottle of brandy, and some glasses.

"I just need more incense, maybe some charcoal to burn it with. Probably not as much as you gave me last time."

The old man reached for the largest earthenware pot in the cupboard. Cambien saw that there were two smaller containers next to it. The gamey smell he didn't recognize seemed to be coming from them. "What's in there?" he asked, pointing.

The elder shook his head, smiling, as he removed the largest pot. "That is extremely powerful, and only for the true masters of the metaphysical. I myself am just learning to make it, and I do not yet understand all the ways to use it. It is—how you say?—*experimental* at this time."

Cambien was intrigued. "Yes, but what does it do? Does it work the same way as the regular stuff?"

The old man pulled two sheets of glossy tissue paper from another shelf and moved to the table before answering. "Yes and no," he said thoughtfully. "Yes, you still rise with the smoke. But there are other ingredients in it that maybe allow you to do something more. But it is not for sale, not yet anyway. Now, how much of this do you want?" he asked, effectively changing the subject and impelling Cambien to leave the cabinet and come to the table to see.

"Let's see . . . yes, that should be enough."

He watched as his companion portioned the amber-like lumps onto a sheet of paper, which he folded carefully into a packet. He then made a second packet of charcoal, which he placed next to the first. He put the lids back onto the containers and carried them to the cabinet, locking them away. He turned to Cambien. "That will be one thousand euro."

Cambien didn't bat an eye. He pulled out a large bundle of money and paid the man, who gave a jolly grin as he pocketed it.

"And now, one more drink, to celebrate our business."

Cambien didn't mind the mellowing effect of the ouzo, so he joined the old man for another shot. They walked back down the trail towards the veranda, the sun setting redly before them.

"Of course, you will stay for dinner?" the old man asked.

Cambien, however, felt the pull of the packets in his pocket. "Thank you very much for your invitation, but I really need to get back to my house. As I told you, I have been working very hard lately. I need to be alone, to relax. I hope you can understand."

Most visits are cause for sharing a meal, according to Greek hospitality, so it was poor form for Cambien to decline the invitation. The old man said that yes, of course he understood, but thought to himself that his former pupil seemed far too anxious.

Cambien commanded himself not to run as he hurried back down the path, through the village, and along the coastal lane. At long last, he gained the privacy of his cottage. Hungering for communion with Maggie, he grabbed the nearest dish in the kitchen and a box of matches and sank onto the middle of the floor. He poured a small measure of charcoal onto the dish and lit it. As soon as it began to burn steadily, he dropped three precious lumps of incense on top of it. The fragrant, blue smoke began to curl seductively under his nose on its way upward. He sat back, crossed his legs, and began to calm his breathing. Before closing his eyes to begin, he took one last look at the physical world around him.

Through the window, he saw the fiery sun settling behind the hills for the night. He thought briefly that it must be past dinnertime as he closed his eyes. He snapped them open again in consternation. *Damn! The time change!* So eager had he been to travel to Maggie, he had forgotten that he was seven hours ahead of her. She would be awake at this moment, would not be asleep for hours. He could not get to her.

And the incense was burning. It would be wasted. Without thinking, he reached into the dish, desperate to separate the amber nuggets from the glowing charcoal. He scorched his fingertips in the effort, but was unable to separate the two elements, the incense having fused to the glowing charcoal.

He carried the dish to the sink and ran water on it to extinguish it, but anxiously turned the handle too far. The water came out of the tap with such force that it blasted the cinders from the dish, washing them down the drain. "Augh," cried Cambien, grasping vainly after them.

Dismayed, he turned the water off. Sweat ran into his eyes, his breath came hard, and his fingertips smarted where he had burned them. He got a glass of water and sat in a chair. He took two of the small, yellow pills from the case he always carried and swallowed them.

Half an hour later, he walked sedately to the taverna in the village. He ordered a late supper for himself, chatting with the proprietor as he ate. In the back corner, he saw two of the old man's black-eyed sons sitting with some other men, watching him. He nodded at them and they nodded back. He knew they would tell their father that they had seen him eating in the taverna, and that the old man would again wonder at his refusal to stay for dinner. But it couldn't be helped.

He went back to his little house, took his Anadreme, and went to sleep, curled up tight, longing for Maggie.

Immediately upon awakening in the pale light of early morning, he checked his watch. She would be asleep now.

Again, he started the incense and prepared to meditate over it. He was worried, because he had nothing of hers to add to the burn, and he was so very far away. He was not sure he would be able to find her. But he was driven to try.

He breathed slowly and deeply, opened his mind, and rose with the ascending smoke.

The blue world swam in a mist before him, and he began to move in what he hoped was the right direction. Water sped beneath him, and still more water, featureless and colorless in the gloom. He could not get his bearings. He let go and drifted higher, trying to gain perspective. But the higher he rose, the more indistinct the earth became, a suggestion of a presence under its blue-grey mantle of atmosphere. He began to move purposefully in one direction, then another, faster and faster. He descended closer to the earth, seeing again only endless ocean. Frantically, he sped towards the darkness.

At long last, the water yielded to solid ground, but something was wrong. He sensed frozen mountains, ice, and an empty wasteland. He tried to recall whatever geography he could. Perhaps he was too far south? He guessed at a northerly direction and began to move at a great rate of speed. Soon he was over water again, with no landmarks or features. This was hopeless. "Maggie!" he called into the vacuum.

He felt himself losing altitude and saw the misted world below him fading into oblivion. Powerless, he closed his eyes and let go, as directionless as he had been in the lightless cave the old man had once shown him.

He opened his eyes. He was sitting on the floor of his tiny house, the sun streaming in the windows behind him and warming his back. In front of him, in the small dish, the last ember flickered out.

22.

When Monday arrived, Maggie dragged herself to work. As she waited for the elevator, she overheard Jill telling someone that Cambien was out of town until Thursday. Only then did she realize how on-edge she had been, anxious about the next face-to-face encounter she would have with him. She understood that she had actually been feeling fear at the prospect.

At her desk, she struggled to work on her story about the plant in St. Louis but found it was impossible to compose an article. Instead, she pulled up a report she had to edit for Dr. Rajagopalan, mechanically proofreading while her mind wandered.

Vicky. Gone. And what a horrible person she had been at the last, refusing Vicky's friendship out of jealousy, choosing instead to conduct a pointless fantasy of a relationship. The thought of Cambien intruded and she felt apprehensive. She supposed he would seek her out to commiserate over this tragedy with when he returned from wherever he was. This prospect made her extremely uncomfortable.

By lunchtime, she had given up trying to be productive. She drove to Vicky's house and parked in the driveway, half hoping to see her friend outside, watering the garden in one of her sleeveless summer dresses, smiling a greeting from under her unruly blond curls. But of course, the garden was empty, the flowers already wilting from lack of care in the late-summer heat. The house presented that terrible stillness that tells, with finality, that the owner no longer resides there.

Washing dishes in the kitchen that night, Rowan asked her how she was doing. She told him that she hadn't accomplished a thing all day; that trying to focus on dull scientific research reports and FDA requirements was torturous in the face of her loss.

"How did your boss take it?" He did not look up from the pan he was scrubbing as he asked.

"I have no idea. He's out of town until Thursday. For all I know, he doesn't even know yet. But God, I really don't feel like going over it with him." She closed the door of the dishwasher, turned it on, and left the room.

Rowan set the clean pan in the dish rack to dry. Perhaps Cuthbert didn't even know yet, eh? Well, as a personal acquaintance of the man, he would be sure to volunteer at work to make the notification. Surely Cuthbert would prefer to hear the news from a friend.

Thursday afternoon, Rowan called his wife to say he would be late and not to hold up dinner. Mike did the same, and the two men went Mooney's after their shift ended. They ate burgers and drank beer and shot the breeze with the other cops and retired guys. A little after seven, they left the bar, got into Rowan's car, and drove off.

It was a little tricky, locating Cambien's address—he kept his information unlisted and private, which was not uncommon among the town's wealthy and celebrated—but the police have ways of finding these things out.

They drove up the long driveway as the twilight came on, noting that the lights were on in the house and a sports car was parked in the driveway. Rowan parked just behind it, right up against the bumper. The two men went up onto the porch and rang the doorbell.

After several minutes, Cambien opened the door. He looked genuinely surprised to see them, though more irritated than unnerved. "Hello Rowan, Mike. What brings you here?" His voice was terse.

"Good evening, Dr. Cuthbert. Can we have a few words with you?" Rowan asked.

Cambien silently stepped aside, opening the door wider so the men could enter.

Rowan and Mike walked past him and into the entry hall, taking in details as they went—the pile of mail still on the table, the bags dropped at the bottom of the stairs—clearly, the man hadn't been home from his trip more than an hour or two.

"Is this a social visit or an official one?" Cambien closed the door and turned to face them.

"A little of both," Rowan said. "Is there someplace we can sit down?"

Cambien had no intention of allowing the uninvited detectives into the recesses of his home. He decided to curtail the intrusion. "If you've come to tell me about Vicky, I already know."

Mike and Rowan seemed surprised. "Oh, we didn't know you knew. How did you hear about it?" Mike asked.

"I just saw it in the paper."

"You seem to be taking it pretty well," Rowan observed.

"What do you want me to do? Slit my wrists?" Cambien could tell by the set of the imbecile's jaw that he was becoming angry. "Listen, Rowan, we're all men here, so I will speak freely." Enjoying himself now, he began to smirk. "There are two kinds of women; those you marry and those you fuck," he said in a poisonous voice. "I think we all know what kind Vicky was."

Rowan had interviewed all manner of despicable people during his career and had long ago learned to do it without emotion. However, his hand now shot out of its own volition, clutching Cambien's shirt tightly at the neck and thrusting up into his throat. "You shut your mouth, you son of a bitch. She was my daughter's Godmother," he spat through clenched teeth.

Mike stood by impassively, wearing the dim expression he adopted for interviews. Rowan and Cambien glared at each other a moment more before Rowan released his grip. Cambien stepped back and drew in a raspy breath, rubbing his throat with one hand. "I think you gentlemen will understand if I ask you to leave now," he growled. He turned and opened the door again.

Rowan, who had hoped to trip him up somehow and had instead lost control, began to storm out the door. Level with Cambien, he stopped and faced him once more. "You know, Doctor, turns out there weren't any skid marks at the scene."

Cambien kept his gaze locked on Rowan's, the smirk back on his face. "Entirely consistent with an alcohol-related crash, as you well know" he drawled. "Face it, she was a hopeless drunk. It was bound to happen sooner or later."

Rowan turned and went out. Mike followed, saying, "You're welcome for the notification," as he went.

As they walked across the lawn, Mike's face returned to its normal, astute expression. "That's your wife's boss, right?"

Rowan answered in a clipped syllable. "Yup."

"You gonna tell her what a charmer he is?"

"Nope." The men got into the car and slammed their doors. Rowan turned his head to look out the rear window as he backed out of the gravel drive. "She gets defensive when I tell her to be careful of him. She already knows how I feel." On the cul de sac pavement, he shifted gears and drove forward, away from the genteel-looking Victorian house. "Anyway, I think she's starting to figure it out for herself."

Very early the following morning, while it was still dark out, Dr. Rajagopalan lay awake. Unfinished lab work filled his mind and he was unable to get back to sleep. This happened to him from time to time; he believed it had to do with age. After watching his wife sleep for a few minutes, he decided he might as well get up and go to the office.

Arriving in the gray dawn, he proceeded to his lab. He walked through the office area that he shared with Maggie and directly to the back of the large room. On the far side of a set of equipment-laden shelving, he set his laptop on a counter. Soon, he was diligently reading and transcribing notes.

Half an hour passed quickly as he immersed himself in his work. Then his concentration was broken by furtive noises from the office area. Curious, he peered around the column next to the counter he was working on. He couldn't see much at first, as he had neglected to turn on the lights in that part of the lab when he came in. But a movement attracted his eye and he could just make out, in the dim early morning light through the windows, the lofty form of his employer, Dr. Cuthbert, walking to the back of Maggie's desk. His actions were stealthy. Dr. Rajagopalan felt the hairs on the back of his neck stand up. He held his breath and watched.

Maggie kept a sweater, a shabby old cardigan, hanging on the back of her chair for days when the office air conditioning was too chilly. Dr. Cuthbert now bent down to this sweater and buried his face in it, holding it up in his hands and breathing in deeply. He seemed almost to be drawing sustenance from the garment. Dr. Rajagopalan's lip curled involuntarily.

Now Dr. Cuthbert had taken a small, plastic bag from a pocket and was examining the sweater. He spent a few minutes collecting something from it and dropping whatever it was into the bag.

A distant noise from the far end of the hall carried into the room, signifying the first employees arriving for work. Dr. Cuthbert straightened.

Dr. Rajagopalan leaned back again, concealing himself behind the pillar. Motionless, he listened intently until he heard footsteps leaving the room. He peeked from behind the column and was relieved to see that the office was empty once again.

Several hours later, Cambien again entered the lab's office and Dr. Rajagopalan again observed him, apparently unremarked by him. Although Dr. Rajagopalan was this time working at his own desk, Cambien spared him not a glance. He strode directly to Maggie's side, perched himself on the edge of her desk, and looked down meaningfully at her. In a honeyed voice of compassion and concern, he asked, "How are you doing, Maggie?"

Dr. Rajagopalan had thought Maggie was sad and distracted lately. But he was pleased to notice, from the corner of his eye, that she seemed annoyed rather than comforted by Dr. Cuthbert's cloying attentions, although she remained polite.

"I guess I'm doing alright," she answered. "A little numb, still. It probably hasn't really set in all the way, you know?" She gathered herself. "Are you okay? You were out of town when it happened, weren't you?"

Cambien looked sadly at his own hands, clasped on his thigh. "Actually, I hadn't left town yet. She...she had said she might drop by that evening. I guess that's why she was in North Stamford at all. If only I had told her to stay home, that the weather was just too awful. I guess I feel responsible somehow..." He trailed off, hanging his head in a posture of guilty torment.

Maggie sighed. "Don't be ridiculous, Cambien, of course you aren't responsible for what happened. That's why they call them *accidents*—no one did anything on purpose." He gazed out from beneath dark brows at her. "Really. Don't beat yourself up about it. It's awful enough without heaping more misery on it." She looked quickly at her computer as her eyes filled.

He laid a soothing hand on her shoulder. Before she could stop herself, she flinched, but he paid no notice. "I'm so sorry you've lost your friend, Maggie."

"I'll be all right," she said in a shaky voice. She stared stubbornly at her screen.

"Maggie," he said insistently, simultaneously giving her shoulder a squeeze and causing her to look up at him. Her eyes blazed with pique but again, he didn't acknowledge it. "Maggie, I want you to promise you'll come to me if you need to talk about it, okay? Just come right to my office. Anytime."

"Okay, I promise," she said quickly, desperate for him to leave her alone. He was making her skin crawl.

But he held her gaze one moment longer. He spoke in a voice that was a study of solemnity. "Don't forget, I loved her, too." With one last, poignant look into her eyes, he released her shoulder. "Take care of yourself, okay?" He conjured up his rueful smile as he stood. Then he turned and left the room.

Maggie rubbed her shoulder where his hand had held her. Her teeth were clenched. Suddenly self-conscious, she turned to see if

Dr. Rajagopalan had watched their interaction. The scientist was staring out the doorway through which Cambien had just exited, his lip curled back in instinctive loathing. He seemed more unsettled by Cambien than she had just been.

He met Maggie's gaze, but his expression remained distant. "We had such a one in my village. I remember when I was a boy," he said. His accent was heavier than usual but without its musical cadence; instead, he spoke in dark, quiet tones. "Filthy night demons."

Maggie shivered. She was surprised to hear such superstitious rubbish from the mouth of a scientist like Dr. Rajagopalan. She was more surprised at her own acceptance of his words.

~~~~

Maggie was making sandwiches at her desk. No matter how carefully she spread the jam on the bread, it managed to get all over her neatly printed reports. She was further distracted because the carp lake, which belonged in the Vale town park, had laid its shores inside her office where the windows used to be, and Charlie and Hazel were playing at its edge. "Kids, please come away from the water. It's steep there and you could fall in," she called distractedly over her shoulder.

She looked up as Cambien entered the lab door. He could see that she didn't want to talk to him. "What are you doing here—"

Maggie, just hear me out," he interrupted. She said nothing but continued to look at him, so he went on quickly. "I don't think you've thought this through. I mean, look at yourself—are you really happy like this?"

She looked at her hands, now covered in a paste of peanut butter and jam that stuck together like epoxy, gumming her fingers. She gasped as she realized she was also wearing her dingiest, oldest nightgown. Behind her, she heard Hazel bullying her brother, who began to cry. "Knock it off, Hazel," she yelled at the child.

Looking back at her desk, she saw that a report she had printed out was ruined with jelly stains and her keyboard was clogged with crumbs that had lodged themselves between the keys. Tears of frustration blurred her vision, and she would not meet Cambien's eyes.

He spoke rapidly. "I just want to make sure you have given full consideration to what I have to offer. I'm offering you the freedom to be you. And I am offering you a love that places you above all else; my work, my company, my life, everything." He said the last word in a whisper, then paused a moment. "Maggie," he said, commandingly this time. She looked into his mesmerizing eyes in spite of herself. "You cannot deny that, during the times we've been together, I have been the most exciting, the most satisfying man you've ever known."

She could not deny it, nor would she admit it. Instead, she flung back something he had said to her the first time they had met spectrally. "Cambien, do you know what this is? It's a dream. It's not real. It's all in my head. But I am a real person, with a real life and a real family, and I'm not going to throw it all away for a stupid dream." He saw that she was adamant. "I don't care how good the sex was, it was imaginary sex. It means nothing."

His black eyes bore dolefully into her. "And the love you had for me? Was that also imaginary?"

She knew it was imperative to answer decisively. "Yes," she said, with all the conviction she could muster.

Yet his smile told her he thought otherwise, and that he was not above pressing his advantage. She found his expression unnerving. But something distracted her. It was the gentle lapping sound of wavelets at the edge of the lake. How could she hear such a soft sound? It was so quiet . . .

She spun frantically, but the sloping, grassy shore behind her was empty, the lake surface rippling placidly beyond it. "Kids!" she screamed. "Hazel! Charlie!" She looked all about, but could not sight them. She turned to Cambien. "Look what you've done! I was supposed to be watching them."

"I'm sure they're fine," he said in a soothing tone.

"Shut up, you freak! Just get away from me!" She turned and ran down the bank, plunging into the lake water. It came up to her chest and was freezing cold. "Kids," she screamed at the silent lake surface. She pounded the surface of the black water with her gummed hands, peering desperately into it, her wet gown wrapping around her legs as she floundered about. "Kids!"

And then Cambien was alone in Maggie's version of her office, her ruined desk and the lake beyond it quiet. She had woken herself.

On Monday morning, Jill stood before Cambien's desk, apprising him of his schedule for the day. Seated, he looked up at her as she read his appointments.

" . . . Then at 2:30, you have that budget meeting with Frank. You should be done by 3:30, and you're free for half an hour." He watched her as she managed his time, pleased. She had a machine-like efficiency and a coolly professional manner. She had a mind like a computer, capable of plotting and tracking appointments and retrieving needed data effortlessly.

"At four, Maggie Moore wants a word with you, and at four-thirty—"

"Maggie? What does she want, did she say?"

Jill looked at her notes. "She wants to review a draft of the newsletter with you."

"Ah. Okay. And then?" But he wasn't really listening as Jill detailed his last appointments of the day. Maggie was coming to see him, of her own accord. A draft of the newsletter could easily be placed in his inbox or emailed for his comments. But she preferred to present it in person. A smile spread behind his folded hands.

At four o'clock sharp, Maggie stood in his office doorway. "Hello?" she said uncertainly.

Cambien looked up from the papers he had been pretending to study. "Hello, Maggie. Please come in." He stood and came around his desk to greet her. "How are you holding up, old friend?" He met her as she stepped into the room, wrapped her in an affectionate hug, and pressed her head against his broad chest. He did this in just such a way, with the door left wide open, as to be above impropriety. He felt her stiffen and tremble slightly in his arms.

She half-returned the hug long enough to be polite, then disengaged from him. "I'm doing okay, really. Thanks for asking."

"Me, too. Soldiering on." Maggie made no reply. "Jill says you have something for me to review. Come, let's go over it." He pulled one of the chairs from in front of the desk around to the back, next to his, as they had used to sit when they had been at their most familiar. He sat in his own leather chair and patted the empty seat of the one beside him.

She did not join him behind the desk. Instead, she walked to the front of it and laid several sheets of paper before him. "I'm not going to take up a lot of your time," she said quietly. He noticed that her hand shook as she laid the papers down and he silently congratulated himself on the powerful effect he had on her nerves. Soon he would wear her down. No woman could withstand him forever. "This is the first draft of the newsletter. I'll just leave it with you and you can let me know when you have it marked up."

Cambien was confused. He looked up flirtatiously from beneath dark brows. "And for this, you made an appointment to see me? To drop something off?" Dimples deepened around his grin.

"No, not just this. There's something else . . ." She seemed quite nervous as she laid another sheet of paper on top of the others. Cambien glanced at it and saw the first sentence, then his mind refused to contemplate it further.

Maggie spoke over the silence. "I wanted to give you this in person because I wanted you to know how really, truly grateful I am for the opportunity you've given me." Her voice was shaky as she rushed through her prepared remarks. "And I wanted to assure you that I will complete this last assignment in a professional manner—"

"You can't just do this, you know," he growled, cutting her off. His eyes blazed with wrath as he looked up at her. She gasped and took a step back. He swept from behind the desk and went to the door in one smooth movement. Closing it, he turned to face Maggie, who had spun to watch his progress. He stepped towards her, seeming taller and more formidable than ever. Maggie retreated until the desk halted her.

"Don't think you can waltz in here, hand me a piece of paper, and just *end* this," he snarled.

He saw she was struggling to maintain her composure. She made a conscious attempt to straighten her spine, though she looked as though she might cry at any moment. "Cambien, I— I'm not sure what you want me to say. I need to stop working for a while. I'm so sorry, but I'm going through a really hard time right now. I just can't concentrate and do the job properly."

"Come on, Maggie, we both know we're not talking about the job right now. This is because of what happened in St. Louis, right?"

She blinked up at him, but would not give him control over the conversation. "No, it has nothing to do with that," she insisted. "I'm just—"

"It has everything to do with that!" he roared. Maggie shrank again from him, and again she willed herself to straighten up and face him. But now she no longer argued, only returned his gaze defiantly.

He approached to within inches of her, close enough to seize her, but his arms stayed at his sides, his hands clenched into fists. Instead, he bore into her with an enraged stare. "This is a complete joke, you know. You can resign from your little job, and you can scurry home to your little *family*," (the last word was pronounced with undisguised contempt), "but this is by no means over." He was breathing hard and his face was red. Maggie trembled with fear but kept her gaze locked on his. "Really, Maggie, do you think you can go as far as we've gone and then just–poof! Make it all disappear?"

His words gave her an eerie feeling. "What on earth are you talking about, Cambien? As far as we've gone? We haven't gone anywhere. Just one loopy, drunken, flirtatious dinner. That's hardly an involved affair."

He was enraged anew by her words. "How do you stand there and lie to my face?" he hissed. "There's almost nothing we haven't done at this point, Maggie. The first time we made love, in the clearing in the woods behind your house—it was windy, and there was a full moon—remember? Or the time you came to me on that wild horse, primly pretending to fight me when you were begging me for it—remember that one, Maggie? How we were both drenched with rain?"

Maggie's eyes widened until they were perfectly round. Her hand became a fist, which she stuffed into her mouth in horror. She felt as though the floor had dropped out from under her, the room was closing in on her. He was overwhelming her. "This is impossible," she whispered. "How could you possibly know these things?"

"How do you think I know these things?" A note of triumph was in his voice. "*Because I was there, Maggie.*"

Her mind reeled, unable to process what he was saying. "But that's impossible," she repeated, clinging desperately to what she knew of the world. "I don't believe you."

"Will you stand here now, look me in the eye, and tell me that you never loved me?"

She pushed past him, stumbling towards the door. She needed to get out of the room, away from him.

"Maggie," he called as she reached the door. She stopped, against her will, listening. "You can't deny that you saw our child. I showed her to you, as we lay in bed, and you loved her too."

How the hell did he know these things? Without looking back, she opened the door and fled the room.

23.

Rowan got home late, after dinner but before the children were asleep. He went upstairs to spend some time with them while Maggie fixed a plate for him.

When he came into the living room, Maggie had the television on and his supper was on the coffee table. There was a cold bottle of beer for each of them. She smiled at him briefly before returning her gaze to the screen, but it was a nervous smile, and he was fairly certain she wasn't really paying attention to the television.

He sat beside her on the couch, glancing at her profile before taking up his plate. "How did the big resignation go?" He ate a forkful of three-bean salad.

Maggie looked straight ahead. "Oh, not very well. I'm not going back tomorrow."

Rowan gave a low whistle. "That well, huh?"

"Dr. Rajagopalan wasn't too bad. He was a little annoyed at first, but he understood. And it helped that I had the name of a temp agency ready for him. They should be able to find him a new proofreader pretty quick."

Rowan munched thoughtfully. "What about your old school chum? How did he take it?" He saw her jaw clench and unclench before she answered.

"That was the part that didn't go so well. He actually got really angry. I thought he would understand; he was close to Vicky, too. But, I don't know, he just . . . he didn't take it very well."

"You know he has the hots for you, right?"

Maggie jumped where she sat, blanched, looked at Rowan in shock, and became quite flustered. "What on earth are you talking about? For God's sake, Rowan, he was my boss. And he was dating Vicky. They were really serious, there's no way he could have been, you know..."

"I'm just saying." He looked at the television and ate a large forkful of cold chicken, letting the matter drop while he chewed. He took a swallow of beer and spoke again. "We want to keep Charlie in pre-K, right?"

"Yes, if you think we can swing it. I think it would be best for him, at least a few days a week. He has his little friends and all the other kids go to pre-K. I don't want him to be the only kid in Kindergarten who doesn't know his alphabet."

"Yeah, we can swing it. I'll sign up for some side jobs, no big deal."

"I'll try to get it together and start working again as soon as I can." She looked miserable but determined as she said it.

He put his arm around her shoulders, pulled her close, kissed the top of her head. "Don't worry about it, babe. You take your time, get over your grief. We'll be fine. We're not in bad shape to begin with."

"Thanks, Rowan." Maggie swallowed the rest of her beer, but it did nothing to calm her nerves. "If it's all the same to you, I'm going to go to bed."

"By all means." Rowan pushed back from his empty plate, holding his beer on his stomach and flipping through the channels.

Maggie took the dishes into the kitchen and went upstairs. Thankfully, both the children were asleep. She had had a trying evening, forcing herself to behave normally for her family.

Already disturbed by the abrupt end to her fantasy affair, Maggie had been deeply upset by Vicky's death and was only beginning her grieving. Rowan had assumed that her emotional state and shaky nerves were due entirely to her loss, and she had not corrected him. In fact, she had gone so far as to use it for an excuse for leaving her job. Rowan had agreed that she should take some time off, to get back on her feet. She suspected he had some lingering guilt for the long emotional desertion he had put her and the children through, and that suited her purpose.

The truth was that she needed space, as much space as a person who lived with her husband and children could carve out for herself, to exorcise herself of her fantasy lover, her broken heart, and her guilt over the entire affair. And now, added to this already daunting task, was the horrifying puzzle of Cambien apparently having been inside her head, somehow present, as she had indulged in her fantasy. And worse, he had promised her that it was not over.

She changed into a nightgown and, restless, went to sit by the open window. A soft breeze cooled her face as she stared out into the blackness. She could not shake the sense of dread that had descended upon her.

She understood her fantasizing to have been of two varieties: daydreams, which she had dictated and controlled completely, and nighttime dreams, which had been unpredictable and wild, and had felt vivid and true.

When Cambien had described her fantasies to her, he had been talking about nighttime dreams, as accurately as if he had indeed been present. Unable to explain his cognizance in any logical way, she reluctantly began to entertain the possibility that, somehow, he had been an actual participant in her dreams.

What if it was true? What if Cambien was some sort of incubus, and she had really been united with him in some incorporeal way? She knew this sounded like madness, and yet . . . what if?

The fragile forgiveness she had contrived for herself, based as it was on the presumption that she had not technically committed adultery, collapsed under the weight of this possibility. She felt her stomach wrench as it struck her anew that she had been unfaithful, maybe even more than she knew.

And there was also the hackle-raising fear of this new threat to her and her family. What if Cambien really could access her mind while she slept? And what if he was true to his word and refused to let it end? How could she ever stop him? She certainly couldn't forego sleep for the rest of her life.

Worst of all, she dreaded that, somehow, Rowan would find out what she had done. She thought of how her faithlessness would hurt him and she wanted to pull her hair from her head in agitation. *Damn you, Cambien! Why did you do this to me?* she railed inside her mind.

An hour passed before she heard her husband turn off the television and start up the stairs. Quietly, she crept into bed. She feigned sleep when he eventually joined her, opening her eyes again only when she heard his breathing become deep and rhythmic.

Propped up on her elbow, Maggie watched Rowan's sleeping face in the darkness of their room. He lay on his side next to her, his eyes closed, his breath coming regularly, the warmth of his body embracing her. She thought of the qualities he had that had made her fall in love with him in the first place: the way he knew right from wrong; his fearlessness; how he always knew what to do; the way he made her feel safe. Surely there was no better place than here, in their bed, with her strong, brave husband beside her, for her to sleep.

She looked at the bedside clock and saw that it was past midnight. Exhaustion dragged heavily at her. Unable to stay awake any longer, she lay as close against Rowan as she could. She draped her arm over his shoulder, drawing comfort from his broad and sturdy back. Sleep overcame her.

Cambien appeared instantly. Maggie sat up and saw him standing by the side of the bed. Fast as lightning, he had slashed Rowan's throat with a short, triangular-bladed knife. Maggie screamed as she saw her husband's blood spurt onto his assailant. Rowan jerked several times but never opened his eyes. Then he became still.

Cambien turned his blazing black eyes on Maggie, his face a demonic, blood-spattered mask of murderous lust. As sometimes happens in one's worst nightmares, she found herself paralyzed. He crawled over Rowan's body and straddled her, leering into her wide eyes.

"How's it going, Maggie? Long time no see." He grinned, his teeth white against the deep flush of his face. He put his hand on her, cupping her breast.

Maggie could not make a sound, nor could she pull her gaze from his eyes. The tumultuous panic in her mind began to crystallize into a command: *fight him*. By a supreme act of will, she regained the use of her arms. She reached up and clawed at his face, trying to reach his shining eyes.

He easily captured her hands and held them over her head. "Come, now, Maggie. That's no way to treat your lover." He lowered his head and closed his lips over hers, his tongue trying to force its way into her mouth. She tasted Rowan's blood. A convulsion ran through her body. Freed from the mesmerizing power of Cambien's eyes, she thrashed wildly, trying to buck him off, kick him, bite him, do anything at all to repel him.

Rowan was calling her. He wasn't dead after all. "Maggie!"

"Rowan! Help," she screamed, her words lost in Cambien's relentless mouth.

Now Rowan's hands were on her as well, gripping her shoulder and shaking her. "Maggie, wake up. It's okay."

Suddenly, mercifully, Cambien was gone. His weight removed from her belly, Maggie was able to breathe and move freely. She sat up quickly, her eyes wide in the dark. To her immense relief, Rowan sat beside her, his hand still on her shoulder. "Are you all right?" he asked.

"Oh, Rowan." She flung her arms around him, collapsing against his chest. Tears flowed from her eyes and she sniffed as her nose ran.

He supported her with one arm, stroking her hair. "Wow, that must have been a hell of a nightmare."

"The worst."

He held her as relief seeped through her body. But still, she was not comforted. A dream, yes, and no harm done: but only the first of many dreams, endless nightmares, for the rest of her life until she was stark, raving mad.

Maggie lifted her head to see the clock. Eight minutes had passed since she last looked at it. Cambien must have been waiting for her to lose consciousness, attacking the moment her mind wandered in sleep.

Rowan yawned against the top of her head. She reached up and kissed him. "You go back to sleep. I'm going to go watch TV for a while."

"You sure?" He was already lying down again, his eyes closing.

"Yeah. I don't feel like sleeping right now. Anyway, it's not like I have to go to work tomorrow. I can always take a nap."

"'kay," he mumbled.

Maggie went down to the living room and turned on every light. She sank into the sofa and turned on the television. The night had become chilly, a harbinger of fall, but she ignored the throw draped on the arm of a chair. If being cold could help her stay awake, then she would be cold.

But staying awake forever was not an option. And the longer she put off sleep, the weaker her mind would become. She needed to figure out a course of action and she needed to do it fast.

Accepting as a fact the improbable notion that Cambien could visit her dreams, Maggie began to wonder how he did it. Was he awake or asleep, or did it matter? Could he do it while he did something else? Maggie was willing to bet he couldn't. She could try napping during the day, when she knew him to be at work. Of course, this was not a permanent solution—how would she explain her new, vampiric schedule to her family? What quality of life would they have?—but it could get her through this crisis, until she could figure out something better.

She sat resolutely through the watches of the night. At six, she went into the kitchen and started a pot of coffee. An hour and a half later she was sitting at the kitchen table, having breakfast with the children. Rowan came into the room, dressed for work. He got a mug of coffee and stood contemplating his wife as he drank it. Her eyes were glassy, her hair limp and greasy-looking, her complexion pale.

"You look like crap," he said.

Hazel and Charlie looked at each other and giggled. "Daddy said a bad word, Daddy said a bad word," Hazel chanted.

"Okay, Hazel, that's enough," Maggie said quietly. She stood and went to her husband, holding him around the waist and laying her head on his chest. "I feel like crap, too. I'll take the kids to daycare and try to get a nap."

Rowan kissed the top of her head. "Okay. I'll call later to check up on you."

⌒⌐

"Jill, cancel my nine-thirty and take my calls for me. I need to concentrate for an hour."

"Certainly, Dr. Cuthbert. Just give me a buzz when you're ready for people again."

"Thank you, Jill." Cambien punched a button on the desk phone and leaned back in his chair.

He felt bad about the night before. He hadn't meant to scare Maggie so badly; God knows he never wished to cause her any sort of distress. It was just that he had been so angry, so frustrated. Yet he smiled as he remembered slicing her husband's neck and watching him die. His unconscious, passive role in Maggie's dream was pleasing to Cambien; it told him that she hadn't confided in her husband about his visits with her. It was their little secret. True lovers always kept one another's confidence. Maggie's loyalty touched him.

Nonetheless, she had stayed away for the remainder of the night and he couldn't blame her, but she must be exhausted by now. If he knew Maggie (and he flattered himself that he did), she would see the fool she was married to off to work, take the maggots to daycare, then go back home and have a nap.

Right about now.

Maggie lay on the sofa, fear and weariness battling one another. Eventually, weariness prevailed and her eyes closed.

Cambien was with her, holding her in gentle arms. The old, plaid sofa had become a simple bed on an iron frame, dressed in striped cotton sheeting and piled with cushions, on which they reclined. She looked around and saw that they were in a whitewashed room. The marble tiled floor was overlaid with woolen rugs. A wall of French doors was thrown open to reveal a small, pebbly beach, an opaque sea, and the red sun setting over distant hilly islands on the horizon. Unseen wind chimes floated winsome notes on the evening air. Small waves breaking on the beach made the only other sound. The setting was the most lovely she had ever seen. A feeling of deep peace and contentment suffused her as powerfully as a drug.

Yet in spite of the restive scene, vague memories of the previous night's horror began to pierce her calm and she tried to move from Cambien's arms. "Shhh," he said, holding her firmly. With one hand, he stroked her hair back from her face, and she felt strangely soothed. She knew she should get away from here, but it was so beautiful, and she was so tired.

Cambien spoke soft and low in her ear. "Feeling better?"

She nodded in spite of herself.

"It's okay now. Things didn't go so well last night, so I thought we'd try my place instead. You like it?"

Another nod.

He spoke even more quietly, almost whispering. "I'm glad you like it, because this is where we'll live, as soon as you say yes. Just you and me, no one to bother us, and all the time in the world." Maggie's clouded mind was steadily becoming seduced by the tempting vision. She wanted nothing more. "And when you're ready, we'll make a baby . . ."

The picture he painted seemed to be the most appealing thing she could imagine. The fear had left her. She marveled at feeling relaxed and well again. She turned her face to Cambien and he looked radiantly attractive. He smiled at her and she found herself smiling back. Slowly, he moved closer and kissed her gently. It was a kiss of profound love, a promise. Maggie's eyes closed as she fell into a rapturous trance. She wanted to stay here forever.

One of the wind chimes had become annoyingly loud, disrupting her reverie. It rang repeatedly, louder and longer each time. She opened her eyes to see Cambien's face contorted with rage, just before he vanished. The serene room, the glowing beach, and the distant hilly islands all went with him.

She was alone on the plaid couch and the phone in the kitchen was ringing.

She leapt from the sofa as though it were full of snakes and did a quick jig of revulsion. Running to the kitchen, she caught the phone on the fourth ring. It was Rowan, calling to check up on her as he had promised.

"Thank God you called," she said, still disoriented. Stars popped before her eyes and the sunlight streaming through the windows hurt.

"Why? What's wrong?"

"Well, n-nothing's wrong, really. I was just . . . just having a nightmare. I'm glad you woke me up."

"Another one? Yeesh. You know, as someone once suggested to me, maybe you should get some help with your situation."

"Rowan, you're a genius. That's exactly what I'll do."

Maggie fixed her hair and drove to her doctor's office. Without an appointment, she sat in the waiting room until the doctor had time to see her. She did not leave until she had a prescription for Anadreme in her hand.

In the fading afternoon sunlight, Cambien stood on the bank of the herring stream. There would be no procreative migration at this time of year, but simply being in this place invigorated him. He stood still as a tree, gazing into the rushing current. He pictured the mass of sleek silver bodies hurtling upstream. Drawn by an ancient design beyond their ken or affect, they were bound to fulfill their purpose. So it had always been, so it would always be.

And so were he and Maggie bound. He was closer than ever to winning her. A few more nights of harrowing sleep disruption (which he would feel bad about putting her through, but which would all be worth it in the end), a few more visions of their idyllic life-to-be, and she would be ready to surrender.

But there was one more thing he needed to do, to turn her his way. He must perform an act that would change her profoundly, join her to him irrevocably. He must visit her fate upon her so that she could no longer deny it and, being transfigured, would come to him willingly.

They were now at a point when he needed to take action. While their metaphysical bond worked steadily to win her heart and soul to him, it could not touch her body. What was needed now was actual, physical contact.

And for that, he needed to see the old man again.

Cambien's travel manager was a miracle worker. She arranged to get his plane winging for Greece that very evening.

By the following afternoon, he was again hiking up the winding path between olive groves and rock outcroppings, the scent of crushed wild thyme wafting up from his footfalls, the gentle sounds of bleating sheep and brass bells drifting on the hot air. The brightness of the sea and the sky dazzled his eyes as the deafening buzz of the cicadas filled his ears.

He was escorted to the terrace beneath the grape arbor by three of the dark-eyed sons, Nikos and two others. The old man scrutinized him as Cambien sat across the wooden table from him.

"Why you are here so soon? You were just here, eh?"

The dispensation of formality made Cambien smile. "It's good to see you, too, old friend."

"Yes, yes, it is always nice to see you. But sometimes you go six months, a year without coming to the island. Now you come every week?" Finally, a spark of humor entered the canny blue eyes. "To what do I owe the pleasure of your visit?"

"That's more like it," Cambien chided playfully. He paused to take a sip of wine from the glass that had just been placed before him. "Mm, excellent. Delicious as always."

The old man continued to watch him as he joined him for a drink. The American sleep doctor behaved affably and seemed healthy and confident, but there was an unmistakable note of urgency behind his casual words. And the briefness between his visits was certainly suspect. He wanted something, and he wanted it badly. The old man's eyes narrowed shrewdly.

After a half hour of sitting, drinking wine, and mellowing in the bucolic atmosphere, Cambien broached the point of his visit. "I have been, as always, most happy with your product. It has performed perfectly on every occasion that I have used it. And I have also always been grateful to you for the things you've taught me. You have opened a world of mind expansion and spirituality to me that most people are not even aware exists."

The old man nodded for him to go on.

"You know that I am a scientist, a researcher, an inventor. That's what I do. It's what I am. My mind is always hungry for more knowledge, for new things to try and new experiences to learn from. I think you are the same way, and so you can understand what I feel."

The old man admired the touch of flattery Cambien had woven into his sales pitch—*you and I are the same, and only you are capable of understanding.* Nicely done. He nodded again, waiting for the kernel of the conversation to be revealed.

"The last time I was here —"

"Last week, eh?" The old man chuckled.

"Yes, just last week—you sold me what you've always sold me, but you let me see that you have other products in your cabinet. At the time, you told me that you would not sell any of it to me, that it was still experimental."

"Yes, I have been working to develop two new formulations." Perhaps the American was right, they were quite similar after all, both inventing ways of mastering reality as they did. A surge of pride struck him; he, a simple island man, crafting concoctions that brought the most educated doctors and scientists of the world to him. He allowed himself to brag a little. "In fact, I have perfected at least one of them."

Cambien leaned towards the old man, his look becoming more intense. "I knew you would, and I know what it does. Yes, I have figured it out. And as you have no doubt surmised, that is the reason for my visit today. I must have some."

The silver-haired man considered this. He was yet overwhelmed by his own success with the new incense and rather in awe of its power. He had not shared it with anyone. It was true that the man who sat across the table from him was his brightest pupil, possessed of both a superior intellect and ability, and would doubtless be successful at using it. But he also had another, indefinable quality, something like ambition or a barely-suppressed ruthlessness, that gave the elder pause. He experienced an odd, anxious sensation, as though he were staring into the eyes of a desperate and dangerous addict. His heart thudded painfully in his chest, though he was sitting still.

Now he regretted bragging that the product was perfected and ready to use. "I have not yet decided whether I will make this new one available to anyone . . ." he began.

The American reached into his pocket and laid a large bundle of money on the table between them. The old man stared at it longer than he ordinarily would have done, shocked by the amount.

Cambien spoke in a voice of solemn respect. "You must know how I feel. I am starving for new experience. I want only to learn from it and to use what I learn to invent better medicines, to help more people. I swear to you that I will honor your invention. There is no one besides you who can make these things." He drew the old man's gaze from the wad of cash to his own, bottomless, black eyes. He said finally, simply, "please."

The combination of the large sum of cash and the humble solicitation of the powerful businessman finally overcame the elder's reservations. Abruptly he stood, picked up the money, and shoved it deep into his pocket. He smiled broadly. "Come."

24.

Charlie had all his machines out. Bright yellow, orange and black, they covered half the living room floor. Legos, wooden houses and tiny plastic people were chaotically laid out to represent what could only be a gigantic construction site.

Charlie was deep into a Big Machine phase. He played with his dump trucks, steamroller, excavator, crane, cement mixer, and steam shovel incessantly. These days, no drive through town was complete without a detour past the future site of a row of townhouses, currently in the early stages of construction. The previous week, the builders had brought in a rock crusher to handle the stone being removed. Maggie had gone through all the mail and paid all the bills while they sat in the parked car, Charlie (and even Hazel) entranced by the activity.

The beeps and rumbles of the toy trucks were accompanied by still more construction noises, improvised by Charlie himself. On the sofa, Hazel had her books laid out around her. In preparation for her imminent entry into kindergarten, she "read" constantly. Although her reading generally consisted of repeating from memory what her mother had read to her earlier, she had an imperturbable air of maturity and dignity about her. She looked up when her brother made an especially loud motor noise and rolled her eyes.

Watching them from the kitchen doorway, Maggie was moved. She looked at the soft curls of her daughter's hair, the jiggle in her son's rounded cheeks, and silently gave thanks for her children.

It had been almost a week since she had quit her job at NarcoDynamics and had begun taking Anadreme. Thankfully, she had not heard from Cambien since. The initial shock of his apparent intrusion into her mind, so improbable by its very nature, seemed by now to be quite removed.

She shuddered as she recalled her state of mind five days earlier. She had been weak with fear at the surreal menace she faced. She had been furious with herself for encouraging such a monster in the first place, for awakening the sort of evil that would follow her home and threaten her family. And she had been utterly alone; she had no one she could discuss the situation with, since to say it aloud would sound like madness, and its genesis was something she would not have anyone know.

But now, with the passage of time in relative peace and with the guarantee of undisturbed sleep (thanks to Dr. Cuthbert himself), Maggie was beginning to regain her confidence. Maybe things would be okay after all. Smiling, she walked into the living room and scooped her son up. He squealed and squirmed as she held him, then he began fussing to get down. "Oops, didn't mean to interrupt the Big Dig," she said, setting him back among his toys.

"Mommy, what about me?" Hazel called from the sofa.

"What about you?" Maggie replied with mock sternness, crossing the room to her daughter. "What about you?" She laughed, dropping onto the couch and tickling the little girl. Hazel shrieked and thrashed until her mother caught her up in a hug. Drawn by the activity, Charlie abandoned his construction site and ran to join them, where he was pulled into the laughing pile.

Later that evening, with the children sleeping upstairs, Rowan commented to his wife that she seemed much better.

"Guess my advice is good for something," he complimented himself.

Maggie smiled indulgently at him. "It's true. A good night's sleep can work wonders. As glad as I am to get away from NarcoDynamics, I did learn a couple things while I was there."

Rowan took a swallow of beer. "So is that what you're taking? One of your old company's medicines?"

"Yup, Anadreme. The stuff that put them on the map."

"What was that launch party we went to?"

"That was for Somnusol, which is a sleep aid marketed to the general public," Maggie explained. "Anadreme blocks people's dreams, and that's what I'm taking. Somnusol is a milder form of Anadreme. It helps calm unpleasant thought patterns, plus it has a mild tranquilizer in it. But I don't need the tranquilizer, I just need not to have nightmares once I'm asleep."

Rowan raised his bottle. "Well, then, here's to Dr. Cuthbert."

Maggie did not join her husband in his toast. "Speaking of going to sleep," she said. She kissed him and stood up.

Upstairs, she washed down a small, cornflower blue pill with a glass of water. She kissed each sleeping child's forehead before climbing into her own bed. Settled back comfortably on the pillows, she read until she began to feel drowsy. Her thoughts became disjointed and aimless and she had a slightly disoriented feeling that she had come to recognize as an effect of the medicine. Calmly, gratefully, she turned off the bedside lamp and lay down for another good night's sleep.

⤙⤚

Cambien was anxious. Whenever he thought of himself, he envisioned an intelligent, confident and important man who competently ran a multi-billion dollar pharmaceutical company. Consequently, he was doubly unsettled when anything made him anxious, both by the nerve-wracking thing itself and the damage it did to his sense of identity.

Still damp from the shower, dressed in charcoal gray pajamas, his black hair sleeked back, he sat cross-legged on the floor of his bedroom. A tray was positioned on the rug before him and on it were arranged a small ceramic dish, a lighter of the sort used to start a grill, a packet of charcoal, a small plastic bag containing several long chestnut strands of hair, and the new packet of incense. He closed his eyes and breathed deeply through his nose several times. Centered, he opened his eyes and began.

The old man had assured him that this new formulation was used in the same manner as the old one. Cambien shook several charcoal pellets into the dish and lit them with the lighter. Once they were glowing, he opened the other packet and shook three small nuggets onto his palm. They were beautiful to look at, rich amber in color and perfectly clear, like semi-precious gems formed from ancient pine resin. They refracted the room's dim light as clearly as yellow diamonds.

Anticipation quickening within him, Cambien carefully dropped the shining pellets onto the burning charcoal. They sparked as they settled onto the bed of coals, immediately emitting rich plumes of yellow tinged smoke. Cambien's sensitive nostrils flared as the pungent new odor wafted up to them. There were the familiar scents of herbs, combined with new, organic, vaguely metallic smells. The overall effect was not as pleasant as the incense he was accustomed to, being somewhat gamier, but it was also infinitely more powerful; he had not even begun to meditate and already he felt a strong pull. Quickly, he extracted a hair from the bag and added it to the burning incense. He did not usually use the crude homing device but decided not to take chances with this new formulation. The burning hair added its own disagreeable perfume to the unsavory odor, but Cambien didn't mind the smell. He closed his eyes and began the most intense journey he had ever experienced.

He traversed the familiar path in record time, in spite of the considerable mass he now carried, and began searching for Maggie. It being after two in the morning, he knew she would be sleeping. He hadn't been to see her in over a week and anticipated catching her off guard.

This new kind of travel was far more forceful than he was used to. Yet instead of feeling disoriented, as he expected, he was aware that he was more powerful than he had ever been in this state. Impatiently, he cast about for Maggie. He should have been with her by now. Why was she so difficult to connect with? His heart hammered against the walls of his chest, demanding to be united with its desire.

Ordinarily, when he was as close as this, Maggie's essence was easily detected. He would home in on it, guiding himself into her mind. Now he knew himself to be in the right location, but there was no sign of her. It was good that he had added the hair to the burning mixture. He used it to locate the precise point of entry to his beloved's mind. Triumphantly, he sought admittance.

The door was closed.

At first, he did not believe it. He assumed he had made some mistake and, stepping back, analyzed his surroundings. There could be no doubt; he was at the very threshold of the treasured sentience. Growing frantic with desire, he again attempted to pass through the barrier, and again. Each time, he was repelled by an energy-deadening impediment. He was dumbfounded that his powerful new form could not gain access where his weaker projections had always met with unopposed success.

Then it dawned on him what she had done. She had used the only known method of barricading herself within her own mind while she slept. The irony that it was he who had made this possible added an excruciating note of bitterness to the rage that erupted within him. Wild with frustration, he roared a string of oaths and curses that trailed off into a demented yowl.

All around him, in the ether, he sensed the disturbance visited upon other vulnerable psyches by his dire outburst. He willed himself calm and hope began to burn within him once more.

She had slammed the door in his face, but so what? He grinned. There was more than one way to skin a cat.

⤚✖

"Mommy, Mommy! There's a man in my room!"

The tiny voice pierced Maggie's dreamless stupor, dragging her vaguely towards consciousness. She was awakened fully by Rowan's explosive departure from their bed as he rushed to his daughter's aid.

Not fully conscious of her own movements, Maggie also rose and followed him into the hall. When she reached her daughter's room, she first looked past her husband, who had halted halfway to the bed, to see her daughter, apparently safe, wresting herself from the grip of a nightmare. Maggie then looked at her husband, trying to understand why he had stopped partway into the room.

He stood frozen, in a defensive stance, staring towards the window.

The double-hung window was open to the night air. A bright moon, which had risen high into the night sky above the house, cast its silver glow down to illuminate the sheer white curtains and glare bluely off the polished wood floor. In this luminescent corner, Maggie saw a flickering, darkly translucent silhouette. It was the shape of a man, tall, broad-shouldered, and stealthy in its bearing. It appeared substantive and yet not; she could see the forms of the open window and the silver-blue curtains through it. She glanced at Rowan. He stared at the same spot, now blinking as though unsure of what he saw. The silhouette wavered, became indistinct, and dissolved into the space of the room. Maggie rubbed her eyes and quickly looked again, but only the window and gleaming floor were to be seen.

Rowan turned to her, searching for confirmation that something had been there. With a jolt, Maggie knew that whatever it was had come at her foolish invitation. She was horrified lest Rowan realize that she had brought this menace into their home to threaten their children. "What?" she asked loudly.

"Did you see anything over by the window there?"

"No."

Hazel, now fully awake, began to cry and call for her parents. Rowan continued to stare at the open window. Maggie brushed past him. She got into the bed beside her daughter, holding her and comforting her and praying she wouldn't notice that her mother was also shaking. She looked up at Rowan. "You go back to bed. I'll stay with her."

"Yeah, just a minute. I want to check around first." He left the room.

Maggie heard Rowan creak down the stairs, pause to step into a pair of shoes, and go out the front door. At the slam of another door, she knew he had gotten his Mag Lite from the truck. It was the kind of flashlight cops use, oversized and heavy; it could be used as a weapon if necessary. She listened as his footsteps crunched gravel before being muted by the grass as he left the driveway and circled the outside of the house. She knew he wouldn't find anything.

Five minutes later, Rowan was back in Hazel's room. He kissed his daughter and his wife and went back to bed. Maggie stayed with Hazel until she was asleep again. She listened for Rowan's soft snores, then got up and went to Charlie's room. The little boy was sleeping soundly. She gently stroked his head and watched over his slumber for a while before returning to Hazel's room.

And so she spent the remainder of the night, watching over her children and fighting her outrage at Cambien for violating her daughter's mind and her revulsion with herself for her own complicity in initiating this living nightmare.

Cambien streaked back across the ether, a mere thread snaking from reality to reality. He felt himself piling back into himself, like handfuls of wet sand dropped onto a growing mound. He sat still, eyes jammed shut, jaw clenched, until the electric jolts stopped shuddering through his body and he was himself again.

He sat for several minutes more, bringing his breathing under control as he took inventory. Aside from a dizzying exhaustion, he was otherwise intact.

He opened his eyes, held his hands out and looked at them. Slowly and with great care, he stood and made his way to his bed. He crawled under the covers, shivering, and lay on his back to contemplate this latest, new experience. Weariness threatened to drag him into unconsciousness. While he was still wakeful enough to do so, he sat up and took the Anadreme pill he had laid out on his nightstand, washing it down with a swallow of water from the waiting glass.

He struggled to stay awake until the drug kicked in. Tamping down his outrage at being frustrated yet again, he forced his mind into its scientific mode and began to analyze the effectiveness of the new incense. It had done what it was intended to do, granting him such enhanced power to travel that he had been able to bring his physical body along. But as sophisticated and incredible as this ability was, once he had arrived, he was still nothing more than a common burglar. And when one visited the home of a law enforcement officer, this was hardly an advantage.

However, he had learned much. He was now an initiate into the realm of actual, physical travel. He understood that this new form of travel was extremely powerful, and that made him more potent than ever.

And he had shown Maggie that she could not hide from him. As he had told her when she fled from his office, she couldn't end this. He imagined what her emotional state must have been when she realized that he had used the little girl as a portal. A wicked grin spread over his face; he bet that gave her pause. She was doubtless reconsidering her options at this very moment.

Patience, he advised himself. He felt like he had told himself this so often in the past few months that it had become a meaningless chant. Yet still it soothed him, reminding him to retain control over himself. All was never lost; one simply had to recalculate sometimes, be flexible, and adjust one's plans to conditions on the ground.

The sheer weight of the exhaustion he felt was dragging him into unconsciousness. Undaunted, his mind continued its empirical analysis of the situation. As he felt the medicine begin to fracture and detach his thoughts from one another, he drew one last conclusion. He knew how he would proceed. Confident of ultimate success, he sank into oblivion and rested.

25.

"The M.E. just filed that report you wanted to know about, Detective." The woman's voice was both professional and solicitous through the phone. "Vicky Bertrand, right?"

Rowan sat up in his chair, suddenly attentive. "That's right, May. She was a friend of my wife's. So, what did he come up with?"

"Let's see. . . ." Rowan heard papers rustling on the other end of the connection. The clerk's voice became rote. "He has cause of death listed as multiple blunt trauma. Wounds are consistent with a traffic fatality. Subject wasn't wearing a seat belt and the vehicle apparently took quite a tumble – went down a 40-foot cliff."

Rowan squeezed his eyes shut and rubbed his temple with his free hand. "Any indication why she might have gone off the road like that?"

More rustling of papers before the woman spoke again. "Yup, here it is. No mystery. Blood alcohol level was point two, more than twice the limit. Plus, he notes that driving conditions were dreadful that night, very dark, heavy rain, ground fog, et cetera."

Rowan didn't say anything. In his mind he saw again the scene he had visited weeks earlier when he had first heard

Vicky's name go over the radio. The morning mists rising over the belly of the car that was inverted and partially sunken in the swamp. And poor Vicky, halfway out of the driver side window, her head and torso pinned beneath the roof of the vehicle, submerged in the muck.

"Detective? Are you still there?"

"Yes, I'm still here, May. That's it, then? Nothing else?"

Her voice became consolatory. "I'm sorry, Detective, that's all. Doesn't seem to be anything to add. Hate to say it, but we see an awful lot of these. Far too many, in my opinion."

"Okay. Thanks for your help, May. I appreciate the call."

"You're welcome. And Detective? I'm sorry about your friend."

"Thank you, May." Rowan replaced the phone's receiver and sat massaging his temples. He could imagine the old medical examiner processing Vicky's body, shaking his head as he wrote up the report. Then, when the toxicology results came in, the man's brow furrowed in frustration as his diagnosis was confirmed: another stupid, pointless, drunk driving death.

Rowan wasn't buying it. He had been doing this job too long not to know when something wasn't right. He was certain Cuthbert had something to do with it.

At least Maggie wasn't spending any more time in the creep's company. Rowan remained seated at his desk, ostensibly engaged in finishing a mound of paperwork, as he fretted about his wife.

For the past two weeks, ever since Hazel had dreamed that a man had been in her room, Maggie had been as jumpy as a cat. She had stopped taking her sleeping pills. He was fairly certain she no longer slept at all. He was sometimes stirred at night by the unprecedented stillness from her side of the bed and wakened to find that he was alone. One time when this happened, he got out of bed and padded around the still house, looking for his wife. He found her in Charlie's room, in the armchair by the window, sitting rigidly upright in the dark, her eyes trained on her sleeping son. When Rowan had entered the room, she had jumped and gasped aloud, startled.

"What are you doing, hon?" he had asked.

"Oh, nothing, just . . . sitting." She had attempted a nervous smile. "I wasn't sleepy, so I came in here. It soothes me to watch the children sleep."

"Seems to me you haven't been sleepy for quite some time. Why don't you take one of your pills?"

She had looked away. "I don't like the way they make me feel."

Rowan assumed she napped during the day, but this did not excuse the anxious vigilance she kept up night after night. In his experience, inability to sleep and paranoia were generally indicators of serious underlying psychological problems. His eyes stung and he paused to rub the back of his neck with one hand. *Not my Maggie*, he thought. She was one of the most grounded people he had ever met.

No, it had to be something else. He knew there was something going on, something she wasn't telling him. He smiled grimly; did she forget she was married to a detective? One of the positive things about their marriage was that they respected one another's personal space, so he hadn't pressed her. But he was fairly certain it had something to do with that ghoul she had been working for, and maybe with Vicky's death as well. He was convinced that the former had something to do with the latter; maybe Maggie thought so too. Maybe she knew more about it than she was telling him.

But why on earth wouldn't she share her burden with him? If he didn't know better, he would have thought she was somehow guilty and hiding illicit goings-on that she was complicit in. But here he came up against another of the good things about their marriage; they trusted one another completely, because neither was the type to be disloyal to the other. So whatever she thought she had done, it couldn't be bad enough to keep her from talking to him when she clearly needed him.

His mind presented another possibility for his consideration; perhaps, during his emotional departure from his family the previous spring and early summer, as he had struggled with his own horror at the little girl's murder, perhaps he had withdrawn so completely that he had damaged his wife's faith in him. Maybe the wounds he had given her were so grossly scarred over she was no longer capable of feeling for him. Maybe she had learned not to include him in her emotional life at all.

He hoped this was not so. It would be a tragedy for their marriage if it were. He looked at the wall clock and then at the pile of reports and paperwork on his desk. Sighing, he picked up his pen and went back to work.

～⊸≺

Rowan was not much of a dreamer. He slept as he lived his life, in an orderly and efficient fashion. He generally crept into bed around midnight, lay next to his wife, and fell asleep within three minutes. The next thing he knew, he was opening his eyes at the sound of his alarm clock.

Yet that night, while he slept, he was visited by a hideous, red-skinned demon. He leapt from his bed and flattened himself against the wall as his mind struggled to reach past its fear, groping for a plan of action. The beast loomed before him, its slit-like eyes gleaming. A trained and seasoned lawman, Rowan was horrified at his own terror. He had no idea what action he could take, no coherent thought at all. Falling back on his training, his body assumed a defensive stance.

The monster did not approach but stood three paces away, its head nearly brushing the ceiling. It looked at his face appraisingly for a moment and Rowan felt as though the beast had some variant of respect for him. It spoke a single word in a powerful, growling voice. "Watch."

Rowan's dream (which he had by now realized this was) changed scenes. He was looking at the exterior of a tall, teal-colored Victorian house with a tower on one side. The lighting suggested early afternoon and rain fell heavily. He thought he recognized the house, but couldn't remember from where.

Now he was looking around inside the room at the top of the house's tower. It was clearly intended to be an observatory; windows lined the walls. He saw a familiar, tall, black-haired man bent over a telescope, looking out across the rain-softened treetops. Staring at the barrel of the telescope, Rowan felt a vertiginous rush as his vision became the view through the instrument. He soared over the wet trees and into the backyard of a large, affluent-looking home. This place felt painfully familiar to him.

Across the early spring colorless lawn, he looked through the sliding glass doors at the rear of the house, into a family room, where he saw a tiny girl curled up asleep on the rug before the television. He felt recognition of her identity hurtling toward him like an oncoming freight train. He tried to shield himself from realizing who she was, but his mind (and here, he felt certain that it was his own mind and not the compelling force of the dream) helpfully showed her to him as he had last seen her, lying in a tiny indentation in the low-growing foliage, her light brown hair matted against her head with rain and blood.

Rowan's eyes snapped open in the dark. The bed beside him was empty, as it always was these nights. Outside, he heard rain falling softly on the world.

The old man toiled up the dusty trail, the late morning sun already too hot on his head and back. Sweat ran into his eyes as the shade of the lush plateau came into view. His breath came hard and tightness, not quite severe enough to be called pain, strapped across his chest.

He felt an aimless anger at his growing infirmity. Not one year ago, he had no trouble moving about his island, overseeing his sons (who were all good men, but let's face it, there were no geniuses among them), gathering ingredients, hauling wood, and doing whatever work he felt he ought to do. Now it was a frustrating odyssey to do something as simple as walk up from the village after a cup of morning coffee.

He could not catch his breath, though he moved slowly, and his limbs felt leaden. He refused to consider that his heart might be weak. If he thought about his situation rationally, he would have to leave the island and travel, perhaps all the way to Athens, for medical care, which would leave him weaker than he was now. It would be extremely painful, and it might even kill him. Even if it did not, there would be the long convalescence and the reliance upon his sons, for his own care and the husbandry of his affairs. None of these prospects were acceptable. So he simply proceeded with his life, come what may.

He slogged slowly onward, at last gaining the sweet shade of his orchard. The path went from dust to grass as it leveled off and he gulped the cooler air, his body attempting to flood itself with oxygen. On trembling legs, he rounded a final curve and the sight of his beloved, vine-shaded veranda came into view.

Relief was dispelled by anxiety as he recognized the silhouette of a tall man already seated at his table. He knew at once who it was and what was left of his poor, tired heart began to pound warningly in his chest. He also knew that he had been seen and had no choice but to proceed, like a man, refusing to be intimidated in his own home. Thrusting despair over his weakness from his mind and forcing his ravenous breathing to slow, he stood straight and continued to the table at an unhurried pace.

The American watched him with an arrogant expression, as though he could easily see the physical struggle the old man sought to conceal. Well, he was a doctor, he probably could. The old man gave him no smile of greeting, but called out harshly, "What you are doing here, eh?"

This time there was no pretense of affection between them and any admiration they once had for one another burned away in the glare of crude need and mutual distrust.

The American waited for him to gain the table and collapse into his chair, panting openly. When he saw the elder begin to revive, he reached into a pocket and pulled out a roll of money, which he laid on the table between them. He didn't speak, but kept his gaze trained on the older man's face. He smiled confidently.

The old man glanced at the money and saw that it was far more than the obscene amount he had been paid the last time. He cringed with regret. He was sorry he had ever met this tall, brilliant, ruthless American, sorrier still that he had befriended him, had once trusted him. He was sorry for the joy he had foolishly taken in his own accomplishments, when he had felt strong and wise, master of his island. He had fancied himself an oracle, a god of the human psyche. He had imparted the secrets he had discovered to the great scientist, who was so impressed by what he knew. Oh, how he now regretted the folly of his own pride, a weakness he had indulged throughout his life; always showing off how much he knew, never considering the danger of passing such powerful knowledge to minds it should never be revealed to.

He raised his eyes, once as brilliant as the sea around them but now a weak, watery blue, to the man across the table. "Put away your money," he said. "Let me show to you something. It is something I should have showed to you a long time ago." He stood up, though the effort was costly, and turned to see if his companion would follow. With a look of consternation, the other rose and shoved his money back into his pocket.

At an infuriatingly slow pace, the old man led the younger one out of the shady orchard and back into the sun. Gradually they mounted an ascending trail of packed red dust, making their way toward the island's central summit. Cambien had been on this trail with the old man before, years earlier. He wondered what the codger could possibly wish to show him as they trudged upward.

Presently they left the trail, wove through a maze of rocky gullies, and stopped at the mouth of cave. The old man drew a flashlight from his pocket and prepared to enter. His impatience getting the best of him, Cambien halted him with a hand on his shoulder. "Look, you've showed me that cave before. There's nothing in there but some bats, a crack in the floor, and a whole lot of darkness. Big deal. Can we skip the tour and get down to business?"

The old man swayed, dizzy from the heat and the climb. He looked into his companion's face and spoke around wheezy gasps for breath. "No, it is important. I think I have understood something. I want to explain to you." He turned from the bright sun and ducked into the cool darkness. Cambien rolled his eyes and followed.

For a quarter of an hour, they proceeded into the cavern. The light from the world outside had long since vanished as they worked their way over the uneven ground, around rock formations, and through narrow passages. At last they emerged in a small chamber. In the center of the floor, a crevice yawned.

They stood at the edge of the abyss and the old man trained his light down into it. They both strained their eyes, following the beam as far as they could before it was swallowed by the blackness. "Thousands of years ago," began the old man, "a very famous oracle lived in this cave."

Again, Cambien sought to cut him off impatiently. "Yes, yes, she threw burning herbs into the pit and the spirits at the bottom sent up visions on the smoke. You've shown me this before."

The old man's gaze did not move from the impenetrable blackness at their feet. "And many years ago, I showed this place to someone else, a beautiful young lady who came to this island. She came with her family, to visit relatives and spend the summer holidays. She was very smart, with nice clothes and the sophisticated ways of the Athenians.

"I was a young man then, with hair as dark as yours. I was handsome and proud, and I wanted to show off. So I told her some of the secrets of the island, and I brought her here." His voice trailed off, his words chasing down the echoing passages, leaving a harrowing emptiness in the air.

Impatient though he had been minutes earlier, Cambien felt oddly unwilling to rush the old man. He waited, forcing himself to stand still in the smothering blackness, the unbearable silence.

At last, his companion drew his entranced gaze from the crevice and looked at Cambien. "You," he said. His eyes were wide with the shock of a horrible realization and his white hair stood on end. "You first came to this island and I saw something in you. Again, I thought, here is someone worthy to share my secrets with. And you did not disappoint! Never I have met a one so gifted, so natural. You were at home in the world I showed you, as though it was where you belonged. I thought, at the time, how this can be? But now, I think I understand."

Cambien did not care to meet the old man's wild eyes any longer and he looked away down the passages on the other side of the room. "What are you babbling on about, you old fool?" he growled.

"You see, when I brought the beautiful young lady here— Helena, your mother—I brought the herbs I had been working with, a big bunch of them. I told her I knew how to talk to the underworld, the way the oracle did. She was laughing, she thought I was a silly island boy, but maybe she was a little bit scared too. So, I put a fire to the bundle and I drop it in the hole. And we sit and we wait.

"It falls for a very long time. We never hear it hit the bottom. She began to laugh again, to tell me I am silly. I was laughing too.

Then, we smell the smoke as it starts to come back up to us. It was very dark, darker than it is now." The old man's eyes were unfocused in the dimness again, seeing the young woman he had brought here on a summer's day many years earlier instead of the man, her son, who stood before him now. "And I don't know how to say, but . . . a very bad feeling had come into this room. We both felt it, Helena and I, and we stop laughing. We looked at each other and we both knew that something was coming up from the hole, on the smoke, and that it was a very bad thing." The old man shuddered in the dark as he remembered. A chill ran down Cambien's back.

"I had to work very hard to be a man, to let her go in front of me, as we ran from here," continued the old man. "It seemed to take forever, and we ran into rocks and walls. Helena was screaming as she ran. I think I was screaming too. We could feel the bad thing coming behind us. So help me, we even heard it laughing, a terrible sound.

"Finally, we saw the bright light ahead and we got to the end of the cave. We were almost outside, but the cavern became full of . . . something. Again, I do not know the words; it was mostly like a very, very bad feeling. It was like you did not want to breathe the air because it was poison. It smelled like things you can't really smell, like hopelessness and fear and death. And it became hard to see, and hard to make ourselves move. Helena stopped running, like she did not care anymore. I kept her in front of me and finally I picked her up and ran outside."

He paused, still reliving that long ago day. In spite of his impatience, Cambien listened. Finally, the old man seemed to come back to the present; at least, he seemed to see Cambien again. He spoke. "Once we got outside to the sunlight, the badness disappeared. It could not follow. Helena could move again, we could both breathe, and we ran all the way to the village. I remember thinking, good, we got away.

"And then, years later, I meet you, and now I am not sure Helena did get away."

The old man stopped speaking, still looking at Cambien with that incredulous expression. Cambien could not see the point of the old man's story, and now he was annoyed that he had been delayed for no apparent reason. He spoke with barely suppressed anger. "I have no idea what you are implying, but I am out of patience. So please, let's leave this cold, dark cave and go to your nice, clean cave, where you keep your ouzo and your incense, and we can finish our business."

The elder made no move to leave, instead shining his light into Cambien's face and gaping at him, studying his physiognomy for traces of something only he could identify. Cambien did not care to be blinded by the beam of light while surrounded by blackness, dangerous passages and bottomless pits. The temporary loss of what little vision he had in that hellhole sparked an angry panic and he swung out at the light. "What the hell do you think you're doing, you old fool," he spat. The flashlight, knocked from the old man's hand, sailed across the opening in the floor and landed behind the rocks on the other side of the chamber. It continued to shine feebly on the far wall, keeping the damp room one degree away from total darkness.

Cambien swiveled his head to follow the flashlight, then spun back to the frail person in front of him. He seethed with fear and rage. "Well, now what?" he roared.

The old man had not averted his gaze when the light had been struck from him and still stood facing Cambien, though his features were now lost to the gloom. It was difficult to tell, in the dimness, whether he was transfixed with fear or sudden comprehension as he spoke in a voice that grew stronger with each word. "I know what you are now," he said. "I can see it so clearly. If only I had seen it the first time I met you, I would never have taught you anything."

Frustrated by long delay and thoroughly unnerved by the blackness of the cave, the proximity of the bottomless pit, and the creepiness of the old man's tale, Cambien no longer had the equanimity to stand accused. Fury with the senile fool welled up in him. He spat words through clenched teeth. "Listen, you stupid old man, I don't care what you think you see. The fact is that you have taught me everything you know and sold me everything you've ever made, except for one last thing. And you're sure as hell not going to stop now. Now go get that light and let's get the hell out of here, so I can get what I came for."

But the white-haired man dropped his gaze and shook his head. "No," he said sadly. "There will be no more."

Cambien read the finality in the man's demeanor and could not fathom that he was being refused. "What?" he yelled. "What?"

The brave, frail voice came through the gloom. "It is finished. I will not give you anything more."

Cambien hissed in the blackness as he drew in a bitter breath.

"I could not live with myself," finished the old man.

"Then don't live at all!" Cambien shrieked. He thrust with both hands on the man's chest, flinging him back with the full force of his rage, his frustration, and his hatred.

Though the room was too dark to see and it had happened too fast, Cambien held in his mind, like a photograph captured at night with a flash, the image of the old man's blue eyes wide with terror as he hurtled back, into the black nothingness. He never made a sound as he fell and Cambien never heard him hit.

By evening, the old man's black-eyed sons had begun searching the island for their patriarch. They found that the locked cabinet in the whitewashed cave had been broken into and an empty space on one of the shelves indicated that something had been taken.

They never found their father.

26.

The entire family rose early and ate breakfast together. Hazel dressed in carefully selected clothing, which had been laid out the night before. Everyone else dressed up a bit, Rowan in the clothes he would wear to work. Maggie polished the children's faces with a damp washcloth. They left the house together. Hazel skipped excitedly down the porch steps, a brand new, pink backpack bouncing on her back.

They walked to the end of the driveway in a boisterous little group. Rowan took pictures of Hazel alone, Hazel with Charlie, and Hazel with Charlie and Maggie. They all peered down the street expectantly.

When the yellow bus swung into view, Charlie and Hazel began to jump up and down, squealing excitedly. Maggie and Rowan hugged and kissed Hazel as the bus pulled to a stop. Charlie hung onto his sister and wouldn't let go until Maggie peeled him off, sobbing. Hazel climbed the first two steps and turned to wave, grinning broadly. Rowan took more pictures.

And then it was over. Rowan got into his truck and drove off. Maggie took Charlie to preschool and returned to her empty house. The unstructured day stretched dauntingly before her.

She had another cup of coffee to ward off the ever-present weariness. Sleep remained a scarce commodity for her, fearful as she was of her lapses into unguarded unconsciousness. She spent the day running errands and it was soon time to pick her son up. They returned home to greet Hazel as she stepped off the bus at the end of the driveway.

Dinner that evening was cheerful and celebratory. Hazel was the star of the hour, and for once, Charlie didn't seem to mind. The little girl regaled her father with tales of kindergarten: "Jenna wanted to play with the blocks too, but she threw up right on the table!" and "Marley has the same exact backpack as me!" and "Miss Janson has three hamsters in a fish tank!"

By nine o'clock, Hazel still hadn't wound all the way down, though Charlie had been asleep for an hour. Maggie sat at her bedside, stroking her hair back from her face in an attempt to quiet her, while an unchecked monologue issued from her mouth. Her eyelids drooped lower and lower until they were closed, and still she talked on. But the words became nonsensical and sentences went unfinished, until the speech finally ceased altogether.

Maggie watched her sleeping daughter's face for several minutes more. Then she went to check on Charlie, who also slept placidly. Satisfied for the moment, she dressed in a nightgown and drifted downstairs to join Rowan on the couch.

She sat upright next to her husband, trying to become absorbed in the show he was watching, which featured a fast-talking young chef with a European accent. Rowan had spread some paperwork on the coffee table, which he perused while keeping one eye on the TV.

Maggie watched the young chef prance through a farmer's market, patronizingly explaining how he selected vegetables. Her head fell forward and she jerked back upright.

"Why don't you go upstairs and get some sleep?" Rowan said. "I'll take the first watch." She looked at him, surprised by his open reference to the nocturnal vigils she thought she had kept hidden from him. He was smiling at her, a smile that said he knew all about it.

"Thank you, I think I will," she said simply. She kissed him and he patted her backside as she passed in front of him to leave the room.

Ten minutes later, lying in bed and knowing that Rowan shared her burden (although he didn't know what, exactly, it was) Maggie gratefully fell into the waiting arms of Morpheus.

An hour later, Rowan stood and stretched. He looked at the clock and figured he could check on everyone upstairs and come back down in time to catch the headlines.

First he looked in on his wife. Her face was peaceful in her repose and he stood watching her sleep. He realized that it had been a very long time since he had seen her like this; even when she lay, apparently resting, in their bed at night, her features were never truly relaxed, as they were now. Whatever she had been going through was certainly taking a toll on her. Regret that she didn't feel comfortable talking to him about it stung him, followed by the now-familiar guilt for how withdrawn he had been. Who was he to demand her confidence now?

He bent and kissed her forehead softly, then went to look in on the children. By eleven o'clock he was back on the couch as the local news broadcast began.

Even in her sleep, Hazel's mind was running as fast as she had been talking all evening. So many new things to do in kindergarten! So many new kids to meet and play with! Posters and pictures of new things to learn all over the walls! New toys! And just beyond the door, down the hall, were even more new kids and posters and things!

Hazel stirred in her sleep, her face screwing up.

She was walking through the doorway of her new classroom with all the other children, down the long hall. More and more children, bigger and bigger kids, were joining the throng. Soon she couldn't see past the backs and chests of the bigger kids around her as she was drawn along in the tide. She tried to stop but the kids behind her pushed her and she had to keep walking or fall and be trampled. For a moment, the tall boy in front of her stepped to the side and she could see the way ahead. The hallway had lengthened itself indefinitely, running on to a vanishing point in the darkness; it had become an endless tunnel, filled with surging humanity, proceeding into blackness. Hazel didn't want to go down the endless tunnel, but the big kids around her pushed her along. She began to cry.

She woke and sat up in bed. The room was dark and scary, like the end of the hall in her dream. Her bare feet hit the floor with a soft thud and she padded out to the hallway. The light was on in the hall, which meant that her daddy was still downstairs. Hazel went to the top of the stairs, but the light in the stairwell wasn't on and the stairs descending down into the darkness reminded her too much of her nightmare.

She turned and went back down the lit hallway to her parents' bedroom. Pausing in the doorway, she looked into the darkened room and, by the light that crept in from the hall, saw that her mother lay asleep.

Hazel went to the bedside. She stood a moment, looking down at her mother. Mommy hadn't been sleeping very well lately, Hazel knew. She hesitated, wondering whether she should wake Mommy up. She again considered going down to her father, but the thought of the dark staircase made her shudder. That settled it. She was still scared and there was no way she could go to Daddy. She would wake Mommy up and tell her about the scary dream.

Hazel reached for her mother. She saw her own small, white hand progress through the darkness, over a brief expanse of blanket, to just above her mother's shoulder. Her hand began its descent to her mother's smooth skin. But instead of meeting the expected resistance of a solid object, it fell all the way to the bed, through the emptiness where her mother had just been. Hazel jumped. She spun wildly, looking around the room.

There was no one there. Hazel looked at the bed again, but her mother had vanished.

❧

Maggie had been deeply asleep when it happened. She only became conscious of her sleeping self when she was already in trouble, when a man had come up behind her and roped one steely arm around her throat, the other around her arms and waist.

Rendered breathless, she felt herself lifted and borne rapidly into nothingness.

She knew it was useless but her panicked body twisted and squirmed nonetheless. Her abductor held her against him as they went at dizzying speed. The arms around her did not loosen, and she felt herself growing weaker and dimmer, barely able to draw the shallowest of breaths. She felt other things, too—weightless, untethered, infinitely potent in some indefinable way—but her agitated mind could not understand these sensations. All her waning energy was directed at fighting both the rising hysteria and the growing darkness of unconsciousness.

Quite quickly, the journey was over. A terrifying free fall of a nature she had never experienced ended in fragmented stages of decreased velocity and increased solidity. The faintness that loomed from fear and lack of air was increased by the bizarre shocks that wracked her. Her body had come to rest on its side, still bound in the unyielding arms of Cambien Cuthbert (for whose else's could they be)? Then she blacked out.

When Maggie regained consciousness, she was lying on her back. She was relieved to feel herself breathing freely, although her body was weak with exhaustion. The air she gulped carried a strong and unpleasant scent, but she greedily inhaled it anyway.

She became aware that another body reclined beside her, stretched along the length of her own, with an arm and a leg draped possessively over her. She opened her eyes. Cambien's face was inches from her own as he leaned up on one elbow, panting as though recovering from great physical exertion, watching her with a rapt expression. When he saw her open her eyes and look at him, he grinned a smile of pure joy. He wore a look of complicity, as though together they had achieved a long-fought-for goal and were now basking in the glow of mutual triumph. His sable hair, usually so sleek, was loose and wild all about his head and his eyes held the gleam of a manic inner drive that was within grasp of achieving its ends.

"Hey," he said. His voice was tender and intimate. Maggie moved to sit up, but the arm and leg across her body instantly stiffened to the consistency of iron. She abandoned the effort at once, struck by the weakness of her body. She felt as though she had just run a marathon.

Instead, she tried to get her bearings. She looked around and was stunned to discover that they were lying on a large, carved walnut bed in a spacious bedroom, neither of which she had gone to sleep in. The air was hazy with yellowish smoke and Maggie realized this was where the unpleasant odor came from. The only light came from two stands of candles, set on either side of the room. As when she had seen them, alongside this bed, in her first ever dream of Cambien, the flames flickered calmly. Outside the windows, the night was moonless and black. She closed her eyes in consternation. "Where am I?"

Cambien lowered his head and breathed in her ear. "You are with me."

Maggie struggled to move her head away. The arm around her held her fast. Words tumbled out in a panic. "Cambien, please. What's going on? How did I get here? Where are my childr—"

"Shhhh." Cambien put his finger over her lips. Holding her face still, he kissed her mouth gently. Maggie went rigid. "Everyone's fine. No one even knows you've gone. By the time they figure it out, we'll be on our way to our new home." He kissed her gently again, taking no notice of her firmly closed, ice-cold lips. "And they'll never find us there," he whispered.

She spoke out again, unable to hide the edge of fear in her voice. "What new home? What are you talking about?"

"I showed it to you once–the whitewashed cottage by the edge of the sea." He nuzzled her neck, burying his face in the luxuriant wealth of her chestnut hair. "You loved it there, remember? And we talked about our future together?"

Abruptly, Maggie remembered the dream she had had two weeks earlier while napping on the couch. She saw herself again, lounging with Cambien, suffused with a feeling of peace and love as they looked out at the sun setting on the sea. He had been telling her that they would live in that place together, that no one would bother them there. She struggled to remember . . . he had said they would have a baby. Her eyes widened.

Watching her, Cambien smiled as he saw comprehension dawn on her face. "Now do you understand, my love?"

Maggie shook her head. "No, no, Cambien, this is crazy. I don't want to."

"Maggie," he cut her off sternly. "Did you forget that I have been inside your mind? That I know the contents of your very heart? Don't try to deny to me that you want a baby."

Maggie squeezed her eyes shut, tears running down her temples to the damp linens beneath. She felt a sickening sense of entrapment. Of course she longed for another baby at times. She also longed to be completely free and independent sometimes, and other times she wished only for Rowan to make her the center of his world. Her heart hungered for so many things, sometimes contradictory things, at all times, that it was utterly unfair of Cambien to select only the few desires that matched his own and hold her to them.

He chose to misconstrue her silence as surrender. "I know it's hard for you. I know you feel like you owe them something. But it's time to follow your heart. Because in the end, that's the only thing any of us can ever do. We have no choice in the matter, really; it's all been decided already. I can't change it any more than you can. We can only follow the path that's meant for us."

He closed his eyes and leaned to kiss her. Maggie again struggled to turn away, but he slid on top of her and held her face with his hands. She felt the trembling weight of his tense, lean body on hers, heard the quickening of his breath as he pressed his lips to hers. She was dismayed at the inadequacy of her gown to protect her from the act he meant to commit. She foresaw his intentions; the destruction of her family's sanctity and the soul-wrenching moral predicament she would be placed in, with no satisfactory solution possible. She understood that, by compromising her and charging her with the ultimate responsibility, Cambien meant to wrench her from her family, weakening her so that the only viable option was to flee with him and bear his child.

She became desperate to free herself. She summoned every ounce of strength in her wracked body and fought. She writhed, screamed, bit, and kicked. But as in her nightmares of late, he simply overpowered her. Her desperation lent new levels of ferocity to her struggle. He countered these by again placing his hand around her throat and pinning her neck against the mattress.

Now fighting just to breathe, Maggie abandoned the struggle to get free. Cambien looked apologetically into her eyes. "I'm sorry, my love, but it's the only way." He spoke in a choked voice, on the verge of tears himself. But there was also a radiant joy in his expression.

Maggie's breath came in gasps. Cambien held her by the neck, her body supine beneath his. He did not permit himself to see her tears.

He shivered with sweet anticipation; here, now, at long last, they would complete the sacred act of their epic love. It was finally going to be all right; she was going to be his, and their mutual destiny would be realized. He held her body, stretched taut and trembling beneath his, and prepared to join to her. His eyes closed in rapture and he threw his head back, overcome with the most intense love he had ever felt. The world held its breath. It was time.

Thus poised on the cusp of fulfilling his life's purpose, Cambien heard a loathed sound that froze the blood in his veins. A derisive chortle, overly loud in the anticipatory stillness, came from the corner of the room.

He whipped his head around to see the horrible demon crammed into his leather armchair, watching him with amusement. This had never happened; the beast had never been able to follow him into the physical world. How could this be?

He looked past the creature and saw that the incense he had burned to enable him to fetch Maggie, that he had traveled to Greece and thrown his mentor into a bottomless pit for, had remained lit and continued to send dirty yellow plumes curling upward. In his haste to be with Maggie, he had failed to extinguish it. Once again, he had foolishly left the door open, and disaster had let itself in.

The sublime joy of the previous moment dissolved before an onslaught of horror and hatred. Cambien rolled to his side and raised himself into a crouching position, glaring over Maggie's body at the monster. A frustrated rage flooded him, and he screamed at the beast. "You! What are you doing here? Why now? Why can't you leave me alone?"

Again free to catch her breath, Maggie dreaded to see the cause of Cambien's sudden terror. She forced herself to turn her head and saw what at first looked like an enormous man, too big to be real. Its naked skin glistened, the color of dried blood, in the flickering candlelight. As she looked at the creature, she realized it could not possibly be of this world. Its huge head sat upon a broad neck, its eyes glowed like yellow embers, and its wide, reptilian mouth was lined with pointed teeth. And stranger still, Cambien was apparently acquainted with this thing, as evidenced by the way he screamed at it. She felt her by now tenuous grasp on reality slipping.

Surreally, the beast sat in a comfortable, semi-reclined position, one enormous leg crossed nonchalantly over the other, speaking cordially as though it were a guest at a cocktail party. "Why can't I leave you alone?" it repeated. Its voice rattled like stone grating on stone. "Surely, you don't mean that. I have to see how my boy is doing, especially at such a momentous time as this." The demon mimed the act of wiping a tear of pride from its yellow eye, sniffling loudly. "You do your old man proud, son. She's a beauty."

Oh God, it can't be talking about me, Maggie thought numbly.

Cambien refused to accept the meaning behind the demon's words. "I am not *your boy*." His voice was strong, yet a tremor belied the conflict between terror and love that raged within him. "You have no claim on me. Now once and for all, leave."

The demon merely shook its head and laughed. "How can you say I have no claim on my own son?"

Maggie wrenched her gaze from the beast and turned to look up at Cambien. He was dumbfounded by the monster's assertion. His face, drained of color, floated ghost-like against the darkness of the room. His black eyes blinked incessantly and his mouth opened and closed wordlessly. She watched as Cambien lost the fight to deny what had been said.

"No, I knew my father. He was a good man." His voice sounded forlorn.

Again, the demon laughed indulgently. "You knew the man your mother married, but he was most assuredly not your father. That distinction belongs to me." The laughter stopped. "Why else did you think your mother didn't survive? You fouled your own nest, you filthy little maggot. No mere woman can endure the seed of ones such as us."

Cambien's head hung to his chest. For the first time in the monster's presence, he felt no fear. Such intense wretchedness filled his heart that it had simply displaced weaker emotions like mortal dread.

The demon mimicked a voice of paternal encouragement. "Aw, come on, son, buck up. Don't be ashamed of what you are."

A last shard of defiance burned in Cambien's eyes. "I'm not like you." His voice rose to a scream. "*I'm not like you!*"

"But of course you are. Why else are we all gathered here? Why else did you think you could visit other people's dreams? Why else have you been so driven to be with this woman? Have you never questioned your relentless impulse to mate with her? To return to spawn in the backwaters where you were bred, like one of those ridiculous herring you love to watch?"

"It's not like that. I love her."

The demon was amused. "Don't kid yourself. It's because of what we are—incubi. Night demons. That's just what we do."

"No! I love her."

"Have it your way, then." The beast chortled. "Who knows? You are half human, after all. Perhaps you do love her."

The room became still. No one moved. Cambien crouched by Maggie's side, denial, terror, rage, desire and love battling within him. His head dropped again and he clasped it with both hands.

The beast watched coldly as Cambien fought the violence within his own mind. Then it stood up. "Well, guess I'd better hit the road. My time's almost up." Everyone looked at the smoldering dish of incense, which was now nearly burnt out. "Anyway, I don't want to interfere here. Who wants their old man hanging around on a date? You kids have fun. And, son," it cocked its head and winked, "don't do anything I wouldn't do." Its face split into a lecherous grin and its raucous laughter rang through the room. The beast's form became translucent, then transparent, mingled with the dissipating yellow-gray curls of smoke, and finally faded altogether. The echo of its vile laughter lingered a moment longer and disappeared.

The room went silent. Maggie lay still, fearful of movement of any sort. She glanced at Cambien. His face, tucked against his chest, was hidden from her. After several moments had passed, she began to wonder whether he was still aware of her presence. She held her breath, mustered the whole of her courage, and slowly, slowly, began to move one leg toward the edge of the bed. A centimeter at a time, she reached her foot toward the floor. She didn't dare to breathe.

When her foot had gone as far as it could go, she carefully began to rotate her hips, orienting herself away from Cambien. Instantly, his arm shot out from his side and his hand was again on her throat. He lunged to his hands and knees, leaning over her, his weight on her neck, his face inches above hers. Maggie choked and sobbed in fright as she looked up into the black pits of his eyes. His face, ashen white a moment ago, was now red. In a voice torn with anguish, he rasped, "You will not leave me now." Hot tears fell on her face. "We have to finish what we came here to do."

He draped himself over her, freeing a shaking hand to push her hair back from her face. Maggie saw that he was wracked by warring passions of great intensity. She prayed he was weakening. "Please, Cambien—"

"Shhh. Everything's going to be okay. We just have to do this. Everything will follow from this . . ." He was again going through the preliminary motions of lovers as he struggled to follow the course of action he had planned for years, to carry on as though no detestable fiend had just entered the room and destroyed the world as he knew it. Maggie turned away and squeezed her eyes shut.

He gazed down upon the beloved face, trying to evoke the sense of triumph he had wielded not ten minutes ago. Devastation after devastation rioted in his brain; the demon he had fought his whole life had fathered him? *Don't think about it!* He had killed his own mother, poisoning her innards in the course of his gestation? *Stop it!* He was the same as the monster? *No!*

He shook his head, desperate to clear it of these thoughts. It was crucial that he bind Maggie to himself—now—with this great, procreative act of love. He forced himself to see the creamy skin, the chestnut tresses, and the crimson lips that he loved. He evoked an image of their ultimate victory, their future life together, in the whitewashed cottage by the sea. He saw Maggie beside him as they lay on a blanket on the sand at sunset. She looked up into his face, her eyes soft with love for him. And between them, on the blanket, their child cooed and smiled. He closed his eyes and clung to this vision with all his might.

But he could not hold it; Maggie vanished from the vision, leaving only a motherless infant that howled at him for a comfort he could not provide. *Why else did you think your mother didn't survive? You fouled your own nest, you filthy little maggot. No mere woman can endure the seed of ones such as us.*

It couldn't be. It was beyond unfair. How could he be driven his whole adult life by his love for this woman, when its consummation would kill her?

Do it anyway. You have to—it's what you do. It's the baby you really want, after all. He snapped his eyes open, shaking his head in an attempt to dispel the base impulse. But a savage wave of lust convulsed his body. He saw Maggie's quivering breast and pawed at it ravenously. He had to—now—it was time, damn it! His destiny, fulfilled at last . . .

An empty space beside him. No one to share the beauty of the child with. No more Maggie. Cambien howled with agony. His head was riven by the painful urge in his loins and the immaculate love in his heart. Something inside him broke.

Maggie opened an eye and saw Cambien, still leaning over her, trembling violently, his face twisted into a grimace of agony. He fell off of her, landing clumsily at her side in a half-sitting, half-reclining position, heaving wrenching sobs.

Somehow, out of all that had happened this night, Maggie felt pity for the tortured man beside her. She cautiously raised herself onto an elbow, her face level with his. "Are you all right?" she asked falteringly. Her voice cracked from the violence her throat had endured.

The sound of her words brought him back to her. For a final time, his black eyes met her hazel ones. He took one last, long draught of the sight of her, reaching for her very soul through the shining orbs. An infinitely deep sigh wracked him. He said, simply, "Go."

Maggie did not need to be told twice. She rolled off the bed and moved swiftly to the door. With a last look back at the broken man, now clenching his eyes against another shudder of wretchedness, she turned and fled the room.

It only took her a moment to find the stairs. Once at the bottom, she was in a large entrance hall. The front door was gained in four running strides. She heard the shot as she pulled it open. She hadn't even known Cambien kept a gun.

She raced out into the cool, black air, down the steps, and onto the dew-wet lawn.

27.

Goose bumps prickling his skin, Rowan took in his young daughter's words.

Mommy disappeared.

He had run upstairs at her calls, seen the empty bed, and listened to her story.

Mommy disappeared.

He searched the room, then the upstairs, then the entire house. He went outside and walked the perimeter, carrying Hazel, who was weeping with fear.

Returning upstairs, he stared at the empty bed. The covers were wrinkled, as from being slept under, but were not turned down, as from a person getting out of bed. He forced himself to be calm, to concentrate.

He recalled the a man's silhouette, flickering in the silver moonlight in a corner of his daughter's room before fading away.

Mommy disappeared.

He abruptly recalled a recent dream, where a hideous beast had shown him the landmark Victorian house he had once visited with Mike, to question Maggie's boss, the disturbing Dr. Cuthbert.

Rowan knew he didn't have cause to bring the police into the situation. It seemed to take forever for Pop to arrive, to be told there was no time for questions, just to watch the two sleeping children piled into their parents' bed.

Rowan erupted from the house into the cool black hush of midnight, dove into his truck, and tore out of the driveway. He saw no other cars as he flew down the parkway. He drove way too fast. In seventeen minutes flat, he skidded to a halt in the gravel of Cambien's driveway. A gunshot punctured the stillness as he jumped from the truck. Ducking, he drew his service revolver and pelted towards the dark house. Wonder and relief overwhelmed him as the front door opened and his wife raced towards him, barefoot and in her nightgown, over the lawn.

He caught her and held her tight. Delivered, she clung to her husband, tears of terror, sorrow and regret flowing freely.

꙳

The following evening, Maggie and Rowan sat side by side on the old, plaid sofa as the late news came on. "In our top story tonight," blared the blond anchorwoman excitedly, "a local business owner, distraught over the recent drunk driving death of his girlfriend, takes his own life."

Maggie turned to Rowan. "I'm ready to tell you what happened," she said.

She told him everything. And once she began to confide in him, once she had torn the scab off the wound, the insidious infection that had been devouring her from within poured forth.

As her story came out, she saw that Rowan was not repelled. Rather, he held her closer with each new revelation. She spoke steadily, and he listened. And after an hour of wrenching, tearful confession, the barrier between them was overcome, and she and he were united in an intimacy of an intensity they had felt only thrice before: on their wedding day and at the birth of each of their two children.

EPILOGUE

After a long day upstate, hiking trails and picking the last apples, the Moores drove homeward. It had rained most of the time, and they were wet and tired. Darkness had fallen.

The parkway was always clogged on Sunday evenings with city dwellers returning home from country weekends, so the Moores hoped to avoid the traffic by wending their way home on a two-lane back road. But the route they chose turned out to be jammed with traffic anyway. They sat in their car, rain pounding dismally on the roof, waiting for the glut of vehicles to move.

Adrift in the darkness, Maggie gazed dreamily through the rain hammering the hood of the car. Droplets rebounded from its surface to obscure the way ahead in a mist. She spread her hands across her stomach and smiled, thinking of the day when she would meet the new one whose tiny heart fluttered within. Her feelings swelled and she turned to her husband. He noticed her glance and smiled, taking his right hand off the steering wheel and placing it over her left one.

She turned her head to check on the children. She was surprised to see they were both awake. They had been quiet for a long time. Each child looked out a window, seeing nothing in the rainy night, lost in whatever thoughts he or she entertained. "Wow, have we been lucky," Maggie said quietly to her husband.

"Huh?" Rowan eased the car forward as the traffic began to creep along.

"The kids," she elaborated. "I mean, it has been a rather crummy day after all, for a kid—too rainy to do half the things we planned. They've been stuck in the car more often than not, all the pretty leaves were already down, and the food at that restaurant was horrible. And here we are, still in the car, still miserable outside, everyone's damp and tired, and now the traffic's horrible too. I can't believe they're not complaining."

Rowan shrugged. "They're good kids."

Finally they reached the cause of the traffic jam: emergency road construction, which was being carried on in spite of the darkness and the foul weather. As they slowly rolled past the site, Charlie stared excitedly through his window. Huge highway department lights flooded the scene and men in hard hats and reflective gear directed the traffic. But best of all, several bright orange and yellow excavators worked only feet from their car. Charlie watched the big machines tearing chunks from the earth as he passed. It was better than a movie.

"Look, Charlie," said Maggie. "See the men working?"

The little boy stared through the window with wide, enraptured eyes, watching the machines working in the night.

And Maggie, at peace, returned her gaze to the misted view through the windshield, settled back against the seat, and began to dream.

About the Author

Kia Heavey lives in Connecticut with her husband, a law enforcement professional, and two children. After graduating from Barnard College with a degree in German Literature, Kia worked as an art director in advertising. She wrote *Night Machines* because it was a book she wanted to read, but no one had written.